Storm Advisory in Effect

In my business, we not only understand chaos theory, we totally abide by it. Chaos happens. Always plan for speed.

Either the Djinn was putting me on, which would be seriously unfunny, or the spell was coming from Elsewhere. I hoped not an Elsewhere that began with the letter Hell.

I got a bad feeling. 'No offence, but can I at least get some proof this message is from Lewis?'

'No,' said a female voice, decisively. Static. The radio clicked off.

It *could* be the Djinn. In fact, it was even likely; I'd embarrassed him, and he owed me payback for that. But he *had* made a call, and I couldn't waste the chance if he was honestly giving me instructions on how to find his boss. Djinn had a host of faults, but out-and-out lying wasn't among them.

And besides, I had to outrun the storm behind me anyway.

'Oklahoma City,' I sighed aloud. 'Home of heavy weather. Fabulous.'

The only redeeming thing about it was that I knew the territory. I hadn't spent a whole lot of time there, but one of my best friends in the world had retired out there. It'd be nice to have a friend right now. Somebody to count on. Some shoulder to cry on.

I had to look on the good side, anyway. Because the bad was pretty overwhelming.

Ill Wind

Ill Wind

Book One of the Weather Warden series

RACHEL CAINE

First published in Great Britain in 2008 by
Allison & Busby Limited
13 Charlotte Mews
London, W1T 4EJ
www.allisonandbusby.com

A CIP catalogue record for this book is available from
the British Library.

First published in the USA in 2003.

10 9 8 7 6 5

ISBN 978-0-7490-7916-1

Typeset in 10.5/14pt Sabon by
Terry Shannon.

The paper used for this Allison & Busby publication
has been produced from trees that have been legally sourced
from well-managed and credibly certified forests.

Printed and bound in the UK by
CPI Bookmarque Ltd, Croydon, Surrey

Rachel Caine is the international bestselling author of over thirty novels, including the *New York Times* bestselling Morganville Vampires series. She was born at White Sands Missile Range, which people who know her say explains a lot. She has been an accountant, an insurance investigator and a professional musician, and has played with such musical legends as Henry Mancini, Peter Nero and John Williams. She and her husband, fantasy artist R. Cat Conrad, live in Texas with their iguana Pop-eye, a *mali uromastyx* named (appropriately) O'Malley, and a leopard tortoise named Shelley (for the poet, of course).

www.rachelcaine.com

To those who inspire:
My husband, Cat (always), and to my dear friends
Pat Elrod, Kelley Walters, Glenn Rogers, Pat
Anthony, and – of course – 'the' Joanne Madge

To those who believe:
Everybody in ORAC (you know who you are!)
and my friends at LSGSC

To those who made it happen:
Lucienne Diver and Laura Anne Gilman

To my musical inspiration:
Joe Bonamassa

**And finally, to the one who taught me to love
the storm as much as the calm:**
Timothy Bartz
Rest softly, my dear. This one's for you.

Thunder is good, thunder is impressive;
but it is the lightning that does the work.

Mark Twain

Excerpt from Owning Your First Djinn *published by the Wardens Association Press, 2002.*

Owning Your First Djinn

By granting you the possession of one of the Association's Djinn, the Wardens Association has recognised that you are among the finest in your area of specialty, whether you control Weather, Fire, or Earth. You should accept this great honour and grave responsibility with humility and courage.

Djinn are a valued, precious resource. Abuses of Djinn or their powers will be prosecuted to the fullest extent of our Association's laws, up to and including execution.

Do

- Use your Djinn to **augment** your powers, and rely upon your Djinn for advice in your area of specialty.
- Guard your Djinn's home (commonly a bottle) with great care. Although your Djinn will (of necessity) be loyal only to you until your death, or until the Association removes the Djinn from your care, misplacing a Djinn is a very serious matter with associated penalties. All Djinn must

be housed in breakable containers (see ARCANE RULES, below) but precautions should always be taken against accidents.

Don't
- Manifest your Djinn in public unless first asking it to remain invisible or to take human form.
- Abuse your Djinn by asking it to perform unsavoury or immoral actions.
- Break your Djinn's container UNDER ANY CIRCUMSTANCES.

ARCANE RULES
- Once Djinn have been assigned a master, they can take orders only from that master, unless the master temporarily assigns control to another Warden for business purposes.
- Djinn cannot break their own containers. They are allowed, however, to trick others into destroying these containers, thus freeing them from their services. YOU MUST BEWARE OF THIS AT ALL TIMES. A freed Djinn is a very serious danger to all of us.
- Never ask a Djinn for the Three Things Forbidden: eternal life, unlimited power, or raising the dead.

ETIQUETTE

You may begin to develop a certain fondness for your Djinn over time. This is normal and healthy. But never forget that your Djinn is a magical creature of nearly unlimited power and lifespan, and *is not human*. The motivations of Djinn are not always understandable. Never trust them completely.

TECHNICAL SUPPORT

If you have questions about the day-to-day administration of your Djinn after the initial training period, please contact our 24-hour hot line for assistance. Specialists are on hand at all times for your protection.

Chapter One

Cloudy and cool, with an eighty per cent possibility of moderate to severe thunderstorms by mid-afternoon.

Well, thank God this is about to be over, I thought as I drove – well, blew – past the sign that marked the Westchester, Connecticut, city limits. Traffic sucked, not surprisingly; rush hour was still in full swing, and I had to moderate my impatience and ride the brake while I watched for my exit. *Calm down. Things will be back to normal in just a few more minutes.*

OK, so I was a little too optimistic. Also unrealistic, since me and normal have never really been on speaking terms. But, in my defence, I needed all the optimism I could muster right then. I'd been running on adrenaline and bad coffee for more than thirty hours straight. I'd been awake for so long that my eyes felt like they'd been rolled in beach sand and Tabasco sauce. I needed rest. Clean clothes. A shower. Not necessarily in that order.

First, I had to find the guy who was going to save my life.

I found the exit, navigated streets and annoying stoplights until I found the residential neighbourhood I was looking for. I checked the scrap of paper in my lap, studied kerbside house numbers, and finally pulled the car to a stop in front of a nice Colonial-style home, the kind of place a realtor would describe as a 'nice starter'. It had flame-red tulips planted in mannered rows under the windows, and the lawn looked well behaved, too. Weird. Of all the places I'd have expected to find Lewis Levander Orwell, the most powerful man in the world...well, this wasn't it. I mean, suburbia? Hello!

I tapped chipped fingernails on the steering wheel, weighed risks and benefits, and finally popped open the door and stepped out of the car.

The euphoria I'd felt when I was pulling into town vanished as soon as my feet hit solid ground, crushed under a load of exhaustion. Too much stress, too little sleep, too much fear. Speaking of fear...I felt wind on the back of my neck, and I turned to look east. A storm loomed like purple mountains' majesty, big cumulonimbus clouds piled on top of each other like a fifty-car interstate pileup. I could feel it noticing me, in the way storms had. No question about it, I needed to be out of Westchester before that thing decided to pounce. I'd been watching storms crawl along the coast, paralleling me all the way from Florida. The nasty part was that it might actually be the same storm, stalking me.

They did that sometimes. It was never good.

Nothing I could do about it right now. I had bigger issues. Up the concrete walk, up three steps lined with geraniums in terracotta pots, to a spacious white front door. I knocked and waited, rocking back and forth on three-inch heels that felt like something from the spring collection of the Spanish Inquisition. Bad planning on my part, but then I'd been expecting a pleasant little business meeting, not a two-day panicked flight cross-country. I looked down at myself and winced; the blue French-cuffed polyester shirt was OK, but the tan skirt was a disaster of car-accordioned linen. Ah well. It would have been nice for Lewis to swoon with desire on seeing me, but I'd definitely settle for him pulling my bacon out of the fire.

Silence. I cupped my hands around my eyes and tried to peer through glass not designed for peering. No movement inside that I could see. With a sinking feeling of disaster, I realised I'd never considered the possibility that my knight in shining armour could be away from the castle.

I knocked on his door once more, squinted

through the glass again, and tried the bell. I heard muffled tones echoing through the house, but nothing stirred. The house looked normal.

Normal and very, very empty.

Out where I was, Westchester was enjoying spring sunshine. People walked, kids whooped around on bikes, dogs ran with their tongues hanging out. Inside the house, there was winter silence. I checked the mail slot. Empty. Either he'd been home earlier, or he'd stopped his mail altogether. No papers on the lawn, either.

I considered my options, but really I had only two: get some idea of where else to look, or lie down and die. I decided to do some scouting. Unfortunately, the grass was damp, and my three-inch heels weren't designed for path finding. With some cursing and tripping and excavating myself from spike-heeled holes, I clumped around the house.

The house had that don't-touch-me feeling that indicated strong wards and protections, but I circled it anyway, checking the windows. Yep, wards on every one, good strong ones. The yard was nice and neat as a pin, with the look of being maintained by a service instead of somebody with a passion for plants. Lewis had a very nice workshop in the back, which was devoted half to woodworking, half to magecraft; that half was warded up the wazoo, no way I could do more than just glance in the window before I had to retreat or get zapped.

Powerful stuff. That was good – I desperately needed a powerful guy.

I banged on the back door and squinted in the square of window. Still nothing moving. I could see the living room, decorated in Basic American Normal – looked like everything in it had come out of some upscale catalogue. If Lewis lived here, he was a lot more boring than I'd ever imagined.

I had plenty of powerful tricks up my sleeve, but they didn't include breaking and entering. The kind of powers I possessed, over water and wind, could destroy a house but not open a door. I could have summoned a hailstorm – a small one, OK? – to break a couple of windows, but no, that would be wrong and besides, I'd probably get caught because it was pretty showy stuff. So I resorted to human tactics.

I tossed a rock at the window.

Now, I was pretty sure it wasn't going to work, but in a way it did; the rock bounced off some thick invisible rubbery surface about a half inch from the window, and the back door slammed open.

'Yes?' snarled the guy who blocked the doorway. He was big, and I mean *huge* – big, tanned, bald, with two gold earrings that twinkled in the sunny Westchester morning. He was wearing a purple vest with gold embroidery over rippling muscles. I had the impression of dark pants, but I didn't dare look down. Didn't matter, his chest was definitely worth checking out. Pecs of the gods, no kidding.

Just my luck. Lewis had left a Djinn at home – his own personal mystical alarm system.

'Hi,' I said brightly. 'Lewis around?'

He scowled. 'Who wants to know?'

'Joanne Baldwin.' I held out my hand, palm up; the Djinn passed his palm over mine and read the white runes that glittered in its path. 'We're friends. Me and Lewis go way back.'

'Never heard of you,' he said brusquely. Djinn are not known for their chatty nature, or their sunny disposition. In fact, they're known for being difficult to handle and – if they don't like you – fully capable of finding some sneaky way to do you in. Not that I was an expert, exactly; Djinn were reserved for bigger fish than me, sort of the equivalent of a company car perk in the Wardens Association. I didn't even rate a reserved parking space yet.

The Djinn was still staring at me. 'Go now,' he rumbled.

I stood my ground. Well, it was really his ground, but I stood it anyway. 'Sorry, can't. I need to talk to Lewis. Urgently.'

'He is not here. Being that you are a Warden, I won't kill you for your lack of manners.' He started to close the door.

'Wait!' I slapped my hand – coincidentally, the one with the rune – flat against the wood. It wasn't my upper body strength that made him hesitate, that's for sure. Even Mr Universe couldn't have held a door against a Djinn, much less a five-foot-five woman with more attitude than body mass. 'When will he be back?'

The Djinn just stared at me. Djinn eyes are colours not found in the human genome, specially formulated to produce maximum intimidation. Some of them are citrine yellow, some bright fluorescent green, and they're all scary. This guy's were a purple that Elizabeth Taylor would have envied. Beautiful, and cold as the colours in arctic ice.

'Look, I need to find him,' I said. 'I need his help. There are lives at stake here.'

'Yes?' He hadn't blinked. 'Whose lives?'

'Well, mine, anyway,' I amended, and tried for a sheepish grin. He returned the smile, and I wished he hadn't; it revealed perfect white teeth that would have looked more appropriate on a great white shark.

'You stink of corruption,' he said. 'I will not help you.'

'That's up to your master, isn't it?' I shot back. 'Come on, he knows me! Just ask him. I know you can. He wouldn't leave you here without any way to contact him. Not even Lewis goes around abandoning Djinn like disposable pens.'

The purple eyes were really, really getting on my nerves. I could feel the Djinn's power burning my skin where my hand touched the door, another spiteful tactic to get me to let go so he could slam it shut and ward me clear out to the street. There's nothing stronger than a Djinn on its home territory. Nothing.

The pain in my hand got worse. Smoke rose from my hand where it pressed against the white-painted wood door, and my whole body shook from nausea and reaction. But I didn't let go.

'Illusion,' I stammered. The Djinn was still grinning. 'Don't waste my time.'

'My powers could not touch a true Warden,' he said. 'If you burn, you burn because you deserve it.'

All right, I'd had about enough of playing with Mr Clean gone bad. I took my hand away from the door and held it up.

The world breathed around me.

I might have stunk of corruption, but I still commanded the wind, and it slammed into the Djinn with force of a speeding Volkswagen. Djinn are essentially vapour.

I blew him away.

He was gone for about a half-second, and then he re-formed, looking ready to pull my brain out through my nostrils. So I hit him again. And again. The last time, he re-formed very slowly all the way across the room, looking pissed off but respectful. I hadn't made the mistake of setting foot across his threshold, so he couldn't strike back. All his awesome power – and it was truly awesome – was useless. So long as I didn't break the wards, I could stand out there all day and toss microbursts and katabatic gusts.

The Djinn muttered something unpleasant. I held my hand up again. A strong breeze shoved my hair around, and I felt the warm tingle that meant I had at least one more good Djinn-blasting gust at my command.

'I really, really don't have time to dick around with you,' I said. 'Give him my name. Tell him I need to see him. Or else.'

'No one threatens me!' he growled.

'I'm not threatening, sweet pea.' I could feel the white runes on my hand glowing. My dark hair whipped around my face in the wind, which I kept coiling around me, building tornadic speed. 'Want to bet I can blow you all the way into a teeny little open bottle and stick a cork in you?'

'You know not what you are doing,' he said, more quietly.

'Wrong, I know exactly what I'm doing. Want another practical demonstration?'

He held up one hand in the universal language of surrender. I let the wind swirl and die. The Djinn reached over and picked up something from the table, and it took me a few seconds to realise it was a cell phone. Good God, the Djinn had entered the age of technology. Next thing you know, a satellite dish in every bottle, broadband Internet, microwave ovens...

The Djinn punched numbers, said something, and turned away from me while he talked. I had the leisure to examine the back of a Djinn, which is something you rarely do. He had a nice ass, but his legs ended in a swirl of vapour somewhere around knee level. Still, not a disappointment.

He finished the call, turned back, and bared pointed teeth at me. *Uh-oh*, I thought.

'Come inside,' he invited. 'No harm will come to you.'

'I'll wait out here, thanks.' I rocked back and forth. My feet felt like somebody had set them on fire from the soles up, and the couch in the living room looked cushy and inviting. I wished the Djinn hadn't started being nice. It was harder to maintain my tough-as-nails bitchy attitude, especially when I wanted to cry and curl up in a ball on those nice, soft cushions.

'Suit yourself.' The Djinn turned away to root around in some drawers in the kitchen. He came up with a battery, scowled at it, and threw it back. A corkscrew. One of those clippy things for opened bags of chips. 'Ah! Here. Take this.'

He tossed something shiny at me. I caught it and

felt a flash of cold, something sharp turning in my fingers, and then I was holding nothing but an expanding breath of mist. I opened my hand and stared down. Nothing to show for it but a faint red mark on my palm. I frowned at it and extended a tingle of Oversight, but there was nothing there. Nothing harmful, anyway.

'What the hell is it?' I asked.

The Djinn shrugged. 'A precaution,' he said. Sharp-toothed grin again, very unsettling. 'In case you lose your way.'

Before I could offer a polite thanks-but-no-thanks, I felt the steel psychic slam of wards coming up to full strength. The Djinn was evidently done screwing around with me, even as a diversion.

He floated up to the doorway, watching me as I backed down the steps while fighting against it.

'Hey!' I fumed. 'Dammit, I just want to *talk* to him! That's all! I'm not going to turn him in or anything!'

'Drive,' he said. 'You'll be contacted with directions.'

I was off the back porch and out of the yard and on the sidewalk before I could even think about fighting back.

I flexed my hand, but it didn't feel any different than it ever had. In Oversight, there was nothing visible but flesh and bone, muscles and nerves, the luminous course of blood moving on its busy way.

The Djinn had smelt the Demon Mark on me. That was bad. Very bad.

It meant I didn't have much time left.

God has a sense of humour, and in my experience, it is never kind. I'd tempted fate consistently for days now…I hadn't packed a toothbrush, a change of clothes, or a tampon. Well, at least I had my American Express Platinum, with the infinite credit limit for emergencies…but then again, I didn't dare use it. My friends and colleagues would be watching for any sign of me, and until I found Lewis – and safety – I didn't dare attract their attention. If the FBI could find me, the Wardens sure as hell wouldn't have any trouble.

I kept myself awake as I drove my sweet midnight-blue '71 Mustang out of town by making a mental shopping list. Underwear: check. Toiletries: check. Clothes: definitely. New shoes: a must.

I sniffed the air inside the car. A shower and a car deodoriser wouldn't hurt, either. Maybe something with that new-car aroma. I love classic cars, but they come with baggage and years of ingrained stinkiness. Feet, sweat, sex, the ancient ghosts of spilt coffee. I smelt it only after a few hours on the road, and maybe it was all in my head, but just now I'd give anything for a clean, fresh scent like they claimed in the commercials.

I rolled down the windows and smelt something else, something more menacing. Rain. The storm was getting closer.

I find that as a Warden, it pays to drive something aerodynamic and fast that the wind will have a hard time shoving over a cliff. Just because I can control weather – with the proper focus – doesn't mean the weather likes it, or that it won't decide to screw with me at the most inconvenient times. In my business, we not only understand chaos theory, but we totally abide by it, as well. Chaos happens. Plan for speed.

I accelerated out of town in complete defiance of traffic laws and headed out on the maze that was the Connecticut road system. Basically heading south and west, because that was away from the coming storm, which had turned the eastern sky a heavy grey green. *You'll be contacted with directions.* Had the Djinn just screwed with me? Possibly; the Djinn were known for their mean-spirited sense of humour. Maybe he hadn't gotten hold of Lewis. Maybe Lewis had told him he didn't want to see me, in which case the only directions the Djinn was honour-bound to give me led straight to hell.

I was in antiques country on CT 66, driving past shops that sold Federal chests and Shaker chairs, some of them even genuine. On a better day, I might have been tempted to stop. My Florida house was due for a redecoration, and I liked the psychic feel of antiques. It was definitely time to get over that Martha Stewart everything-in-its-place phase; I was so tired of pastels and good manners, I could yak. The fantasy that I would be going home – ever – to a normal life was something I was clinging to like a spar on a stormy ocean.

I was just passing a shop that housed every piece of junk from the nineteenth century when suddenly the radio crackled on. Hair on the back of my neck stood rigid, and I knew there was a spell travelling with me. A big, powerful spell, coming, no doubt, from my friendly neighbourhood Djinn.

The radio spun channels, picking out its message like words on a ransom note.

A high female voice. 'Drive...'

Midrange male. 'To...'

Full-throated Broadway show tune. 'Oklahoma is OK!'

'What?' I yelped. 'You're kidding, right?'

The radio flipped stations again. It settled on classic rock. 'No-no, no, nuh-no, no, no-no-no-no-no no no no, nuh-no.' Either the Djinn was putting me on, which would be seriously unfunny, or the spell was coming from Elsewhere, I hoped not an Elsewhere that began with the letter Hell.

'Very funny,' I muttered. I shifted gears and felt the Mustang stretch and run beneath me like a living thing. 'Any special place in Oklahoma? It's not exactly Rhode Island. There's a lot of real estate.'

Letters this time. 'O...K...C' Oklahoma City.

I got a bad feeling. 'No offence, but can I at least get some proof this message is from Lewis?'

'No,' said a female voice, decisively. Static. The radio clicked off.

It *could* be the Djinn. In fact, it was even likely; I'd embarrassed him, and he owed me payback for that. But he *had* made a call, and I couldn't waste the chance if he was honestly giving me instructions on how to find his boss. Djinn had a host of faults, but out-and-out lying wasn't among them.

And besides, I had to outrun the storm behind me anyway.

'Oklahoma City,' I sighed aloud. 'Home of heavy weather. Fabulous.'

The only redeeming thing about it was that I knew the territory, and one of my best friends in the world had retired in OKC. It'd be nice to have a friend, right now. Somebody to count on. Some shoulder to cry on.

I had to look for the silver lining, anyway. Because the storm cloud was pretty damn dark, and only getting worse.

I'd met Lewis Levander Orwell at Princeton. He was a graduate student – already had a degree in science, then a Juris Doctor to practice law. His explanation, strangely, had been that he'd wanted something to fall back on, in case the whole magic thing didn't work out. Apparently he had the whole Magical Arts thing mixed up with Liberal Arts.

And for a while, it looked like having a fallback career was a good idea. Lewis had been recruited – or drafted – after demonstrating some definite weather-working abilities at the age of fifteen, but that talent had seemed to fade. He had loads of potential but no actual…nothing concrete to show what his powers might be or what form they might really take. Then, his second year in the Program, he was spotted working in the garden. In the winter, knee-deep in snow. Growing roses.

Red, blooming roses the size of dinner plates. He was honestly surprised that it was hard to do.

He was originally identified as an Earth Warden – someone who could shape living things, alter the land itself, make crops grow in fallow fields, prevent or cause earthquakes and volcanoes. A strong, deep power, and very rare. Then, in his third year of the Program, they'd discovered he also had an affinity for fire. Dual specialties are vanishingly rare. Only five other Wardens in recorded history had ever commanded earth and fire together. Water and air – that was expected, even typical – but earth and fire didn't blend well. Lewis was talked about a lot. He was, we all heard, expected to do Great Things.

Must have been a lot of pressure, but you'd never have known it from the way he acted. Lewis was quiet; he did his work, went to classes, had some friends but gave the strong impression that if any man was an island, it was Isla Lewis. I admit, I pined after him. I had my reasons.

Unfortunately, Lewis avoided Program girls like the plague – which was kind of my fault, because our first encounter had been, shall we say, memorable. Anyway, he deliberately went for the normal girls. Sociology majors, psych grad students, the occasional goofy art student. Girls whose biggest aspiration was to get a secretarial job at Smith Barney and vacation with their bosses in the Bahamas...unlike those of us in the Program, who dreamt of facing down F5 tornadoes and calming raging rivers.

Because I was not stalking him, just keenly aware of his presence, I happened to be around for The Event, which was what we began calling it later when there was some perspective on what had happened.

That was the night Lewis got the shit kicked out of him by six frat boys on a bender.

It was the Kappa Kappa Psi party, which was a music fraternity...for some odd reason, the band geeks always knew how to throw a bitchen party. Four of us from the Program crashed the scene – Lewis, who came on the arm of some miniature brunette flute player; and Paula Keaton, Ed Hernandez, and me, who came looking for free drinks and the slim possibility of getting charmed out of our underwear. I glimpsed Lewis early on, talking to his flute player but not looking very comfortable; he didn't drink much, and the party was rolling pretty well.

Flute Girl eventually got swept away on a tide of Everclear punch, and Lewis was left to ramble around on his own. He knew I was there – I think – but we didn't hook up. If we had…well. Water, bridges, et cetera.

Sometime around 2 a.m., he knocked over a guy's drink. Pretty stupid reason for what happened, but the reason ceased to matter after the third or fourth round of insults, and suddenly there were six of them and one of him, and punches started flying. Two of them held him down, the others took turns kicking him when he went down. Like everybody else standing around at the party, I was frozen in shock, cold beer in hand. Violence happens so quickly. Unless it's you taking the beating, it takes time for it to sink in, especially when alcohol's involved. If you're an onlooker, reaction comes later, when you're asking yourself why the hell you didn't do anything to help.

It couldn't have been long as serious beatings go, maybe less than a minute, but a guy can get really fucked up in sixty seconds when it's a free-for-all, six on one. About the time some of the other guys at the party realised they should be doing something and I opened my mouth to scream, Lewis got kicked in the head and he rolled on his side toward me, and I saw his face.

Bloody. Scared to death. Desperate.

He reached out to me. No, that's wrong; he reached out toward me. He reached for power, as unconsciously as a child reaching for its mother.

The Mother Of Us All reached back.

I felt power sweep over – out of me – in a storm of pins and needles, felt the air gasp around me, felt water drops pulled off my skin and my beer bottle by the sheer power of his call.

The wind hit with the force of a freight train. It was targeted, specific, and it was hungry. I felt its tugging passage, but it barely ruffled my hair; it slammed into the six frat boys and picked them up and swept them across the parking lot, into the side of a brick building, and pinned them there thirty feet off the ground.

Nobody except those who study weather really understands the incredible nature of wind. A fifty-mile-an-hour gust is brutal, but a seventy-five-mile-an-hour gust is more than twice as powerful as that because of the increased pressure per square inch. A ninety-mile wind, three times worse.

These college boys were crushed by, at minimum, a wind of above 120 miles per hour. Enough to fracture bones from the sheer force of the impact. More bones broke from the pressure acting on them as they were held up against the wall. I remember thinking, as I looked at this incredible display of power, *My God, he's going to squeeze them into jelly*, but in the next second Lewis blinked and the wind died and they fell thirty feet to the grass.

Chaos followed. Lewis lay on the ground, gasping for air, staring at me. I stared back in total shock. After what seemed like ages, I hurried over to him, hunkered down, and put my hand on his forehead. He felt burning hot.

'Jesus, Lewis, you called the wind,' I blurted. 'You've got everything. *Everything.*'

He just managed to nod. He probably didn't understand exactly what it meant, the state he was in. The Association got there before five minutes was out, and he was loaded into an ambulance accompanied by three of the most powerful Wardens in the entire world, all of them arguing furiously about what had just happened.

He looked afraid. And woozy. I keep thinking that if I'd done something then, said something to him, tried to stop them from taking him away, maybe things would have been different.

But, realistically, probably not.

I drove for about half an hour before I decided the radio wasn't going to make any more mystical-musical pronouncements. I fished the cell phone one-handed out of my purse and checked the battery level. Two bars. No chance of recharging; I hadn't had time to pack for basic hygiene, much less handy phone accessories. I paged through the numbers in memory – Mom, Sarah, my dry cleaners, my massage therapist... Ah. Estrella Almondovar. Just who I was looking for.

I punched the speed dial and waited through the clicks and rings, lots of rings, before a sleep-mashed voice mumbled, 'This had *better* be important.'

'Kinda,' I said, with as much fake cheer as I could pack into my voice. 'Gooood morning, my little jumping bean.'

She cleared her throat. I could just see her dragging a hand through midnight-black hair, trying to rub away the dreams.

'I got your salsa right here, bimbo,' she said. '*Jesus Maria*, what time is it?'

'Eight a.m. on the East Coast.'

'Yeah, that's like *six* here. You know, big hand on the six, only you can't see it 'cause it's *dark*? What, they don't teach you time zones in Florida?' I heard sheets rustling. Static clawed the line. 'I guess you want something.'

'Great sex,' I sighed. 'With a gorgeous man, with a great big—'

'Bank account,' she finished. 'Some things never change, eh? Sad thing is, you'll probably get it. Meanwhile, I get to listen to your wet dreams at you've-got-to-be-fucking-kidding-me in the morning.'

I downshifted and drafted behind a semi tractor-trailer hauling ass in the fast lane. With cars like my lovely Delilah, and ever-rising gas prices, it pays to conserve all the fuel you can. The Mustang shuddered from the buffeting before we settled into the slipstream, then purred out her pleasure.

Somewhere in the wilds of Oklahoma, Estrella banged what sounded like metal around, dropped the phone, picked it up. 'It's your dime, Jo. You've got until my coffeemaker fills up the first cup, and then I'm gone whether you're finished or not.'

'Places to see, people to do?'

She snorted. '*Chica*, you ought to cut down on the crack. I got no place to be and nobody to do, as usual.' That was closer to the truth than either of us wanted to explore.

'Then this would be good news: I'm headed your way.'

'Seriously?' Her tone turned guarded. 'What's wrong?'

'Wrong? Why would it be wrong?' I thwacked myself on the forehead. Estrella – Star, to her friends – knew me too well.

'You're kidding, right? *You* – leave a life of topless beaches and hot hard bodies to vacation in *Oklahoma*?'

'Dying to see you!'

'Right.' She dragged the word through three syllables. 'How long has it been?'

'Um...' I couldn't remember. 'A year?'

'Try two.'

'Hey, I keep in touch. Don't forget the phone calls. Or the Christmas cards.'

'The Christmas cards show up in February,' she said. OK, she had a point, I wasn't exactly the most reliable friend in the world. 'So what's the deal, Jo? You need crash space?'

'Maybe. Well. Yeah.' I heard her pouring liquid into a mug. 'I should be there in a couple of days. You think I can stop in, maybe just catch a shower and some rest? I may not need it. I'm just saying, maybe. I'll pay for dinner, honest. And at someplace good, not the local roach factory.'

Star sipped coffee. I was desperately jealous; my mouth watered at the thought. 'Tell you what, you maybe show up, I'll *maybe* let you in. That's if you swear there's not going to be any trouble, like you were in last time.'

'That was *so* not my fault. Tornadoes are a perfectly natural phenomenon. Not my fault you live where they go for vacation.'

'Hey, we live *la vida loca* around here, girlfriend. So. Why are you really coming out to the ass-end of nowhere?'

'It's not the ass-end of nowhere. And besides, you're there.' I winced again. That sounded suspiciously like what my buddy Andy had said when I asked him if I was getting fat. You're not fat

– you're my friend! Well, at least it had made me go on a diet.

'Actually… I wasn't being completely honest before. Something's kinda wrong. I have to find somebody. It's important.'

'Somebody around here?'

'Last I heard, he was somewhere close.' I was reluctant to say the name, but hell, Star was right; she knew everybody and everything that went on in that part of the world. 'Um, it's…Lewis.'

'*Qué?*' she blurted. 'You know, I was only kidding about the crack, but seriously, are you high? You got any idea how many people have been looking for him since he disappeared?'

'Yeah, I know. Pretty much everybody in the upper circles.'

'What the hell you gonna do when you find him?'

Not anything I could admit to, certainly not to Star. 'Look, let's not get into it, OK? Let's just call it catching up on old times.'

'Sure. OK.' She banged more metal – probably skillets. Star was a hell of a cook. 'So I'll watch for you, then.'

I sensed something on her end, something she wanted to ask, so I waited. She finally said, 'Hey, you haven't heard anything, have you? About me?'

'From who?'

'Forget it.'

'No, really? From who?'

Another long hesitation. It wasn't like her. Star was a do-it girl. 'I just get worried sometimes, you know? That they'll change their minds. Come and finish the job.'

That hit me hard, in unguarded places. I hurt for her. 'No, baby, that's not gonna happen. Everybody agreed, you deserve to hang on to what you have. You know that. Why would they change their minds?'

'Why do they do anything?' She forced a laugh. 'Hey, no worries, I'm just freakin' paranoid – you know that. I listen to the little voices in my head too much.'

I would, too, if I were Star. Which led down paths of speculation where I didn't want to follow. 'Well, now I'm all jealous. I wish I had little voices in my head. Guess I'll just have to settle for people *really* being out to get me.'

'Bitch,' she said cordially.

'Bimbo.'

Three or four uninspired insults later, we mutually hung up. I tossed the phone back in the passenger seat. Star would give me shelter, and she'd never rat me out to anyone looking for me, but she was really, really vulnerable. A few years ago, Star had taken a tremendous hit, both physically and emotionally, and she'd been forced to leave the Wardens. Usually, when people leave, they get blocked – a kind of magical lobotomy, to ensure they can't go rogue. It had been a close thing with Star, but they'd let her keep what little she had left. Provisionally.

And Star was absolutely right – that didn't mean that somebody wouldn't show up on her doorstep with official sympathy and orders to rip the essence of power out by the bloody roots. They'd damn sure hop to it if they found me conspiring with her, what with me bearing the Demon Mark and all. *God.* I shouldn't be dragging her into this, but there were only a few people in the world I could trust with my CD collection, much less with my life. In fact, there were only three.

Lewis and Star and Paul.

It'll be OK. If I found Lewis, if he did as I asked, if everything worked out OK…I wouldn't need to put her at risk.

If. If, if, if.

It was a small word to hang the rest of my future on. Star's, too.

When I was fifteen, my mother fell in love with a guy named Albert. First of all, I ask you – Albert? I guess it could have been worse. He could have been named Cuthbert or Engelbert, but at fifteen it was still a crushing horror to me. Albert the Bear. Big, hairy guy, with a laugh that sounded like a rusty chainsaw and a fashion sense second only to Paul Bunyan for addiction to flannel.

Albert wanted us all to get closer to nature. Even then, knowing next to nothing, I knew it was a really bad idea, but Mom thought he not only hung the moon but painted it, too, so we all packed our outdoorsy equipment and flannel shirts and hiking boots, and headed off into the Big Empty.

Actually, it was Yellowstone National Park, but same diff.

All right, it was beautiful – breathtaking, even to a disaffected fifteen-year-old girl who didn't want to be pulled away from the mall and her friends for the summer. Beautiful and wild and powerful.

But mostly I was bored, and I wished for TV and MTV and boys. Awesome geysers: check. Incredible vistas: check. Crushing ennui: gotcha.

We hiked. And hiked. And hiked. I wasn't much for that, and when my boots rubbed blisters on the first day, Albert the Bear wouldn't let me rest; he told me it would toughen my feet. I sulked and snapped at Mom and wished desperately that I would fall and break my leg so that a good-looking rescue party of tall, dark-haired men would come carry me away. Occasionally I wished Albert would get eaten by a bear, but that was before I actually saw one; once I had, I didn't wish *anybody* to get eaten by a bear.

Somehow, we got to the top of whatever ridge we were trying to climb, and while Mom and Albert were admiring the downhill view, I was looking up.

'It's going to rain,' I said. The sky was a perfect ocean-deep azure, the sun a hot gold coin glittering like sunken treasure. I sat down on a rock and started to take my shoes off.

'Don't take 'em off,' Albert advised me in his rumbling bass voice. 'Feet'll swell. And I think you're wrong, Jo. It doesn't look like rain.'

I craned my neck, shaded my eyes, and looked up at the thick black bulk of him standing over me. Nice to be in the shade. Not so nice to be in Albert's shade.

'See that?' I pointed to the thin, wispy clouds in perfect waves. 'Cirrus clouds, coming out of the east.'

'So?' For some granola-chewing, tree-hugging forest nut, Albert wasn't very weather wise.

I smiled. 'Look.' I grabbed a stick and drew a circle in the dirt. 'The planet spins this way, right? East to west.'

'Just figured that out, did you?'

I ignored him and drew an arrow the opposite direction. 'Wind moves west to east, against rotation. So why is the wind coming out of the east?'

This time he didn't say anything. That was fine; I wasn't listening anyway. 'It's coming out of the east because there's something rotating—' My stick drew a spiral somewhere over where I guessed we were. '—that's changing the direction of the wind. Rotation means a storm.'

He looked over at my mother. She looked back. I figured the silent conversation had something to do with what a freak I was, what the hell were they going to do with me, and on and on and on. Not like I hadn't already said it and wondered it myself.

I drew some wavy lines in the sand next to the spiral. 'Cirrus clouds form way up high – ice crystal clouds, running ahead of a pressure system. So. It's probably going to rain. Based on how fast they're moving, it'll probably be here before dark.'

A freshening eastern breeze frayed my hair out of its braid and plastered strands to my sweating face.

Somewhere out there, beyond the trees, beyond the place where morning started, I could feel it growing, pulling energy from the collision of warm and cold air, condensing water and energy, sucking micro-drops together to form mist, mist to form clouds, clouds to form rain.

I closed my eyes and I could almost taste it, cloud-soft on my tongue, the taste of brass and ozone and cool, clear water. God, it felt good. Tingles all the way inside, deep down. I'd never been out in the open before to a storm forming. It had a raw, wild power I'd never expected.

'Bullshit,' Albert said bluntly, and laughed. 'Pretty good try, Jo, Hey, you've got quite the con artist there, Nancy.'

My mother wasn't smiling, and she wasn't laughing. She looked at me gravely, thumbs hooked in the straps of her backpack, and shifted from one foot to the other. Mom wasn't used to hiking, either, but she hadn't complained, hadn't talked about blisters or being thirsty or being tired.

'Are you quite the con artist, Jo?' she asked me. I didn't say anything. She turned back to Albert. 'We'd better start back.'

'Oh, come on, Nancy, you don't buy this stuff, do you? She's fifteen years old, she's not some damn weatherman. You can tell the weather around here for days around, anyway. Clear as a bell, that's what this is.'

'There's high pressure to the south,' I said, lacing up my boots. 'Wall cloud forming over the horizon to the east. It'll be bad by nightfall – it's moving fast. Warm air always moves faster than cold.'

'We should start back,' Mom repeated. 'Now.'

And that was that. Albert the Bear grumbled and muttered, but we started back down the ridge. The first darkness edged over the eastern horizon, like early night, at just after three in the afternoon, and then it flowed like spilt ink, staining the sky. Albert shut up about coddling my fear of nature and devoted his breath to making good time. We scrambled down sheer slopes, jogged down inclines, edged carefully past crumbling paths over open gorges. People talk about nature as a mother, but to me she's always been Medea, ready and willing to slaughter her children. Every sheer drop we navigated was an open mouth, every jagged rock a naked tooth.

I wasn't attuned to the land, but even I could sense the power in it, the anger, the desire to smash us like the intruding predators we were. I felt it from the storm, too; the storms that made it into cities were less self-aware, more instinctual. This one pulsed with pure menace.

Warmer air breathed through the trees, rattled branches, and fluttered leaves. The breeze picked up and it carried the sharp scent of rain.

'Faster,' I panted as we hit easier terrain. We ran for it as the storm clouds unfurled octopus tentacles overhead and the rain came down in a punishing silver curtain. Overhead, lightning forked purple white, and without a city to frame it, lightning was huge and powerful, taller than the mountain it struck. Thunder hit like a physical body blow. It rattled through my skin, my cartilage, bones. We're mostly water, our bodies. Sound travels in waves.

Above us on the ridge, a tree went up like a torch.

Albert was yelling something about a ranger station. I could barely see. The rain stung like angry wasps, and under the trees the blackness was complete. Better not to stay under the trees anyway, too much risk of drawing another lightning strike.

Pins and needles across my back, at the top of my head.

'Get down!' I yelled, and rolled into a ball on the ground, trying to present the smallest exposure to the storm. I could feel it now – it was like a blind man with an axe hunting a mouse. It wanted me. It was drawn to me.

It *hated* me.

Lightning hit close, very close. I felt the concussion and heard something that was too loud to be just a *sound*, it was a *force* with energy and life of its own.

I was sobbing now because I knew the next time it would get me. It knew where I was. It could smell my fear.

Somebody grabbed my arm and dragged me to my feet. We ran through the darkness, slipping on grass and mud. Deer burst out of the darkness and across our path like white ghosts fleeing a graveyard.

We made it to the ranger station, and I realised only when I saw Mom and Albert were already there, wrapped in blankets and shivering, that the person who'd dragged me up and out from under the storm wasn't anyone I knew.

She was small and golden skinned and dark haired, and she was laughing as she swept off her park ranger hat and hung it up to dry.

'Nice day for a walk' the other ranger said, the one handing Mom and Albert steaming cups of coffee. My rescuer grinned at him and looked out the window. Rain lashed the glass as if it were reaching inside for us.

'Yup,' she agreed. 'Just about perfect.'

She glanced over at me, and I felt it like a current humming between us. We were the same, shared something fundamental.

The storm wasn't hunting me. It was hunting us both.

'You should be more careful,' she said. 'Some people just aren't cut out for communing with nature.'

'What's your excuse?' I shot back. She lifted one shoulder.

'Somebody's got to be on the front lines,' she said. 'Estrella Almondovar. Star, for short.'

I told her my name. We shook hands. She got me a blanket and, instead of coffee, hot cocoa. As she handed it over, she lowered her voice and said, 'You have a notice? From the Association?'

'Yeah. I'll have an Intake Board at eighteen.'

'Well, don't wait. Start getting the training now, like me – this is my internship. You need it. I've seen the Park react like this to only one other person before.'

'Who?' I asked. She gave me a teasing little wouldn't-you-like-to-know smile.

'You don't know him,' she said. 'But his name is Lewis.'

She went back to the cabin window and stood

watching the fire up on the ridge, the one that the first lightning strike started. As I watched, it flickered, sizzled, and went out.

That's when I knew. She wasn't a Weather Warden, not like me. She had power over fire.

From that day, we were friends. I don't really know why; we didn't have all that much in common, beyond the obvious, but we had a kind of vibe. Energy. We resonated to the same frequencies.

We ended up roomies at Princeton, shared a thousand joys and tragedies and triumphs. She was the best friend I ever had, and it looked for a while like we were going to live charmed lives forever. Smart, beautiful, gifted. Two peas in a pod. Perfect.

And then Yellowstone burnt, and everything changed for both of us.

I gloomily considered Oklahoma City. The most direct route was to follow the Connecticut toll roads until I could get on I-90. It would be the better part of a two-day journey. The coffee I'd slammed down in a caffeinated frenzy at 4 a.m. was no more than a memory, and my stomach rumbled to remind me that delicious as it was, mocha was not a food group.

So should I stop to eat, or pile up the miles? My decisions almost always depend on the forecast, so I flipped stations until I got a weather channel.

The storm that had followed me out of Florida was now ravaging the eastern seaboard. I could see darkness amassing on the horizon behind me, and a flanking line at the edges of the supercell. It was starting to turn, driven by Coriolis effect and the powerful internal engine of water heating and cooling; when it completed its rotation, it would be that most dreaded of East Coast storms, the nor'easter.

I didn't intend to be anywhere near it.

You might wonder why I didn't just give it a wave of my hand and get rid of it – which was entirely within my powers. Well, Newton was right: action gets reaction. Every time a Warden balks the weather, the power has to go somewhere, and believe me, you don't want the power of a supercell discharging through *you*; it's something on the order of three or four larger-than-average nuclear bombs. If I'd tried directly to make my stalker-storm disperse – waved my hands and parted the winds, to give it a biblical interpretation – I might have succeeded here and created the world's largest-ever tornado whirling its way directly at me from the opposite direction. Plus, I wasn't an official Warden in this area...or anywhere, come to that. Not anymore.

Still, I'd been one of the most subtle weatherworkers in history, all my performance reviews said so; I could probably slide it under the radar of anyone who might be looking for me up there in Oversight. Not that I had a lot of choice, really… No matter how fast I drove, this storm was bound to catch me. It had the scent of me now.

I turned the radio on, settled myself comfortably in the body-hugging seat of the Mustang, and began humming while Jim Morrison sang – funnily enough – about riders on the storm. As I drove, I shifted – not gears, but the air above. Cooled it here, warmed it there, slowed the elevator-fast updrafts that were feeding the storm its power. It was delicate work, making sure the energy expended didn't add up to another problem, and still making enough changes that the storm weakened. Also, I had to do it quietly. Last thing I wanted to do was attract attention from the local officials.

It took about two and a half hours to reduce it from a badass mofo to an inoffensive low-pressure system, which is nothing much if you're driving a Mustang and listening to a Doors album marathon. I pulled off the road in the parking lot of a roadside diner called the Kountry Kafe, put the car in neutral, and closed my eyes as I left my body to check out the results.

In Oversight, the world looks very different. I lifted my hand in front of my face and saw a tracery of crystal, my aura cool blue edged with flashes of green and – most unsettlingly – streaks of red. Red was bad. Red was trouble. No wonder the Djinn had smelt the Mark on me.

Nothing I could do about it now. I stepped out in my astral form and admired the crystalline perfection of the Mustang, which was even more beautiful in Oversight than in the mundane world. A real magical beauty of a car. One look at the Kountry Kafe convinced me I didn't want to eat there; it pulsed with bad vibes, like a quaking mass of rancid Jell-O.

I spread my weightless arms and went up. There was no sense of speed – not in this reality – and no sense of resistance, either. I glided up, and up, and up, until the earth curved off beneath me. From that dizzying height, I studied the deforming spiral of the storm. In Oversight it looked almost the same as in the real world, only instead of lightning, the energy displayed in colours – brilliant, vibrant colours that a trained Warden could interpret. I'd done enough with it, I thought. Its overall rotation had been disrupted, and the lightning flickers were showing in golds and greens, sheets of positive and negative charges in scattered glitter. If I'd missed the mark, I would've seen reds and a steady photonegative undertone.

I let go, and the planet rushed back at me. The first time I'd travelled in Oversight, I'd absolutely freaked, and no wonder: the sensation of falling back into your body is one of the most terrifying feelings in the world. These days, I enjoyed it like a thrill ride. Few enough thrills in my life recently. Not to mention fewer dates.

I filled my body again, and the world took on weight and form and dimension. Delilah the Mustang assumed her familiar glossy midnight-blue paint job.

My stomach rumbled again. With one last, regretful glance at the Kountry Kafe, I eased on down the road.

The diner where I finally stopped looked outwardly a lot like the last one, but its Oversight characteristics were more encouraging. It was called Vera's Place. Vera, it turned out, was long gone, but the owner and operator was a perky thirty-year-old named Molly with hair that showed several indecisive home dye jobs and the kind of creamy milkmaid skin that every Hollywood actress wants.

'Pie?' she asked me expectantly as I polished off the last of my open-faced turkey sandwich and mashed potatoes. There wasn't a lot of commerce going on inside Vera's Diner; I counted about six old coots and a yuppie couple dressed from the LL Bean catalogue who sneered at the menu selections and would never even have considered eating something as middle-American as *pie*. Which decided me.

'What, you think I'm hungry or something?' I asked, and scraped up the last of the delicious pan gravy with the edge of my fork. I got a dimpled smile in response.

'Last one we had in here didn't eat pie was some hot-shot defence lawyer from LA,' she confided. I passed over the turkeyless, gravy-free plate.

'Wouldn't want to be included in that company,' I agreed. 'What kind of pie you got?'

She raised an eyebrow. 'You really want the whole list?'

'Just the high points.'

The high points could have filled a couple of pages, single spaced. I decided on chocolate.

'German, cream, or meringue?'

'I'm sorry, is that a choice? Meringue, of course. Definitely.'

The meringue was taller than most three-layer cakes, a hugely delicious confection that went down perfectly cool with the rich, creamy chocolate beneath. The crust was to die for, crisp and delicious. Best pie I ever had. Honest. The Oversight never lies about the quality of food, especially pies.

While I was savouring the last few bites, I took out a road map and looked over the route. Long. Long and boring. I asked Molly about good places to stay and got two recommendations, visited the little Wardens' room, and went back to my car full of chocolatey satisfaction, with the full intention of finding a Holiday Inn with adult channels and a minibar. One gets fun where one can.

Just as I reached for the car's door latch, a feeling swept over me, pins and needles, unmistakable and terrifying. I snatched the door open and dived. My feet had just left the ground when lightning hissed up from the dirt where I'd stood, down from the grey clouds, and met in the middle with an awesome snap of power. The flash blinded me. My ears rattled from the force of the boom. I smelt harsh, metallic ozone and thought about how close I'd come to being a fuse in that current.

Lightning can come from a clear sky, but it has to be driven by energy from *somewhere*, and the storm that I'd doctored no longer had the charge necessary. There wasn't any potential – and yet, I could feel it all around me, a strong positive charge in the ground, negative charges building overhead in the clear but humid sky.

In Oversight, chains of electrons formed and rippled like translucent snakes in the sky – a cold hard glitter striking straight for me. Dear God, somebody was doing this. Somebody really powerful.

I rolled over, clawed hair away from my face, and saw that the ground was blackened and smoking where I'd been standing. The diner's front door banged open, and Molly and the other patrons – even the yuppie couple – crowded around the opening. Too sensible to come outside, too interested to be really safe. I waved at them to show I was all right and started to pull the door of the Mustang shut.

The interior of the open door was charred in a straight line, up and down, poor baby. I hesitated, touched the metal carefully, and found it hot but not scorching. It squeaked in protest when I hauled it closed, but the engine started and the gears still fit.

I had to put some distance between me and what was going on. And I had to undo the damage that had been done up in the atmosphere before lightning started striking like blue-white cobras all over the county, mindless and vicious and enraged. I pulled out on the road and started trying to reverse polarity on the charged particles in the air overhead. The trick was not to try to change everything, just enough links in the chain to break the connections. I chose the particles by feel and instinct, turning *that* one, and *that* one, then flipping a whole section like a pancake on a hot griddle.

Breaking the chain of destruction.

The particles rolled back over, connecting faster than thought, heading for me and Delilah.

Dammit!

I hit the gas and Delilah jumped, raced like her life depended on it. I abandoned the sky and focused on the thin line of moisture on the road beneath the tires. I couldn't change the charge in the earth, couldn't even sense if the ground had been sensitised, too, but I *could* control the water. It was something my enemy – whoever that was – might not have thought of.

In the split second before lightning discharged through the open particle chain, I reversed the polarity of the water and snapped its energy feed to the ground.

The circuit broke, and the energy bled off harmlessly in a million directions.

I waited, watching in Oversight, while my body took care of controlling the Mustang's wild gallop on damp pavement. Watched the living, thinking particles turn and turn and turn, whirring, searching for another circuit to complete.

I watched them suddenly revert to their natural random state as whoever was behind it let go.

I pulled in a deep breath and realised I was sweating. The car reeked with it.

I rolled down the windows and kept driving, not daring to slow down.

The weather isn't what you think it is. Not by a long shot.

It's a predator. In fact, the whole world around you is full of predators you can't see, can't sense, that are held in check only by their own whims and the power of about one per cent of the human population. You want to know why the dinosaurs died out? Look around. They didn't have any Wardens.

We come in three basic flavours. People who control water and air are Weather Wardens, and we're in charge of keeping the furious storms the planet stirs up from scouring mankind off the face of the planet. Earth Wardens keep us from joining the great march to extinction by diverting dozens of planet-crushing catastrophes every year. Fire Wardens control – or try to control – the tendency of the planet to burn things to crispy ash. Mother Nature is schizophrenic and homicidal, and the only thing that stands between you and hideous, painful death is a couple of thousand people worldwide hanging on by their fingernails. Happy, huh? Most people don't want to know that. Hell, most of the time *I* don't want to know.

The Wardens are people with one hell of a lot of magical ability, but the Wardens Association is, foremost and always, a bureaucracy. Oh, sure, we're public servants, saving lives, doing good works, blah blah, but hey, we get paid, and we have structure and job duties and a very nice dental program. Sort of like the IRS, if the IRS kept you from being horribly killed on a daily basis.

In charge are the High Wardens who make up the World Council (which is, oddly, based in the UN Building in New York, although not on any floor most people are likely to visit). Below them you have your National Wardens, who control entire countries, and beneath them Sector Wardens, Regional Wardens, Local Wardens, and Staff.

Nobody expected there would be anything more powerful than a World Council Warden, but then nobody had expected Lewis to pop up, controlling all the elements. Lewis didn't fit. Or...to be more accurate...he fit in right at the top. A true master of the craft, absolutely unique. Nobody in the great big machine that made up the Association much liked the idea, except they couldn't very well doubt it, not with Lewis demonstrating it every time they asked by calling fire, water, air, earth. For a while after the incident with the frat boys, Lewis lived like a lab rat, hemmed in by people who desperately wanted to control him, disprove him, understand him, stop him, worship him, destroy him. And some who just wanted his autograph.

I tried to find out what was going on, but I was just an apprentice, even if everybody agreed I had lots of power and promise. There was no way I'd be kept informed about decisions made at the World level. But at some point – and this is just a guess – I think they decided that it would be safer for everybody if Lewis just didn't exist.

I think somebody tried to kill him. Worse. I think they were stupid enough to miss.

Anyway, we know that Lewis flew the coop. He

vanished with three – count 'em, *three* – of the precious bottles of Djinn from the Association vaults. Poof. Crime of the century, committed by the most wanted man on earth.

Since then, seven years ago, a lot of people have been looking for Lewis.

I was just the latest.

Lightning bolts out of the blue. Great. Somebody was trying to kill me. Actively. This was new, different, and not very welcome.

It was possible – OK, likely – that this had to do with a guy named Bad Bob Biringanine. Bad Bob was not quite two days dead, I'd been there for his big finish, and it was entirely conceivable that I was going to be held responsible. I *might* have a slim chance of avoiding that, but only if I came in from the cold and talked to the Wardens Council...and if I did it wearing the Demon Mark, well, that would be the ball game. I could explain, but they'd never believe me. Never.

And in any case, whether they believed me or not, they couldn't help me.

I was just praying hard that Lewis could. The problem was getting to him before somebody else got to me.

It was possible that the lightning had been an official warning from the Wardens, in which case

I was in really deep, no shovel in sight; I needed to know for sure before I decided on my next move. There was only one person I could trust to ask, these days, who was still on the inside. I retrieved the cell phone, checked the charge – down to one slender bar – and speed-dialled another number.

I got Paul on the first ring.

'Jesus fucking *Christ*, Jo, what did you just do?' It was a bellow, not a question, and I jerked the phone away from my ear, then tentatively moved it back. 'Fuckin' power surge the size of fuckin' New Jersey, and it's right in the middle of my Sector! And don't tell me it wasn't you, I know your style!'

'It wasn't me. Well, it was *aimed* at me, but I didn't start it,' I said, and waited out the gush of curses. Paul Giancarlo was one of the good guys. His temper was mostly a lot of sound, very little fury; for a guy with Family connections – in the Cosa Nostra sense – he was surprisingly sweet. However, I was in Paul's Sector, and within it, he was lord and master of the weather, and he took that responsibility *very* seriously. If I'd been careless with lives, he'd hold a grudge.

Paul bossed about a hundred Regional and Local Wardens, and his chunk of the world ran from somewhere around Montpelier down through Philadelphia, Pennsylvania. I was smack in the middle of it. He had the power to make my trip very uncomfortable indeed, since Paul was great in small scale. He could deliver a monsoon with pinpoint accuracy, hang it right over the Mustang no matter where I turned. He could funnel-cloud me up to Oz, if he chose. And I didn't have time. Besides, conflict between Wardens is rarely good for anybody.

'They're looking for you,' he said more quietly. 'Guess you already know that, since you dropped out of sight like that.'

'Yeah, well, not like I had a choice,' I said.

'What with the murder charges and all,' he agreed.

'It wasn't murder! It was—' Boy, it sounded lame. '—self-defence.'

He grunted. 'You know, Jo, that defence don't hold up all that well even in the regular courts, especially when the guy was three times your age and unarmed.'

'Like a Warden's ever unarmed. This was *Bad Bob* we're talking about, after all. Not some helpless old guy I knocked over the head for his wallet.'

He sighed. It rattled the speaker in the phone. 'He had a lot of friends. Lot of powerful friends. What the hell possessed you to take it this far? I mean, he could be a bastard, but Jesus, you fucking destroyed his house with him in it, Jo. Not to even mention that this storm you cooked up through all that crap has been focused on you like a guided missile.'

I didn't want to talk about that, too many things to explain about Bad Bob and Florida. 'Later. First things first. Somebody set up an unpredicted lightning bolt.'

A long, expressive whistle. 'That'd explain the fucking up of my weather. You're saying somebody threw it at you? Specifically?'

'I'm saying somebody really good threw it at me. I kind of need to know who. Was it…you know…official?'

'As in, did anybody clear it with me first? Hell no. Take my word for it: This didn't come through the chain of command.' He paused for a few seconds; I could almost hear him thinking. 'Jo, look, this is getting too serious. You'd better come see me. Albany. You know the address.'

I did. 'Paul?'

He understood the question before I had to ask it. 'I'm not turning you in, babe. I don't exactly come from a family history of ratting out.'

That said, he hung up. I clutched the phone for a few seconds, trying to decide, but really, I didn't have a choice. Paul's suggestions were just polite orders.

I urged the Mustang up another notch on the speeding-fine scale and hauled ass for Albany.

☙ ☙ ☙

I met Paul when I was eighteen, at my official intake meeting for the Wardens.

It was scheduled at a Holiday Inn outside of Sarasota. I had directions and an appointed time to appear, all on official Warden stationery, and I spent most of the drive wiping sweat from my palms and wishing I could keep on driving and disappear. But the Wardens had made it crystal clear that my presence was required, not requested. They'd also mentioned that they could not only make my life miserable, but if they wanted to, they could put a real unhappy ending on it, as well.

So I walked into the modest little hotel and looked over the meeting-room signs on the board, CULLIGAN COMPANY BOARD MEETING. Nope. LADIES ASSOCIATION OF ROSE GROWERS. Probably not. METEOROLOGICAL RESEARCH INSTITUTE. That looked like the right one. I tugged down my skirt one more time, wished I'd worn something businesslike and conservative, and walked down what felt like the Last Mile. The door was closed. I knocked.

That was the first time I met Paul. He made an impression. He opened the door, and for a frozen second, all I could think of was *Oh, my God, he's gorgeous*, and he made it that much worse by letting his eyes go wider and giving me that quick, comprehensive X-ray scan men are so good at delivering. He was six feet tall, olive skinned, with dark hair and designer stubble. Body by some very expensive personal trainer, or incredibly good genetics.

'Joanne Baldwin?' he asked, still standing in the doorway. I nodded. 'You're late.'

His voice didn't match his body; it was low, gravelly, rough. But then again, maybe it did match, because it vibrated in parts of me that generally don't react to voices. I swallowed hard and hoped my legs weren't shaking too badly, and I followed him into the room.

Of the seven people there, Paul was definitely the standout for looks, but that didn't mean anything; I felt potential power zip up and down my spine the minute I stepped inside. Ugly or beautiful, any one of these people could lay waste to entire countries.

The man sitting at the head of the long table stood up. He was older and blank faced, with grey eyes that looked as warm as polished marble. I didn't know it then, but I was meeting the man in charge of the weather for the entire continental United States, a man who did not generally concern himself with assessing the fitness of some little girl from down in Florida.

'Joanne Baldwin,' he said. It was by way of a formal introduction, and I nodded and fought an impulse to curtsy, which would have been disastrous in the miniskirt anyway. 'My name is Martin Oliver. You've just met Paul Giancarlo—' A nod from the stud muffin. 'Let me introduce the rest of the panel.'

It was a who's who of People Who Mattered. State Wardens from Texas, Arkansas, Montana. Marion Bearheart, an American Indian woman with kind eyes and an aura powerful enough to shatter glass...and the State Warden for Florida, Bob Biringanine. Bob was a short Irish-looking fellow with a perpetual blush, feathery white hair, and steel-blue eyes. He didn't like me. I could sense it at his first uninterested glance.

'Sit,' Martin Oliver invited me, and demonstrated the process. I carefully lowered myself into a squeaky black chair. Everybody stared at me for a few seconds. 'Coffee?'

'No thanks,' I managed. 'Look, I'm not really sure why—'

'You're here because either you need to be accepted into the Program, or you need to have your powers blunted,' Bob said. 'Somebody like you is too dangerous to leave running around wild.'

Martin's cold grey eyes flicked at him, but Bob didn't seem to feel the impact. I tried to think of something to say. Nothing volunteered. Bob – Bad Bob, I later learnt he was called – shuffled papers and found something that apparently interested him. I couldn't see what it was.

'There was a storm,' he said. 'One year ago. You vectored it around your house.'

Oh. That. I hadn't thought anybody noticed. My lips were dry again, and so was my mouth. 'I had to,' I said. My voice sounded childish and soft. Bad Bob's gaze pinned me like I was an insect.

'*Had to?*' he repeated, and traded looks with a couple of the others. 'Weeping Christ, girl, do you understand what you did? Your interference added force to the storm. What would just have caused minor damage to *your* house ended up destroying six others. Because of *you*. You lack judgment.'

I hadn't known that. I thought – I thought I'd done the right thing. Carefully. Precisely. The idea that I'd made things worse elsewhere was a completely new one.

'That's a little harsh,' said Marion Bearheart. She leant back in her chair and studied me. 'We've all screwed the pooch from time to time, Bob. You know that. Just last year, Paul dumped seventeen inches of rain on a floodplain when he was supposed to produce a summer shower. How many houses did you wash away, Paul?'

'Five,' Paul grunted. 'Thanks for bringing that up as often as possible.'

Bad Bob ignored him, staring straight at Marion. 'Paul didn't get anybody killed.'

My heart froze up. There was silence around the table. Bob shuffled papers and came up with a newspaper clipping. 'Dead in the wreckage of the house were Liza Gutierrez, twenty-nine, and Luis

Gutierrez, thirty-one. Three children between the ages of nine and two years escaped with the help of neighbours before the home collapsed.'

It was like listening to someone reading my own obituary. I tried to swallow. Couldn't. Looked down at faux woodgrain and blinked back tears. *I didn't know I didn't know I didn't know.* The mantra of the helpless.

And then, a low gravelly voice. 'Bullshit.' I looked up to see Paul staring at Bob. 'Come on, Bob, she deflected the storm, sure, and she didn't take the force vectors and wind speed into account, but it still wasn't a bad job. But then, *you* didn't recheck for changing conditions before you started lowering the ceiling up in the mesosphere. You want to sling some blame, I think you ought to get a little on you, too. And for God's sake, people die. Without us, the whole Atlantic seaboard would be a pile of corpses – you know that as well as anybody. Sometimes you can't save everybody. Sometimes you can't even save yourself. You know that. You of all people.'

'Paul,' Martin Oliver said quietly. 'Enough.'

Paul shut up. So did Bad Bob, who closed the folder. Martin Oliver opened his own.

'Joanne, maybe what we should be talking about is a great deal more basic. Do you *want* to be a Warden? It's not an easy life, and it's not especially rewarding. You'll never have fame, and even though you'll save a lot of lives, you'll never receive gratitude or recognition. You'll need to go through another six years of training, minimum, before you're trusted as a Staff Warden.' His grey eyes studied me with absolute impartiality. 'Some people don't have the temperament for it. I understand that you're prone to act first and think later.'

I licked my lips. 'Sometimes.'

'Under what circumstances would you believe it was permissible to use the kind of powers you've been given? To, for instance, get rid of a violent storm?'

'To – save lives?' Nobody had told me there was going to be a test. Dammit.

Martin exchanged a look with Bad Bob. 'What about saving property?'

'Um...no.'

'No?' Martin's eyebrows levitated, making his grey eyes wider. 'Is there no time when saving property might be preferable to saving lives?'

My heart was beating too fast; it was hurting my chest. I could hardly swallow for the lump in my throat. 'No. I don't think so.'

'What if the property were, say, a nuclear reactor whose destruction might result in the deaths of thousands more?'

Oh. I hadn't thought of that one.

'What if the property were the central distribution centre for food in a country full of starving people? Would you save the property, or the lives, if by saving lives you starved even more?'

'I don't know,' I whispered. My hands were shaking. I made them into fists when Bad Bob's laugh sawed the air.

'She doesn't know. Well, that's typical. This is what we end up with these days, a bunch of kids raised on free lunches who never had to make a decision in their lives more important than what TV show to watch. You want to trust her with the power of life and death?' He snorted and shoved my folder into the centre of the table. 'I've heard enough.'

'Wait!' I blurted. 'I'm sorry. I didn't understand.'

Marion Bearheart looked at me from the other side of the table, her warm brown eyes full of compassion. 'And do you understand now, Joanne?'

'Sure,' I lied. 'I'd save the power plant. And – and the food.'

Silence around the table. Bad Bob stood up. Nobody argued with him; nobody moved so much as a muscle as he raised his hands at shoulder level.

A cloud started forming above our heads. Just mist at first, clinging to the ceiling like fog, and then getting denser, taking on form and shape. I felt humidity sucking up into that thing, fuelling power.

'Hey—,' I said. 'Um—'

Power leapt through the air, jumping from each one of the Wardens in the room and into that cloud.

It was feeding on them, drawing energy. It was... It was...

...alive.

Bad Bob watched me with those eerie, cold eyes. 'Better do something,' he advised. 'Don't know how long it's going to be content to just sit there.'

'Do what?' I yelped. I didn't remember standing, but I was out of my chair, backing away. The power in that room – the uncontrolled, unfocused menace – the sense that the cloud overhead was *thinking*—

I felt it click in on me as if a channel had opened, and something hot and powerful tore out of the cloud at me. I didn't have time to think, to do anything but just *react*.

I reached up into the cloud and ripped it apart. No finesse to it, no control, just sheer raw power – and power that got loose, manifested in arcing static electricity from every metal surface. Glass shattered. The pitcher of water on the table hissed into steam.

I ducked into a crouch in the corner until it was all over, and the room was clear and silent.

Very, very silent.

I looked up and saw them all still sitting there, hands on the table. Nobody had moved an inch. Marion was the first to get up; she walked over to a covered cart and took out a thick beach towel, and went about the business of mopping up beads of water from the conference table. Somebody else

– probably a Fire Warden – brought the lights back online. Except for a couple of burn marks around the power outlets, it all looked normal enough.

Bad Bob sat back down in his chair, slumped at ease, and propped his chin on his fist. 'I rest my case,' he said. 'She's a menace.'

'I agree,' said the snippy-looking librarian type from Arkansas. 'I've rarely seen anything so completely uncontrolled.'

Martin Oliver shook his head. 'She has plenty of power. You know how rare it is to find that.'

They went around the table, each one putting in a comment about my general worthlessness or worthiness. Marion Bearheart voted for me. So did two others.

It came down to Paul Giancarlo, who stood and walked over to me and offered me a hand up. He kept holding my hand until he was sure I wasn't going to collapse into a faint on the floor.

'You know what this is?' he asked. 'What it is we're deciding here?'

'Whether or not to let me into the Wardens,' I said.

He shook his head, very kindly. 'Whether or not to let you *live*. If I say you can't be trained, you go into Marion's keeping, and she and her people try to take away your powers without killing you. Sometimes it works. Sometimes...not so well.'

If he was hoping to scare me, he'd succeeded

brilliantly. I wanted to say something, but I honestly had no idea what to try. Everything I'd done so far was wrong. Maybe keeping my mouth shut was the best thing I could do.

He finally smiled. 'Not going to beg, are you?'

I shook my head.

'That's something,' he said, and turned around to Martin Oliver. 'I'll take her on. She can't cut it, it's my responsibility. But I think she's going to be a damn good Warden someday.'

Martin winced. 'Not quite yet, though.'

'Yeah, well. Who is, at eighteen?'

'You were,' Martin said. 'I was.'

Paul shrugged. 'We're fuckin' prodigies, Marty. And neither one of us ever had half the power this girl does coming into it.'

'That's what I'm afraid of,' Bad Bob said. 'That's *exactly* what I'm afraid of.'

It was four to three to make me a Warden.

Two hours later, I made it to Albany. Not a bad town, Albany – nice, historic, a little run-down but still the kind of kid-and-dog place that people boast about. Probably smaller than the residents preferred it to be, considering it was the state capital and all. I'd hit it in pretty season – tulips bloomed in shocking rows of red and yellow, like velvet rings of fire rippling in the wind around trees and home gardens. I passed through the industrial area near

Erie Canal, past narrow brownstones with soot-dark stoops, and turned toward the south end – up Hamilton toward the part of town called – appropriately – the Mansions.

Paul lived in a house that had to cost at least a cool quarter million…with spacious lawn, gracious styling, and a lacy white gazebo in the back overlooking a rose garden. I pulled into the drive and parked the Mustang, let the engine rumble to a stop, and took a little peek into Oversight.

I almost wished I hadn't. Paul's house was a castle in the aetheric, I'm talking *castle* here, with battlements and flags and arrow slits. Not too surprising, since Paul had always been a knight – in the warlike sense, the old-fashioned, bloody, mace-and-sword kind. And his Sector was a fiefdom. Paul's world was heavy on the black and white. Bad news for Team Me, whose colours these days were grey and greyer.

I dropped back into tulips and Doric columns on the portico as the front door opened. Paul walked out to meet me. However knightly he might have looked in Oversight, in the real world, Paul was pure Italian Stallion…strong, muscular, with bone structure that bordered on godlike. He still had designer stubble, except I'd long ago learnt it was really just a permanent five-o'clock shadow. Paul had turned forty a couple of years ago, but it hadn't slowed him down any, and *damn*, he was still gorgeous.

Also unfortunately mad as hell at me, at the moment.

'Outta the car,' he said, and jerked a thumb at me.

I rolled down the window with the hand crank. 'Not yet.'

He glowered. 'Why the fuck not? You don't trust me?'

'Check out the door,' I said. The marks of the lightning strike had certainly not done wonders for Delilah's paint job. 'C'mon, somebody tried to fry me in my Stuart Weitzmans the last time I got out. I'm not falling for it twice.'

Some of Paul's anger melted as he looked at the evidence. But, being Paul, he didn't express any shock or sympathy or ask any touchy-feely questions, either. He said, 'You're scared.'

'No shit. You'd be scared, too.'

'What? You don't think I could defuse a little lightning bolt?' he asked.

'Let's just say I'd rather you had four rubber tires between you and it when you give it a shot. C'mon, Paul, get in and well talk. Comfy vinyl seats—'

He grunted. 'You know as well as I do that rubber tires won't do a damn thing against half a million amps.'

'No, but my car has a steel body. It won't melt like that plastic POS you're driving over there.' I jerked my chin at his late-model Porsche.

He looked wounded. 'Don't badmouth Christine. She could give you a five-second start and still blow your doors off.' He let the smile come out, finally, and I felt it warm me like a bonfire. I'd lost count of the times we'd debated cars, discussed the finer points of auto repair, trash-talked about who'd win the fantasy drag race. 'Jeez, Jo, it's good to see you. In spite of every little damn thing. Listen, come inside. I promise you'll be safe.'

'No offence, Paul, but I can't exactly trust you, can I? You're a little too far up in the food chain not to know the orders are to detain me for questioning.'

'Sure, I got the memo,' he said. 'I'm willing to hear your side of it.'

'You'd be the only one.'

'Not the only one. You may think you're on your own, kid, but you don't have to be. You've got friends. Now's the time to count on them. Have a little faith in the system.'

I wanted to – dear God I wanted to – and if it were just a matter of a death and some questions, that would be one thing. The Demon Mark was something else entirely.

'OK, if Muhammad won't come to the mountain, whatever,' he said. 'Open up.'

I popped open the passenger door. He walked around the car and got in; the springs shuddered at the addition of his weight. Paul, not a small guy, looked uncomfortable squeezed into the shotgun seat, and we fiddled with adjustments until he had circulation, if not leg room.

The smell that filled the car was warm, sexy, and familiar. I sniffed closer to him and raised my eyebrows. Paul's face reddened. 'Oh, for Christ's sake, it's just a little aftershave, OK? I got a date for lunch.'

'Lucky her,' I said. 'So who's trying to kill me?'

'Wish it were that simple,' he said, and shifted uncomfortably. 'Jesus, would it kill you to do a little reupholstering here? It's more springs than padding.'

'Yeah, your big fat ass is just used to that luxurious German craftsmanship.' But I knew that what was making him nervous wasn't the springs in the seat. 'Come on, Paul, you have to have some idea.'

'There's a lot of folks that loved Bad Bob. Personally, I thought he was a gigantic pain in the ass, but that's just me. No question, he was one hell of a Warden.' Paul shrugged, looked down at his large, strong hands. 'I know you two didn't get along.'

There was a lot I could say about that – a lot I wanted, desperately, to say – but it wasn't the right time or place, and I wasn't sure Paul could ever really understand anyway. Things were simpler in Paul's world. I wish I lived in it.

'You need to tell me what happened that day,' he said when I didn't start talking. 'It's important. Unless you're planning on pleading guilty, you need to think about mounting some kind of defence. I can help you. I want to help you.'

'I can't.'

'Jo.' He twisted in the seat with a creak of springs and looked directly at me. Nothing soft in his eyes now, nothing but direct, unmistakable warning. 'You have to. I'm not saying this as your friend, I'm saying it as a Warden. You don't give yourself up and start telling your side of the story, you know they're coming after you. You can't run around loose like this. One of the most powerful guys in the world is *dead*.'

'You're going to call the Power Rangers?' That was our own private joke...Marion Bearheart's division of the Association had no official name, but they were the justice system of our screwed-up little world. Quietly took care of the problems. Calmly dispensed justice when required. No arrest, no jury, just the gentle, final judgment of the executioner.

He held my eyes. 'I don't have to, and you know it. They'll find you. They're already on your trail.'

I had a very cold, cold thought. 'You think the lightning bolt—'

'I think it's a warning, Jo, whether it came from the Rangers or not. This is a serious thing you're

into. You don't want to laugh it off. Not this time.'
He reached out and took my hand, and even in that
gentle touch I knew he had enough physical
strength to crush my hand like paper. If Paul
wanted to restrain me, it wouldn't exactly be a
challenge – unless I wanted to fight on the aetheric.
Which made me think of Bad Bob, and I felt a wave
of sickness break over me. It left me shaking.

'Stay,' he said. Still a request.

'Thought you had a lunch date.'

'It can wait.' He was looking at me again,
watching me in that half-lidded, intense way that
carbonated my hormones. And worse, he knew it. If
I stayed, I was going to get myself in trouble, one
way or another. 'I don't believe you did anything
wrong. I think Bad Bob lived up to his reputation,
things got out of hand – is that how it was?'

'I can't do this,' I said, and pulled my hand free.
Paul was staring at me with big, calculating brown
eyes. His eyebrows pulled together. The smell of
aftershave reminded me that I wanted to kiss him,
and I sank farther back in my seat, trying not to
give in to temptation, trying not to notice the way
sunlight slid warm across his cheekbones and
turned his skin to gold. God, I wanted comfort. I
wanted someone to make everything...*better*.

I knew better than to believe I could find it
anywhere except inside myself.

'You need my help to stabilise the system?' I

asked him. The lightning bolt would have torn his careful manipulations to shreds, sending the weather into chaos even if it wasn't yet visible to the naked eye. He shook his head.

'I've got three people on it already. The less work you do in the aetheric, the better,' he said. 'And stay the fuck out of Oversight. Especially if you're determined to keep on with this. You glow like a heat lamp.'

'I don't have a choice, Paul. I've got to keep on with it.'

'I could stop you, you know.'

'I know.' I leant forward and kissed him. Caught him by surprise. After a few seconds, those sensual full lips warmed under mine. The fantasy had been good; the reality was better. When I pulled back, he had a glazed look in his brown eyes, but he blinked and it cleared up. So much for my ability to cloud men's minds...

'Jesus,' he breathed.

'It wasn't *that* good,' I protested. But he wasn't kidding. He was looking at me with wider eyes, really staring now. Seeing.

'There's something wrong with you,' he said. 'I can't see it, but your aura's turned red. Blood colours, Jo. You know what it means—'

When I looked down at myself, I saw the black writhing form of the Demon's Mark on my chest, over my heart. It was working its way down. I focused hard and halted its progress, but I couldn't hold it for long. When I looked up, Paul was in Oversight, right in front of me – layers of green and gold and blue, perfect in their intensity. He'd see it. He *had* to see it in me.

Back in the real world, he only said, 'Are you sick?'

I wanted to tell him. I didn't know why he couldn't see it in me, but I needed him to know, to *help* – to get this thing out of me. I was shaking all over with the desire to tell him.

And I couldn't afford to. That was the one thing he wouldn't let slide.

'Sick,' I finally agreed.

'Let me help you. Please, just let me get Marion. She can help you—'

'No!' The protest ripped out of me with so much force, I felt it slam into him like a punch, and he pulled back. I struggled to get my voice under control. 'No, she can't. Nobody can. Understand?'

He kept looking at me, studying me. I felt like he was seeing all the way through to the black shadow of the mark. God, I couldn't risk that.

'I've got to go,' I said. 'Are you going to turn me in?'

It was so quiet in the car that I could hear the ticks and pops of Delilah's engine cooling, hear my own fast heartbeat. Somewhere off in the distance, thunder rumbled. He reached out and touched my cheek with one thick finger, caressed the line of my cheekbone, and then sat back like he wished he hadn't touched me at all.

'I'm not going to get on the hot line just yet. I'll give you that much. But we both know Marion's people will find you. And if they don't, when the Council calls me to join the hunt, I'll come at you, sweetheart. You know I will. I have no choice.' He let out a long breath. 'Maybe that's for the best. Because if you're really sick—'

'I know.' I was no longer looking at him, and I concentrated instead on my hands. My fingernails were ragged and torn. I picked at one and focused on a shiny red bead that appeared at the corner of one cuticle, lifted the hand to my mouth and tasted the warm copper tang of blood.

'You have five hours to get out of my sector,' he said. 'Try to come back, and my Djinn will stop you. You don't set foot in my territory, Joanne. Not until this is over. Understand?'

'Yes.' One-word answers were possible, but just barely. God, this hurt. I'd anticipated everything but how much it would hurt.

Paul reached over and took my hand in his. His skin felt very warm and, startlingly, very rough. He worked with his hands, I remembered. On his car.

'Tell me,' he said. 'Tell me where you're going. I swear, it won't go anywhere else. I just want to know.'

'I can't.' And I didn't dare. Finally, I pulled in a deep breath and said, 'I'm going after Lewis.'

He looked confused. Bothered, even. 'Lewis?'

'Lewis Orwell.'

'I know who the fuck Lewis is. Everybody knows. Why Lewis?'

'Because he has three Djinn. I met one at his house, so he still has two more. I just need him to give me one.'

'At his *house*?' Paul repeated. He wasn't a guy who was surprised often, but his eyebrows shot skyward. 'What do you mean, at his house? How can you know where he is?'

'He told me.' I sounded smug when I said it, but there, I'd kept the secret a long time. I deserved a little round of I'm-cooler-than-you, especially with Paul, who was rarely out of the loop. 'Long time ago.'

He gave me a richly deserved glare. 'I'm not even asking what you did to get it.'

'Hey, I can't help it if I'm irresistible.' Yes, definitely, that was smugness in my voice. I was comfortable with it. 'Which is why he's going to help me out and give me a Djinn.'

He stared. 'You're fuckin' crazy. Why the hell would Lewis do that?'

'Because,' I said, before I could think about it, 'I think he used to be in love with me.'

Paul shook his head, got out of the car, and then

leant in the passenger side window. An east wind ruffled his hair – storm on the way.

'Jesus, Jo, he's not the only one,' he said, and walked back into his castle.

I drove out of Albany not knowing exactly how to feel. I loved Paul. I'd always loved him. Paul had written my introduction letter to the program at Princeton. It was because of him that I had the degree and the training to become a real Warden.

It was because of him I wasn't a drooling shell screaming out my lungs in an asylum, because I knew that despite Marion's gentle touch, I couldn't have gone on without my powers. I would have cracked. Paul prevented that.

All the good things in my life had happened because of Paul.

All the bad things had happened because of Bad Bob.

The Wardens have a big fancy home office where they hang plaques of outstanding performers, and Bad Bob's name was covering the walls. One of the most talented Wardens ever to join the team, he was also one of the most controversial.

He had been a brilliant, temperamental teenager; he'd grown into a brilliant, tantrum-throwing, bad-attitude adult. People feared Bad Bob. Nobody in their right mind wanted to be under him. Even at his own level, or above it, people hated to see him coming.

I got him as a boss.

I'd heard all the stories – Bad Bob threw a drink in the face of the President of the United States, and it had taken all the resources of the Association to get him sprung from Secret Service custody. Bad Bob had walked into a going-away party for a retiring National Warden in England and swilled down an entire bottle of Cristal champagne, when he didn't even like to drink, just to spite the old boy. He was feared, he was revered, and he was legendary for a reason. It was considered a badge of honour to have a run-in with Bad Bob, something you could dine out on for months.

Weather Wardens sometimes resemble a Keystone Kops comedy more than they do an actual professional organisation. That's because no large organisation composed of mavericks with superpowers can ever be said to be truly *organised*. Yet, somehow, we manage to protect human beings from about eighty per cent of the crap that Mother Nature throws at us, in our arrogant, mostly chaotic way.

Nobody, however, had been able to stop Hurricane Andrew.

It had swept in from the Hurricane Zone, looking very much like all its wimpy cousins who'd taken no more than a few well-chosen pressure shifts to counter. Nobody in the Florida office was much worried. Bad Bob, Sector Warden back then, hadn't even been informed. He had Staff to handle those kinds of things; his responsibility was looking after the macro events and keeping the whole Sector stable over time.

Andrew got out of hand. First two Staff Wardens worked on it, then five, then more. Before it was over, there were literally hundreds of Wardens focused on it, trying to defuse the ticking bomb of the storm.

Even Wardens have to be careful in dealing with a storm of that magnitude. It killed more than twenty of them, shattered the powers of at least ten more, and by the time Bad Bob physically made it to the scene, it had already hit the coast of Florida and begun its raving march of destruction.

I wasn't there, of course. Too young. But I heard all about it in school.

Bad Bob walked along into the centre of the storm and stopped it. All alone.

Oh, damage was done – the worst hurricane to hit the coast in a century. But even in the middle of all that devastation, *we* knew how much worse it could have been. Andrew was a sentient storm, a storm that had gathered sufficient energy to hold its form and continue to ravage a path of destruction over land for a thousand miles or more. Andrew was *angry* and *hungry* in a way few things on this planet can be. And yet Bad Bob had faced it down and made it bow to his will.

After that, even those who thought he was a jerk and an asshole wouldn't turn down a chance to be on Bad Bob's team. It was considered both a nightmare and an honour. A badge of courage second to none.

By the dawn of 2002, I'd been a working Warden for four years, mainly up and down the Atlantic coastline. Technically, I was working for Bad Bob in Florida, but as with CEOs of major corporations, his presence was mostly made manifest by phone calls to those far above me, or with a scrawled signature on memos. I reported to Regional Warden John Foster, a capable, easygoing man with a penchant for tweed jackets and pipes, the kind of guy you half expected to have a plummy Oxford accent instead of the North Carolina drawl that came out of his mouth. We did the usual – more rain here, less there, smoothing out a tropical storm into a squall, diverting storms from heavily populated areas. Nothing really dramatic. Nothing important. I screwed up a couple of times – everybody does – and got bawled out by Bad Bob via telephone. It was nothing personal. Everybody gets reamed by Bad Bob at least twice, if you survive on his team at all.

And then in August, Tropical Storm Samuel came calling. Early for hurricane season, but in my experience the worst came early, or it came late. Samuel had some very unusual patterns in it, patterns that reminded us of Andrew. The decision was made, all the way up at the World Council level, to stop the storm before it came anywhere near to posing a threat. Nobody was complacent about that kind of thing anymore.

I'm still surprised that my name came up for that, but then it was still a small-sized thing, not a major event, and I had a solid rep with warm-weather storms. No doubt John Foster had thought it would be good training for me, since it involved working with a Warden on the other side of the pond – Tamara Motumbo, from Mauritania. I'd done tandem manipulation before, but in classroom and lab settings, nothing like the kind of power-sink that lurked out in that womb of storms called the Bermuda Triangle.

The National Weather Service has some nice offices in Coral Gables, Florida – rebuilt after being smashed to scrap metal and splinters by Hurricane Andrew. I arrived that morning feeling loose and relaxed and ready for anything; working in Florida had given me a chance to indulge myself in the quest for the perfect tan and the perfect bikini, and I was feeling confident that I'd finally mastered at least one of them. Six square inches of aqua-blue Lycra priced at about fifteen dollars per square inch. It was in a tiny little shopping bag on Delilah's front seat, my personal reward-in-advance for the job I was about to do. The plan was to finish up ridding the world of Tropical Storm Samuel, change into the bikini, and hit the beach for the rest of the day.

There was nothing unusual about visiting the NWS offices. We – meaning the Staff Wardens and Regional Wardens – did it all the time. Our badges said VISITOR or RESEARCHER, but at least half the building suspected we were something more, although nobody said it out loud and nobody asked any questions. Lots of significant looks, though. And people handing you free Cokes.

That morning, I signed in at the reception area, clipped my tag on my loose white shirt – which was subbing for a cover-up later at the beach – and exchanged chitchat with the receptionist, a gorgeous African-American woman named Monet. We exchanged bikini-shopping stories, and as we did, I happened to glance down at the visitor log. My eyes froze on a name.

Robert Biringanine.

'Bad Bob's here?' I asked Monet.

She glanced up at me, looked around, and leant over closer. 'Meeting with somebody,' she confirmed. 'I didn't ask who.'

'Well, I think I'll just sacrifice a small furry animal to whatever god spared me from *that*.'

'Baby, I'd sacrifice more than that just to make sure I got *out* of the meeting all right.' Monet rolled her eyes. 'That man eats his own children, I swear.'

'He damn sure eats his Staff's children. And his Staff.' I checked my watch, which told me I had five minutes to launch. 'Better get in there. Later?'

'Later,' she confirmed. 'Cuban sandwiches for lunch. There's a great place about six blocks down. Be there.'

I waved and was buzzed through the door into a high-tech wilderness of cubicles, glass conference rooms, arrays of computers blinking in machine dreams. Two or three of the analysts and meteorologists looked up and watched me pass, but nobody spoke. I knew where I was going, and so did they.

Situation Room B is, technically, a secondary crisis centre, but it's rarely in use; the Wardens use it for an informal office most of the time. I'd been in it five or six times already, so I knew what to expect when I opened the door.

Except that there was someone else already there.

Bad Bob Biringanine stared out at the cloudless blue sky, his feet up, drinking a glass of water with bubbles. I hadn't seen him in the flesh since my nearly disastrous intake meeting, and I felt myself turn small and weak at the sight of him. Especially when those laser-sharp blue eyes considered and then dismissed me.

'Baldwin, right?' he asked. He had a light tenor voice, neutral with indifference.

'Yes, sir.'

'Just here to observe,' he said. Observe. Like that wasn't worse than any trouble I might have been in already. Having Bad Bob staring over your shoulder was bound to make even the best Warden nervous, and I wasn't quite arrogant enough to consider myself the best. Yet.

I sucked it up and sat down to review the file: maps of pressure systems, satellite photos fresh off the printer of the growing circular mass of Tropical Storm Samuel, still lashing empty ocean beyond Bermuda. My opposite number was waiting in a seaport town in Mauritania named Nouakchott; the phone was pre-programmed for speed dial to reach her. Voices don't carry so well in Oversight. Landlines are always a plus for long-distance work.

'You getting on with it while I'm still young?' Bad Bob asked. He hadn't moved from his kicked-back spot, was still staring at the view. Funny how I think of it as a view, even though both of us were looking at a clear blue sky, not even any clouds in sight; we were drawn to the boundless and limitless possibilities. When I swallowed, I felt my throat click. There was a carafe of water on the table, sweating diamond drops, but I didn't feel like showing him that my hands were shaking. I wiped palms against blue jeans.

'Sure,' I said. 'No problem.'

I speed-dialled. Tamara Motumbo picked up on the second ring, and we exchanged some nervous pleasantries, through which Bad Bob drummed fingernails against the table. I hurried along to Step One, which was confirmation of the scope of our work. It's always good to go into a powerful situation with a clear expectation of what you're supposed to walk out with.

We decided we wanted to disrupt Samuel enough to make it just another squall; no point in trying to wipe out the storm altogether, since it would only move the energy someplace else that might spawn something just as bad. I made notes as I went, and my writing was shaky. Nothing like knowing every move you make is on the record.

'Ready?' I asked Tamara. She said she was, though I'd lay money that neither of us was really sure.

I sucked in a deep breath, let go, and floated out of my body and into Oversight. The room turned grey and misty, but Bad Bob was like a brilliant neon sign, lit up with so much power, it was hard to look at him directly. Red tinged. I wondered if he was sick, but I wasn't about to ask after his health, not now. I turned away from him, oriented myself with the vast voiding power of the sea, and let the waves of its energy carry me up and out, far up, flying without sound or pressure through the liquid we call air. No clouds in Oversight, either, but there was a low red band of energy over the ocean and a corresponding white one coming down from the mesosphere – clouds later, then, and rain in a day at most. Warming and cooling ocean air is the unimaginably powerful engine that drives the machine of life. Connecting to it like this, right on the coast, was a sensuous, dangerous experience.

I soared. In Oversight, crossing huge distances takes a fraction of real time, but it still felt like a long trip by the time I saw the swirling entity we were calling Samuel. He was a big, growing boy, already well into rebellious adolescence and halfway to becoming a dangerous hooligan. Facing that kind of storm makes you feel small. No, not just small: non-existent. The forces that formed him and drove him dwarfed anything I could summon out of myself.

I shifted just enough of my consciousness back to my body to ask Tamara on the phone if she had a Djinn.

'Yes,' she said. 'You don't?'

'Getting mine in about six months.'

'So you want me to source.'

'Yeah, please.'

'No problem.'

Technically, I should have been sourcing the power out of a Djinn to do what we were supposed to do...The Warden nearest the storm usually had the responsibility. Using a Djinn for a source was sort of like having a superconductor in the circuit – it augmented and amplified your power, and assisted in channelling it accurately. The fact that I'd been assigned to this storm without a Djinn to source me was, I realised, not an accident. It was a test.

And Bad Bob was my proctor. Wow. No pressure.

I fought off a cold shiver and got down to business. After about thirty seconds of real time, I saw a shape approaching in Oversight – Tamara. Tall, bright, unusually vivid in her aura colours, with a clear white line of energy linking her back to her home in Mauritania. As I watched, power surged along that link. Her Djinn was delivering the goods.

I reached out to her, and our aetheric bodies touched. Energy jumped the barrier and shot into me, and I had trouble holding on to it; I was not used to Djinn-sourced power at such levels. It felt like being drunk and being dizzy and being in love, and connected to that kind of power I could feel every molecule in the swirling air, every slight variation of temperature between them. It was like…

…like playing God.

Somewhere, Bad Bob was watching. That thought shook me out of any sense of divinity and got me to work. There was, predictably, a ridge of high pressure riding in front of Samuel. Seen from Oversight, the whole thing looked remarkably like a freeze-framed explosion, with a pressure null in the centre and force travelling out in all directions. You don't stop a thing like that.

You just weaken the forces that drive it your direction.

Tamara and I worked quickly and – if I may say so – efficiently to smooth out the temperature variations at surface level to cut off the flow of energy up into the monster, and raise the temperature at the top end to create a shorter pressure wave. Small changes, followed by detailed analysis of the effects. One step at a time, always going back to the source...the ocean...for the next tiny change.

The weatherworking took no more than thirty minutes, real time, and Tropical Storm Samuel was reduced to nothing more than a stern southeast wind with some fluffy, rain-heavy clouds. I let go of Tamara – reluctantly – and felt all that power drain away.

I fell back into my body with a rushing suddenness that scared me and told me just how tired I really was. Normally I have more control than that. I'd had no idea how addictive that kind of power could feel, and how ridiculously pathetic I'd feel once it was gone.

Tamara was saying nice things about working with me, in the real world, on the real phone. I remembered how to move my lips and thanked her.

Bad Bob reached across to punch the button to hang up the line.

'Joanne Baldwin,' he said. 'Funny. I voted against you that day, you know. At your intake session.'

Like I'd ever forget.

I was too tired to be scared of what he was about to say. I'd just have to eat whatever crap he dished out and try not to yearn for that feeling of being God, because it would be so nice to smack a nice lightning bolt down on his ass. To feel powerful, just once, in his presence.

He put a heavy hand on my shoulder, squeezed, and then patted twice.

'Well, maybe I was wrong,' he said. 'You're not half bad, Baldwin. Got a lot of raw power, that's for damn sure. More than I've ever seen, to be absolutely truthful. I figure with power like that, you might be able to do a lot of damage.'

I wasn't entirely sure I'd heard that right. I blinked and tried to get my tired brain to follow what he was saying. 'Damage? I didn't...?'

'Oh, no, just the opposite. You really brought home the bacon today.' Now he had both hands on my shoulders. I wondered, for a creeped-out, crazed moment, if he was trying to cop a quick feel. Sexual harassment wasn't limited to just the normal outside world, after all. If anything, men who held the power to destroy whole countries might have a greater tendency to it. I wondered exactly what to say to get myself out of it.

And then I realised he wasn't rubbing my shoulders in any suggestive kind of way. It was more like he was holding me down in the chair.

'OK,' I said slowly. 'Well, I really ought to get—'

'Damage is what you'll do when you go out of control, Baldwin,' he interrupted. 'I've seen hundreds of kids like you. Jumped up, arrogant little boys and girls who have no idea what the real price of power is. And no respect for it, either.'

'Sir, I'm all about the respect. Promise.'

'No, you're not,' he said. 'Not yet. But you will be.' He didn't let me go. 'You've got no idea what I'm talking about, do you?'

I didn't want to admit it. He didn't care, anyway.

'God, the strength in you,' he said, staring down at me with those merciless eyes. 'All that strength, going to waste. You don't need a Djinn. You don't need a damn thing. I remember what it was like, being young and stupid. You know what happens, little girl? It goes away. Sooner or later, you get old, you get slow, you lose the edge. And when that happens, people screw you.'

I was too scared to say anything. He wasn't talking to me, not really; there was something bad going on here, something underneath. His fingers dug into my shoulders like iron spikes.

'You going to screw me, little girl?' He showed his teeth. 'I mean in the figurative sense.'

'No, sir,' I whispered. 'I wouldn't.'

'Damn right you wouldn't.'

I could almost feel something in the room with us, something huge and dark and malevolent. Something violent.

It wants something. Something I have.

Bad Bob seemed to realise it, too. He blinked, shook himself, and took his hands away from my shoulders. I felt the sting of blood rushing back and knew I'd have bruises there later.

'Go on,' he said. 'Get out of my sight.'

I suppose I must have walked out, past the meteorologists, through the security door, signed out, handed Monet my badge, probably even said something. But I don't remember a thing from the getting up part to the part where I was sitting inside my car, gasping for breath and on the verge of tears.

I couldn't possibly have known how close I came that day to dying, but I sensed it. On some level, *I knew.*

I headed for the comfort of a beachside bar. On reflection, not the best answer to coping with crisis, but you go with your instincts.

Mine were just...bad.

❧ ❧ ❧

Chapter Two

Scattered thunderstorms, possibly heavy and severe, in the afternoon hours. A Weather Advisory is in effect for the area beginning at 11 a.m. EASTERN TIME.

Paul had given me five hours to make it out of his Sector; it wasn't a generous head start, but he knew the Mustang could make it. I had to slow down around Philadelphia, wary of speed traps, but I was still making pretty good time. By my calculations, I'd be out of his territory with about a half hour to spare. I knew he'd set his Djinn to monitor me, so it was no surprise when one appeared – *poof* – in my passenger seat.

Unlike Lewis's house Djinn, who had favoured the traditional look, this one was hip to the new. She was a well-groomed young black woman, glossily perfect, with cornrowed hair and wraparound dark glasses and a sunshine-yellow pantsuit. I especially liked the yellow nail polish. It was a nice touch.

I managed not to drive the car off the road, though I did fumble a gear change.

'You've got a lot of people very upset,' the Djinn said. She had a nice, smoky voice, contralto, with a bit of a whiskey edge. 'While it might be amusing, it makes more work for me.'

She skinned down the shades, and I got a look at her beast-yellow eyes. Horror movie monsters never had eyes that scary, or that beautiful.

'I can see it in you,' she said. 'It's burrowing.' She made a clicking sound with her tongue that sounded dry and insectile.

'Paul didn't see it.'

'Wardens don't,' she murmured. 'Unless they ask us to show them. Which they don't, because they don't know the right question to ask.'

Oh. 'Want to take it off me?' I asked.

She smiled. 'You know the rules,' she said. 'A Djinn doesn't do favours. A Djinn takes orders from her master. You, sistah, are not *my* master.'

'What if Paul ordered you to take if from me?'

'I think he would not, considering it would destroy me and he would never get another Djinn.' The Djinn put the glasses back on. 'You're already corrupted, I can smell it on you like a rotting wound.'

'Cheer me up some more,' I invited.

She smiled. Long canines showed white in her smile. 'Would if I could. You going to make the border?'

'If you don't fuck around with me.'

She laughed. 'Now why would I do that? Everything I do must be in my master's best interests. Rules of the game. Although if you'd slow down, you might at least make it interesting.'

She seemed oddly talkative, for a Djinn. I decided to indulge my curiosity as we cruised in on I-95 toward Philly. 'Must be a bitch, being enslaved and all.'

'Enslaved?' she asked. It didn't seem to bother her. 'We are not enslaved.'

'That's what they teach us in school.'

She sniffed and drummed yellow talons on Delilah's window glass. I hoped she wasn't leaving scratches. 'Your school is sadly free of knowledge. Djinn are the children of Fire. We serve as we must serve, as Fire serves when chained and devours when freed.'

'Freed? I thought you were – sort of eternally – um, damned.' Which wasn't the best way to put it, but I couldn't think of a politically correct phrase.

She shrugged. 'Fire serves no one forever. It is always ready to burn the hand it warms.'

The Djinn were rare – we all knew that. Precious resources. One Djinn per lifetime, no more, and when a Warden died, his or her Djinn just went back into rotation, assigned a new master. Nobody had said anything about them ever getting freed.

She gave me another cool smile. 'Too bad you're going to die. I rather like you. A favour, then. Ask a question.'

'Did Paul tell you to kill me if I don't make it out of his territory?' I blurted.

She smiled. 'That was a poor question,' she said. 'Care to try again? Secrets of the universe? Lotto numbers? Whether your true love will be tall, dark, and handsome?'

I thought about it. Never look a gift Djinn in the mouth. 'Where's Lewis?'

She took her glasses off again, and even though I didn't look at her, I could feel the pressure of those horrible, beautiful eyes. She was a dangerous pet to keep, a sleek predatory beast with bloodlust kept in check only by a constant flow of Kibbles 'n Bits and a great big magical leash.

'You already know the answer,' she purred.

'Oklahoma? What the hell's he doing in Oklahoma?'

She looked away. 'Saving someone. Is that not what he is always doing?' She practically steamed with contempt. 'One of these days, it will cost him.'

'Can we cut out the middleman, here? Just take me to Oklahoma?'

Teeth flashed. 'Your favour has been spent, Snow White. Choose better next time.'

ILL WIND 105

'Great. Forget favours. Got any advice?'

'Be kind to your Djinn.'

'I don't have a Djinn.'

She shrugged. 'You will, if you survive. I can smell that on you, too.'

'Wait!' I sensed she was about to poof again. She slid her sunglasses back on and sat, politely bored, swinging one hand in time with Ozzy Osbourne belting out a ditty about war pigs. 'Can you give Paul a message for me?'

'I can,' she agreed. 'It remains to be seen if I will, Snow White.'

'My name is Joanne.'

'I like Snow White better. I am Rahel,' she said, and pointed toward herself with one neon-yellow talon. Were they longer than they had been? Her teeth flashed into a smile. 'Speak.'

'Tell Paul that I'm sorry. And that I still love him.'

She shuddered delicately. 'I try to stay out of the sexual business of mortals.'

'Yeah, well, we're just friends.'

'So say you,' she said, and cocked an elegantly shaped dark eyebrow. 'You did not see him later.'

That led to things I shouldn't be thinking about, not when driving a speeding car. Rahel flicked her fingernails together in a dry, yellow clatter and disappeared.

I tried not to feel quite so relieved.

I didn't know the Warden in Philadelphia, and I

was just as happy to breeze by without making his acquaintance, but I needed a pit stop. I pulled off the highway for gas at the Independence Hall exit. After taking care of the bladder problem and filling up the Mustang, I scouted around for a likely spot to grab a quick cheeseburger for the road. Weariness was starting to liquefy the edges of my brain, and I could have used a nice long nap in a Motel 6, but I was taking Paul seriously. I needed to get out of Philly on time. The idea of Rahel's having any power over me at all was extremely motivating.

Independence Hall would have made a nice diversion and a great place to stretch my cramped, exhausted legs, but I wasn't about to risk another lightning bolt in a crowded place. What I saw of it was nice. As I cruised by, I couldn't help but notice that Ben Franklin – little specs and all – was sitting on a bench reading to a group of absolutely spellbound children. There was no way I wanted to bring my problems into that world. That world didn't know the sunshine was provided for them, just like the rain, or that somebody had to protect them daily from the fury of the earth and the weather.

It was a nice world to visit, even if I couldn't live there.

On the way out of town I checked both the horizon and the weather forecasts; the storm was still out there, moving inland in my wake, but Paul's folks could take care of anything still to do. I could relax and enjoy the drive.

Hopefully.

It was a good seven hours to my next safe haven in Columbus; between here and there lay cities with Wardens I barely knew, not likely to be friendly toward me. The Sector Warden from Philly to Columbus was Rashid Al-Omar, a beautiful man about seven or eight years older than me, known to be a straight arrow and conservative both in weather and everything else you could name. For some reason, most Weather Wardens were conservative; it was the tie-dyed hippie Earth Wardens who'd cornered the liberal market.

Weather Wardens on the right, Earth Wardens on the left...that left Fire Wardens in the middle. My friend Estrella had been a Fire Warden, once upon a time – one of the best. But fire's a funny thing. Like Rahel said, fire is always ready to burn the hand it warms.

I felt a hot knot of tension ease in my gut as I passed the city limits sign of Philadelphia and America stretched out before me. I was out of Paul's jurisdiction.

When I checked the rearview mirror, I saw Rahel standing there next to the sign, clicking her cheerful neon talons, watching me with beast-yellow eyes. She waved.

I shivered.

My cheeseburger was greasy but filling. I wasn't overly concerned about cholesterol; with the Demon Mark on my chest, I wasn't likely to live long enough to care. I felt it moving, and I flattened my palm over my breast. I wanted to squash it flatter than the tattoo it resembled, but it existed mostly in the aetheric, and there was nothing I could do. I felt its pulse against my fingers. Ick. I wiped my fingers on my blue jeans convulsively and tried a sip of Coke, aspirated down the wrong pipe, choked and coughed. Maybe it was my nerves, maybe it was something more, but I let the Mustang slip the leash a little too much.

I was blasting along at eighty miles an hour west on I-70, just passing Harrisburg, when I heard the wail of a siren start up and I looked in my mirror to see cherry lights popping blue and red behind me.

Well, that was just perfect.

No point in making the evening news by trying to outrun them; I gulped deep breaths and fumbled the Coke back into the cupholder. Downshifted. Pulled over to the side. Delilah's engine growled, frustrated at the delay, and I sympathised.

My hands were sweating as I waited. The cops didn't get out of their cruiser for a good three minutes, probably checking the car's registration and me for outstanding warrants...which, unless they were Wardens, I didn't have. I wiped my palms on my knees and watched as they got out, one on either side, and did a slow, menacing walk up toward me.

I had already rolled down the window, and the smell of early spring wafted in, sweet with wild-flowers. I knew I looked a mess, and I verified it in the mirror – yep, circles under dark blue eyes, no make-up, lank, needed-to-be-washed black hair. I smelt, too. I needed a shower and sleep.

The cop appeared at my window so suddenly I thought that, like Rahel, he'd planned it for effect.

His mirrored sunglasses reflected my pallid face and mooncalf expression.

'Hi,' I said weakly.

'License, registration, and insurance.'

I handed them over. He took them without comment, but didn't look at them yet.

'You from Florida, miss?' he asked. The plates on the Mustang were from the Sunshine State. It wasn't a psychic leap.

'Yes, sir. Saint Petersburg.'

'Uh-huh.' He made it sound suspicious. 'You were pushing this beauty pretty hard.'

'I'm sorry about that. It sort of got away from me.' As if a car had ever gotten away from me in my entire life.

'You really have to watch it, a car like this. It's a lot of power for—' He had been, I thought, about to say *such a little lady*, but sensitivity training had paid off, '—for everyday driving.'

'Thank you, sir, I will.' Was that a dark cloud moving too fast overhead? I had only the reflection in his glasses to go by, but I could have sworn there was a cloud...

'Just a minute, miss,' He went away with my papers. I leant over and tried to figure out what was going on above me. I let go of my body just enough to shift into Oversight, and saw myself flickering gold and violet and red, the Mark moving like a nest of worms above my heart. Then I looked up, through the crystalline roof of the Mustang, and I was staring straight down the throat of Hell.

What was happening up there wasn't obeying any natural laws. It was being *forced* to happen. I tried to reach for the clouds, the winds, the pressures, but I got shoved aside like a child. Something incredibly strong was manipulating everything from the exo-sphere on down, all the way to the friction layer. Red flickered in the clouds, and as I watched, it shifted spectrums, into photonegative.

Whatever was about to fall on me, it was going to fall very hard.

The cop popped back in my window, and this time I did flinch – in Oversight, he was a burly, twisted-looking bastard, probably neither good nor bad, but nothing I wanted to tangle with. He handed me a clipboard with something signable on it. I signed. He probably said something. I probably responded. He handed back my papers.

I badly wanted to scream at him to get back in his car, but it wouldn't have been a good idea; I clutched the ticket in one sweaty palm, fired up the Mustang, and eased it into gear. Carefully. The cops got in their cruiser and sat there, writing up records. I felt a lurch of relief... At least they weren't going to be fried like eggs on the pavement. Now all I had to worry about was me.

'Easy,' I chanted to Delilah. 'Easy, easy, easy.' We drove, holding it to the speed limit, and overhead the storm grew and swirled and muttered its hatred. It followed. Again, I tried to defuse it, but whatever force controlled it had effectively shut me out.

I had seven hours left to go. I wondered if Hell planned to wait that long.

The storm stayed with me into Pittsburgh, travelling like a balloon tethered to the antenna of my car. The weather channel was in a panic. Meteorologists, not being in the know or having Oversight, were unable to predict the consequences, but their outlook was grim. Hell, I *knew* the consequences, and they were right – the outlook was grim.

After five long hours of steering, I was sweaty and trembling; the Mustang practically drove itself, but I'd worn myself out, trying to get a grip on the factors that were driving the weather system overhead. I could feel other Wardens trying to work on the storm, but it laughed at us. Heavy magic. Big weather.

It was a special kind of torment. The person who'd created the storm knew I was trying to stop it, and the stress of my not knowing when and where it would strike was half the fun for the sick bastard. I thought longingly of Paul. Maybe if I called him…or Rashid… No, they were in this up to their necks already, and if they hadn't already solved this problem, they weren't going to be able to do anything for me. So who was doing this? Somebody had come along and brute-forced this thing together, and if it hadn't been broken up yet by the combined power of the Wardens, it had one hell of a power supply behind it. When I looked at it in Oversight, there was no clear identification, nobody lurking nearby to blame it on. Which meant it was somebody strong enough to do it at a great distance *without* travelling in Oversight to touch it. That was – incredible. And really, really scary. Who the hell could manage that kind of thing? Very few, I thought. Senior Wardens, World Council members… Lewis.

I had a very bad feeling suddenly.

The world slid by, shadowed by hovering clouds. Spring still tried to be cheerful but lost colour as the sun disappeared. Birds fled with me, heading west.

Other cars moved in formation, too, their drivers either oblivious or trying to make it despite the odds; I didn't have a choice. Stopping would be suicide. Driving on was just as bad.

I'd be out of gas by Columbus.

Think. I was a Weather Warden, dammit – maybe not holding on to the best possible reputation these days, but I was damned good at my work. My palms were sweating again. I wiped them, one at a time, and took another swallow of soft drink. My throat was so dry, it clicked. On the seat beside me lay the crumpled wad of ticket that I hadn't even bothered to read. If I survived this drive, I'd survive a fine from the Pennsylvania State Troopers.

Back at school, old Yorenson had always said there was no such thing as an unstoppable weather system. Weather was as delicate as a house of cards. Remove one card, and the structure would start to collapse; the trick was to plan the collapse. A perfect execution, he'd said, would negate the threat *and* create a beneficial environment at the same time.

Maybe I'd been thinking about it wrong. I'd been prodding at the storm itself, trying to loosen the magic that bound it together; maybe all I needed to do was change its location. I reached for my cell phone and dialled it one-handed from memory.

Paul's growling voice. 'You've got to be kidding.

Are you crazy, calling me? I thought we had an agreement.'

'Listen. I know you're tracking this thing—'

'Yeah, I know it's cantered right over you.' He sounded depressed; I wondered if there was someone listening in. 'You know what they taught you, Joanne. You fuck around with the weather, it *will* fuck around with you.'

'This ain't a storm cell with a grudge, Paul. Somebody's driving.'

'The brain trust thinks it's you. That you've gone over the edge.'

'Brilliant,' I sighed. 'Just brilliant. You know better.'

'I'm just sayin'.'

I bit my tongue hard enough to taste blood. Blood and ozone. The storm was getting stronger overhead, rotating like a pinwheel. Other cars had run for cover. I was driving all alone now, and up ahead I saw another small town on the horizon.

'Listen, we're running out of time,' I said. 'Help me.'

'We're trying, dammit, but if you didn't put this thing together, I don't know who the hell did. It's stronger than anything I've ever seen—'

'We need to do this together. I need you to create a cold downdraft over the top of this thing. You're going to do it fast and hard.'

He grunted. 'We tried that. Didn't work.'

'You do it at the same time I create a hot-air mass underneath. We ought to be able to pop this sucker straight up about twenty miles and start kicking the crap out of it with an adiabatic process. I need it in the mesosphere, Paul. We have to rob it of the fuel or we can't pull it to pieces.'

Paul was quiet for a few seconds, then said, 'Give me two minutes.'

'It's got to be precise.'

'It'll be precise.'

I sensed he was about to hang up and talked fast. 'You got a line to Rashid?'

'Yeah.'

'Apologise for me in advance, and tell him to watch out for the shears,' I said, and hung up.

Basically, the plan was for me to drastically warm and expand the air underneath the entire storm, shoving it upward while Paul created a vertical process to drag it all the way up to the mesosphere, where we could work on it with much greater forces until it fell apart. The downside of it was that creating that kind of sudden, drastic updraft was going to rip apart the stability of this area. Wind shears were a distinct probability – the kind that knocked planes out of the sky. Hence, my warning to Rashid; it would be up to him to handle the devastating side effects.

I watched the digital clock on the dashboard. It took forever to flick over one minute. I felt something happening overhead, a kind of power gathering, and I couldn't tell if the storm was about to strike or if Paul was marshalling his forces. Either way, not a pleasant sensation seen from my perspective.

The digital clock finally flickered a new number. I reached up, grabbed air, and poured in heat...heated it so rapidly, the molecules had to expand, no matter what the cost. The storm pushed back, but it couldn't fight two fronts; I felt it being dragged upward by Paul's cold air funnel, sucked up through the friction layer, the troposphere, the stratosphere. Slowing as it reached the arid, chilly spaces of the mesosphere.

My enemy – whoever he or she was – would have to power that storm with the equivalent energy of fifteen or twenty nuclear reactors just to keep it together, and trying to bring it back down would be almost impossible, given the warm air column I'd created and was maintaining. Warm air beats cold air, given a short time frame. Elementary weather physics.

I felt the moment its creator let go of it. It was impossible for a storm that big to fall apart, but it did – blown apart, just like a puffball. Without the magic that sustained it, it was just random water and gas. I could feel the pressure easing inside my head.

Going, going...gone.

My phone rang. I flipped it open.

'Nice,' Paul said.

'You, too.'

'I can't change my mind, kid. Don't come back.'

'I didn't think you would,' I said. 'Don't worry. I'm not your problem anymore.'

Paul chuckled, a sound that left me warm inside. 'That'll be the day.'

I had just hung up the car phone when the first microburst slammed into the car with the speed of a bullet train and knocked me off the road. I fought the wheel, heard the Mustang scream as it grabbed for traction, but the road might as well have been ice and oil. I skidded. The world lurched. And oh, God, there was somebody in the way, somebody standing by the side of the road, I was going to hit him...

I spun out in a spray of dust, felt a dull *thump* of impact. My tires caught the grassy edge of the shoulder, and physics took over, giving the car a sickening tilt.

Not the car, I thought in utter despair. Please, not the car.

And then something caught me and steadied me, and Delilah thumped four tires back on the ground. I had the breath knocked out of me, but apart from some tread loss, neither one of us had been hurt much. Delilah was shaking all over. So was I.

I turned off the engine and put my burning

forehead on the steering wheel and gulped in air that tasted now as much of fear as of all the old ghosts of fast food, but it was still delicious.

'Sorry, baby,' I whispered to Delilah. 'Thought we were both headed for the junkyard.'

It took me a second to remember the rest of it. The dull *thump* of impact.

Oh, Jesus, I'd hit somebody...

I fumbled with the seat belt, frantic. *Oh, God, no – let him be OK...*

Somebody tapped on the window. I gave myself whiplash coming around to stare, and saw a shadow...large, dark, and threatening. I sucked in breath to scream.

I blinked, and the shadow resolved into just – a guy. A guy with brown hair that needed trimming and some silly-looking round glasses that reflected blazing sunlight. A nice face, with smile lines around the eyes that said he was older than first glance would take him for. He was wearing a patched olive-green trench coat that for some reason reminded me of World War I – a vintage clothing enthusiast, or somebody who could afford only Salvation Army couture.

I rolled down the window.

'You OK?' he asked, and adjusted a backpack on his shoulder. Oh. I got it. He was a road dude, somebody who walked for a living, hitching when possible. Homeless by choice, maybe, instead of circumstance. A guy in search of adventure.

Well, he'd sure as hell found it this time.

'Fine. I'm fine,' I croaked, and dragged lank, oily hair back from my face. 'You're OK? I didn't hit you? No tire tracks on you or anything?'

He shook his head. An earring glinted. I tried to remember which ear meant he was gay, and then doubted myself; the earring thing might be an urban legend. I concluded it was either bullshit or the glint was in the heterosexual ear, because he smiled at me in a warmly non-academic way.

'So, can you believe this weather? Some crazy stuff going on,' he said. I could imagine...a cloud levitating with the speed of a freight train, straight up, then blowing apart like God himself had smashed it to pieces. Plus Delilah roaring along at top speed and spinning out like NASCAR roadkill. Not something you see every day, even if you are a road dude. 'Thought we were really in for it.'

I hoped the *we* was a generic kind of thing, not a hello-I'll-be-your-stalker-this-evening warning sign. 'Gee, bad weather? I didn't notice.'

He hitched the backpack again, as if it were giving him some trouble, and nodded as he straightened up. 'Well, be careful. Too nice a car to end up in some ditch. Not to mention too nice a lady.'

Gallant, but he was a genuine guy – he'd put the car first. Somehow, that won me over. I wasn't getting any weird vibes from him, and even the company of some dude smoking grass and getting as one with nature might be better than talking to my car on a hell-drive like this. He even had a nice smile.

I looked at him in Oversight, just to be sure, but there was nothing special about him, nothing dark, nothing bright, nothing but plain old Joe Normal. I opened the passenger door and said, 'Need a ride?'

He stopped walking away and looked at me. He had really dark eyes, but dark in a warm, earthy kind of way. If he were a season, he'd be fall.

'Maybe,' he said. 'Pack's getting kind of heavy. What's the price?'

'Nothing.'

His eyebrows twitched like he thought about raising them. 'Nothing's for nothing.'

'Pleasure of your company.'

'*That* can be taken a couple of ways,' he said, and shrugged off the pack. It fit into the backseat like a second passenger. He didn't need as much leg room as Paul. 'Not that I'm complaining or anything.'

I felt strongly that that should offend me. 'You really think I look like a chick who'd pick up some skanky guy on the side of the road?'

'No,' he said with a sly, Zen-like calm. 'And just for clarification, I take exception to the skanky. I have had a bath.'

I waited until he'd strapped himself in safely before Delilah rolled again. Sunlight flickered through trees, tiger-striping the road. A gentle west-to-east breeze rustled leaves. I hadn't closed my window, and the smooth, cool scented air blew my hair back from my face. It felt good on my flushed skin.

'Not skanky,' I agreed finally. 'Rough?'

'You think I look rough?'

'Maybe a little grubby.'

'I'll accept grubby.'

When I looked over, he chuckled. I laughed, caught the edge of my hysteria, and blamed it on exhaustion and fear. I caught my breath and wiped my face.

He said, 'My name's David, by the way.'

'Joanne.'

'How long have you been on the road?'

'Isn't that my line?' I asked him. 'I think it's been about thirty-six hours, but I'm really not too sure anymore.'

'Any sleep?'

'Not so much.'

'I guess you know it's not safe to drive like that.'

'Safer than stopping,' I said, and then wondered why I had; I don't confide, especially not in normal, mundane people. David nodded and looked out the window. 'So how long have you been on the road?'

'A while now. I like it. It's beautiful out there.' He

nodded toward the other side of the glass, where things were whipping by at Mustang speed. 'Everybody should get out in the world for a while, just so they know who they are, and why.'

It sounded philosophical and New Agey to me, but hey, I freely admit I'm cynical. 'Thanks, I'll take indoor plumbing, cooked food, and reliable heating any time. Nature's great. I just don't think she likes us very much.'

'She likes us fine,' David replied. 'But she doesn't stack the deck for one side or the other, and we seem to think she should. Cockroaches get the same shots as humans, in her view. And I think that's fair.'

'I'm not about fair. I'm about winning.'

'Nobody wins,' he said. 'Or don't you watch the Discovery Channel?'

'More of a Comedy Central fan, myself. And don't tell me that you've got a cabin with cable stashed in your backpack.'

He out and out grinned this time. 'No, but sometimes I take a room at a motel so I can cleaned up and sleep in a bed for a change. You got something against the Discovery Channel?'

'Adult pay-per-view,' I advised him. 'Only way to go.'

Strangely, I felt less sleepy and less fogged over with weariness since he'd gotten in the car. Maybe there really was something to misery loving company. Plus, a little casual flirting never failed to get my blood moving.

He looked over at me with a smile that was just saved from being cynical by his gentle eyes.

'Real life,' he said, 'is always more interesting. You just never know what will happen.'

What happened was that we drove for another thirty minutes, and the skies were clear and menace free, and I finally was able to pull in for a pit stop at a place called Krazy Ed's Gas 'n Food. Krazy Ed himself ran the register. I don't know if he was Krazy, but he was meaner than a pit bull, and I'd have been willing to bet that he'd killed a few would-be burglars in his time. David stayed quiet, polite, and he got out as quickly as possible with his haul of cheese doodles and Twinkies and diet soda. Evidently his oneness with Mother Nature did not extend to eating organic – or even partially organic – food.

Delilah drank her fill at the pumps, I slid my feet in and out of the now-torturous high heels and asked Krazy Ed if there was anyplace in town he could recommend as a clothing store. Apparently there was. It was a little place called the mall.

'Mall,' I echoed after David and I were back in the car, safely out of Krazy Ed's reach. 'How big a mall can there be in a town this size? A Wal-Mart I could understand, wherever two or three of us are gathered together, but...'

David didn't say anything. He just pointed to the road sign directly in front of us. It read, GREEN HILLS OUTLET MALL, BIGGEST IN PA! Although, by my calculations, we were just wee miles short of being out of Pennsylvania altogether.

'Oh,' I said. 'Pretty big, I guess.'

So we followed the signs.

Big wasn't the word; the place was frigging enormous. I'd seen major airports that covered less land mass, and the cars – you could have taken a dozen big-city car dealerships and stuck them together in one contiguous lot, and you'd still have fewer vehicles than were choked into narrow rows around the Green Hills Outlet Mall. I offered David the chance to get a ride with some of the thousands of other mall shoppers, but he politely declined and walked into the place with me, hands in his overcoat pockets and eyes full of sly amusement as if he were on some sociology field trip. I wondered how many malls he'd ever been to. The clothes he was wearing weren't really hand-me-downs after all – blue checkered flannel shirt, blue jeans, lived-in hiking boots, that vintage overcoat. It all looked good quality, with no ground-in dirt – in fact, recently washed. Like David himself. He smelt lightly of male sweat, but nothing stinkier. If he'd been living rough, it certainly hadn't been any rougher than most vacationers.

Which raised a question, because most guys on

the road for a couple of years tended to wear miles on their faces. His was mileage free.

Still. I checked Oversight. He was placidly unmenacing.

'I just need a few things,' I told him. 'Clothes. Stuff like that. You can go to the food court if you want to and eat something with some actual nutritional content for a change. My treat.'

We were, in fact, looking at the food court, which was larger and noisier than Barnum and Bailey's big top. Even the pickiest taste could find something in that maze of colour and plastic – from hamburgers to Szechuan, curry to pork pies. David looked mildly impressed. I handed him a twenty-dollar bill. 'Knock yourself out. See you back here in an hour. If I don't see you, I'll assume you've caught another ride, OK?'

He pocketed the twenty without protest and nodded without looking my way. 'I'll be here,' he said. 'Don't forget me.'

Not likely. I looked back over my shoulder when I got to the escalator and saw he was standing there, watching me. The round circles of his glasses caught neon fire as he turned his head, and he walked off into the crowd with his overcoat swinging gracefully around him.

He really was – something. I wasn't quite sure what. Why the hell had I picked him up? No, that wasn't the question. A girl could have the occasional weakness for a cute, mysterious stranger. The question was, why the hell was I still with him?

I made the decision that when I was done here, I'd slip out the side exit and leave him on his own. Hell, I'd given him a ride, contributed a twenty to the cause – I'd done more than my duty, right? And there was, well, me to consider. I had my own problems, dammit.

Yes. Definitely. That's what I would do.

The escalator delivered me to a whole different level of colour, this one full of clothes. Trashy clothes, flashy clothes, trendy clothes, clothes even my grandmother would have found too dowdy to wear. I picked a place called Violent Velvet and decided that it deserved a once-over for the name alone.

The colour of the season, I discovered, was purple – well, last season, because it was an outlet mall and they were unloading stock that hadn't sold, but that didn't matter. I liked purple. I liked purple velvet even better, and since the spring wasn't so warm, it constituted a comfort-versus-fashion challenge.

Half an hour later I emerged from the fitting room wearing purple hip-hugger pants, a stretch lace white shirt, and a flared purple jacket that harked back to Edwardian styles. Everything I was wearing, from underwear out, was new. It felt so good, it was almost sexual. I paid up, bagged two more outfits and a pair of purple satin pyjamas, and revelled in the feel of flat-heeled, fashionably clunky shoes. My feet were shell-shocked but grateful. A quick fifteen-minute stop at the nearby convenience store netted me tampons, toothpaste, toothbrush, travel-size mouthwash, makeup, and – because a good Girl Scout is always prepared – a discreet travel-size package of condoms. But, I reminded myself again, I was ditching David. So the condoms were more in the way of wishful thinking.

Anyway, it had nothing to do with him. In the outfit I was wearing, I might have a date before I even made it down the escalator.

I was basking in girl power when suddenly the hair along my scalp prickled, and I knew something was wrong. Weather? No, that was OK, a quick survey of Oversight told me all was well. Something else. I couldn't pin it down, but the feeling persisted. Something was wrong here, in the middle of all these busy people, all these stores chewing money at a Las Vegas rate. Something to do with air, I thought. But not weather—

I realised I was feeling faint, and I didn't understand why. I'd been feeling great just a few seconds ago, loving my violent velvet, ready to take on the world. Now I needed to sit down.

I found an unoccupied Victorian-style wrought-iron bench and sat down next to some squatty pine trees. They looked unconvinced by the skylight above, but a finch had somehow found its way in and was perched on one of the branches, watching me with beady finch-eyes. It made a sharp sound that sounded dull and smeared to me, as if I were hearing it underwater, and it snapped its wings and flew away.

Fainter. Sounds fading. I couldn't understand what was happening. I was breathing faster, but the part of my brain in charge of total freak-out was shrieking that something was wrong, wrong, wrong.

I was still trying to figure it out when I slid sideways and fell over on the bench. Cool white-painted iron against my cheek. Felt good. So tired.

People gathered. Lips moved. No sound reached me. I was gasping now, panting fast, and because my hand was by my face, I could see that my fingernail beds were turning a pure, delicate blue.

Something about – about – experiment at school –

Oh, God, I couldn't breathe. No, that's not right, I was breathing, but there just wasn't anything there *to* breathe. Nothing but my own carbon dioxide.

I remembered, as suddenly and clearly as if it were happening in front of me, that I'd done this before. Not as the subject. As the experimenter.

I'd done this to a lab rat. Removed all the oxygen from the air surrounding him and made it a clear poisonous shell around him, so no matter where he ran, no matter how he tried to get away.

I hadn't killed the rat. I'd popped the bubble once I'd mastered the technique, and the rat – white, with a pink nose, funny how you remember those things – had scurried off unharmed.

But whoever was practicing on me wasn't popping the bubble.

Focus, dammit!

My brain was starting to send out hysterical flashes, distress signals. Flashes of colour across my eyes. A strangely realistic memory of my mother reaching down for me, giant-size in my perspective. Delilah spinning on the road. Lewis, lying on the ground, blood dripping down his face, reaching out for the last key to his power.

I realised I had stopped breathing and couldn't seem to make myself start again.

Something wrong. What was it?

Clear as a bell, I heard my mother say, *I wish this didn't have to happen.* She sounded so disappointed in me.

Yorenson. Disappointed. Standing at the head of the class, listening to my wrong answer. *Really, Joanne, you know this. You know how to do this.*

Couldn't remember. It was dark. Very dark. Warm in there, in the night, but no stars, no moon.

No. Hallway. Something at the end. I was moving toward it without any sensation of moving, there was light, and light and—

I was sitting in a creaking wooden school chair,

and the room smelt faintly of Pine-Sol and chalk, and Yorenson pulled at his tweed jacket like a fussy girl and asked me a question that I didn't understand, and I felt panic rising like storm surge along the coast. I had to get this right, had to. He looked at me in disappointment and turned back to the blackboard. He drew an air molecule, chalk squeaking.

I was the only one in the room. Staying after class. Remedial weather theory. No, that wasn't right, I had never—

Pay attention, he said, without turning around. Squeaking chalk. *This takes delicacy, my dear.*

On the board. The answer was on the board. All I had to do was – was—

Crystal sparkles around the edge of Yorenson's blackboard, eating. Darkness all around, eating the answer.

No.

I reached out with my hand, and the chemical structure on the board became reds and blues and yellows, three-dimensional, spinning, and I plucked away one thing that shouldn't be there – a yellow grape in the wrong place on the stem – and stuck a blue one in its place.

Again. Faster. Reaching for thousands of spinning models, millions, billions, and it wasn't my hand that was reaching, it was my mind, it was me.

Yorenson turned from the blackboard and put

the chalk down and smiled at me.

Breathe, he said. Don't forget to breathe—

—and suddenly there was sweet, sweet air in my lungs, and the noise, my God, the noise was terrific, people shouting, feet running, voices, some kind of alarm going off in a store, the hyperactive beat of music in the distance, sweet, sweet chaos.

I swept in breath after breath after breath and listened to my pounding heart and thought, I *hated that goddamn class.*

Someone was cushioning my head. I blinked and focused and saw that it was David. He looked deathly pale, and I could feel his hands trembling. For some reason his glasses were off, and his face looked different. Stronger. His eyes glittered with flecks of copper.

'Hi,' I whispered. He started to say something, but didn't.

Somebody slapped an oxygen mask I didn't need over my face.

Funny how a near-death experience can make you hungry. I sat in the food court with David and gulped down a heroic meal of beef kebab, saffron rice, samosas, and some kind of designer water without bubbles or aftertaste. David still looked spooked. He hadn't said a word to me during the hysteria of the paramedic visit, or the argument over whether or not I was brain-damaged enough to go to the hospital…hadn't, in fact, said anything to anybody. He'd just stood there at the edge of the chaos, arms folded, watching me with a frown curved between his eyebrows.

It was kind of cute, really.

I had to sign releases and I-won't-sue waivers, not to mention endure dire predictions of disability and death from the local doc-in-a-box who'd arrived on the scene with personal injury lawyer in tow.

By the time it was over, I'd grabbed David by the elbow and said, 'I'm starving,' and he *still* hadn't said anything through the entire walking, ordering, and eating process.

Now, as I gulped the last of my water and scooped up the last errant grains of orange-specked rice, he leant forward and asked, 'Done now?'

'Guess so.' I ate a last mouthful of naan, licked my fingers, and used the napkin as a last resort. People were still watching me, either because of my excellent fashion sense or because they were waiting for me to fall down and foam at the mouth again. Probably the most exciting thing to happen in the mall since the Christmas pageant.

He was watching me that way, too. 'You want to tell me what's going on with you?'

'Not really,' I said. 'Listen, no offence, but I think it's better if you just take the twenty I gave you and look for another ride. It isn't that I don't like you, it's just that—'

'You might have another one of those?'

Yeah. I might, this time while driving Delilah at top speed. Or next time, my invisible enemy might decide to wrap a mantle of poison around David instead of me, to distract me while he pulled another little trick out of his magical hat. Somebody really didn't want me to reach Lewis. Who? Why? Who even knew I was looking? The Djinn, of course, but Djinn didn't act without orders from their masters. And that Djinn was Lewis's, and if Lewis had given me the directions to meet him, he'd hardly be trying to kill me, too. Well, Paul knew, sort of. And Star. *Shit.* Speculation was getting me nowhere.

'If you have another one of those fits, you're going to need help,' David said. 'Besides, I get the feeling you're driving a long way. I could use the lift. Really. I've got a long way to go.'

'Yeah?' It was the first information David had offered, however oblique. 'To where?'

'Phoenix,' he said. 'My brother's in trouble. I'm trying to get to him.'

I found a last grain of rice and coaxed it onto my fork. 'What's his name?'

David hesitated, then looked away. 'Joseph.'

'Biblical theme.'

'We're a very religious family.'

I shoved the tray away and put my hands flat on the table. They weren't shaking anymore, which was an improvement. And I didn't feel anything much happening around me, not from an eldritch standpoint, anyway – plenty of screaming kids, arguing adults, booming bass from stereo stores, babble in a hundred languages. All in the real world.

What had almost killed me didn't belong here, in this world. My enemy had been precise this time, tried to get at me personally. Now that I was on my guard, he wouldn't have as much opportunity. Next time, he might try something messier.

I couldn't afford to be around people when that happened.

'Phoenix,' I repeated. 'Look, seriously, it's not safe to be around me, OK? Call it what you want – epileptic fits, demonic possession, poison, Mafia enforcers. It's just not safe. So do yourself a favour, buy a bus ticket, catch a commercial flight, rent a car, just turn around and walk away. Right now.'

He looked at me seriously from across the teal blue plastic table. Behind him, a neon light sculpture of a parrot climbed a tiled pillar. The brilliant colours made him look drab, a bird in winter colours.

'You're serious?' he asked.

'As a heart attack.'

He finally nodded and said, 'OK.'

Well, what had I expected? Argument? Heroic measures? Declarations of undying love and loyalty? Hell, he was a road dude, just a guy who'd asked for a ride and gotten in over his head. Cute, but not playing at my power level.

Still. I hadn't expected him to just say OK and walk away. Not really. Not without even another word. It was a little bit ego-bruising.

Well, as a matter of fact, that wasn't what he was doing. He had my plastic tray with the empty disposable plates and tableware. He opened a trash receptacle and dumped stuff, slid the tray into a stacker, and ambled back with his hands stuck in his coat pockets.

'I meant to tell you, you look incredibly good in that,' he said. 'Purple really likes you.'

He was still waiting. I raised my eyebrows. 'Anything else?'

'My backpack,' he said, perfectly reasonably. 'It's in the car.'

'Oh.' I shoved a shopping bag at him. 'Make yourself useful.'

He had a truly wicked smile. 'I often do.'

We hiked a Yellowstone distance to the car, and even though the sky was clear except for some high cirrus wisps, I kept an eye on it. Lightning had been known to form chains hundreds of miles from a storm centre – been known to strike people dead from clear skies. In my case, it wouldn't be an accident.

Poor Delilah waited where I'd left her, scorched

door and all. I unlocked the back and got out David's backpack. It was surprisingly heavy. He rescued it from me when I almost dropped it.

'What the hell's in there?' I asked. 'Did you rob Fort Knox?'

'Yeah, this is my idea of a quick getaway,' he said, and shrugged into the thing like he'd been doing it all his life. 'Tent, portable stove, cookware, clothes, extra boots, and a few dozen books.'

'Books?'

He gave me a pitying look. 'You don't read?'

'I don't carry the New York Public Library on my back. Hell, I don't even carry it in the trunk.'

'Your loss.' Now that he had his belongings, he seemed to still be waiting for something. 'You going to be OK?'

'Me? Sure.'

'You want to explain what happened back there?' he asked.

'The whole curry thing? Really, I just like Indian food.'

'Funny.' He waited. I waited, too. 'You're not going to explain.'

'That's the general idea,' I agreed. 'You don't want to know. It's better that you don't. Safer.'

He shook his head. Before I could stop him – or figure out if I wanted to stop him – he leant forward and kissed me lightly on the cheek. I stepped back, raised a hand to touch burning skin, and was surprised by how high my heart rate spiked.

'Take care,' he said. 'And take care of Delilah.'

'Yeah,' I wanted to say something profound, but I could barely manage the one word. He turned and walked away, heading back for the mall. Ten steps away, he turned with a dramatic flare of his coat.

'Hey!' he called as he kept walking backwards.

'Yeah?'

'You look like you shopped at Prince's garage sale,' he said, and smiled – a real, full, beautiful smile.

'Hot, aren't I?'

'You're a regular fire hazard.' He waved and turned again, a perfect balletic turn, and kept walking.

I watched him all the way until he disappeared inside. I had opened the driver's side door, but I didn't really remember doing it. Warm metal under my hand. I got in and smelt a ghost of his aftershave – something cinnamon, exotic, warm. Turned the ignition key. Delilah started up and purred.

'Just the two of us, baby,' I said. I didn't like the sound of it nearly as much as I'd thought I would.

When I was ten, I went on vacation with my mom to Disney World, just the two of us. Dad was gone by then, vanished into the sunset like Roy Rogers, only instead of riding Trigger, he was riding his secretary, Eileen Napolitano…not that I knew that when I was ten, I knew only that he was gone and Mom was pissed, and anytime I whined about wanting to paint my toenails orange, she told me she didn't want me to end up a secretary.

Mom and I went to Disney World together – my sister, Sarah, older than me, had opted snobbishly for two weeks of band camp instead. We arrived in Orlando in the middle of a clear and sunny March afternoon, and by seven o'clock, the weather guys were saying hurricane season was coming early. Nobody believed them. We rode the monorail to our hotel, and I splashed in the pool and squealed over the cartoons on TV as though I hadn't already seen them twenty times. And Mom looked out the window a lot at the cool velvet sky, the hurricane moon floating in specks of stars.

The following morning we arrived at the Magic Kingdom with clouds boiling from the east – a big black storm wall riding the tide. My mom was never one to let a little rain get her down. We rode the Mine Train and Space Mountain and Haunted Mansion. We rode every ride I was tall enough for, even the ones that made Mom queasy. We bought souvenirs for Sarah, even though I didn't think she deserved it, after rolling her eyes and being a fourteen-year-old superior little drama queen.

When we were taking pictures with Mickey and Minnie, the rain started. It was like somebody had turned a lake upside down, and the Magic Kingdom turned into the Kingdom of the Sea. If you wanted your picture taken with Charlie the Tuna, it was perfect. By four o'clock, the hardiest Mouseketeers had taken shelter in the hotels, away from the windows and the lightning. Even Pluto got in out of the rain.

Not me and Mom. We were already soaked stupid, so it didn't really matter much anymore. We whooped and hollered and splashed down Main Street USA, played shark attack in Tomorrowland, and pretended that we'd rented out the whole Disney empire for ourselves, just for one day.

It was the best time we ever had together. And yeah, the rain could have been a coincidence. But when I look back on it now, that was the beginning. Every major moment in my life has been accompanied by dramatic weather, and for a long time, I didn't know why.

Even after I knew, even after I accepted it was all true, my mom couldn't. Parents almost never did, apparently; she never really had a chance to come to terms with it. Heart attack at the age of forty-nine. There one minute, gone the next, a shock like a bolt of lightning from a clear blue sky.

It had occurred to me to wonder, much later, if that had been arranged. I tried not to think about it too much, because it made me consider the path that I'd chosen, or had been chosen for me.

I didn't get close to people. Not anymore.

Which perfectly explained why I'd had to leave David behind, the way I'd left every part of normal life behind me when I'd taken the oath and joined the Wardens. I was risking my life every time I reached for power. I didn't have the right to risk anyone else's along with it.

Too bad. He was really, really cute.

Just outside of town, two miles over the state border, Delilah sputtered. It was just a tiny hitch, but I felt it like a spike driven between my ribs. *Oh, God. Not now.* Nothing menacing on the weather front, but that didn't mean opportunity couldn't knock. Or smash me flat.

Maybe it was nothing, I told myself. Just a ping, just a coincidence, a one-time-only—

Fuck. She chugged again. And again. The engine sputtered and roared back to life.

'Oh, baby, no, don't do this, don't—' Delilah wasn't listening. She gulped air, coughed gas, choked.

We coasted to a halt on the gravel shoulder, next to a road sign proclaiming the wonders of a McDonald's just five miles ahead on the right. Under Ronald's cheery leer, I got out and resisted the urge to kick tires. I could fix her. I always fixed her.

But not wearing the new purple velvet. *Dammit.* I'd bought some more practical clothes, but they were still in the plastic shopping bags in the trunk, and there wasn't a changing room in sight. Ah well, the road wasn't that busy, and I was desperate. I grabbed jeans and a button-front shirt and climbed into the backseat.

Getting out of velvet pants is not as easy as it sounds, at least not in the backseat of a Mustang. Not that I hadn't had practice, but still, there was the embarrassment factor; every time I heard a car, I had to duck down and hold my breath. Finally, I was down to the purple satin panties and lace shirt – no bra, because I'd wanted to make a good impression on David. Which apparently I hadn't, because he wasn't here to appreciate it.

I was completely naked except for the panties when I heard a tap on the window behind me, screamed, and threw my velvet jacket over as much of myself as it would cover.

Of course. Why had I ever doubted who it would be?

'You bastard!' I yelped. David looked puzzled and far too innocent to really *be* innocent. 'Jeez! Turn around, would you?'

'Sure.' He did. I scrambled around, pulling on blue jeans first, then making sure I had my eyes boring into his back while I put on the denim button-down. I had a bra somewhere in the shopping bag, but I didn't want to take the time.

I knocked on the window and slid across the seat, opened the passenger door, and got out to face him.

'It's a funny story,' he said. 'I was just walking along—'

'As if I want to hear it,' I snapped. 'Jesus, you scared the crap out of me!'

'Sorry.' He didn't look sorry, but there was a little colour in his cheeks that hadn't been there last time we'd said good-bye. A little glitter in his eyes that probably wasn't regret. 'I thought you were in trouble.'

'Genius! I *am* in trouble.' I stomped around, popped Delilah's hood, and set the prop in place. 'The engine folded.'

'Yeah?' He looked over my shoulder. 'What is it?'

'Hell if I know.' I started examining hoses. He didn't bother me, which was odd – how many guys do you know who wouldn't stand over you and offer advice even if they don't know a radiator from a radish? After a few minutes, I looked back and saw he'd taken off his pack and was sitting quietly on it, leafing through a paperback. 'What the hell are you doing?'

'Reading, what does it look like I'm doing?' He turned down a page at the sound of a car approaching, stood up, and held out a thumb. The truck blew past in a smear of wind and chrome.

'You're hitching?'

'Beats walking.'

He held out his thumb again. I checked more hoses. They all looked good. The clamps were intact. Dammit. I didn't think it was a valve problem, but with vintage Mustangs, you never knew. I'd already had Delilah's engine rebuilt twice.

I spun away from the car, put greasy hands on my hips, and stared at him. 'OK. I may be slow, but eventually I get it. You're following me.'

He concentrated on trying to flag down a bright yellow Volkswagen bug the exact colour of a lemon drop, but it didn't even slow down.

'It's the main road out of town,' he said. 'And I'm heading for Phoenix, remember?'

'You are *following me!*' I resisted the urge to kick Delilah's tire; there was no reason to take it out on the baby. 'And you know something.'

'Like what?' He didn't look concerned. In fact, he didn't even look interested.

'Like who's doing this to me.'

'Well, I know it's not me. Does that help?' He gave up on the road and went back to the easy-chair comfort of his backpack. I gave him a glare and went back to checking hoses, but Delilah didn't give me any hints.

'Try it again,' David suggested. He was back sitting down, reading. I checked the oil and ignored him. Nope, it was full and grime-free. Double dammit. I couldn't see anything blown, no telltale sprays of oil or fluid. The block looked good.

No sense in delaying the inevitable. I dropped to the gravel, rolled over, and squirmed under the car.

'Need any help?'

'No,' I yelled. 'Go away!'

'OK.' I heard David get up and walk over to the road as another car approached. It slowed down, then sped up a squeal of tires. 'Jerk.'

'Not everybody's as nice as I am,' I agreed. 'Shit. Shit shit shit.' The engine looked good from down here, too. I was getting oil-smeared and gravel-gouged for nothing. 'This is just great. Come on, baby, give me a break here.'

I slid back out, cleaned gravel out of the palms of my hands and brushed off my blue jeans, shook dust out of my dark hair, and announced, 'I'll try it again.' David remained unimpressed. He had taken his pack and moved about twenty feet farther down the road and was sitting with his back against the pole of the McDonald's billboard, reading.

I slid into the driver's seat and turned the key.

Delilah hummed to life, smooth and even as ever. I idled her for a while, gave her gas, revved her, closed my eyes, and listened for any hitches.

Nothing. I let it fall back to idle and felt the vibration in my skin.

David was reading *The Merchant of Venice*. He was kicked back, relaxed, feet up. His brown hair gleamed red highlights in the sun, and overhead the sky was blue, blue, merciless blue.

I popped the clutch and rolled past him, accelerating. He never looked up.

Ten feet past the billboard, I hit the brakes and skidded to a gravel-spewing stop. In the rearview mirror, I saw him turn down the page, put the book back in his backpack, and heft the thing like it weighed no more than my purse.

He stowed it in the backseat and got in without a word. As he got in, I grabbed his hand and held it palm up, then passed my hand over it and concentrated.

Nothing. If he was a Warden – Earth Warden, I suspected – he had no glyphs. Maybe a Wildling? They were few and far between, from what I'd ever heard, but it was possible he had some kind of talent. Maybe.

He took his hand back, frowning slightly. 'And that was—?'

'Checking to see if you washed your hands.'

He looked doubtfully at me – oily, dusty, grimy. I accelerated out onto the open road.

'How'd you find me?' I asked.

'Luck,' he said.

'Yeah,' I agreed gloomily. 'Luck. I'll bet.'

Five miles down the road, I spotted a cloud on the horizon ahead of us. Just a little cloud about the size of my hand. Hardly anything, really.

But I could feel the storm coming back. *Son of a bitch.*

❧ ❧ ❧

By the time the sun went down, I was exhausted. I planned to have David take the wheel, but there was a hitch in my brilliant plan.

David didn't drive.

'At all?' I asked. 'I mean, you *can't*?'

'I'm from New York,' he explained. As if that explained it. To me, it was like meeting somebody with three heads from the planet Bozbarr. It also caused a big sucking hole in my plans – I hadn't wanted to pull over at all on the way to Oklahoma, beyond gas and bathroom stops. But the world looked sparkly and jagged, I was floating about an inch outside my body, and my muscles trembled like soggy rubber bands.

I'd kill us both if I tried to go on much longer.

'We're stopping for the night,' I announced. 'I need some rest.'

David nodded. He had a little clip-on light on his book, and he was deep in the perils of one of John Grisham's lawyers. I wished he would get a little more interested in the prospect of spending the night in a hotel with a hot babe who owned a purple velvet suit, but apparently not happening.

I tried a hint. 'Any preference? Trashy decor? Adult channels?'

He turned a page. 'Indoor plumbing's a plus.'

Bigger hint. 'Two rooms or one?' I kept looking at the road and the sunset. In my peripheral vision, he still looked relaxed and unfazed, but he marked his place in his book and turned the light off.

'Kind of takes the mystery out of it if you ask,' he said.

'Just thinking out loud.'

'One's fine.'

Well, that was an answer, but I wasn't getting the come-hither vibe. David was just about impossible to read, which was funny, considering how much time he spent with the printed page. Ah, well. Truthfully, I was too wasted to be seductive anyway.

Up ahead, the cool blue glow of a motel sign floated like a UFO above the road. Clean sheets, fluffy pillows, little complimentary soaps. It sounded like heaven. Up close, it looked a lot more like purgatory, but any afterlife in a storm.

I checked us in, getting absolutely no reaction from the wall-eyed clerk to any of my quips, and paid with my fast-dwindling supply of cash. I signed the slip and got the room key and went back out to the car. The chunky orange tag attached to the key said we were in room 128. It was, naturally, on the other side of the building, the dark side, where half the parking lot lights were dead and the other half terminally ill. I pulled Delilah up in a parking space directly in front of the door.

Well, one benefit to the place: it was quiet. Awesomely quiet. Nothing but the wind whispering through trees and rattling a stray plastic bag across the parking lot.

'Shall we?' I asked, and reached down to grab my duffel. David took out his heavy backpack and camping kit. I doubted he would need all of it, but I supposed living on the road makes you less than trusting about that kind of thing.

Once we were inside, my visions of gleaming chrome bathroom fixtures and deep-pile carpeting were crushed. The carpet was indoor-outdoor, the bathroom had last been upgraded in the 1950s, and the sad-clown prints on the walls could never have been remotely fashionable. But it had clean sheets, reasonably fluffy pillows, and (I saw during a fast reconnaissance) complimentary little soaps. So OK. Next door to heaven.

David leant his backpack against the wall. 'One bed,' he said.

'Lucky for you, you brought camping gear.' I flopped down on the bed and immediately felt gravity increase by a factor of ten. The mattress was old and sagged, but it still felt like a cloud under my aching back. 'God, I could sleep for days.'

The bed creaked. I hoisted one eyelid and saw that David had perched on the edge, looking down at me. In a perfect world, he would have been all choked up with romantic desire. In my all-too-real reality, he said, 'You look terrible.'

'Thanks,' I murmured, and let my eye drift shut. 'You charmer. Sheesh.'

The bed creaked again, and I heard him

rummaging in his backpack. Footsteps on the carpet. The bathroom door closed, and the shower started up with a stuttering hiss.

Sometime a few minutes later, the sound of running water melted into the steady, stealthy sound of rain. It was raining. That was bad, I could feel it, but I couldn't think why. Rain tapping the windows, polite at first, then beating harder, impatient to be inside. Wind whispered and rose to a roar, and I heard a rumble of thunder and felt the cold hair-raising frisson of electrons aligning.

A flash of lightning, blue-white, outside the window.

It was coming for me—

I pulled awake with a gasp and found David tucking a scratchy blanket around me. I flailed my way out of it and stumbled to the window, ripped aside the curtains, and stared out at the dark.

Quiet. Quiet as the grave. No rain. No thunder. No lightning stabbing at me from above.

'What?' he asked.

It's looking for me, I wanted to say, but there was no way I could explain that sort of thing. I was so tired, I was incoherent, shaking, almost crying. *It's out there.*

'Did it rain?' I managed to ask.

'Don't think so. Maybe you heard the shower. You haven't been asleep long.'

Oh. I remembered now. The shower. He'd been taking a shower.

When I turned around, I realised he was wearing nothing but a towel and some well-placed water drops, and it hit me with a cattle-prod jolt that he was absolutely, unquestionably *gorgeous*. Skin like burnished gold, and under it the best kind of muscles on a man – long, lean, defined without bulging. A gilded thatch of hair on his chest that narrowed to a line down his stomach, pointing the way under the towel.

'Oh,' I blurted. 'Wow. You – don't have much on.'

'No,' he agreed gravely. 'I don't usually sleep in footie pyjamas.'

'Would it be too personal to ask what you do sleep in?'

'Pyjama bottoms. Unless that bothers you.'

Bothered me? Hell, yes. But in that nice, liquefying, warm-silk way of being bothered, as in 'hot and.'

'No,' I said weakly. A drop of water glided down over his shoulder and melted into his chest hair. I had a fantasy so vivid, it raised my skin into goose bumps.

'OK. You planning to sleep in that?' he asked me. I was still wearing the gritty, oil-stained denim from my try at fixing Delilah, and looking at him in all his glory, I felt grubby and short and smelly.

'Um, no,' I said, grabbed my duffel, and escaped to the bathroom.

Funny how a nice flare of lust can burn off the fog of exhaustion; I stripped off my clothes and kicked them under the sink, stepped into a shower he'd left warm for me. Shampoo and conditioner clustered considerately on the floor near my feet, open bar of soap in the tray...all the comforts of somebody else's home.

I scrubbed myself pink, washed and strangled the water out of my hair, and wrapped myself in one of the motel's thin, stiff towels. Record time. I considered shaving my legs, decided no, reconsidered, and then managed to get depilated in under four minutes, with only one tiny little cut near my left ankle.

When I came out into the bedroom, the bed was empty. No David.

He was zipped into a sleeping bag on the floor.

I stood there, dripping and steaming, and said, 'You're kidding.'

He didn't open his eyes. 'You've said that to me before. Do I really look that funny?'

'Bastard.' I flopped down on the bed again, squirmed under the covers, and stripped off the towel beneath. 'You made me get up for nothing.'

'No,' he corrected. 'Now you're clean and you'll sleep better.'

He turned over on his side, away from me. I

wondered if he was naked inside the sleeping bag, growled in frustration, and put a pillow over my face. Suffocation had no appeal. I took it off and said, 'You can bring your sleeping bag up here, you know. Beats sleeping on the floor.'

He didn't answer for a few seconds, long enough for me to experience total rejection, and then he turned over and raised himself up on one elbow to look at me.

I expected some quip or some question, but he just looked. And then he flipped open the sleeping bag, slid out, and walked over to the bed.

He hadn't lied. Pyjama bottoms. They rode low on his hips.

I folded back the covers. He got in. I lowered my head to rest on the pillow, still watching him, and he rolled up on his left side to face me.

Some sane part of my mind was telling me that this was just some guy I'd picked up on the road, for God's sake, some guy who could be a rapist or a killer, and that part of my mind was completely right and completely wrong. I knew him in places that had nothing to do with my mind.

'Turn on your side,' he said. I did, feeling like I was already dreaming. The slide of sheets felt cool and soothing on my overheated body.

I could feel him warm at my back, not quite touching. He put a hand on my hip, slid it gently up.

I couldn't breathe.

He put his fingers at the base of my neck and drew them lightly down the curve of my spine, all the way down. I felt my muscles contract and shiver, and I wanted to stretch like a cat against him; it took all my control not to do it.

If I'd been melting inside before, I was boiling now.

'I'll have to call a penalty,' he said. His voice sounded far away. 'You're not even wearing a T-shirt. Definitely a violation of the rules.'

His fingertips followed the curve of my hip again.

The tacky room had dropped away, and it was just the two of us, suspended in time and silence. There were no rules for this, none that I'd ever known. Just instinct. I started to turn toward him, and his hand spread out, holding me in place. His breath was warm on the back of my neck, his lips barely touching skin.

'You're afraid of me,' he whispered. His hand moved into the demilitarised zone of my stomach. 'Don't be afraid.'

It wasn't him – I was scared of myself. I was tired, vulnerable, frightened, lonely, desperate. I couldn't trust my own senses, much less...whatever this was. Whoever he was.

I hadn't thought about the Mark for hours, but now I could feel it moving inside me, turning restlessly as if it hungered as much as I did. Oh,

God, I couldn't concentrate enough to hold it back, not with him so close, so warm.

'Shhh,' he whispered, even though I hadn't made a sound out loud. His hand moved again, gently, tracing a line of fire from my stomach up between my breasts. Flattened out over my heart. 'Be still.'

I felt a lurch inside, a chill, a burst of heat.

The Demon Mark stopped moving.

'How—?' I blurted, and instantly stopped myself from asking. I didn't want to know. There was so much here I didn't want to know, because if I knew, then I would have to move away from him, give up this warmth, this beautiful peace.

'Shhh,' he said, and his lips touched the back of my neck. 'No questions, no pain, no fear.'

I glimpsed something then, just the edges of something vast and powerful, and I almost knew—

His hand moved again, gliding down, drawing my mind away from what it chased in the dark. His fingers brushed gently over my aching nipples, settled back on my stomach.

'You should sleep,' he whispered. As if I could. As if I could ever sleep again, after feeling this, knowing this...

But it was all slipping away, water through my fingers, air flowing free through the sky. I was falling, and falling, and falling.

His hand moved slowly down and came to rest over the aching emptiness of my womb. It pressed flat and burnt his warmth into my deepest places.

'Dream well,' he whispered.

Pleasure came in a wave, drenching me from head to toe, and it went on and on and on. It was the last I knew, except for the dreams.

I dreamt of rain.

It was raining the night Lewis showed up at my door...the slow, steady, nurturing rain people believe is their birthright on this planet, the kind that had to be squeezed out of Mother Nature with a fist of power. I'd been working at it all damn day, and by the time I got home and sank into a hot bath, I was worn out.

I'd been soaking for about ten minutes when I heard the doorbell ring. *Let it ring*, part of me sighed. The other part reminded me that I was a responsible adult, a Warden, and besides, the visitor might be either Ed McMahon with a Publishers Clearing House check or – even more unlikely – a gorgeous hunk.

It was the gorgeous hunk possibility that lured me out of the bath. I wrapped a thick ratty blue robe around myself and made wet footprints to the door.

I swung it open to find...nobody there. And then I looked down.

There was a guy huddled in a sitting position against the wall, soaking wet, his brown hair sticking up like porcupine quills. He was shaking, hugging himself for warmth. It took me a full ten seconds to recognise his face and feel the shock.

'Lewis!' I blurted, and before I could think what I was doing, I got my hands under his arms and tugged. No way I could have lifted him myself, but he cooperated and stumbled over the threshold and into my living room, where he proceeded to drip and shiver uncontrollably. I slammed and locked the door, ran to the hall closet, and came back with the warmest blanket I had – considering it was Florida, not so very warm.

When I came back, he was sitting down again, this time on the tile floor of the entryway.

I used a tiny jet of power to suck all the water off him and out of his clothes and directed it down the kitchen sink, where it gurgled and drained away. I warmed the blanket at the same time and threw it around his shoulders.

'Hey,' I said, and crouched down. 'Not that the floor's not comfy, but I do have a couch.'

He opened his eyes, and I was surprised by the fear in them. Lewis, *afraid*. What could scare the most powerful Warden in the world?

'Can't make it,' he admitted. He did look bad – skinny, almost skeletal, with dirty-pale skin as if he'd been someplace dark for a long time. 'Thanks.'

'I vacuumed you off and gave you a blanket,' I said. 'Don't thank me yet. Come on, up.'

We repeated the grabbing-and-hauling and got him to the couch, where he sprawled and proved that a normal-size couch wasn't designed to accommodate a six-foot-plus guy at full length. I spread the blanket over him. 'When's the last time you ate?'

'Don't remember,' he murmured. I started to go into the kitchen, but he caught my wrist. 'Jo.'

The touch, skin-to-skin, started a burn between us. He let go the second he felt it.

'You're in trouble,' I said. It wasn't exactly a stretch. 'I get it. And no, I won't call anybody.'

It was what he wanted. He nodded and closed those warm brown eyes.

When I came back with a microwaved cup of soup, he managed to squirm to a sitting position and sipped it faster than good sense allowed. I pulled up a pale plaid hassock, sat down, and watched him. When he'd sucked the last noodle out of the cup, I took it and laid it aside on the coffee table.

'Good,' he murmured. I put a hand on his forehead. He was burning up with fever. 'I'm all right.'

'Yeah, like hell.' I fetched cold medicine from the bathroom and made him swallow two gel capsules with another cup of soup. All nice and domestic. No sound in the apartment except for the steady tick of rain on the roof and windows.

He didn't say anything until the second cup of soup was finished. He rolled the empty ceramic in his hands, watching me with fever-bright eyes, and finally said, 'You're not going to ask?'

'Do I have any right?' I took the cup and set it back down. 'You're the big boss, Lewis, I'm just a Staffer. You say *frog*, I jump. You say nurse you back to health—'

He made a rude noise. 'Yeah. You're the mothering type, Jo. And the no-questions-asked type.'

He had a point. 'OK. What the hell are you doing here, showing up starved and sick on my doorstep? It isn't like we know each other, Lewis. At least, not in any way that matters.'

Cruel but true. Lewis's eyes widened, and he looked down. 'I know you,' he said. 'And I trust you.'

'Why?' He gave me an off-kilter smile for answer. I felt myself blush hot up around the cheekbones. 'OK, rephrasing the question. What kind of trouble are you in?'

The smile disappeared, and he looked ill and tired. 'The worst kind,' he said. 'Council trouble. I broke out.'

I froze, my own mug of soup halfway to my lips. Steam tickled my nose with ghosts of spices. 'Broke out?'

'They were keeping me in a hospital, the one

where...' He had an inward look, and what flashed across his face didn't look like a pleasant memory. 'They were keeping me at the Pound.'

The Pound was a nickname among the junior Wardens for the hospital Marion Bearheart oversaw, where Wardens checked in and walked out – or were carried out – as regular human beings. The place where we got neutered, or in my case, spayed.

The place where our powers could be ripped away at the roots.

'No,' I whispered, and put the soup down to take his hands. His felt cold, still. 'God, Lewis, they *couldn't*. Not you.'

'They hadn't decided, but I knew which way it was going to go. Martin didn't want it, but the others—' He shrugged. 'I don't fit, Jo, I have too much power, and they can't control it. They don't like that.'

No wonder he'd run. He had so much to lose, so much... I couldn't imagine Marion agreeing to it, but she was sworn to obey, like all of us. Lewis was right not to take the chance.

It explained why he'd come to me like this, wet and sick; he couldn't use his powers, not even to protect himself from the rain or burn the virus out of his bloodstream. Lewis lit up Oversight like a Roman candle every time he called power. Until he was back at full strength, he couldn't defend himself.

I put a hand on his burning forehead and stared into his eyes. The sparks jumped between us, weak but still there.

'Trust me?' I asked. He nodded. 'Then sleep. Nobody's going to get you here.'

He fell asleep within minutes, curled under the blanket. I washed the mugs and put them on the dish drainer, went back and let the cooling water out of the bathtub. By the time I'd exchanged the robe for a comfortable tank top and drawstring pants, he was snoring.

He looked very young, but then he *was* – older than me, but a lot younger than most other Wardens. I sat down on the floor next to the couch, leant my back up against it, and listened to him sleep while I watched TV with the sound turned down. I didn't dare close my eyes; I kept watch in Oversight, alert for the approach of anybody who might be on his trail.

Toward morning, the rain stopped, and whether I meant to or not, I fell asleep. When I woke up, Lewis was gone from the couch. I heard the shower running. The floor had taken a horrible toll on my muscles, and by the time I'd worked myself into a standing position and hobbled my way into the kitchen to put on coffee, he was back, dressed in my ratty blue bathrobe. It actually fit. Where it dragged the ground for me, it maintained a politically correct mid-calf length on Lewis, and he didn't have to roll up the sleeves.

'How do you feel?' I asked, and poured him a mug of liquid morning magic. He sipped it, watching me. His eyes were clearer, anyway, but his hair still stuck up in wet porcupine quills and gave him a vulnerable look.

'Better.'

'Good.' I reached for the coffee cake I'd put out on the counter and winced as another muscle group went on strike. 'Wish I could say the same.'

I didn't see him move toward me, and the shock of his warm hands on my back came as a surprise.

'Do you mind?' he asked.

'Um, hardly.'

He moved his large, capable hands down to my waist and dug his thumbs in, right where it hurt in the long muscles. Slow, deliberate pressure that hurt at first, then dissolved into absolute pleasure. I pulled in a slow breath, let it out, and felt tension leak away from shoulders to toes. 'Whoa. Ever consider a career in massage therapy?'

'I'm open to new ideas.' I could hear the smile in his voice. His thumbs pressed more lightly, in slow circles. 'Feel good?'

'Any better, I'd lose motor skills.'

'I'm sorry I pulled you into this,' he said. His hands moved up, chasing the tension. 'It was – a bad night.'

'I've had a few,' I admitted. 'It's OK, you know.

You can stay as long as you want to.'

His hands made it to my shoulders and squeezed away hours of stress. 'No, I really can't,' he said. There were a lot of ways to interpret that, but if Lewis meant anything more intimate, I couldn't tell it from the slow, steady pressure of his fingers on pressure points. His thumbs dug into the nerve clusters just behind my shoulder blades, and I felt my knees go weak.

'So you're leaving.'

I felt that smile again. 'What can I say? I've always been a one-night stand.' He smoothed my back with gentle strokes. 'I have to go. If I stay with you, it just puts you in the fire with me. You don't need to attract their attention.'

'Me?' I turned, startled, and found myself chest-to-chest with him. He didn't step back. 'Why?'

'You know why.' His brown eyes were bleak, but they never quite lost their edge of amusement. 'They only like Wardens to have so much power. You – you're different. Not to mention uncontrollable.'

'Hey!' I put my hands on his chest and shoved him back a step. 'Watch it, buster.'

'I didn't mean it in a bad way.' He shrugged. 'I mean *they* can't control you. So they'll be watching you, Jo. Don't give them a reason.'

'You must still have a fever. I'm just *Staff*, for God's sake. Why would anybody be watching me?'

Lewis held up his hands in surrender. 'Point

taken. I'm probably wrong.'

No, he wasn't. I could tell. I glared at him. 'Don't bullshit me.'

'Don't pretend you don't know what you are.'

'Well, I *don't* know.' I felt my face set into a frown. 'You tell me.'

He reached out and took my hand in his.

Skin on skin.

Sparks. Waves of power echoing through me, back to him, amplified as they returned to me.

I pulled free and stepped back until I felt the kitchen counter behind my back. For a few long seconds we just looked at each other, and then he nodded, reached around me to pick up his cup, and wandered back to the bathroom, sipping it.

I barely tasted mine, even though I drank the whole cup while watching the closed door.

When he came back out, he was dressed in the blue jeans, a loose green knit shirt, and hiking boots he'd been wearing when he arrived. Dry, at least. And with some colour back in his too-thin face. I went in the bathroom and grabbed the box of cold medicine, added it to a bag of snacks and bottles of water. As care packages go, it wasn't much. I tossed in the contents of my wallet, which didn't make an impressive addition, and handed it to him.

His fingers brushed mine, drawing those sparks again. He craved it, I knew. So did I. And neither one of us could afford that.

He'd left something behind in my hand, a folded piece of paper with meticulously crisp corners. I started to unfold it, but he stopped me. 'It's an address,' he said. 'If you need me, that's where you'll find me. Just don't—'

'Tell anybody?' I finished, and gave him a faint smile. 'You know better.'

'Yeah.'

He leant forward and folded his arms around me, pulled me into a full-body hug that sent waves echoing and crashing in my head.

When he kissed me, it was like floating on a sea of glittering silver light. So much power...

He was gone before the dazzle cleared. I locked the door behind him and stood for a long time, my hand on the knob, thinking about him. Not that I knew what I felt, or what it meant, or anything at all, really.

But I was worried for him. And about him. And about myself.

Two hours later, the doorbell rang again. This time it was three polite, poker-faced Wardens who had lots of questions to ask me about Lewis.

He was right. From that moment on, they never took their eyes off me. *They'll be watching you, Jo. Don't give them a reason.* I hadn't meant to, ever.

Just like I hadn't meant to ever unfold that piece of paper.

And then...Bad Bob had happened.

It was time for Lewis to give a little aid and comfort of his own.

I woke up in the motel one body part at a time – toes first, where sunlight striped warm across them. Legs...thighs...hips... by the time I opened my eyes, I was feeling drowsy and completely relaxed, happier than I had in years.

I felt like I'd had the best sex of my life. But I hadn't. Had I? No, definitely no merging of body parts had occurred with David. But of course, today was another day, with endless possibilities...

I was lying on my stomach. I rolled over, which should have been one of those graceful movie-star manoeuvres, but ended up as a Three Stooges wrapped-in-the-sheets farce. By the time I'd clawed out of the cocoon and pushed tangled hair back from my face, I saw it was all wasted, anyway.

David was gone.

There was a cold hollow in the sheets where he'd been. I let my hand explore that for a few seconds; then I hugged the rumpled bedclothes to my chest and looked around. No sleeping bag on the floor. No backpack leaning against the wall.

I'd been dumped. Comprehensively dumped.

I got up and walked around the room, but there was little sign he'd ever been there, nothing but the outline of his head on the pillow and a single used towel on the counter in the bathroom. I stood there in the antique-white tiled chill and stared at myself in the mirror. The shower and night's sleep had done me good – still some dark smudges under my eyes, but I looked presentable. And dammit, even though he was gone, I was still humming all over with the aftermath. I closed my eyes and went up into Oversight. My body was glowing honey gold, with a flare of brilliant warm orange cantered low, just over my womb. A flare in the shape of David's hand.

I put my own hand over it and felt something there, almost an electric tingle. *Dream well.* His whisper moved through me again, and I felt that stirring again, like my whole body wanted to answer.

Dammit. I didn't know whether I wanted to get on my knees and beg him to come back, or kick his ass from here to California. No, I knew, I just didn't want to admit it. Tears burnt at the corners of my eyes, which was *ridiculous*, I didn't even know this guy, how could I possibly be disappointed in him? In myself?

And yet I was. Once again, I'd trusted a guy. Once again, I was on my own, scared and desperate and lonely.

I sat down on the bed and tried not to let it take me over. My hands were shaking, my breath unsteady, and I knew if I started crying, I wouldn't be able to stop until I was screaming. Too much. The feelings weren't about David, not really, they were about *everything*, about the Mark, about Bad Bob, about the helpless sick feeling that I was no longer in control of anything in my life.

I *would not* cry. Not for this. Not over him.

I ripped the tags off a fresh pair of panties and dressed in my stretch lace shirt and purple velvet. I was going to be defiantly, look-what-you're-missing-you-asshole gorgeous. I spent time in the bathroom on hair and makeup, and when I was done, it wasn't like *Vogue* would be banging down the door, but I looked yummy enough to turn heads. And my hands were almost steady again.

I didn't have a lot to pack, just the one duffel bag. I jammed things in, zipped it, and was ready to go. I yanked open the door and started to leave, but something stopped me.

The room still felt like David. Still smelt like him. I couldn't shake the feeling, even though I knew it was crap, that he was still in there somewhere, just out of sight, hiding. But there was no place to hide, and no matter how much of a practical joker he might be, this joke just wasn't funny.

I'd been intending to slam the door, but instead I closed it quietly, the way David must have when he left me alone with my dreams.

Pretty Miss Delilah glinted and glittered in the parking lot. I unlocked the driver's side and tossed my duffel in the back and thought about breakfast. I could, I decided, have breakfast, since my stomach was rumbling like an unexploded volcano. And coffee. Thick truck-stop coffee that was more like day-old espresso.

I needed something to live for.

Waffles sounded like as good a place to start as any.

The Waffle House came in the usual yellow, brown, and orange colour scheme, bringing back all that nostalgia for avocado appliances and rust-coloured shag carpeting from my childhood. I suppose the fact they were still stuck in the '70s was lucky, all things considered, since their prices shared the same time warp. I ordered a large pecan waffle with powdered sugar and crispy bacon. The waitress poured me a gallon-size cup of generic black caffeine. I fiddled with silverware until the food arrived, then gulped down juicy syrup-rich bites, alternating with crunchy bacon nibbles, until I felt better about my world and David's absence from it.

Business was sparse. Just me and four tired-looking men all in grimy baseball caps, sporting the bouncy physique of guys who spent most of their time driving and eating Ho Hos. Everybody had coffee, straight up, nothing froufrou like latte or decaf; we were all here for the straight stuff, mainlined in big chunky ceramic mugs.

Three extra-large cups later, I was ready to rock 'n' roll. I paid the tab to the ancient cashier and turned to look out the big picture windows. In between Day-Glo advertisements for the manager's specials, I saw that the storm was crawling closer. Not hell-driven, but making a pretty good clip. Still, not a problem yet. I could still outrun it. I didn't want to do any manipulation; too much risk of discovery by either my secret stalking enemy or the Association, and I wasn't so sure which, at this point, would be worse. Paul's tolerance had probably expired at about the point his time limit had clicked off. By now, every Warden in the country might be looking out for me.

As I shoved my wallet back in my pocket, I accidentally knocked over a saltshaker sitting on the counter. The silver top spiralled off, made loopy progress to the edge, and spun in a circle.

I hardly noticed, because of the interesting thing the spilt salt was doing.

It was...talking.

It mounded itself into little white salty letters, which said, *Joanne*.

I looked around. The cashier had moved on; the waitresses were all making rounds with coffeepots. Just me and the talking salt.

'Um...yeah?' I asked tentatively.

The salt dissolved into a flat white heap again,

then scattered wider over the counter. More words. These said, *South 25 mi, L on Iron Road.*

My heart started pounding harder. I stared at it and finally whispered, 'Is this Lewis?'

A pause. The salt wiped itself into one snowy drift, then scattered back out across the faux-wood counter.

Ya think?

'Very funny. I have to get condiments with a sense of humour.' Salt was, technically, of the earth... Lewis would be able to control it. In fact, in a place as generally unnatural as this, it might very well be the only thing he *could* control enough to get his point across. I was just happy he hadn't tried to spell out things in runny egg yolks.

Got your attention? the salt asked. Not only arrogant, but pushy, too.

'South twenty-five miles, left on Iron Road,' I repeated. 'Got it.' I took in a deep breath and blew it out, scattering the words into tiny white random grains.

It didn't seem to like that, and sucked itself up into a pile, then flattened out again. A moving finger wrote one word: *Good.*

It then made a little white smiley-face that immediately blew into randomised scatter as a waitress marched up, *tsked* the mess, and wiped the spill up with a damp cloth.

'You OK?' I must have had a bizarre look; she was staring at me.

'I'm talking to salt,' I said numbly. 'What do you think?'

She shrugged and kept on wiping up. 'Missy, I think you should've probably gone with the decaf.'

Chapter Three

*The National Weather Service has issued a
severe weather advisory for a four-state area
including Ohio, Indiana, Illinois, and Missouri.
Hail, severe winds, and tornadic activity are
possible. Please stay tuned to your local
weather sources for more information.*

Twenty-five miles down the road, there was a
battered, shotgun-riddled sign for Iron Road. I
slowed down and coasted to a stop at the side of the
road, looking down the turn-off and wondering
what exactly a smarter, saner person than me would
do.

I inspected the place while my blinker clicked.
Iron Road was a small two-lane affair that
disappeared into some dense, overhanging trees,
dappled with sunlight and shadow. Picturesque,
which was another word for isolated. Why would
Lewis want me off the beaten path? Why wouldn't

he just show up in the diner and, say, order an eggs Benedict and chat about the good old days? Well, of course, he had reason to be careful, too. Lewis was, in many ways, the most wanted Warden in the world. In comparison, I hadn't even made the top ten.

'What the fuck,' I said to Delilah, and eased her back into gear as I turned the wheel. She purred effortlessly down the hill onto Iron Road, into green shadow and smooth, deserted blacktop. I kept the speed down. On a rural road like this, anything was likely to jump out and present a road hazard, especially wildlife and farm animals. The last thing I needed was to end up picking cow out of my grille while a storm rolled up on me.

Fields stretched beyond the trees, sun-drenched and extravagantly green. I rolled down the window and breathed in cool, clear air spiced with earth and new leaves. Lewis hadn't said how far to proceed down Iron Road; I could only guess there'd be another sign.

At the crest of the next hill, I saw a neat red farmhouse with a matching barn behind, the kind of thing people paint for craft fairs; I'd never really seen one that, well, perfect before. It even had a windmill and some paintworthy Hereford cows chewing cud in the fields, ringed with a tumbledown rock fence and a riot of new wildflowers in neon purple and buttercup yellow.

Perfect Thomas Kinkade. Wind rippled the grass in long velvet waves, and I remembered one of my instructors – who knows which one – remarking how similar the seas of water and air were to each other. *We swim in an ocean of air*. Come to think of it, that probably wasn't a weather class. It sounded like English Lit to me now.

Iron Road didn't change names, but it should have; after the pretty little farm, it turned into Dirt Road, rutted and uneven. I slowed Delilah to a crawl and fretted about the state of her suspension. Nothing up ahead that I could see except a hill looming green and tan, more trees stretching out their arms over the road.

Delilah slowed down more, without my foot pressing the brake.

It's funny how you can just *know* these things, if you're true partners with your car. I could feel, as if it were my feet instead of Delilah's tires on the road, that something had gone wrong. Badly. It felt as if we were driving through deep mud, but the road was dry, the ruts hard-caked and laced with brittle tire treads. What was slowing us down?

I heard something hissing against the undercarriage of the car. I knew that sound. It sounded like...

Delilah shuddered, and I heard her engine take on a plaintive, unhappy tone. She was struggling to move, but it was getting harder, and harder, with every rotation of the wheels.

It sounded like loose sand.

The road was turning to sand, and we were sinking into it.

'Shit!' I yelped, and went up into Oversight. As soon as I soared out of body and above the car, I could see it; the earth was dull red, moving, churning like a living thing. The rough dry soil was being crushed into tiny, slippery grains. No, not sand...the road was turning to dust, finer than sand, and not just on the surface – this went deep, ten feet at least.

I yanked the wheel, trying to get Delilah off the road and into the trees, where roots and plants would slow the progress of liquefying earth, but it was already too late, the wheel turned loosely in my hands, the tires spun without traction. Dust geysered into the dry air and puffed away on the waves of the ocean of air. The car settled about a foot, and I knew that there was nothing keeping it up now except an even distribution of weight over a large, flat undercarriage. That and possibly someone's goodwill.

We floated, me and Delilah, unable to escape.

In Oversight, I spotted my enemy before she ever pushed through the underbrush – a blue-green aura, laced through with pure white for power, gold for tenacity, cold silver for ruthlessness.

Marion Bearheart had found me.

I dropped back into my skin and saw her coming

out of the trees to my left. She was just about as I remembered her from my intake meeting – middle-aged, dignified, skin like burnished copper and hair of black and silver hanging loose over her shoulders. Marion still had kind, gentle eyes, but there was nothing weak about her.

'Joanne,' she said, and her low voice seemed welcoming, somehow. 'There's no point in trying to run. Wherever you go, I can dissolve the ground under your feet, tie you down with roots and grasses. Let's make this easy.'

Of course. I'd forgotten. Marion was an Earth Warden.

A rustle of underbrush on the other side of the car drew my attention to someone else – younger than Marion, male. I didn't know him, but he had Scandinavian white-blond hair, fair skin, and summer-blue eyes. Like Marion, he had on a plaid shirt and blue jeans, practical hiking boots. Another Earth Warden. Their fashion sense – or lack of it – was unmistakable.

The third one, standing next to him, was so small I almost didn't see her – small, dark, delicate. Nothing delicate about her clothes, though, which featured a lot of leather and attitude. Her hair was cut pixie-short, streaked with unnatural greenish highlights, and she had face jewellery – a nose ring, to be exact, with a stud to match in the other nostril.

'You brought friends,' I said, turning back to Marion. She smiled faintly.

'Against you? Naturally.' She nodded toward them. 'Erik and Shirl If you're thinking of calling a storm, I'd advise you not to try it; Shirl is a damn fine practitioner, but she has a tendency to be a little heavy-handed.'

Pieces of the puzzle started to drop together. 'Oh. The salt?'

This time I got a full, delighted smile. 'I just wanted to talk to you, Joanne. It seemed like the best way to arrange it. I knew you were looking for someone. It stood to reason it was another Warden. I was only hoping it was someone with an Earth power, or that would have seemed a little odd.'

Since Lewis had the whole collectible set, nothing would have seemed odd to me…and didn't that just sum up the Wardens in a nutshell? We only thought talking salt was odd on a percentage basis.

Just my bad luck she'd gambled and I'd fallen for it.

I had a slightly darker thought. 'The lightning bolt?'

Marion looked startled. 'Of course not! We just want to talk to you, not kill you. Shirl's specialty is not weather, in any case.'

I saw something flare bright out of the corner of my eye, and turned to see Shirl holding out a palm in front of her. Fire danced on her skin, flickering gold and orange and hot reds. It reflected in her dark eyes, and I felt a surge of dislike for the arrogance I saw there. *I know better Fire Wardens than you, sweetheart. Ones who don't have to show off for the boss.* Still, fire gave me the willies, always had. I'd seen what it could do, close up.

'So talk,' I said. 'Or give me back the road and let me out of here. There's a storm coming.'

'I know,' Marion speared Shirl with a look, and Shirl put the fire back where it came from. 'Let's take a walk, Joanne.'

She reached out and opened the car door. A square stepping-stone of solid earth formed in the shifting dust, just big enough for me to stand on. I eased out, feeling Delilah rock like a boat in a pond, and bent down to test what my car was sitting on top of.

My fingers passed into the dust with barely any resistance at all; it was so fine, so frictionless than I felt a second's dizziness. Fall into *that*, and you wouldn't be coming up.

'This way,' Marion said, and turned away. I put my hand on Delilah's dusty finish for a few seconds, trying to reassure her – and me – that things weren't as bad as they seemed, and then stepped off the square of solid ground and into the shadows of the trees.

It felt like another world. Marion's world. The Earth spoke to her, the way the sky did to me:

whispers of leaves, dry creaks of branches, the padding footsteps of living things, small and large and minuscule, that made up her realm. I thought about the farm back there, the picture-perfect setting. That had been Marion's equivalent of doodling, while she waited. Perfect grass, artistic dottings of wildflowers. Marion created beauty from chaos, or maybe just demonstrated how beautiful chaos could be when seen through the right eyes.

We came out of the trees into a meadow filled with knee-high grass stalks, silver tipped, that rustled and murmured and bent under the touch of a brisk northeast wind. Overhead, white cirrus clouds shredded into lacework. A plane crawled the blue and threaded a white contrail through the lattice. It all looked flat, but I knew the plane was barely above the troposphere. The cirrus clouds were at least twenty-five thousand feet, maybe higher, well above the level of even a weather balloon. And those peaceful clouds were scudding fast, dragging the storm behind.

Marion turned her face into the wind and said, 'The Zuni always said, first thunder brings the rain. But we're far from Zuni country.'

'Everybody says something about the weather. Most of it's nonsense.'

'Most of it,' she agreed, and looked at me with those tired, patient, gentle eyes. 'Murder's a serious charge, Joanne. Running from it makes no sense. You know you'll be found.'

'I didn't murder him.'

Her dark eyebrows rose, but her face stayed still and closed. 'You argued, he's dead. Do we really believe this is an accident?'

Well, no. It hadn't been an accident. I'd been *trying* to kill Bad Bob Biringanine.

I just hadn't expected to *succeed*.

She took my silence at face value. 'You were to wait for me in Florida.'

'I couldn't. I had things to do.'

'Such as?' She shook her head, brushed hair back from her face when the wind played it into a veil over her eyes. 'Tell me what happened between you and Bad Bob. Maybe I can help you.'

I opened my mouth to tell her about the Demon Mark, but of course I couldn't; it would be suicide. And she couldn't see it – otherwise, Marion or a hundred other Wardens would have known about Bad Bob's condition long before he passed the infection on to me. Rahel had told me as much – they were impossible for humans to see, even Wardens, unless they asked their Djinn the right questions. I felt sick and trapped and more afraid than I'd been in a long time. *Help*, I wanted to say. But I didn't dare, because I knew there was no help, no cure, nothing but a long and terrible dying. If I didn't get a Djinn, I would never survive, and the

Association would never give up one of their precious store to save my life. They were very firm on that point. One Djinn per customer, rationed strictly on rank, and I'd blown my chance before I got my own. Giving me a Djinn now would just be a waste of a good elemental. They certainly wouldn't sacrifice one just for little old me.

I hedged. Some of the truth was better than none.

'There was something wrong with him,' I said. 'Bad Bob, I mean. I don't know what it was, but he attacked me. I thought he was going to kill me. I had to do it.'

'You pulled lightning,' Marion murmured. She crouched down and plucked a weed out of the ground, held it lightly between her fingers. It sprouted a bud, which exploded into luxuriant colour. Red, this one. Brilliant blood-red, with a black centre like an eye. 'You didn't try to, say, immobilise him instead, as you must have been trained to do.'

'Hey, this was *Bad Bob*, not some fifth-year apprentice with a bad attitude. The higher level a Warden is, the worse the consequences if he loses control – hell, Marion, you know that. Power and responsibility. Well, I had to fight him, and I had to use the big guns to do it. You want me to say I'm sorry?'

'No,' she said. The flower in her hands blazed brilliantly through summer, faded, withered into

winter, and died. A life in less than a minute.
Marion's little silent demonstration: *You control the
weather. I control life itself.* 'I want you to
understand that you will have a chance to tell your
side of it. But when the judgment comes, it is final.'

'Bullshit. You've already decided, all of you. You
think I'm a danger. You want to—' To neuter me.
Scrub my head with steel wool. Take away
everything that I love.

'I don't, actually,' Marion said, and dropped the
flower. 'But if the Council decides that you cannot
be trusted with the powers you control, then those
powers have to be taken from you. I know you
know this. You can't keep running like this. You
have to go back.'

'I can't. Not yet.'

'The Council meets *tomorrow*. Nobody sent me
after you today, but if you don't submit yourself for
judgment tomorrow at the Council offices,
somebody will, and my orders will be very
different.'

'You're travelling with a hunting squad,' I
pointed out. 'Two Earth Wardens and a Fire
Warden. That's to counteract my powers without
fighting me on the weather front. Right?'

She didn't answer. Didn't have to, in fact.

'Tomorrow's tomorrow,' I said finally. The storm
had crawled closer on its little cat feet, and I could
feel distant tingles at the edges of my awareness; the

storm talked to me, the way that the forest and this meadow talked to Marion. My power, and my enemy, all at once. 'You going to let me go or what?'

Marion smiled, and I knew what *that* meant.

I felt tiny, stealthy ropes of grass moving around me, sliding over my shoes, climbing my legs, and I yelped in absolute disgust and ripped free, hopping from one foot to another. The earth softened under my feet, and even though they were relatively low-heeled, my shoes sank in fast, heels first. I kicked them off, scooped them up, and ran like hell.

It was like running on razors. Every stone turned its sharpest edge toward me; every branch whipped at my body or my face. Grass struggled to slow and trip me. I broke into a cold sweat at the thought of having to flail through those trees, but I didn't have a choice; I huddled low, below the reach of most branches, and tried to hop over the thrashing whirlwinds of grasses and roots that reached for me.

Fire blasted bright in a straight line between me and Delilah's open door, and on the other side of the car I saw Shirl, her hands outstretched, placing the fire and directing it toward me. *Damn*, I hate fire.

There was plenty of fine dust afloat, exactly what I needed to condense water in the air; I quick-froze the air in a twenty-foot circle, crowding molecules closer, forcing water molecules to attach around the tiny grains of dust. Mist hazed the air, and I felt my hair crackle and lift from the power. I poured energy into it, never mind the consequences; out here in the country, there wasn't as much damage to be done by a mistake, and I was damn near mad enough not to care.

Within ten seconds, I had a thick, iron-grey cloud overhead. I flipped polarity above it, and the charge began the process of attraction and accumulation, drops melting and merging and growing until their own weight overcame the pressure of droplet attraction.

The cloudburst came right on cue and right on target. Cold and hard and silver, slicing down from the sky in ribbons. The fire sizzled; Shirl cursed out loud and tried to counter for it, but I'd saturated the whole area with as much moisture as possible, and physics were against her. She couldn't get the core of the fire hot enough, not without pouring more energy into it than most Fire Wardens possessed. Their talent was in controlling fire, not sourcing it.

'Joanne, don't!' Marion was right behind me. I eyed the unstable pond of dust on which Delilah floated – quickly becoming mud as the deluge mounted – and swallowed my fear. Cold rain down the back of my neck, soaking my hair flat, drawing a full-body shiver. I had to bet that she wouldn't let me die.

I jumped for the car door.

A leafy vine tangled my foot and tugged me off balance. My fingers brushed the cold wet metal, and then I was falling, falling—

Falling into the soft quicksand.

'No!' Marion screamed.

It wasn't like falling into mud; mud has resistance and weight. This was like falling into feathers.

My instinct was to gasp, but I conquered it, clamped my mouth shut and tried not to breathe, because sucking a lungful of this stuff would be an ugly death. I squeezed my eyes shut against dust abrasion. No sound down here, no sensation except falling, falling, falling. How deep would I go? Marion couldn't possible have softened the earth deeper than ten feet; there wouldn't have been any point. Didn't matter. Ten feet would be more than enough to bury me.

The important thing was that Marion was just as handicapped as I was. She could harden the earth again, but that would kill me just as quickly. This wasn't exactly science; it was art. This was her ocean, her solid ocean, and I was drowning in it. She'd try to save me; there was no percentage in killing me, at least not yet, and she'd have to think of something fast. Maybe she'd be trying to harden the earth in an upward path, like a ramp to the surface; I'd just have to find it.

Find it how? God, I wanted to take a breath. *Needed* to.

That, at least, I could fix. I pulled at the air trapped in the fine dust and formed it into a cocoon around me. It made a shell a few inches thick all around me, not enough to keep me alive for long, but enough for me to take a couple of quick, clean breaths. I needed to get up, but I didn't know how to do that. There wasn't enough volume in the air to create any kind of warming and cooling effect that might serve as an engine. Flailing around in the dark, I couldn't feel anything solid.

I was stuck.

Something touched the back of my neck, warm and solid, and I reached desperately for it.

Skin. Human skin. It was too dark to see anything, but I was touching a living person. Not female, I discovered – even the most flat-chested woman has some softness to her in that region. I extended my bubble of air to fit around the newcomer and spared a precious breath to whisper, 'Erik?' Because at least the blond-haired Earth Warden would have been a lifeline, even if it was a lifeline into a cell.

But it wasn't Erik.

Lips touched mine, gentle and warm and entirely tasty, and I knew him in deep places where his touch still lingered.

'David?'

He didn't answer, and I felt his lips fit back over mine. Fresh air puffed into my mouth, and I opened myself to it, to him.

Both of us floating together in the dark, close as lovers.

He grabbed the hand not still clutching shoes, and swam sideways. Which was wrong in so many ways... First, there was nothing to swim *against* – this stuff had no resistance, hence, no propulsion. But he was propelling just fine. Second, *sideways* should have taken us right into the solid walls of the channel where Marion hadn't softened the earth, but we just kept right on moving, going and going and going. My lungs burnt for air. As if he sensed that, he turned and breathed into my mouth again. That shouldn't have worked; his lungs should have already scrubbed the oxygen out, given him back only waste products to share with me.

I breathed in pure sweet air, or as near as made no difference. It was like a shot from a diver's tank, and I felt energy shoot through me like white light.

After who knows how long, David began to swim up at an angle. I felt things brush my reaching free hand and arms – tendrils – grass roots.

We broke the surface in an empty meadow, where grass shivered and whispered and bent silver heads to the freshening wind.

I didn't have to climb out. The ground hardened under my feet, pushing me up, until I was standing barefoot on the grass, Venus born dusty from the ground.

David was still holding my hand. He had come up with me, and dust fell from the shoulders and sleeves of his coat in a thin dry stream. He shook his head and let loose a storm of it. Behind the dust-clouded glasses, I saw his eyes, and this time he didn't try to hide what they were. What they meant.

His eyes were deep, beautiful, and entirely alien. Copper-coloured, with flecks of bright gold. They flared brighter as I watched, then faded into something that was nearly human-brown.

'You *bastard!*' I hissed.

'Just a thank-you would have been good enough,' he said. 'Want to call a cloud for us? I'm in desperate need of a bath.'

'You're a *Djinn*!'

'Of course.'

'*Of course?*' I repeated. 'What do you mean of course? I was supposed to *know*? Hello, didn't hear the clue phone ringing!'

He just looked at me. He took off his glasses – glasses he could not possibly need – and began cleaning them on the edge of a dark blue T-shirt that advertised *The X-Files*. Mulder and Scully looked bad-ass and mysterious. His brown hair had coppery highlights, even under the coating of dust. Except for the eyes, he looked entirely human.

Which, I now knew, was entirely his choice.

I was so mad I was shaking. 'Whose Djinn are you? Did Lewis send you?'

He put his glasses back on, grabbed me by the arms, and used some martial arts trick to sweep my feet out from under me. I fell backwards into the grass with a bone-rattling thud, and he caught himself with outstretched hands just above me. More dust sifted down on me. He muttered something in a language I couldn't catch, and the dust swirled into a compact little ball and dropped away from us.

Somehow, it just made me madder. I opened my mouth to yell at him, and he put his lips down very close to my ear and said, 'If you scream, they'll hear you. I can't prevent that.'

I caught the scream and held it in because I heard, just about two feet away, the crunch of footsteps in grass. A shadow blocked the light overhead, and I peered past David to see Shirl standing there, looking puzzled.

'Anything?' Marion's voice, coming from the left, coming fast in our direction. Above me, David's face was blank and still, and I could see he was doing something – whatever it was, it was blocking them from seeing us in either the physical or aetheric realms. Unless they stepped on us or I made some inappropriate noise, they wouldn't find us.

'Nothing,' Shirl confirmed. Marion's shadow joined the other woman's. 'Dammit, this isn't possible. She was down there, I swear she was. But Erik said she was gone when he went down.'

'I saw dust here,' Marion said. She paced slowly back and forth, too close to my head for comfort. 'Right around here. But I don't know how she could possibly have done that. She's not an Earth power.'

'Maybe somebody's helping her.' Shirl was too perceptive for my taste. That and the nose ring were putting her on my bad side. 'She got any Earth Warden friends?'

'A few, but I can't see them sticking their necks out like this, not when they know what she's accused of doing.' Marion hesitated again, and I could see her looking down, looking right at me. I didn't even dare to breathe. David wasn't touching me, but I could feel the heat radiating off him – what if they could feel it, too?

'Maybe you should bring in your Djinn.' A new voice – Erik. He came trudging up from the other side. 'Just set him to tracking her.'

'I have other things for my Djinn to attend to,' Marion said in a way that convinced me Erik shouldn't have made the suggestion. It apparently convinced Erik, too. He shut up. After another few fast heartbeats, Marion said, 'All right. We have her car. She's not going anywhere, at least not fast. We'll wait for her to come back to it.'

'What if she doesn't?' he wanted to know.

Marion smiled. 'You don't know much about Joanne, I see.'

The three of them tramped off through the grass. I didn't dare move, breathe, or speak as the sound of them receded. When the only thing left was the dry whisper of the grass, David let his arms bend and slowly lowered himself to lie on top of me. Sweet, hard pressure that made it hard to breathe.

'Get off,' I ordered. His eyes flickered, brown and copper and gold, all the richness of the earth.

'Kind of you to offer, but don't you think we'd better get moving?' With no transition, he was on his feet. He was so fast, I couldn't even see him move. Dammit, he'd been playing with me all this time, playing at being human. That little drama he'd orchestrated back at the motel, that had just been *fun* for him.

I ignored the inconvenient fact that it had been fun for me, too.

I scrambled up and faced him, very aware that I was filthy and tired and scratched and bruised. At least I wasn't shoeless. I dropped the low-heeled pumps I was holding and stepped into them, ignoring the grit inside. 'I am *not* going with you, not until you tell me whose Djinn you are!'

'You want to go with them?' he asked, and looked in the direction Marion had gone. They were still visible, just at the edge of the trees, heading for my car. Poor, abandoned Delilah. 'Just say the word – I can remove the veil and you can go right back to what you were doing. Which was, if I recall, dying.'

'You didn't answer my question! Whose Djinn are you?'

David smiled. Not the full, delighted grin of a being of limitless power, but the tight, unhappy smile of a man who knows too much. 'My own,' he said. 'And I was really hoping you wouldn't ask that three times.'

Three times. I hadn't meant to, but it was a ritual number, and he had to answer.

He meant he was free. Not bound.

A free Djinn.

That was...impossible. Absolutely—

It meant – oh, God, it meant *I could claim him.* And once I'd claimed him, I could make him take the Mark. He was exactly what I was looking for. He was the thing I had been hell-bent on asking Lewis to give me.

And now I didn't need Lewis at all.

He looked at me steadily, with eyes that were not quite human and not quite Djinn, that copper-brown hair blowing in the northeast wind. Thunder boomed in the distance. The storm was moving this way, and all things being equal, it would be drawn to me because I was its opposite.

I felt the Demon Mark stir in my chest, and the sensation was enough to make me want to gag in horror. I could get rid of it, now and forever.

All I had to do was...

I could see fear flickering like heat lightning in the far horizon of David's eyes.

He'd saved my life – not once but several times – I knew that now. Was this really how I was going to repay him? Enslave him? Force him to be a host to this filthy thing? Trap him into never-ending agony?

Djinn don't die. At least not that anyone has ever recorded. They get the Demon Mark and they go insane and they're sealed away, for all time, with this poison eating away at them. Screaming for eternity.

I could do it to him. All I had to do was say the words. It hammered my heart faster, made me weak in the knees. Made me light-headed and sick to my stomach. *Come on*, the logical part of me insisted. *Don't go soft on me now!*

But when I opened my mouth, I found that all I had to say was, 'I don't suppose you know how to get my car back.'

I was stunned by the flash of relief in his eyes. I didn't want to see it, either, because that meant I had to think about it, and what it meant. He wouldn't be relieved if he hadn't dreaded it. And if he dreaded it...

I can't think about this right now. Self-preservation first, compassion second, right? I wasn't thinking straight. Later, I'd do what had to be done.

David must have sensed that, because he looked away from me for the first time.

'No,' he said. 'But if you're not that picky, Marion came in a perfectly good Land Rover with a full tank of gas.'

The Land Rover – a massive white beast, liberally splashed with mud to show it wasn't just a suburban wannabe's dream – sat unattended in a grove near the wildly unlikely beauty of the farmhouse. All around it, I could see evidence of either Marion's or Erik's tinkering – grass just a bit greener, trees surreally gorgeous, perfect flowers spreading petals to the sun.

The Land Rover looked like a massive mechanical roach on the wedding cake.

I tried the door, hoping Marion wouldn't have been anal-retentive enough to turn on alarms in the country...no panicked shrieking followed, but the handle clicked and failed to open.

'Locked,' I said to David. He reached over my shoulder and touched the door. Metal *thunked*.

'Open,' he disagreed. The door swung wide.

We climbed inside in silence – for me, tired and hurt as I was, it was like scaling K2 – and once I was perched in the comfortable seat, looking out through the smoked-glass windows, I let the flavour of another woman's car flow over me. Subtle scents, not as well aged as Delilah's odours...herbs, mostly, and fresh grass, dirt. Nobody had abused this baby with decomposing fast food or spilt coffee; if Marion spilt anything, I guessed it would have been herbal tea. There was a single silver thermos lying on the backseat. Coffee, I hoped. Erik looked like he was manly enough to swill a cup now and then.

David must have thought I was waiting for divine inspiration about the lack of car keys. He reached over and touched the ignition with one finger. A blue spark jumped, and the engine purred.

'You're handy if I ever want to get in the grand theft auto business,' I said. 'Any other neat tricks you can do I should know about?'

It was a loaded question, and he was right not to answer it. He sat back in the seat and fastened his safety belt. I attached mine, slipped the Land Rover in gear, and bumped gently out of the meadow and back up onto the blacktop of Iron Road, where I hit the accelerator hard. There were a few tense moments for me, watching the rearview mirror, but I didn't see the Wrath of Marion pursuing, and there wasn't a lot she could have done to affect us at this distance, in a car, on a paved road. Earthquake, maybe, but that would put others in danger, and Marion had scruples.

Hopefully.

Even so, I felt tightness ease in my shoulders as I made the left turn from Iron Road onto the highway again.

I turned right, heading north. David stirred, but I beat him to the comment.

'They're expecting me to head south,' I said. 'And I will, but not this way. I need to get lost before they think about using the mundane cops to track us – this tanker truck isn't exactly inconspicuous.'

'And a vintage Mustang was?'

Well, he had a point. I sped north to the next farm-to-market intersection, took a random turn to the west, and followed some roads that didn't have signs and probably didn't need them; if you didn't know where you were going, local theory was, you didn't belong there anyway. I studied the dashboard. Marion had popped for the addition of a global positioning system. I activated it and looked the map over while I was driving. So did David, intensely interested; he traced routes in silence with his fingertip, showing me alternatives, until we locked in one that took us through midsize cities in Kansas, heading for Oklahoma City.

'There's a shorter route,' he pointed out.

'I'm starting to worry about the shorter routes. Anyway, I have a good friend who lives near Oklahoma City, so we'll go there first.'

'And—?'

'And I'll figure it out from there.'

'Well, that's a hell of a long-range plan.'

'You're shutting up, now, right?'

He did. It was kind of a shame, because I had a lot of questions. One of them was, of course, what would happen to Delilah, my sweet midnight-blue baby. The idea that Erik or – perish the thought – Shirl might end up driving her made me almost turn the Land Rover around and go back.

We must have gone about thirty minutes in silence before I asked him, 'So you really don't have a master?' Because I still couldn't believe it. Well, sure, in the stories...there were always old copper lamps lying around waiting to be rubbed for three wishes. But real Djinn don't work that way. Real Djinn are numbered, assigned, and accounted for like precious jewels, and their service is eternal.

David was looking out the window at the rolling pastoral countryside, sparsely dotted with cows and neat-rowed fields. He didn't turn his head. 'You know that's one of the few questions I had to answer honestly, since you asked it three times. No. I don't have a master.'

Djinn could lie about most anything except who they were and who they served – but you had to ask them directly, and be really focused, because they were also Zen masters of the obscure; and weren't afraid of resorting to trickery to misdirect the questioner. But David's answer didn't seem obscure; it seemed simple and to the point. He was that impossible dream, the free-range Djinn. Which meant – no, I didn't want to think about what it meant. Far too tempting. Far too easy.

He turned his head then, and he wasn't troubling to disguise his eyes anymore; they were bright copper, beautiful beyond words, scary beyond measure. His human disguise, I saw now, had been pretty minimal; just a muting of his eyes and hair, an inward turning of his powerful aura.

'You hid in Oversight,' I said, instead of what I was really thinking. Djinn weren't the only ones good at avoiding questions. 'How'd you do that?'

'It's different when we're free. We come into the full range of our abilities only when we're working for a master. Outside of that, we just have camouflage and some small talents, hardly more than what you have yourself.' This from a guy who could start cars with his finger and swim through solid earth like water. But then, I realised, those were things a properly trained Fire Warden or Earth Warden could do. So maybe he wasn't dishing crap after all. 'I appear as your subconscious shapes me.'

'Human?'

'Mostly. I can be hurt.'

'Killed?'

He shook his head. 'Maybe. It's been a long time since I've been free. I don't know. But hurt, yes.'

'And if I go into Oversight now—'

'You'll see me as human.' He shrugged. 'Not for your benefit, though. That's just how we look when we're free.'

It made sense, actually. Djinn, like any living thing, would have developed the ability to hide themselves from predators. In a very real sense, that's what magic-wielding humans are to them – predators, waiting to pounce and devour. Or at least to enslave. It was an extremely interesting and unsettling thought, because it meant that there might be more than just David out there. A *lot* more. Hiding in plain sight. Hoping nobody with the right set of facts twigged to their true identity, because it would be so easy to...

I wrenched myself away from temptation. Again.

'You've been following me,' I accused. I took my foot off the gas and let the Ranger coast for a while, because we were coming up on one of those small-town speed-trap zones. Not a big town, Eliza Springs. Not much of a town at all. A speed limit of thirty miles an hour smelt like the ubiquitous traveller tax.

David didn't bother to answer.

'Somebody sent you,' I continued. 'Maybe not your master, OK, maybe that's true. But somebody.'

More silence. Then again, I wasn't asking a direct question. If I were magically compelled to answer questions, I'd resent it like hell, so I kept it conversational and declamatory. 'You caused that spinout.'

His shoulders tensed, just a bit. He relaxed them. No answer.

'I felt the car tip. I was going to roll over.'

'Yes.'

'And you stopped it.' No answer. It was time for a little force. 'Why?'

'Seemed like a good idea at the time.' His warm-metal eyes flicked toward me, then away.

I reminded myself that even though he had to answer questions, he wasn't under any obligation to tell the truth, not unless I asked him the same question a ritual three times, and even then only if it fell within certain guidelines. I didn't want to do that, because he also wasn't under any obligation not to disappear at the next blink of an eye. This was a little bit like dealing with a skittish, beautiful wild thing…too much heavy-handed crashing around and he'd run.

'You were going to let me crash and burn.' I made it a statement. 'Why save me?'

'I liked the way you looked,' he said. 'I saw you at the diner, when the lightning came for you. You could have run back inside. Why'd you get in the car?'

'You're kidding, right? There were all those—'

'People,' he finished for me. 'You didn't want to put them in danger. I told you. I liked the way you looked.'

'In Oversight.' He didn't confirm or deny. 'I didn't see *you* in Oversight, and I was *looking*.'

'We've had this conversation. You can't see me

when I don't want you to.' He flickered, suddenly, like a failing TV picture, blinking in and out in strobe patterns. I almost ran the SUV off the road. 'Sorry. Just a demonstration.'

'This morning at the motel – you didn't leave. You were just—' Hiding. I had another thought. 'You watched me! You watched me change clothes!'

He closed his eyes and made himself comfortable. The smile on his face made me smack him on the shoulder. Hard.

'Hey! I'm talking to you!' I said. He didn't move, just sat there, relaxed and limp, eyes still closed. 'Right. As if Djinn nap.'

'We do.' He did sound tired. 'And I'm going to.'

'Whatever.'

'Fine.'

I fiddled with the radio and worried more about cops, and Marion, and cell phones, and the fact that this damn British boat was all too conspicuous. Of the three stations available, two were country and one was rap; I settled for rap. If David had an objection, he didn't wake up long enough to voice it.

We made it safely past the six intersections and one Dairy Queen that made up Eliza Springs, and hit a farm-to-market road that headed vaguely west. I notched the Land Rover up to a comfortable purring speed and frowned at the speedometer, which told me kilometres per hour instead of miles per hour. Close enough. I had bigger problems than a speeding ticket.

One of them snored lightly at my right elbow, all the way to the state line.

Something about the way David affected me – and he *did* affect me, no doubt about it – reminded me of my first date. As dates go, it wasn't supposed to be very adventurous; Mom drove me and Jimmy to the movies at the mall. She bought our tickets, Cokes, and popcorn, wished me a nice time, kissed my cheek, and strolled off to go shopping.

Jimmy was sweating. He was trying so hard to be a gentleman that he slapped my hand when I tried to open a door, which sort of went against the basic principles of gentlemanly behaviour. I managed not to smack him back. We seated ourselves in the theatre with snacks and drinks, sat stiffly next to each other, and prayed for the lights to go down so we wouldn't have to fumble through too much conversation. We exhausted the bad points of Mrs Walker, the math teacher, and Mrs Anthony, the English teacher, and Mr Zapruzinski, the boy's gym coach who always smelt like old sweat and cigarettes, and there weren't any girl-boy subjects either of us felt competent to attempt.

We had just added the band teacher to our mutual-enemies list when the lights went down. Way down. Like, out. And outside, the storm that had been looming overhead and shaking its fist for three hours...

...let me have it. Oh, yeah. It was pissed off. Thunder roared so loudly, I thought we were already watching Star Wars. As I sat there in the dark with a bunch of shrieking preteens and a few panicked adults and my (literally) blind date Jimmy, I heard rain hammer the roof like a million stones from an angry mob. It was a riot storm. An assault storm. I knew, immediately, that things were bad and going to get worse.

Jimmy tried to kiss me. It was a panicked, sweaty attempt, and he missed and smacked his forehead into mine, and for a second I saw *Star Wars* warp effects to go with the roar, and then he corrected and got his lips on mine and—

Oh.

Well.

That wasn't so bad. He sat back quickly when the house lights flickered on again and looked triumphant. As well he should. I felt – curious. Warm all over, especially in the middle, as if I had started to melt.

'Maybe we should go,' I said hesitantly to Jimmy. The theatre was emptying out, parents herding kids like frightened sheep, a few teens slouching away and trying to look cool and uncaring and maybe a little bit to blame for all the uproar.

'You want to go?' he asked. He really was kind

of nice, I decided. Dark hair, thick and straight, pale blue eyes, and long soft lashes, sensitive looking. We were the last two left in the theatre, with hail hammering the roof, thunder booming like a foot kicking the door.

Jimmy had pretty eyes.

'We could stay,' I said, attempting nonchalance. 'Want some popcorn?'

It was my first try at seduction. It succeeded.

Jimmy reached over and kissed me, more enthusiasm than skill, and we spilt popcorn all over the sticky theatre floor, and my warm liquid centre heated up some more and started a rolling boil. This kissing thing, this was fun. It went on for a while, and I guess the storm was still raging but I wasn't exactly paying attention, and Jimmy was breathing like a steam engine in my ear and he put his hand on my breast and *oh, my*—

The lights flickered again and went out. I was grateful.

Jimmy's hand moved, and my nipple went hard, and in that moment I think I even would have let him put his hand down my pants, except that at that particular instant, the roof of the theatre peeled open, shedding ceiling tiles and metal struts and cement.

I screamed. We jumped apart, and rain dumped over us again, freezing cold, and hard little nuggets of ice spat out of the dark and shattered on the concrete floor, stuck to the purple plush velvet, stung like wasps on my exposed arms and face. Jimmy put his arms around me, and we stumbled toward a dim EXIT sign.

The wind howled like a knife-wielding maniac. A chunk of ice the size of a golf ball hit Jimmy hard enough to make him yelp, and I wrenched away from Jimmy's arms and screamed at the top of my lungs:

'Hey! Stop it!'

I looked up into the heart of it, this angry temper-tantrum-throwing child of a storm, and I put everything I had into the scream. I shoved at it with muscles in my head that I'd never really exercised.

'I mean it! Quit!'

A ball of ice the size of a soda can smashed at my feet and scattered like broken glass, glittering me with shrapnel. I drew in breath for a third scream. No need.

It stopped.

Silent. Dead still. Overhead, clouds lazily rotated like a watch running down. Lightning laced in and out of the edges.

Raindrops pattered on the ruined roof. Thunder muttered darkly.

Sound of my heart beating hard, hard and fast as a rock 'n' roll drum, and I heard Jimmy make a puking sound and run for the door.

The clouds rotated again. I looked right into the

hard dark centre of it and it looked back, and we understood each other, I guess. I sat down on a cold, wet seat and looked at the movie screen that would never show me *Star Wars* because it had a jagged rip down the middle, like a lightning bolt.

I never saw Jimmy again.

I wasn't sure if David reminded me of that divine burst of first lust, or the terror of knowing I no longer controlled my life.

I strongly suspected it was both.

By the time David woke up, we were in Battle Ground, Indiana, and I was pulled over to the side of the road and doing a little car maintenance on a stubborn air filter. It left me even dirtier and grimier than before, and I slammed the car door extra hard because having David peacefully snoring in my ear was just about more than I could stand.

He came awake at the noise like a cat, completely alert and looking neat and self-satisfied.

'Good morning,' I said. 'We've been on the road for about nine hours, and we're—'

'Outside of Battle Ground, Indiana,' he said. 'I know.'

I'd turned the GPS off, so he didn't get it off the computer screen, and we were nowhere near a road sign. 'And you know this—'

'You missed the part where I admitted I was a Djinn?'

'C'mon. Really?'

'Yes.' David smiled slightly. 'I haven't been completely sleeping. I've been keeping us unseeable.'

'As opposed to invisible?'

'Unseeable just means that people don't look at you, not that they can't see you. It takes less effort.'

'I thought you were asleep.'

'We don't sleep the same way you do. Keeping us unseeable doesn't require much thought, and neither does knowing where I am.' He shrugged. 'I suppose in the computer age, you'd call it operating system software.'

It brought on an intriguing question. 'How many ages have you been through, anyway?'

He shook his head. I'd have to ask two more times to get a straight answer, and frankly, it wasn't worth the wasted breath. I was tired and cranky, and I needed food. I was also wishing he'd told me about the whole unseeable thing earlier, because I would have felt safe enough to park and grab a Big Gulp and cheese crackers from a convenience store. Then again, I might have decided to try a drive-through fast food place and they probably wouldn't even have noticed me.

'I'm thinking about pizza,' I said. 'Deep dish, lots of cheese, maybe some pepperoni. They've got to have good Chicago style around here. Wait, I don't suppose that's one of the handy cool tricks you can do, is it?'

'Make pizza?' He gave it serious thought. 'No. I can't create something from nothing, at least not while I'm free. I could probably transmute it for you, so long as what I made it from contained some of the same elements.'

'Like?'

'Tomato into pizza sauce. Grain to bread crust. Although I'm not exactly sure how to get pepperoni.'

'I think you start with a pig, but let's not get too far into that. Man, what I'd give for a Moon Pie right about now.'

David turned and looked around in the backseat; I could have told him the prospects for scavengable food were slim. Marion kept a clean car, something I'd never really been able to do, as much as I loved Delilah. I tended to accumulate slips of paper, receipts, scribbled directions, paper wrappers from straws...

But there was something, I remembered it. 'Hey, I think she left a thermos in here. Coffee would be incredibly good.'

He didn't see it. I leant back and spotted a silver gleam under the passenger seat, just about popped a vertebra rooting it out, and came up with the goods. I was just about to check it for caffeine content when David said, 'Do you feel that?'

I forgot all about caffeine. The jolt of adrenaline

went straight to my heart and tingled in every soft tissue on my body. I put the thermos aside. 'Yeah.' The hair on my arms was standing up. 'Don't get out of the car.'

'I wasn't planning to.'

I had long ago outrun the storm, but there was a line of clouds dark on the horizon ahead. I'd been playing with the idea of doing some sabotage on the cold front coming down out of Canada, but that was just plain selfish. Bad weather was both natural and necessary. The only time I was really morally allowed to tinker was if it posed a clear and imminent danger to human life...not necessarily including my own.

What I felt wasn't the storm ahead, and it wasn't the storm behind. It wasn't a storm at all. I wasn't entirely sure *what* it was, except that it was strange.

'Any idea—?'

'No,' David said. 'Not yet. Maybe you should start the car.'

I did, and eased the Land Rover into gear and back onto the road. We accelerated without any problems. After half a mile I remembered to breathe. Nothing fell on us out of the sky or rose up out of the ground, which was downright encouraging.

'So,' David finally said. 'Exactly how many enemies *do* you have?'

'Marion's not an enemy.'

'She buried you alive.'

'It's complicated.'

'Apparently.' He settled back in the seat...not relaxed, exactly, but cautiously watchful. 'Tell me about what happened.'

'You know what happened. You were there.'

'Tell me why you're running.'

I felt a lurch somewhere in my gut. 'You know, I really don't want to talk about it. If I'd wanted to talk about it, I would have done the whole This-Is-My-Life thing with Marion, where it might actually matter.'

'You need to tell someone,' he said, which was very reasonable. 'And I don't have a stake in the matter.'

In other words, he was Djinn. He could walk away at any time. I wasn't even a flash of a second in terms of the eternal life he could look forward to. My story was something to pass the time. Hell, *I* was something to pass the time.

'I killed somebody,' I finally said.

He was unmoved. 'So I heard.'

'Somebody important,' I said, as if he'd contradicted me. I was surprised to feel tears burn at the back of my throat. 'I had to.'

David reached over and touched my hand. Gently. Just the tips of his fingers, but it was enough to send a warm cascade of emotion through me that I didn't fully understand. Was it a Djinn thing or a David thing? Was there even a difference?

'Tell me,' he said. 'Please.'

I told David about the first encounter I'd had with Bad Bob at my intake meeting, and then the weird showdown we'd had at the National Weather Services offices, the time I'd worked the Bermuda Triangle and stopped Tropical Storm Samuel.

And then I told him the rest.

After I'd calmed down with a few drinks at a sand-side bar, I'd decided to put Bad Bob's bizarre problems behind me and just be a girl for a change. I'd strolled down to the sea in my fancy new few inches of perfect spandex. Beautiful girls are a dime a hundred on Florida beaches, so I didn't feel special... Well, OK, maybe I did, a little, because it was a *really* good bikini. Beach studs checked me out, and there was nothing bad in that. I staked out a section of warm white sand as far as possible from screaming kids and teenagers blaring the greatest hits of Eminem on boom boxes, applied sunscreen and dark glasses, and settled down on my beach towel to soak up the love of Mother Sun.

There's nothing like a good day on the beach. The warmth steals slowly into every muscle like an invisible full-body massage. The dull, constant rhythm of the seas counts out the heartbeat of the world. The smell of fresh salt water, banana and coconut oil, that ripe undercurrent of the cycle of life turning somewhere under the waves. The sounds of people talking, laughing, whispering, kissing. Happy sounds. Somewhere out there, in the wet darkness, sharks hunt, but you can forget that, lying there in the sun, letting your cares slide away like sand through your fingers.

I had almost succeeded in forgetting about everything that was bothering me when a shadow cut off my sun and sent a chill running through my blood. It didn't move away like it should have.

I opened my eyes and peered up, dazzled, at a dark shape with a brilliant white halo of windblown hair...then blue eyes...the face of Bad Bob Biringanine.

I sat up fast. He was crouching down next to me. I did one of those involuntary female things one does when wearing too few clothes in the presence of an intimidating man...I put on my cover-up, then crossed my arms across the thin fabric.

'That's too bad,' Bad Bob said. 'It's a nice look for you.'

'What?'

'The suit. Designer?'

'Yeah, right. On what you pay me?' I shot back. 'Don't think so.' I glared. In my experience, guys who gave grief and then came bearing compliments were not to be trusted. Especially guys who held my future in the palm of their hand.

His face was different out here in the world –
more natural, I guess. There was something that
hummed in tune out here, near the sea and sky. This
was what true power looked like in its element –
not dealing with people, which annoyed him, but
being part of the vast moving machine of Earth.

'I scared you this morning,' he said. 'That's not
what I meant to do. It's not personal, Baldwin. It's
not that I think you're a crappy Warden. It's that
I've seen too many turn out that way.'

'Thanks for the warning. I got the message.'

'No, you didn't. And hell, I can't blame you, I'm
the king of arrogance, and I damn well know it.
Anyway, you did good,' he said. 'Most people screw
it up their first time out in the Triangle. There's
something out there that isn't anywhere else on the
planet.'

'Really?' I shaded my eyes and tried to see if he
was kidding me. 'What?'

He eased himself down to a sitting position on
the sand. 'If I knew that, I'd probably be National
Warden by now instead of some cranky old bastard
with a nasty reputation. Maybe someone with more
guts and less self-preservation than me will find out.
They don't call it the Mother of Storms for no
reason.'

'A discovery like that could really make a
reputation,' I said.

He grinned, and it was a street urchin's grin, full of Irish charm, and I had the sense he'd done some sweet-talking of girls in his immoral past. Lots of girls. 'Oh, I think my reputation's secure, don't you?'

It was, of course; whatever else Bad Bob Biringanine got up to, he was bound to be a legend for generations to come. I sighed. 'Why'd you come down here? Just to get in my light?'

He dropped the grin and just looked at me seriously. 'I liked your work. Steady, calm, never mind the bullshit. You didn't let me get to you, and that takes guts. I've rattled plenty of cool customers in my day just by looking at them, and you looked right back. That's impressive, girl.'

Oh. Now that my heart rate was slowing to under two hundred, I realised that Bad Bob was trying to make a connection with me, not just ruin my afternoon. Had he ever done this before? Probably, but the stories of Bad Bob that play well are the confrontations, not the conciliations. Nobody would buy me a drink to hear that Bad Bob patted me on the back.

But it still felt good.

'I've been looking for somebody with steady nerves,' he said. 'Special project. You interested?'

There was only one sane answer. 'No offence, sir, but no. I'm not.'

'No?' He seemed honestly puzzled. 'Why the hell not?'

'Because you'd crush me like a bug, sir. It was all I could do to get through an afternoon with you staring down my shirt. I don't think I could handle a full eight hours of it a day.'

And had I said that out loud? Yes, I had. And he *had* been checking out my boobs all morning there at the Coral Gables office. So there. Let the charming old bastard chew on it.

He stared at me steadily, with those eyes like pale blue glass, and said, 'Oh, it wouldn't be eight hours a day. Twelve, minimum. Possibly as much as eighteen. Though I will give you time off for good behaviour, if you keep wearing that bikini.'

'No.' I settled back on the sand and closed my eyes. 'If you're going to keep sexually harassing me, could you do it from about three feet to your left and quit blocking my sun?'

He didn't move, of course. He stayed solidly in my light. After a few dead moments, when I didn't open my eyes or try to fill the silence, he said, 'You're still six months away from qualifying for a Djinn. I can make that happen in two weeks. Or I can make sure it never happens. Your choice, sweetness.'

I threw an arm over my eyes and groaned in frustration. Of course, it would come to this. Blackmail. Perfect.

'Come on, Baldwin, you're an ambitious little ladder-climber. We both know you'll work for me just for the bragging rights. Quit playing coy. Here's the address.'

He dropped a business card on the bare skin of my stomach. When I opened my eyes, he was walking away, a bandy-legged white-haired man still broad in the chest, muscular in his arms and legs.

An ageing tough guy. A hero of the kind they don't make anymore.

On the back of the business card was his home address. On the front was his name, *Robert G. Biringanine*, and in very small letters below it, *Miracles Provided*.

I held the card in my hand for the next thirty minutes as I tried to empty my head and concentrate on sunshine, but the cold, pitiless blue of his eyes kept intruding. By four o'clock I'd had enough, and trudged back to my car, lugging beach bag and beach umbrella. Two hunks in Speedos – six-pack abs and all – tried to convince me to do some snorkelling in one of their beach houses, but I had things to think about. Big things.

At six, I called Bad Bob's, got his answering machine and left a message that I'd be at his house at 7 a.m.

See, I'd like to blame it on Bob's cynical little threat-and-reward strategy, but the fact of the matter was, I found him interesting. More than twice my age, white-haired, wrinkled, bad-tempered, notoriously difficult...and there was something intensely *alive* behind his eyes that I'd never seen before. Well, not since Lewis, anyway.

Power calls to power – always has, always will.

Two minutes before seven the next morning, I was standing on Bad Bob's porch, which had a stunning view of the blue-green ocean. It rippled like blown silk and flowed up on sand as white as snow. He had a private beach. It was a measure of who – and what – Bad Bob really was. As was the house, a post-modern sweeping dome with lines that reminded me of wind tunnels and race cars.

'No bikini?' Bob asked me when he opened the door. That was his version of good morning, apparently. He had a coffee cup in his hand as big as a soup bowl. His striped bathrobe that made him look like a disreputable version of Hugh Hefner, and he had the moist, red-rimmed eyes of a morning-after drunk.

I hesitated over choices of responses. 'Do I have to be polite?'

'*Polite* isn't a word people often use to describe me,' he answered. 'I don't suppose I can expect it from you, either.'

'Then no more cracks about the bikini, or I turn around and walk. Seriously.'

He shrugged, swung the door wide, and turned away. I followed him into a short hall that opened up into a truly breathtaking room. It must have gone up thirty feet in a curve, with windows overlooking the ocean all along one side. Carpet so deep I wondered if he hired a lawn service to maintain it. Leather couch, chairs, furniture that combined style and comfort. All unmistakably masculine, but with a finer taste than I would have expected from somebody of Bad Bob's reputation.

'Nice,' I said. People expect that kind of thing when you first see their home.

'Ought to be,' he said. 'I paid a fortune to some unspeakably horrible woman named Patsy to make it that way. Through here. Coffee?'

'Sure.'

He led me into a vast kitchen that could have catered dinner for a hundred without breaking a sweat, poured me a cup, and handed it over. I sipped and found it had the rich, unmistakable taste of Jamaican Blue Mountain, fifty dollars a pound. Not the kind of thing I'd give away cups of to marginally welcome guests. I took as big a mouthful as I could get away with, savouring that smooth caramel aftertaste. I could get used to all of this...fancy house, ocean view, fine imported beverages. I had no doubt his collection of whiskey was first-rate, too. And he struck me as the kind of guy with a killer DVD collection.

'So,' I said. Bad Bob leant against a counter, sipping coffee, watching me. 'Staying off the subject of the bikini, what exactly am I here to do?'

'You're here to work as my assistant. I need a good, solid hand in manipulating some small-scale weather patterns for an experiment. Nothing I couldn't do myself, but it would save time to have another pair of hands.'

'Hands?'

'Metaphorically speaking. You've worked with Djinn before?'

'Sure. Well, not closely. But I've been linked to them.' Man, the coffee was *excellent*. He'd poured a pretty generous cup; I wondered how open he'd be to the concept of refills. I was going through this mug pretty quickly. 'I can handle it.'

'I'm sure you can,' he said. 'You know, I have the feeling you're going to be absolutely essential to the success of this project. It's groundbreaking. I think you'll be truly impressed by the scope of what we can accomplish together, Joanne. By the way, how's the coffee?'

'Fabulous. It's—' My eyes blurred. I blinked, felt the world slip sideways, and reached out to brace myself against the counter. I could hear my heart beating, suddenly. ' – it's Jamaican Blue—'

I must have dropped the cup, but I didn't hear it shatter on the ceramic tile. I remember my knees letting loose, I remember sliding down with my back to the cabinets, I remember Bad Bob taking another long drink from his cup and looking down at me with those pitiless blue eyes.

He smiled at me. His voice sounded slow and wrong and far too friendly. 'We're going to do great things together, you and I.'

I woke up on the edge of panic, fighting nausea, with no idea where I was or what the hell had happened to me. It took a full minute for my brain to start connecting chemical chains long enough to remember Bad Bob, the tainted coffee, the collapse. Jesus, what kind of a bastard ruins *Jamaican Blue Mountain* with knockout drops?

I was lying on the leather couch, and my hands were tied behind my back. I could barely feel them, but I knew it was going to be painful if – when – I worked my way free. I blinked shadows from my eyes, shook my head to get hair out of my way, and found Bad Bob sitting in the leather armchair just about five feet away. The bathrobe was gone, replaced by a pair of khaki pants and a loud Hawaiian print shirt. He was holding a half-empty glass of something on the rocks, which might have been apple juice but probably had a lot more punch.

'Don't struggle,' he said. 'You'll just dislocate a shoulder, and I'm not much on the medical stuff.'

My tongue felt thick as a sausage, but I managed to fit it around words. 'Fuck you, you bastard. Let me go.'

His bushy white eyebrows rose. They curled up and out, and reminded me of a lynx. The eyes were predatory, too.

'Ah, ah, be nice,' he said. 'My offer to you was absolutely valid. We're going to do some great work together.'

'What in the *hell* do you think you're doing? You think you can just abduct me and—' My brain caught up with my mouth and told it to shut up, because he had abducted me, and chances were he was going to get away with it, too. Nobody knew I'd come here. I had no close friends, no confidants. I hadn't spoken to my sister or my mother in a month. John Foster might wonder where I'd gotten off to, but like most Wardens, I wasn't a slave to the nine-to-five. Could take weeks for anybody to begin to worry.

'You'll be fine,' he said. He took a long slug of his drink, made a face, and put the crystal tumbler on a glass table next to him. There was no sound of anybody else in the house, just the usual everyday hum of electrics and air circulation. The surf hitting the shore came as a dull, unceasing drum. 'I have something important for you to take part in, and I want your word that you're going to take this responsibility seriously. You're going to change the world.'

I had a lot of ambition, but changing the world was a little outside the scope. I tried the ropes again, felt sharp pain dig into my shoulder, and decided to work on things a little less directly. I couldn't go head-to-head with Bad Bob Biringanine...few people on the planet could. But maybe I could take him from behind.

I started slowly, slowly working the oxygen out of the mixture in the room. Nothing obvious, because obvious would get me swatted like a fly. At the fastest rate I dared to work, I needed to buy at least ten minutes for the O^2 levels to drop far enough to put him to sleep. *If* he didn't realise what I was doing. The alcohol would help that, slow his perceptions and make him more susceptible to nodding off.

'I – I came here to work for you,' I said. 'Really. You didn't have to drug me. You could have just explained it to me.'

'Sweetheart, I couldn't really take the chance you wouldn't agree. I need you. It's more of a draft than a volunteer army.' His eyes skipped away from me, toward the windows, where the Atlantic rolled endlessly toward the Pacific. 'Stop fucking with the air in here or I'll knock you out and do this while you're unconscious. It doesn't really matter, either way. I just thought you'd like to be a witness.'

I swallowed hard and let my manipulations of the oxygen drop. 'To what?'

'To your transformation. I'm about to transform

you from some second-rate, arrogant little weatherworker to a world-class talent. And in return, you're going to save my life.' He got up, stretched, and went to refill his glass from a crystal-stoppered decanter on the sideboard, near something that looked like an authentic Chinese terra-cotta solider, like, the ones found in the emperor's tomb. It almost looked real enough to walk across the room.

'Sir, please, I have no idea what you're—'

'Shut up.' He didn't raise his voice, but there was something dark and violent in it that made me instantly seal my lips. Liquor splashed ice in his glass, and he took a drink. 'How do you think all this works, Baldwin? You think the Wardens Association is just some not-for-profit do-gooder fraternity, like the Lions Club or the Shriners? We *run the world*. That takes power. More power than you can even imagine.'

I had no idea what he was talking about, but so long as he was talking, I had breathing time. I worked on the knots with numbed fingers. It was all I could think of to do.

'When Hurricane Andrew hit the shore in '92, it was a killer of the worst kind. It was all set to destroy us, singly or in groups. Somebody had to take on the responsibility to stop it.' He snorted and tossed back the rest of the liquor. 'Some poor bastard like me. But humans aren't built that way,

Baldwin. They're built to come apart under that kind of pressure.'

He was talking. I decided I should be cooperating. 'That's why we have the Djinn. To take the stress.'

'What crap. You don't know dick about Djinn, girl. They have power, but they dole it out in little bits and pieces, always looking for ways to screw us – they hate us. They'd kill us if they could.' He rattled the ice in his glass and tried to suck the last drops of his drink from between the cubes. 'Rely on the goddamn Djinn, you get killed. No, to stop Andrew I needed something else. Something bigger.'

He was insane. Bad Bob was literally insane. There wasn't anything bigger than the Djinn except...

I bit my lip and felt a fingernail rip off against rope, but that was nothing compared with what I was afraid he was about to do to me. It was all falling together now, and it made a hideous kind of sense.

'A Demon,' I whispered. 'You took on a Demon.'

'Smart girl,' he answered. 'Too bad, really. I can't afford to put my Djinn out of commission with this thing – level of Demon this is, it'd probably eat him alive, but it'd damn sure poison him past usefulness – so it has to go somewhere. My heart's going. Can't die with this bastard in me.'

'Wait—'

'Sorry, time's up.' Bad Bob put his drink down, walked over to me, and put his hand on my forehead. His skin felt ice cold. It might have been a compassionate gesture, but he put some strength into it and forced my head down, pinning me against the leather couch. I kicked out at him, writhed, wriggled like an eel regardless of how much pain tore at my arms and wrists. 'Don't worry. This'll be quick. Demon goes in, and then I burn you. You probably won't feel much pain at all.'

He tried to pry my mouth open. I fought back with every muscle in my body, desperate to get him off me, *away*, because I could feel it in him now, a black cold hunger devouring him from inside.

'Dammit!' He backed off, blue eyes glittering with rage, and reached out for a bottle of wine – very old, with a flaking, yellowed label and a cork that looked fossilised. He worked the cork out of it, set the bottle on the floor, and said, 'I need you.'

In the movies they always show Djinn coming out of the bottle in a puff of smoke, but that rarely happens, unless the Djinn is a traditionalist with a sense of humour. Bad Bob's Djinn just appeared – *blip* – without any dramatics at all. I've always wondered how Djinn decide how to look, and why they always seem to look so nearly human; this one was nearer than most. He looked like an accountant. Suit, straight black tie, pin-striped shirt. Young, but ancient around the eyes. The eyes, of course, gave him away: a kind of phosphorescent green that caught daylight the way a cat's eyes reflect at night.

'Sir?' he asked. He didn't even look at me.

'Hold her down,' Bad Bob said. 'Don't kill her like you did the last one. It's hard enough to find a match, you know.'

The Djinn leant over and put his hand on my forehead. Instantly, gravity tripled and pinned me down; made it an effort to drag in a breath, much less fight, I wanted to say something, but I knew it wouldn't do any good; Bad Bob wasn't listening, and his Djinn couldn't do anything against his orders. *Don't kill her like you did the last one.* His Djinn didn't want the Demon moved. Maybe, if I could think fast enough, I could get his help...

'Open her mouth,' Bad Bob said. The Djinn laid one fingertip on my lips, and even though I clenched my jaw muscles, I felt it all slipping away, felt my lips parting. *Oh, God, no.* Maybe I imagined it, but the Djinn's touch seemed to make it less painful, less horrific. *Help me. Please stop this.* But if he could, or if he even wanted to, there was no sign of it in those inhuman green eyes, clear as emeralds. I felt grey edging in around the knife-sharp spike of fear, the desperate desire to *get away.* Maybe I could pass out. I wanted to pass out. Anything not to feel this.

The Djinn's touch burnt. My lips slid open, and cool air hit the back of my throat with drowning force.

Bad Bob bent over and touched his lips to mine. Not a deep kiss, just a touch. Just enough to create the bridge of flesh. He tasted of booze and stank of fear, and I tried to scream...

Too late.

I felt it squirming in my mouth, shooting tendrils down my throat, invading me in a way that even the worst rape couldn't equal – it was inside me, ripping furiously through my flesh, looking for a place to hide. I tried to scream, tried to vomit, tried to *die*, but it just kept going, down my throat, burning in my chest, squirming and moving through me like a hand until it closed into a fist around my heart.

The pain was so bad, I left my body and escaped into Oversight, and that was when I saw the Demon Mark for the first time. A black nest of tendrils writhing around the core of my magic, my life, feeding. The last of it slid out of Bad Bob and left him shining and clear of taint.

And utterly devoid of power. He'd carried it for so long that it had eaten away the power he'd started with. He was an empty shell of a man whose heart continued to beat, but I felt the horrible hollow space where this *thing* had been.

And then his heart jumped, shuddered, and froze

in his chest. His face took on a dull sheen of surprise.

Can't die with this thing inside me.

Oh, God, no. This couldn't be happening.

I felt the particles charging around me, and it reminded me suddenly of Lewis, turning his bloodied face to me, holding out his hand for power. Because it was power forming around me, funnelling *through* me. Taking the last of the energy that kept Bad Bob alive. I could taste the drowning blackness of his despair, the wailing terror of his death. The Demon Mark sucked it down and began to taste what was inside me, too, and the sensation was so bitterly wrong that I couldn't help but fight back. It was as instinctive as gagging.

I reached for power, and it came, a rolling white wave through Oversight, circling me like a tornado. It would wreak havoc on the real world, but I didn't have a choice. Every cell in my body, real or aetheric, was screaming to get that *thing* out of me.

In the real world, the dome house literally exploded. Glass blew out from the windows in a pulverised mist. Wind tore through the room at speeds impossible to withstand and shredded wood to splinters, plastic to shards. The terra-cotta warrior exploded into dust. Charged particles glittered and flashed and rolled like crystal waves around me, storm-ready. So much potential energy, my hair lifted and crackled with it, on the verge of burning. Every circuit in the house blew, frying electronics, starting fires in the walls. In Oversight, the power draw flared photonegative, out of control, and ice crystals began to form around minute particles of dust in the swirling air of the living room.

Outside, steaming hail the size of baseballs, soccer balls, hit the beach; I heard the hard, brittle impacts all over the house. Temperatures soared, then dropped, as pressure rose. Outside, over the sea, clouds massed with incredible speed, darkened, began a lowering rotation.

Bad Bob fell to the floor, a lifeless lump of flesh, already being torn apart by the forces in the room. By my own power, out of control.

His Djinn disappeared into the maelstrom, and I saw the wine bottle picked up by the wind and hurtled against the far wall with so much force, it literally vanished into crystals no larger than sand.

The leather couch I was still lying on was blown back with a tidal force of wind, and I rolled over debris. Shards of glass everywhere; I barely noticed the cuts, but I managed to get my fingers around a sharp needle-edged piece and slashed at the ropes that held my hands until they parted with a moist snap. It hurt, but my standards of pain had changed; a little flesh-and-blood agony was nothing to worry about.

I scrambled until I found a wall at my back.

Lightning flashed, and I could feel the thing feeding inside me, out of control; greedy little bastard sucking down every mote of energy. It fed off storms. It fed off the power burning inside me.

I had to shut it off. Somehow, I had to reach down into that – *thing* – and force it to obey. It was growing inside me, growing angles and cutting edges; it would burst out of me like some evil child and then...and then...

Something warm and gentle touched the back of my neck. *Breathe,* a voice whispered inside me. Under my skin. *Child of air, breathe in your strength.*

I gasped in a breath. Another. The air felt warm, smelt faintly of ozone.

The Demon is of the darkness. Use your light.

I opened my eyes and there, in front of me, was the Djinn. Bad Bob's Djinn. He was a column of living fire, a pair of golden eyes, something wonderful and terrible at the same time.

Breathe in your strength, it said again, and when I inhaled, I felt the fire go into me, burning like raw lava down my throat, into the darkness.

Now go.

I was outside in the rain, in the cold, with my arms wrapped around my body, shivering. The surf pounded the dome house, sucked at it like a tasty treat. Overhead, the eye of the storm whirled and stared down on me.

Inside me, the Demon Mark shuddered and went quiet.

I breathed out mist and steam, and around me the energy levels faded. Lightning flashed, hit close, and I felt the burn of ozone on my flesh like the heat of a distant cold sun.

And then I slammed back down, *hard*, into reality. Cold, wet, windy reality, the storm screaming over tortured waves, the stench of burning and dead things and my sweat. There was *something inside me*, stuck inside me. I ripped open my shirt, expecting to find – something – some horrible black tangle under the skin. There was only a faint, intricate black scorch mark. I touched it, trembling, and felt the thing underneath stretch and murmur in its sleep.

I went to my knees, hard, and threw up.

I don't know how long I was there, huddled near the ruins of Bad Bob's house, but I felt the Wardens when they arrived – Janice Langstrom, Bad Bob's exec, and Ulrike Kohl. Ulrike concentrated on the storm raging out at sea, but I could have told her it was useless; the storm was mine, keyed to me, born of my fury. All she could do was tame it down to a sullen retreat.

It was Janice who found me. 'Joanne?' We knew each other. Not well, but enough for nodding acquaintance. I let her help me up to my feet and pulled the tattered halves of my blouse together, more out of an instinctive desire for her not to see the Mark than any impulse to modesty. 'Oh, my God! What happened here?'

I opened my mouth to tell her...and then didn't. I couldn't even begin. Something in me – that wily, scared-to-death primitive part of my brain – told me that if I said anything about the Demon Mark, I could kiss my ass good-bye.

I just shivered.

She searched my face, her frown deepening; she was an older woman, younger than Bad Bob but not by much. Moderately powerful. Extremely perceptive.

'That storm has your smell all over it,' she said, and her grip on my arm tightened. 'Where is he? Where's Bob?'

I didn't answer. I saw the blooming of anger in her cool grey eyes, and then there was a wind-torn shout from the ruins of Bad Bob's house, and Ulrike staggered out.

'He's dead!' she screamed.

Cold grey eyes snapped back to me and narrowed. The grip on my arm was as tight as a vise. 'You killed him?' she asked, and didn't wait for the answer. '*You killed him!*'

She shoved me backwards. I felt energy gathering around her, phasing in blacks and reds. No, I couldn't fight her. Couldn't fight anyone.

I couldn't control this thing inside me, and it *wanted* to fight.

I reached out and physically shoved her, and ran like the Demon itself was after me.

Miraculously, Delilah was still untouched, up on the road. I jumped in, started her up, and hit the gas, spinning tires and leaving a scream behind as Ulrike and Janice pelted out after me, both yelling.

I had killed Bad Bob. Bad Bob was a legend, and I was the one who'd called the storm. The Wardens wouldn't listen to what I had to say; if they could sense this *thing* inside me, they'd cut me apart to destroy it.

I had to get rid of it. Bad Bob had passed it to me. The idea of passing it on made me sick. Everything I'd ever read about Demon Marks had the same grim message attached: no way to get it out of you once it was in, except by giving it to some other poor bastard, the way Bad Bob had given it to me. God, no.

I can't afford to put my Djinn out of commission with this thing, he'd said.

I could give it to a Djinn. Only I didn't have one, did I? Bad Bob's Djinn was gone. That meant I had to find one.

It all came together in a brilliant flash in my head.

Lewis. I could get one from Lewis.

❧ ❧ ❧

It was dead silent in the Land Rover when I finished. David wasn't looking at me. He wasn't looking anywhere, exactly, just staring straight ahead. I couldn't tell what he was thinking.

'Now you know,' I said. 'You know what you're risking just being around me. Because I swear to God, David, I can't have this thing get loose again the way it did on the beach. I'll kill myself first.'

'No!' He lunged at me, and I almost ran the truck off the road. He held up his hands, more to stop himself than to reassure me. 'You can't. Listen to me, you *cannot* die with this thing in you.'

'Well, I can't let it just destroy everything, either! I have to control it, or get rid of it. Or die.'

David sucked down a deep breath. 'If you die with the Mark, the Demon will tear itself from your body, and it will walk the aetheric. If that happens, the destruction you saw before will be *nothing* next to what it can accomplish in its aetheric form. It will take more power than all of you have to stop it then.'

'Well, I'm not just passing it on to somebody like the goddamn herpes virus.' He was watching me with that creepy intensity again. 'What?'

'Give it to me,' he said. 'Say the words, bind me, and give it to me. You can. You have to.'

'No!' The idea gave me chills. Worse than chills. I had no idea what the Demon Mark would do to a Djinn, but I had no doubt that if the Mark fed off power, it would find an all-you-can-eat smorgasbord inside a Djinn.

'It can't overcome me,' he said. 'It'll be trapped inside of me, forever.'

'It'll destroy you!'

'No worse than it will you, in time,' he said. 'I can be contained. Once I'm sealed inside a bottle and put back in the vault, I'm no danger to anyone. You—'

'No!' I shouted, and slammed my hands on the steering wheel like I wanted to beat sense into him. 'No, dammit, I said *no!*'

David was so very reasonable, so convincing. 'I'm what you were looking for. I'm a Djinn, Joanne. I'm your way out.'

I felt tears burning in my eyes, couldn't get my breath around the lump of distress in my throat. God, no. Yes, it was what I wanted, and I couldn't do it. *Couldn't.* There had to be something else, some other way...

'I'll find Lewis,' I whispered. My head was pounding from the force of my misery. I wanted to cry, or scream, or just whimper. 'He'll know what to do.'

'Why?' David's voice was so soft, so reasonable.

I felt a surge of absolute panic, because I realised...realised I didn't know. Why *would* he know any better than I did? Lewis was more powerful, all right – more powerful than anybody. That didn't mean he could save me, except by presenting me with the same choice I had right now. Destroying someone else. A Djinn, maybe, but in every way that mattered, a real person.

'I'm so tired—' It came out of me in a rush, uncontrolled. 'I can't think about it. Not now.'

'You have to,' David whispered. 'Let's just get this over with.'

The car lurched, sputtered, and coasted to a stop. Dead. 'No,' I whispered. 'I won't let you...take it...' I'd fight him with my last breath, if I had to. I wouldn't be the cause of his destruction. If there was any right thing left in my life...

The lights flickered and died, and in the ghostly whisper of the fan spinning down, I felt David reach across and draw his hand gently across my forehead.

'Then rest,' he said.

I woke up in the passenger seat, belted firmly in place, cramped in places I hadn't known I had muscles. The clock made no sense. My mouth tasted like the bottom of a fish tank, and I needed to pee so badly, it hurt.

'What...' I mumbled. David was driving. 'Thought you couldn't drive.'

'I lied,' he said. 'Djinn do that.'

I muttered something about his mother under my

breath – did Djinn have mothers? – and squinted at the clock again.

'Wait a minute,' I said. 'I've been asleep for only thirty minutes?'

He didn't answer.

'Oh. Twelve and a half hours.'

'We're an hour outside Tulsa,' he said. 'We should be nearing Oklahoma City.'

There was a brilliant blaze of light on the horizon, like frozen gold smoke against the cloudy sky. Still light rain falling, but when I checked Oversight, I found everything even and steady. No storms chasing me, for a change.

'Let's stop,' I said.

David glanced aside at me. 'Where?'

'Anywhere with a bathroom.'

'I'll find something.'

I nodded and ran my hands through my hair. That didn't cut it. I hunted around in Marion's glove compartment, came up with a brush, and attacked the tangles in my hair until it was shiny and smooth. Nothing much I could do about my generally gritty condition, but Marion had also left behind some nice wintergreen gum that took care of evening breath. I was starting to feel caffeine deprived, but just about the time I thought about complaining, a sign appeared in the distance: LOVE'S. The billboard text underneath Said GAS – FOOD – BATHROOMS.

'Miracles provided,' David said. I froze for a second, then remembered to breathe. Surely he didn't know that was Bad Bob's tag line. Surely.

At exactly 9 p.m. we pulled into a parking lot big enough to hold at least thirty or forty long-haul rigs; it was a little more than half full. Oklahoma was having a damp spring, it seemed; the clouds overhead were inoffensive nimbus, spitting light rain, and we hurried inside to a warm, well-lit vestibule. On one side was a convenience store, on the other, a traditional sit-down diner; straight ahead was the sign for bathrooms. I left David to his own amusements and headed for the relief station. On the way, I ran across a gleaming bank of pay phones, and I remembered something I'd forgotten to do.

Star. I'd meant to call Star and tell her I was coming.

I picked up the handset and thought about it for a while, hung up, then finally completed the call. She wasn't there, but her answering machine took my message. *Coming into town tonight or tomorrow. See you soon.*

I hoped I would, anyway. I was feeling desperately alone. I wanted to count on David, but I was such a danger to him... It was like travelling with someone bent on suicide. If I said the wrong thing, got desperate... I had to be on my guard. Always.

When I came back, I found David sitting at a table in the diner, contemplating a menu. He had a cup of steaming coffee in front of him. I gestured at the waitress for the same and picked up my own copy of the house specials.

'Any ideas?' I asked.

I got a quick flash of copper eyes over the top of the menu. 'A few,' he said. It sounded neutral, but his eyes weren't. They were verging on Djinn again, not enough human camouflage to matter. 'You need to end this. Now. Before it's too late.'

'Get stuffed.' I studied choices. The waitress – who, amazingly enough, had pink hair to go with her pink uniform – delivered my coffee, and I made an instant decision. 'I know it's weird, but I want breakfast. Got any blueberry muffins?'

'Sure,' she shrugged. 'What else?'

'Pancakes. And bacon.'

Pink hair nodded. 'For you, handsome?'

David shrugged. 'The same.' She folded our menus and was gone in a flash of a cotton-candy skirt.

Which left us looking at each other in uncomfortable silence.

'You *have* to stop,' David said at last. 'You're running out of money. You have no friends, no family. You don't even know if Lewis will help you.'

'I've got you,' I pointed out.

'Do you?' A flash of hot-metal temper in his eyes. 'Not unless you say the words.'

There was no way to answer that, and I didn't try. I looked down at my hands, adjusted the silverware into neat rows, and finally sipped coffee.

'You're a fool,' he finally said, and sat back. 'Marion's hunters will be coming for you, and how will you fight them?'

'Same way I already did.'

'The Mark is taking you over. It's moving slowly, but it's moving. It's filtering into your thoughts, your actions – that's why you won't take what I'm offering. It isn't because you care about me. It's because the Demon won't allow it.'

He touched a nerve I didn't think was raw. 'Shut up,' I snapped. 'Enough. We're going on to Oklahoma City. I've got friends there. Besides, Lewis will know what to do.'

He leant across the table and fixed me with those eerie, inhumanly beautiful eyes. 'What if he doesn't?'

'Then I guess Marion's people are going to get a big surprise when they try to give me a power-ectomy.'

He sat back as the waitress slid plates of food between us. We ate in silence, avoiding each other's gazes like old married folks.

When we were finished, there was still a basket of blueberry muffins between us. I asked for a sack and bagged them up. Not like there was a chance in hell I'd live to starve to death, but still. Reflex.

We got back in the Land Rover and drove into the surreal yellow glow of Oklahoma City.

I don't suppose anybody ever forgets how they lose their virginity. I certainly can't forget. And, of course, it involved a storm.

Rain is a mixed blessing when you're in college. Everybody likes rain, to a point, but when you're trudging around campus, soaked to the skin and looking like something the Red Cross would put on a poster, it loses its charm. So there I was – cold, wet, eighteen, and a virgin. Yes, really, eighteen. I wasn't saving myself or anything noble like that; the simple fact was that I thought most guys who wanted to drag me into the backseat were losers, and I had more standards than hormones.

College was different. Here I was at this great school, with all its rich history and good-looking young men, and even better, I was in a program that not only didn't punish me for my weirdo status, it *valued* me. After four months, I was blooming. Putting away the baggy shirts and shapeless sweatpants, indulging in clingy, flirty clothes my mother wouldn't approve of.

That was how it happened: clingy, flirty shirt, tight blue jeans, and a storm.

I came into the Microclimate Lab blown on a

cold gust of wind, dropped my backpack to the floor with a *squish*, and leant against the wall to catch my breath. My lab partner was already there and looking so dry and comfortable, I knew he hadn't been out of the building all day.

'It's about time,' he said. 'You're thirty minutes late. We've got to map the pressure streams and have all this done for Yorenson by noon tomorrow—'

He was turning around, and about the time he got to that part of the sentence, he saw me standing there and stopped talking. I wiped water out of my eyes and saw him staring at me. Well, not at *me*, exactly. At my chest.

The clingy, flirty shirt? The rain had turned it about as transparent as fishnet.

I wasn't wearing a bra. And my nipples were as hard as thumbtacks from the cold wind.

I crossed my arms over my chest and tried not to look too much like the fool I felt. My lab partner – somebody I'd had a crush on from about the first ten seconds of laying eyes on him – didn't care how much of one he looked, apparently, because he just blinked and kept staring.

'You were saying?' I asked.

He clearly drew a blank.

I sighed. 'Yes, I'm a girl. Don't tell me you never noticed before.'

He had the grace to blush, and he did it well –

one of those neck-to-hairline flushes that makes some men look all the more attractive. He was one of them. Dark hair, bedroom eyes. Not that I cared, of course. Much.

'Here,' he said, and stood up to take off his jacket. He started to hand it over, then hesitated. 'Maybe you should, um, turn around first.'

When I did, he draped the jacket over my shoulders and let me situate everything to my not-so-high standards of modesty. The jacket was warm dark leather, and it smelt like aftershave and male sweat. When I turned around, he was working hard at being the gentleman the jacket offer implied. I was frankly a little disappointed.

'Guess we'd better get to work,' I said.

'Not yet. You're freezing.'

I was shaking, all right, but it was half hormones; the lab was empty except for the two of us, and we had it scheduled for the entire afternoon. Rain lashed the windows, and thunder rumbled so deep, I felt it like a caress.

Showing off, he warmed up the room by about five degrees. I was grateful, but we both knew it was a violation of the rules. No adjusting of temperature for anything but assignments. Still, no teachers taking notes.

'I'm OK,' I said, and took my seat at the table. My hair was still wet and dripping, so I bent over and squeezed as much out of it as I could. When I straightened up, the jacket gaped open, and I saw his eyes dive to get another look.

We pretended to work for a while – OK, maybe we even *did* work for a while – and actually came up with some right answers for the day and recorded them in our logs. Fast, too; we finished the assignment and had at least an hour left. The storm was still blowing outside, and the energy tingled all over, begging me to come out and play. I was almost dry now, but still wore his jacket, and he hadn't asked for it back.

'Well,' I said, and stood up. 'I guess we might as well get out of here.'

'Might as well.' He stood up, too. Taller than me. Broader. Standing too close.

I looked up into his eyes and slid the jacket slowly down my arms, and held it out to him. He took it and dropped it on the floor somewhere behind him.

I looked down at myself. The blouse hadn't quite dried; my nipples were still clearly visible through the thin fabric.

He took one step forward and put his hands on my waist. When I didn't step back, he moved his hands up along my sides, thumbs out, up, along the underside of my breasts. Those thumbs settled on the second most sensitive area on my body, where he moved them in a slow, gentle circle that took my breath away.

'So,' he said, and his voice was coming from somewhere much deeper than it had before, 'we're supposed to be researching energy, right?'

'Energy,' I agreed. My voice was shaking.

'Heat.'

'That, too.'

He leant down, and our lips met and melted. No shortage of heat there, or friction. I was shaking all over again, but I'd never felt so alive, so fully in my skin as I did at that moment.

Rain, and rain, and rain. His jacket made a pillow on the floor behind the lab table. We fumbled at each other's clothes until they slid away. The sting of cool air on naked skin, then the flare of shared warmth. Not a lot of foreplay, but hell, I didn't need it; the storm combined with the energy passing between us had made me as ready as I'd ever be. The pain took me by surprise, and so did my sudden desperate desire to make it stop, make *him* stop.

And with the tearing of my hymen, something else happened. Power. Power raced into every nerve in my body and snapped me into full awareness. I *knew* the man who was making love to me, every cell, every nerve, every pulse beat that echoed between us. I felt...*everything*.

I felt the huge rumbling cascade of his power as it flooded me, making me arch hard against him, and the extreme pain of it, the *pleasure*...sparks

snapped between us, blue-white, bleeding off
energy that our bodies weren't built to contain.
Power, echoing between us, waves bouncing from
one of us to the other and getting stronger with
every second.

He wasn't prepared any more than I was. We were
swept away on a rhythm like the sea, and when the
tide came, it came high, and I drowned on waves and
waves of a pleasure I'd never felt before, felt him
drowning with me, clung to him for dear life.

I heard things shattering around us. Light bulbs.
Glass windows. I felt wind scream over us in
whipping, out-of-control gusts.

And then it was over, and we were lying together,
sweating, weak, and *still* feeling the power building
between us.

He realised how dangerous it was before I did.
He pulled away from me and kept going, far away,
scrambling backwards until his back touched the
wall. I scuttled back and hid under the lab table. All
around us, the wind whipped and screamed and
overturned tables and chairs until it finally faded to
a breeze, then a sigh.

Stillness.

'God,' he whispered, and put his head in his
hands. I sympathised. My head was pounding, too.
Every nerve in my body felt crisped.

I licked my lips and said, 'It's not supposed to
happen like that, right?'

There was blood on the floor where I'd been lying. I stared at it for a few seconds and saw he was staring at it, too.

He looked utterly stricken. 'No,' he whispered. 'God, I'm so sorry. I didn't know—'

I didn't know whether he was apologising because I'd been a virgin or because we'd almost destroyed the campus. I didn't really have time to find out.

The man was, of course, Lewis Levander Orwell. And so far as I know, he never again touched a girl who was in the Program.

I was still looking for my panties when Professor Yorenson arrived to find out what the hell was going on.

I don't know what I'd been expecting. A message from above, complete with cherubs and singing choirs, inviting me to join Lewis in whatever hole he'd crawled into? Crap.

We cruised around I-40, looking for signs from the heavens while I restlessly cycled through radio stations, hoping for a cryptic message.

Nothing.

If Lewis was here, evidently he didn't want to talk to me.

I finally pulled up in the parking lot of a La Quinta Motor Inn.

'He's here?' David asked, frowning. I was on the

verge of hysterical tears or worse, hysterical laughter – worn down to nothing by the strain.

'He's around,' I lied. My voice was shaking. 'I need a shower and a good night's sleep in a real bed. If you've got a problem with that, thumb a ride.'

He shook his head and followed me into the hotel lobby.

I checked us in with the last of my cash. I was so tired, I would have taken a cell in a monastery, but La Quinta turned out to be quite a showplace, with an indoor pool and a bubbling jewel of a hot tub that we passed on the way to the elevators. They'd booked me third-floor accommodations, facing the parking lot and the approaching storm. That was perfectly fine with me. Always best to keep your eye on what's coming.

The room was spacious, tasteful, with a huge king-size bed and pillows big enough to qualify as mattresses in their own right, or maybe that was just my exhaustion talking. David went straight to the far corner and set his backpack down.

'Why the hell do you carry that? It's just window dressing, right?' I was pins and needles all over, aching, itching for a fight. 'Like the clothes. To make me think you're really human. Well, give it up. I know better now.'

'Do you?' He sat down on the bed and put his hands on his knees, watching me pace back and forth. 'I doubt you know any more about the Djinn than you do about the Demon Mark.'

I couldn't look at him. I liked the way he looked, and I knew what I saw was constructed, artificial, something he'd put together to please me. Which was just – wrong. Obscene. And it pissed me off. 'I know everything I need to know about the Djinn.'

Dangerously quiet on that end of the room. I paced restlessly to the windows. Rolled the curtains open on a night sky rich with stars.

'Maybe I *will* claim you,' I said. 'Maybe I'll claim you and order you to get the hell away from me for a change. Wouldn't that be a stitch?'

He knew I was baiting him. 'Don't start this, Joanne. I don't want this.'

'Well, news flash, I didn't want *any* of this! I didn't want to be gang-raped by Bad Bob and his pet Djinn. I didn't want to end up with this *thing* inside me. And I didn't ask for *you*, either! So why don't you just—?'

He stood up. I turned to face him. Energy crackled the air, and it wasn't entirely emotional; it couldn't be separated that way. Djinn were creatures of fire, and I was…whatever I was becoming. Water. Air. *Darkness*.

'Just what?' he asked in a soft, dangerous, purring tone. 'Let you throw yourself on the pyre of your own arrogance? Don't tempt me.'

'Just get the hell out,' I said flatly. 'I thought you didn't want to fight.'

'I don't! I've tried to help you! I've tried to make up for—' He stopped himself. His eyes were molten bronze, glittering with gold flecks. Shimmering hot. 'Say the words. It's the only way you're going to get out of this alive – you know that.'

'Oh, so now *you're* going to kill me? Oh, hell, why not? There's probably a Let's Kill Joanne club, with cool little membership cards and souvenir rings. You can be the president, and Bad Bob the Ghost of Honour—'

He grabbed me by both arms and shook me. Hard. 'No! Stop being a smart-ass bitch and listen to me! You have to say the words and give me the Mark, *now!* Just do it!'

I put my hands flat against his chest and shoved. It was likes pushing at a block of David-size concrete.

'Say the words!' He yelled it at me. Shook me harder, so hard my head snapped back and forth, my hair fell in a blinding curtain over my eyes. 'In the name of the one true God, *say it* or I swear I will hurt you so badly, you'll beg me to kill you! I *will* hurt you!'

He was hurting me. His hands were tight as vices, crushing skin, bending bone. God, it hurt. It was like dying from the inside out, and the Mark, the Mark was fighting back, ripping at my flesh with invisible claws...

'Say it! Be thou...'

I wanted it to stop. I wanted the pain to stop. 'Be thou bound to my service!' I screamed. 'There! Happy?'

His face went pale, but his eyes burnt brighter. His fingers squeezed tighter. 'Again!' He shook me again, just to be sure, as if he could rattle it out of me. 'Say it again!'

'*Be thou bound to my service*!' I didn't want to say it, but it was ripping itself out of me, the words like knives in my throat. The pain was incredible, blinding, suffocating. My skin was burning where he touched me. Scorching. I could smell my skin cooking under his hands...

'Again!' David shouted. 'Say it again!'

Three times the charm. Three times would bind him to me for the rest of my life. Three times for him to trap me into doing what I *did not want to do*.

I remembered Lewis's Djinn back in Westchester, burning my hand where it touched the door of the house.

I choked on tears of rage and pain and croaked out, 'Nice try, asshole. No way.'

He froze, staring at me, and I saw something incredibly vulnerable in his face – a kind of ashen despair. It was instantly gone.

The pain vanished just as instantly – bruising, no broken bones, no burns. Illusion.

He hadn't even left a mark. His hands were

gentle on me, and the only heat there was skin on skin. Human heat.

'Say it,' he whispered. 'Please. Just end this, and *say it*. Please don't make me watch it rot you inside. I can't stand that.'

I sank down on the bed and cradled my head. 'Why the hell do you want to do this for me?'

He went down on his knees on the carpet next to me, started to touch me and then stopped as if he didn't trust himself. 'It's the Mark. Can't you feel it? It's seeping into your thoughts, your feelings. Soon you won't *want* to be free of it. It's got to be now, or you're lost.'

He was right, of course. That's where the anger was from, the constant, itching fury. From the Demon Mark. It was growing, developing, taking me along for the ride. I could feel it tapped into me now. Its power was at least partly mine. Soon, we'd be joined, and there'd be no going back unless I was ready to give up my soul with it.

When I looked up we were at eye level, close as lovers. I put my hand on his cheek and said, 'I swear to the one true God, David, you will *never* take this Mark. So give it up. Just go away. Let me have a little peace, while I still can.'

It hurt, that moment. It was a wire stretched between the two of us, buried deep in our hearts, pulling and singing with tension.

I broke it. I got to my feet and stepped around

him. He caught my wrist. 'Where are you going?'

'To take a shower,' I said. 'I stink like a cattle truck. Don't worry, I don't think the Mark is going to wash off and spoil your chance to be a martyr.'

I walked calmly to the bathroom, shut the door, and locked it. All the normal bathroom hotel amenities, like a coffeemaker and a hair dryer, complimentary shampoo and lotion...Life looked so normal in here, preciously, wonderfully normal.

I sat down on the closed toilet seat and stared at the spacious bathtub for a while. I was too tired to think, but luckily there was no need for it; I stripped off my filthy clothes and piled them in an untidy mess under the bathroom counter, started the water, and got in while it was stingingly cold. As I started to cry, I felt the Demon Mark moving inside me, stretching lazily, like a bully waking up from a nice long nap. I sank down to my knees in the tub, hugging myself, letting the warming water pound my neck and back. Water sluiced away, sluggish with dirt, but even when it ran clear, I felt far from clean. I would never be clean again.

Soaping and rinsing my hair was oddly therapeutic, though. By the time I rinsed for the third time some of the chill in me had started to thaw.

I was going to live, I discovered. Even though turning down David's offer had effectively signed my death warrant, there had to be something left. If Lewis came through, fine. If not...there were options. There had to be. I could read, research – find out how to fight this thing.

Still, it took every ounce of courage I had to get myself out of the tub and through the ritual of drying off.

When I ventured out of the steaming bathroom again, David was gone. His backpack was there, still leaning drunkenly in the corner; his long olive-drab coat was hung neatly in the closet, and his clothes were in a drawer. Even his shoes were present and accounted for.

As I hunted around for clues, I discovered he'd left me a present. There was a bikini laid out neatly on the bed. Turquoise, teeny, outrageously daring. I stared at it, baffled; the hotel gift shop was long-ago closed, and I hadn't rescued any clothes of my own; surely David wasn't in the habit of carrying around a thing like that in his pocket.

I remembered the beautiful blue jewel of the pool below and the quietly bubbling hot tub. Ah. Of course. The invitation was silent, but it was there. I could either accept or crawl in bed and go to sleep.

I dropped the towel and put the two tiny pieces on. It fit like it had been made for me. Which, I knew, it had been. It had that aura about it, that warmth of David's skin.

I checked it in the mirror.

It was...the perfect bikini.

I grabbed a hotel towel and the key card, and went to find him.

David was sitting in the hot tub. Bare-chested, eyes like shimmering copper that got brighter when he saw me. I laid my towel and key on a nearby table. He held out his hand to help me down the steps into the hot, silken water. I eased in slowly, one inch at a time; it felt like I was dissolving, all my worries and cares bubbling away. The kindest acid in the world. I sank down to my neck, then back up, slowly, gliding closer to him.

'Ground rules,' I said. 'Don't you *ever* threaten me again, or I'll bind you all right, I'll bind you into a bottle of drain cleaner and bury you at the bottom of a landfill. If you're lucky, some archaeologist might dig you up in a few thousand years.'

His hair was damp at the ends, dark and curling. I lifted my hand and touched it, trying to comb the curls back under control, but my fingers weren't interested in his hair, not really; they glided down to the smooth, hot landscape of his skin. Down the column of his throat, to that sexy bird's-wing sweep of his pectoral muscles, and I felt him tensing in a slow, pleasurable way.

'I'm going to die,' I said. The tension turned dark. 'No, it's OK. If I can die and take this bastard thing with me, I'm doing the world a favour.'

'No.' His eyes burnt, shimmered, not human and not concealing it. Somehow, that made the absolute humanity of his body that much more powerful. He was human because...because he wanted to be human. Because of me. 'You can't.'

I put a damp finger on his lips. 'Ground rules, David. You don't tell me what I can and can't do. If you like me even a little bit, you'll let me have this freedom, OK?'

His hand came out of the water and traced the line of my bare shoulder. Where he touched, shivers followed. God, such a touch...caramel warmth, spreading through me like a slow orgasm. Maybe it wasn't magic, but it felt that way. Felt...bewitching.

I felt him surrender to it, too.

'I don't like you,' he said. '*Like* has no pulse. No fever. No fire.' His right hand came out of the water now, joined the left in gliding up my shoulders, my neck. I could feel my pulse pounding wildly. Both my hands on his chest now, mapping the golden territory of his body. 'Like isn't what I feel for you. It never was.'

Our lips met, slowly. Damp, hot, hungry. He tasted darkly exotic, like a fruit from deep in an undiscovered jungle. Jets from the tub pushed us closer together, closer, until all that was separating us was the practically nonexistent fabric of my bikini and whatever he might have been wearing under the bubbles. It felt deeply right, utterly wrong. Forbidden. Natural. Perfect.

He'd been so careful to stay in control, but now I could feel the fire in him, wild and raging like a nuclear core. His hands touched my breasts and traced the hard outlines of my nipples under the water, and the bikini might as well have been imaginary, the way my nerves caught fire. I didn't want to ever stop kissing him, but I had to breathe; when I pulled back for a gasp of air, he let me do it, and a necessary rush of sanity came between us.

'A little too public,' I managed to say, between deep breaths. His hands were still on my breasts under the water, thumbs gently caressing thickened, aching nipples under thin turquoise fabric. His eyes weren't anything like human now; they were glorious, alien, beautiful beyond anything I'd ever imagined. I couldn't fathom how I'd ever mistaken him for just a guy, no matter what kind of magic he'd worked.

'Don't worry,' he murmured. His voice was deeper now, richer, almost a purr. He drifted closer again, put his lips right next to my ear. 'They can't see us.'

There were jacketed hotel employees at the desk right beyond the windows, chatting among themselves. Nobody looked in our direction. A grumpy-looking businessman wheeled his suitcase past and didn't spare us so much as a glance.

David put one finger under the stretch turquoise fabric of my top and pulled me right up against him. I couldn't stop touching him, tracing the hard, yielding planes of his chest, the flat ridges of his stomach. My hand slid down, and I felt a thin layer of waterlogged fabric gathered at his waist.

'If they can't see us,' I breathed into his mouth, 'get rid of the bathing suit.'

Before the words left my lips, there was nothing under my fingers but wet skin. Nothing to hold me back.

David braced himself on the ledge, watching me with those unbelievable eyes the colour of burning pennies, as I stripped off the wet bikini top and tossed it onto the side of the hot tub. Before I could reach for the bottoms, his hands were on the job, sliding them down my legs.

'Is this against the rules?' I asked. I grabbed the edge of the hot tub, one hand on either side of him, and straddled his lap. 'Tell me this is against the rules. It feels too good to be legal.'

His voice was a hot, breathless growl. 'You refused to bind me – I don't have to tell you anything. Ah!...'

He was hard as steel, hot as fire, and he felt so good going in that I shuddered and collapsed against him, holding him in me and feeling life pulsing between us. 'Tell me,' I whispered. His breath was fast and hot against my neck.

'It's forbidden,' he said. 'And it's stupid. I need to – to stay – don't—'

'Don't what?' I moved my hips slowly, a liquid circle, and felt him tense against me. 'Don't do this?'

His hands came up, gliding up over my breasts, my neck, to hold my face like something precious and fragile. No more words. No more anger. We lost ourselves, fire and water dissolving into each other in a perfect union of opposites, and when I cried out, it was into his mouth, and all his strength, all his magic didn't keep him from joining me.

At the very second that I was completely alive, completely alight, I felt the Demon Mark make its move, like a taloned hand clenching around my heart. I came crashing back to reality with a jolt like electrocution, and the sensation of being violated, being ripped away from him, was so real that I panicked. Lost control. Lost myself. I felt it pushing deeper in me, pulsing like some terrible child, and on the outside David's strength kept me from going under the water, but I was convulsing, crying out, and all the fire in the world couldn't melt the ice forming in me, forming in sharp angles and ridges and forming into...

'No!' I heard him say, and there was helpless pain and fury in it. Not just flesh, not just fire – passion. 'Stay with me. Don't let go!'

My body was going limp, shutting down, all my resources turned inward against the invader. Was this how it had been for Bad Bob? Had it really hurt this much? God, I didn't want to hurt. I wanted to go back to that warm, sweet place in heaven, go back to David's arms.

David put his hand flat above my heart.

Hot gold poured into me, melting ice, forcing the black tendrils of the Demon Mark to a stop, but it held tight to what it had gained. It was bigger now. Darker. Full of cool, malevolent life. Tapped deep into the roots of where I lived.

When the pain receded and I could breathe again, I realised David was holding me against him like a child, my head on his shoulder, stroking aimless patterns on my bare skin. No, not aimless. Where his fingers touched, I felt stronger. Warmer.

'Shh,' he whispered, when I tried to speak. 'My fault. My fault. Let me help.'

'Your fault?' I repeated blankly. It was a huge effort to raise my hand and touch his face, but a rich reward when I saw some of the tension ease out of him. 'How the hell is this your fault?'

'You asked me if it was forbidden. I shouldn't have let myself do this—'

I put my fingers over his mouth to shut him up. His lips moved, not with words, but with silent kisses.

'Don't ever say that,' I said. 'Don't ever.'

❧ ❧ ❧

We stayed like that, him on the ledge, me cradled in his arms, for more than an hour. No words, no impulse for more; he stroked my hair in a slow, hypnotic rhythm.

'I'm waterlogged,' I finally said, and raised my head from where it rested against his chest. 'Going on raisin skinned.'

I caught the edge of his smile.

'You're the mistress of air and water,' he said. 'I can't believe you couldn't fix a thing like that.'

'True. But I'm too tired. Can't you just – blink us back up to the room?'

'No,' he said. 'I can move myself anywhere I like, but taking you is a bit more difficult.'

'You tunnelled through the earth with me,' I reminded him.

'And I'm recovering my strength,' he said gravely. 'I assume you want me fully restored.'

'Bet your ass.'

The Demon Mark was silent again, almost invisible; still, it was hard to move, because I kept waiting for it to strike again. David understood. He let me sit up slowly, watching my face, and reached out to place his hand over my heart again.

'It's quiet,' he said.

'What if it gets noisy again?'

'It won't. Not tonight.' He didn't make any promises for tomorrow, I noticed. Well, I was getting out of the habit of thinking about tomorrow anyway.

I got out of the water, weak-kneed, my bits of Lycra back in place for the trip upstairs. David surged out of the hot tub next. I found myself fascinated by the way water caught and tangled in his hair, flecked his entire body with light. God, he was beautiful. I couldn't quite believe that I'd drawn passion out of that perfection, because he looked so controlled and untouchable now.

'Put some clothes on,' I said, 'before I have to fight off the desk clerks to hang on to you.'

He reached for my towel and wrapped it around his waist. That did not make him any less attractive. If anything...

'Upstairs,' he reminded me. I took his arm, and we walked out of the pool area onto the deep pile carpet past the front desk. One of the clerks looked up, frowned slightly, then realised what she was doing and gave us a brilliant smile.

'I'm sorry, I didn't see you in there. The pool area's closed for the night,' she said. David – just human David again, brown hair and brown eyes, just another guy – nodded and apologised. We strolled back up the hall to the elevators, where we waited politely until one dinged open for us.

I shivered in the air-conditioning as the doors rumbled closed; David noticed, made a casual gesture, and instantly I was warm and dry.

'Wow,' I said, surprised. He raised his eyebrows.

'Nothing you couldn't do yourself.'

I moved closer to him and found him dry, too; warm as if he wore summer under his skin. He put his arms around me, but he did it carefully. Too carefully.

'David.'

'Yes?'

'I'm not fragile.'

He didn't smile, didn't look away from my face. Close up, the colour of his eyes was a deep, rich gold-stone. 'Compared with me?'

'OK, granted, more fragile than you. But don't treat me like I'm dying, I'm not dying, I'm just – living until I don't.' David still didn't look away. 'Promise me you won't let all this stop you from throwing me up against the wall right now and kissing me like my life depended on it.'

It was a short ride to the third floor, too short for the kind of reassurance I wanted, but he did manage to make me feel better. And warmer.

In the room, with towels and swimsuits discarded, he proceeded to raise my body temperature considerably. This time, there was no demonic tantrum to spoil it for us, just long, slow, delicious heat that kept building and building until I burnt.

I fell asleep curled against him, with his hand over the Mark, holding it still.

❧ ❧ ❧

I woke up alone in a well-mussed bed, felt the cold hollow in the pillow where David had lain, and I felt that cold certainty sweep over me that it was like the first night: I was going to open my eyes to find him gone as if he'd never been.

But when I looked, he was standing at the window, looking out. He was already dressed in a gold flannel shirt and blue jeans, feet bare, and he had his glasses on again. Human disguise firmly in place.

I stretched and let the sheet slip down. David didn't take the bait. He looked uncommonly sober for so early in the morning, especially after a night that had left me still tingling and vibrating all over.

'No good morning?' I asked. 'What's so fascinating? Cheerleaders practicing naked in the parking lot?'

He didn't answer. I got up, wrapped a sheet around me in the best movie-star fashion, and togaed over to join him at the plate-glass window. The sun was above the horizon, but not by much; it was layered in pinks and golds, floating just under a grey layer of low-hanging, rounded clouds. More rain up there. And a darker line to the south that I didn't like.

'Nasty,' I said, pointing to it. He *still* didn't answer. 'Earth to David? Hello?'

And then I saw where he was looking, down into the parking lot. For a few seconds, it didn't register – cars, lots of cars, nothing special...

...and then my eyes settled on a midnight-blue Mustang with a charred driver's side door, parked innocently in the fourth row. Next to the white Land Rover.

Marion's hunters were here.

'Shit!'

I dropped the sheet and ran into the bathroom, scooped up clothes from the floor, and pulled on stretch velvet pants without bothering with underwear. The lace shirt tore at the bottom as I yanked it over my head. Jacket and shoes went on practically simultaneously, and while I was dragging my tangled hair out from under the coat collar, I yelled at David, 'Come on!'

He was still at the window. Shoeless. I grabbed his arm and towed him toward the hotel room door.

He stopped two seconds before the knock came. His face was focused and pale, eyes as dark as midnight.

'Get in the bathroom,' he said. 'Shut the door.'

As if that would do any good. 'I'm going down fighting, not hiding.'

'Just *do it!*' His fury was sudden and hot as nuclear fire, and before I could even try to argue, he took me by the shirt and shoved me into the bathroom, banged the door shut, and I heard a huge concussion of sound, of *pressure*. What the hell—?

I opened the door and saw the glitter of glass all over the carpet. The curtains were blowing in, straight in, like gale flags. The windows were completely gone, nothing but a sugar-dusting of glass left at the corners.

David turned, grabbed me by the hand, and pulled me to the window. Picked me up like a toy in his arms. Behind us, the door to the room shuddered and jumped on its hinges, then caught fire with a red-orange *whoosh*.

David jumped out into open air.

I didn't know how indestructible free-range Djinn might be, so I formed a thick cushion of air under us, an updraft to counter our fall. It was still a jolt of an impact, but even before my mind could register it, David was already running.

'Put me down!' I yelled.

'Shut up!' he yelled back. There was raw ferocity in his voice, too much to argue with. He skidded to a halt next to Delilah. 'Get in the car!'

The door was unlocked. He put me down, and I slid into the driver's seat; no keys, but he reached in the open door and touched the ignition to start her up.

'David—'

'Drive! Don't stop for anything!'

Before I could protest, he was running back toward the hotel, looking up at the black gaping hole that used to be our window on the third floor.

Someone was standing there. I couldn't see who it was, because at that moment the curtains fluttered and started to blow out instead of in. I felt the shock wave of it a second before it hit – straight-line winds, running at least a hundred miles an hour. I felt Delilah shudder and roll backwards; I jammed on the brakes. David hadn't moved, but his shirt was being pulled right off him by the merciless pressure. As I watched, buttons popped and the fabric slid down his arms; the wind took it and it whipped away toward the horizon.

There was a terrible concussive *pop* from the direction of the hotel.

Something coming at us. Glittering. David turned, screaming at me to *drive, now*, and it was more the stark urgency in his face than understanding that made me scratch rubber in reverse out of the parking space. When I realised what it was that I saw flying toward me across the parking lot, I hit the brakes again and screeched to a bone-crunching halt.

Every window on this side of the hotel had shattered, and the glittering, slicing fragments were hurtling toward me.

Toward a family of four clinging to the door of a red minivan down the row.

Toward a pregnant woman huddling out in the open, caught between rows of cars.

Toward *David*.

I threw myself up into Oversight and grabbed for what I could reach, which wasn't much; this was brute-force stuff, and my enemy already had control of just about everything there was to use. I grabbed air and forced molecules to move, *move*, never mind the chaos factors that introduced; that wall of broken glass was going to shred us all to hamburger if I didn't.

I jammed on the car brakes, abandoned the idea of retreat, and focused everything I had on the moment. I superheated the air and released it in a hard, fast, focused pulse. It didn't have to be much, just enough to disrupt the wind for a fraction of a second; glass is too heavy to continue at right angles to gravity without a clear kinetic force acting on it.

My microburst – five hundred yards wide – blew into the opposing wind-wall and shattered the momentum, and for a second there was a haze there of power meeting power, glass turning over and over like windblown confetti, and then the shards rained down to the asphalt with a sound like a hundred bags of dimes breaking open. The hurricane attack started up again, but it was too late; glass isn't easy to get airborne once it's on the ground.

I realised I could no longer see David. God, I'd been too late, too late to keep the glass from hitting him – he was down somewhere, between the cars, down and slashed to ribbons—

The passenger door yanked open, and David threw

himself in, bare-chested and bleeding. 'I told you to go!' he shouted. I jammed Delilah back in gear, popped the clutch, and squealed rubber in a turn that any stunt driver would have been proud of. We screeched around the corner, heading for the street—

—and almost crashed headfirst into a Winnebago blocking the exit. I jerked the wheel and got us around it, barely, registering the shocked faces of Ma and Pa Retirement as the Mustang roared past.

Hair on the back of my neck hissed and prickled, and I knew it was coming again, could feel those ions turning and connecting overhead. Not just one lightning bolt this time, but hundreds, *thousands*, a sky full of falling razor blades, and I couldn't stop all of them. People were going to die.

'David!' I screamed. He grabbed my hand, and I smelt the actinic charge in the air, heard the hissing sizzle of it overhead. That power had to discharge, needed to discharge, and it was going to go somewhere fast and hard. It would settle for anything that would form a satisfactory current. Buildings...trees...flesh and blood and bone.

I felt David's strength pouring into me. Not the same magnitude as what I'd felt from other Djinn, but then David's strength wasn't fully sourced until he was bound.

No time to plan, no time to do anything but what I knew, at heart, was right.

I built an invisible road for the power to

discharge, working fast, touching and turning polarities a billion atoms at a time. I'd never worked on such a scale before, but I had to reach, and reach, and reach without stopping to doubt myself. I stretched myself over the aetheric as thin as a spider web, armouring the innocent, leaving a clear and unmistakable path for the strike to follow. A lightning rod with a silver ground wire unreeling back to me.

It had to be back to me. It was the direction all the power was being pushed, anyway.

David felt it. 'No! What are you doing?'

'Not now,' I snapped, and felt the Mark wake and move inside me. I tightened my grip on David's hand. 'Keep it still!'

I felt warmth pulse through his flesh and into mine, strike deep. The writhing inside me went quiet.

The last chains of power snapped together. In Oversight, the silver line went white-hot with potential.

'Hold on,' I whispered, and closed my eyes.

The lightning flashed blue white, brighter and hotter than the sun – silent, because sound would come later. I opened my mouth to gasp and tasted the bitter tang of ozone. Pins and needles blew over my skin in a wave, from my feet to the crown of my head.

And then the lightning hit Delilah dead on.

❧ ❧ ❧

Chapter Four

Wind shears and lightning strikes are likely
in the Norman area, with a large high-pressure
system advancing from the northeast; possible
severe weather is likely for this evening.
Residents are urged to stay aware of
changing weather conditions.

People were talking.

I didn't think they were talking to me. They were talking about...about somebody being dead. There was shouting and noise. Metal.

Somebody was saying my name, over and over. I tried to open my eyes, but then I realised I couldn't because they were already open. There was nothing to see, though. Just light. Bright blue-white light.

Was there something wrong with me? I tried to blink my eyes, but nothing seemed to move. If I had something wrong with me, I'd be in pain, wouldn't I?

Maybe I was just tired. I'd been tired for so long.
Maybe now I could sleep.

I wished people would stop talking to me. It was really annoying. And there was something touching me, something hot.

And then there was something cool on my face. Wet and cool.

Water.

The second time was easier. I came almost all the way up from the dark, heard voices, recognised David murmuring something soft and liquid that didn't sound like words, not any words I knew. That was all right. Just the sound of his voice was all I needed.

There was another voice, too. A woman's. I knew it, but...but I couldn't remember. Eventually I felt something soft under my head, felt road vibration quivering in my skin, and knew I was lying down in a car. The hard lump of an unfastened seat belt lay under my left hip.

I opened my eyes on a dull carpeted roof the colour of nothing, heard the humming of tires on wet road, and smelt – weirdly enough – blueberry muffins. I moved a hand, carefully, and it hurt – hurt everywhere. It felt like every nerve in my body had been mapped in hot wire. There was an aching sore spot on my right foot, another at the top of my head.

No question about it, I was lucky to be alive. If I hadn't been insulated by Delilah's steel frame...

My hand was still in the air. I stared at it, baffled, and realised I'd forgotten to let it fall down. Before I could do so, somebody reached back and captured it.

David. He looked back over the passenger seat at me. Dressed again in his road-dude disguise, complete with glasses. No sign of the cuts and scrapes he'd had back at the motel. No sign of any damage to him at all, except in the wounded darkness of his eyes.

'You're OK?' I whispered. My throat hurt like hell, and I was so thirsty, I felt like I'd been freeze-dried. And cold. Very cold. His hand radiated warmth into me.

The Demon Mark moved inside me, just a slight stealthy crawl. I closed my eyes and fought it, but I was so tired, so drained.

It kept moving. I felt David trying to stop it, but he was drained, too. Too tired to save me now. I had to save myself.

I reached down and choked the black terrible thing with as much self-control as I had left in me. It writhed and tried to slither around me, but I held it until it stopped its quivering progress.

'I'm OK,' David answered me when I opened my eyes again. 'Easy, take it easy. Rest.'

'She's awake?' The woman's voice, the one I

RACHEL CAINE

almost recognised. Spanish accented. Slightly slurred. I squinted, but all I could see in the rearview mirror was a flash of dark eyes. '*Mira*, JoJo's back among the living.'

And then I knew who she was, with a burst of happiness that exploded right out of my core. It hurt to smile. I did it anyway. 'Star light, star bright, first star I see tonight...'

She laughed that silvery laugh I remembered so well, and glanced back from the driver's seat. Still beautiful, Estrella Almondovar, my good friend. At least on that side of her face.

She joined in with me in a duet. 'Say a prayer, say a Mass, keep this fire off my ass.' It wasn't the way the children's rhyme went, but it was our variation. And she finished by holding up the middle finger on her right hand in the universal screw-you symbol. A tiny flame danced on its tip.

'*Chica*, you're still crazy,' she said. 'But then that's why I love you so much.'

After my disastrous Yellowstone getting-back-to-nature camping trip, Estrella and I talked every week. I ran up my mom's phone bill to outrageous levels; like the teenager I was, I could talk about nothing for hours, and Star was more than happy to go along with it. She was lonely, and we were soul mates; somehow, we could find a telephone book funny, if we talked about it for more than two minutes.

Star was the only friend I had who *understood*.

So. My intake meeting happened, Princeton happened, graduation happened (and wasn't that something, but that's a story for later). Fast-forward to 1999, and my rotation as a Staff Warden on the Help Desk. We call it something more official than that, of course – the Crisis Centre Support System – but really, it's a Help Desk, just like ones computer departments all over the world have in place, and for much the same reasons. When things go wrong for the Association, they go wrong in a big way, and communication is everything because the aetheric doesn't carry sound for shit. Everybody gets a turn in the hot seat at the Help Desk, which is run 24/7 with a minimum of twenty staffers, who are empowered to do everything from troubleshooting to calling National Wardens out of bed in the middle of the night.

About six days into my tour, I got a phone call from – who else? – Star. There was a wildfire out of control in Yellowstone, and the Regional Warden was on vacation; Estrella and her boss felt that it was serious enough to escalate it and get specialty teams on the job. A Yellowstone fire is no laughing matter. It's one of the richest natural preserves left in the United States, and it's also a sinkhole of random energy; put the two together, add any kind of instability, and you get disaster.

We laughed, we chatted, we talked. Two friends catching up on time lost. She wasn't really worried.

Except it got worse. I could tell that from the tone of her voice. It changed from light to businesslike to dead serious as she fed me map coordinates, burn rates, wind speeds, all the alchemical elements that went into making up a disaster.

'Got it,' I said, typing the last of the data into the system. There was a dull sound in the background, like airplane noise. 'Hey, you want to turn the stereo down? It's getting a little loud on this end.'

She coughed. Dry coughs at first, but they raised goose bumps on my arms. 'No can do, babe. Guess you'll just have to yell.'

'Is that the *fire*?' Close enough to roar like that? Oh, God. I knew that Estrella was calling from a Ranger Station somewhere near the edge of the blaze. As a Fire Warden, she had to be close to work her magic – not like Weather Wardens, who can manage things from miles or even countries distant. Fire was too interactive. It required real risk on the part of those who engaged with it. But I'd never imagined how close, or how much risk.

'That or somebody's throwing one hell of a barbecue.' She started coughing. Thick, choking coughs. I was sitting in a Situation Room on the nineteenth floor of the Association offices in Chicago, and I could still hear the crackle of the fire; it wasn't just close, it was *right there*. All around her. 'Aw, shit.'

'What?'

More coughing. When it stopped, I heard the sound of things bumping, crashing. 'It's blocking the front. Hang on, I'm going for the back door.'

'Estrella?' No answer. I could hear her hoarse, heavy breathing, could almost taste the smoke.

'Bastard's cut me off,' she said at last. I could tell from the shaking in her voice that she was really scared this time. 'Hey, JoJo? This is really getting screwed up. I need out of here. 'Cause I don't look good in black, know what I'm saying?'

I was already typing in alerts, ringing pagers and cell phones with the necessary codes to let people know the situation. Within ten minutes, there'd be a Situation Team convened, with Weather and Fire Wardens, maybe even Earth Wardens to help organise the rescue of trapped animals and energise the forest itself to fight the fire. But that wasn't going to help Estrella.

'Can you make a path through?' I asked. I could hear things popping loudly in the background, like gunshots. 'Jesus, what is that? Is somebody shooting?'

'No, it's the trees. Trees exploding. Sap boils—' She coughed again, deep aching coughs that made my chest hurt in sympathy. '*Shit!* Can't do it. Too hot. Can't get the fire down long enough to get out.

Dammit. I'm toast.' Her laugh was rich and thick with phlegm. 'Burnt toast.'

'Hold on,' I said. I pulled up the Wardens Map, overlaid Fire Wardens on top of it and got Estrella's location. Once I had it firmly fixed in my mind, I went up into Oversight. My body receded and I flew straight up, arrowing as fast as I could through grey ghostly layers of concrete and steel and wiring, up into hot summer air, up higher where the layers cooled and storms were born. There was disturbance up here, caused by temperature shifts. I oriented myself and moved toward Yellowstone. As I did, I had to buck the currents; force lines were vibrating, bending under the strain. A lot of heat being generated up there. Pushing hard, I flew against the currents until I could see the whole of Yellowstone laid out in front of me.

It was *boiling*. Not in the physical sense, but in the aetheric; something had gotten the land stirred up, all right, and the turbulent, angry pulses were enough to make me want to drop back into my safe, secure little cubicle far from the danger. Fires were combusting everywhere... It didn't take much, in such an angry mood, for a forest to start self-immolating.

I pinpointed Estrella's location – she was broadcasting desperately in the aetheric – and went up, way up, until daylight gave way to twilight, which gave way to the false night of the highest levels of the mesosphere. Fifty thousand feet above it, the disturbance was more like a gentle current; I could start to manipulate things to my advantage.

Within a minute, I had formed a cold arctic-fed breeze by tunnelling a channel for it through the superheated Yellowstone air. When I had it flowing where I wanted it, I let it collide head-on with a column of heat, controlled the agitation of the molecules to keep it localised, and dropped halfway back into my body in Chicago.

'Star, listen to me, I'm about to drop a very heavy cloudburst right on top of you, understand? It'll hold the fire down long enough for you to make a hole and get out of there. Star?'

Her croak barely sounded human. It was hard to make anything out over the roar of the fire. 'Fucked up, JoJo. Damn. We all fucked up.'

'Star, stay with me. Hey, you remember the rhyme? Star light, star bright—'

'You crazy?' A bare whisper of air.

I kept going. 'First star I see tonight – come on, you know this one…' It was hard, so hard to move the clouds into the right position. I could feel her there, reaching out to me. I could feel the despair and fear. 'Wish I may – wish I might—'

I flipped the switch on the storm, and I heard the roar of rain pour down. I hoped the hiss I heard was steam, not fire.

And then I heard Estrella laughing. 'Say a prayer,

say a Mass...keep this fire off my ass!' She collapsed into a coughing fit. Then whooped.

I let myself relax. Fatal mistake. I felt – heard – saw the aetheric boiling back, rebounding at us like a snapped rubber band. 'No, Star, listen, don't yell, *run!* Now!'

She didn't hear me. She was still whooping in celebration.

The line went dead.

I sat tensely, answering lines and connecting up Wardens with each other – it was a big coordinated response, and my little cloudburst ended up as the anchor point for six other Wardens to form a true stormfront, driving down temperatures and dumping nature's fire extinguisher at volumes rarely seen in this country. Meanwhile, the Earth Wardens were trying their best to protect fleeing animals and build up earthen firebreaks, and the Fire Wardens... Well, you can guess the hell they were in.

Six minutes later, I had an incoming line light up, and a brisk British voice said, "You're looking for a Fire Warden coming out, right?'

'Estrella Almondovar,' I said. 'Did you get her?'

A brief, pregnant pause. 'Got her. We have one of the best Earth specialists with her right now, seeing to her.'

'How bad—?'

'Bad,' he said flatly. 'Third degree burns over thirty per cent of her body. Lucky.'

'*Lucky?*'

'Twenty Fire Wardens in the Park today,' he said. 'Sixteen dead so far.'

Say a prayer, say a Mass, keep this fire off my ass. You did it, chica. Otherwise, I'd be a pile of ash in hell.

It was the first thing she'd said to me when she'd gotten healthy enough to call from rehab. I'd held her hand that day in the hospital when Marion had broken the news to her that her powers had been shattered, that she'd never again be able to control fire. She still had her life. After a fashion, she had her health. After everything the Earth Wardens and doctors could do for her, she even had a passable face.

I'd never shaken the feeling that I should have done more and done better. And yet Star had never complained, never second-guessed, never blamed me.

I only, ever, blamed myself.

I must have fallen asleep again. When I woke up, we were still driving, and Estrella was singing under her breath to a Madonna song. She couldn't carry a tune worth a damn.

I realised – finally – that we were back in the Land Rover. No wonder I could stretch out in the backseat. 'Hey,' I croaked. 'Water?'

'Sorry,' Star said cheerfully. 'Can't stop yet. We

want to make sure they're not on the trail.'

'They?'

'You know.' She gestured with her left hand, and something about it caught my attention. It was skeletal. Leathery. Scarred. *God*. I'd forgotten for a second about the damage to her body. 'Marion and her merry men. You know they tried to kill you, right?'

I tried sitting up. My body ached like I'd come down with the mother of all flu viruses, but everything seemed to still function right. Toes and fingers wiggled. My nose reported the unpleasant lingering smell of burnt hair.

'You're one lucky girl,' Star continued. 'My money would've been on that polyester crap you're wearing melting all over you. You got only a couple of spark burns, that's all.'

I took a deep breath and asked for the worst of it. 'Delilah? My car.'

'She's a real fixer-upper. Time to trade up to something made in the last twenty years, I'd say. Hey, what do you think about this one?' Star gestured out at the hood of the Land Rover. 'Marion, pretty good taste, eh? I always wanted one of these. Weird that she left the engine running, but our gain.'

David was in the passenger seat of the truck. Left the engine running, my ass. I wondered how he'd managed to do it without her noticing.

Then again, I had a better question. And a more pressing one.

'How'd you know where to find me?' I asked. Star grinned and steered around a cattle truck; the smell of scared beeves and cow pies overrode my burnt hair, at least for a minute.

'You're kidding, right? I get your message, I see the aetheric get all fucked up, and I think...JoJo! And there you were. I got to the parking lot just about the time the freaking sky started falling. Man, that was one big lightning bolt. Biggest I ever saw.' Star shook her head. 'Like I said, you're lucky.'

'You should let me out somewhere,' I said. 'Ditch the truck before you get home. This is serious, Star, I don't want you in the middle of it.'

'Yeah, no kidding it's serious, La Quinta looks like a hurricane hit it.' She looked over her shoulder at me. 'Yeah? Did it?'

'Sort of.' I rested my elbows on the seat backs and leant closer. 'I really don't want you in this.'

'Hey, Queen of the Universe, nobody asked what you wanted. I don't ditch the girl that saved my life.' She glanced over at David. 'Or her *verdaderamente lindo* boyfriend.'

'Star!'

'What? You don't think he's cute?'

'He's sitting right there!'

'And so grateful I am.' She flashed him a half-crazy grin, which seemed to have no real effect on David. '*Chica*, you always did have good taste.'

I sighed. No way to reason with her when she was in this kind of take-no-prisoners mood, and besides, it was nice to hear somebody was enjoying themselves at my expense. 'OK, right, he's definitely *lindo*. Um, where are we, exactly?'

'Exactly?' Star punched the GPS keyboard.

I rolled my eyes. 'Come on.'

'Aw, you're no fun. OK, *approximately*, we're about two hours outside of OKC. Back roads. I didn't want to stop too long, 'cause, you know, you're on the run.'

I looked at David, who hadn't said a word. He shrugged. 'I didn't think it was worth the argument,' he said. 'You needed help. She offered. And she said she knew you.' And, I sensed, he'd been in no position to refuse. Probably out of it himself. That power surge had been enough to knock the stuffing out of a Djinn as easily as any Warden.

I agreed. 'Oh, she knows me. Too well.' David didn't look reassured. In fact, now that I was getting a look close-up at his expression, it looked guarded and worried. 'It's OK. Star's a friend. A long-time friend.'

She muttered something that might have been *bet your ass* and changed lanes, whipped around two eighteen-wheelers and back before another truck blasted by. Wherever we weren't going, we were getting there awfully fast.

David captured my hand in his. 'You OK?'

'You know me, Energizer Bunny.' The feel of his skin was distracting. I wanted to feel the rest of it, all over me. 'Hungry, though. And I think I mentioned thirsty. And in need of a pit stop, so if you see any convenient gas stations...'

Star checked the rearview mirror. I got the sense that she was checking out the aetheric, too, in Oversight, but I was too tired to try to rise up there with her; I leant my cheek against David's shoulder. He felt real, and human, and warmly male. Hard muscles under soft skin.

'We're about forty miles from the next town,' she said. 'I don't like it out here – too open, too much room for ambush – but hey, if you've gotta go, you've gotta go.' She fumbled in a fringed leather purse lying like roadkill in the space between the seats, fished out a small metal square, and handed it over. 'Cell phone. Hang on to it. Yours was probably toasted, right?'

'Right.' Cell phones had gotten smaller and cooler since the last time I checked. Hers flipped up like a *Star Trek* communicator, complete with colour screen and more controls than a 747. 'Thanks.'

'Just to be safe. If we're gonna split up, even for a few minutes, you got the 911 security blanket.'

She applied brakes and eased the Land Rover over to the shoulder in a hiss of gravel; the cattle truck she'd passed blasted by us with a car-shaking gust. Star aimed off the road, into the flat grass prairie and toward a stand of scrub trees. 'Hope you're not picky about accommodations.'

'You're kidding.'

'Hey, you said pit stop, I'm getting you a pit stop. Besides, drivers have to pee, too.' Star put the truck in park and hopped out to the cheery accompaniment of warning bells for leaving the engine running. On the passenger side, David did the same, then opened the back door for me and handed me out like a gentleman. Good thing he did; my legs felt like water balloons. I clung to his hand for a few seconds until muscles firmed up and informed me they were ready to take my weight.

Star turned, and the sunlight fell down full on her face.

Even though I'd seen it dozens of times, it was still a shock. Half her face gleamed bronze gold, perfect; the other half was seared and scarred the colour of old liver. They'd given her a left eyelid, after a fashion. Her lips twisted into a curl on the burnt side, and the scar continued down into the neck of her white peasant blouse. I knew it dripped down past her waist on the side and back. It looked like melted wax.

'Still gorgeous, huh?' she asked. There was no hurt, no surprise, no disappointment in her voice. Certainly no embarrassment. 'Looks worse instead of better, I know. Not everything improves with age.'

She turned on her heel and limped her way toward the scrub trees. I realised I was still holding David's hand, almost crushing it, and I kept my eyes on her as I asked, 'What did she see?'

He shrugged. 'At the hotel? I don't know. I blacked out when the lightning hit. When I woke up, she was there, pulling you out of the car.' David was watching her, too, and I couldn't mistake what was in his eyes for anything but worry. 'She kept the car from catching fire until we were both out. Otherwise I think you'd be dead.'

I took a breath, let it out, and nodded. 'Does she know about you?'

'I don't think so. I've been careful.'

That didn't unknot the tension from my shoulder blades. 'Yeah, well, keep it up. I love her, but – you be careful.'

I went after Star toward nature's Porta Potti. She was already taking advantage of the lack of facilities, and she looked absolutely comfortable doing it, but then she was the outdoorsy L.L. Bean type. Me, I circled around, looking for a comfortable piece of ground free of any hint of fire ants, wasps, or other hazards to my exposed behind. Star finished up and went back toward David. I skinned down my pants.

'Is this a bad time?' a voice asked me when I was halfway to a crouch. I yelped and scrambled back up, tripped over my pants and almost fell. 'Over here, Snow White.'

I turned while I yanked up my waistband. Paul's Djinn, Rahel, still in her sunshine yellow suit, sat primly on a tree stump, inspecting her nails.

'Please, go ahead,' she invited. 'You're not bothering me. I have all the time in the world.'

'What do you want?' Although I figured I knew... This was what I'd been dreading. Marion, for whatever reason, hadn't used her Djinn against me, but there were plenty of Wardens willing and able to do so – Paul, for one. I couldn't take Rahel in a straight fight. Nobody could, except another Djinn.

Which was why there weren't a lot of territorial disputes at the upper levels of the Wardens. I was worn out, maybe David – no, it would be suicide for David to get into this. He was depleted, and he was masterless; she'd break him with a snap of her well-manicured fingers.

'Your attention, please,' she said, and clicked her nails together. They looked glossy and sharp. Her hundreds of braids rustled as she turned her head toward me, a dry sound, like bones rattling. 'You're going the wrong way.'

Not what I'd expected. I was braced for a fight, and the lack of one threw me. 'Excuse me?'

Rahel hopped down from her perch and slinked in my direction. I fought the almost uncontrollable urge to back up; my heels were already sinking into damp ground. 'I said...you're going...the wrong...way. Snow White. Go back where you were told to go.'

I was feeling difficult. 'Or?'

She lunged at me, caught my arm in one hand, and levelled the other right in front of me, claws out an inch from my eyes. 'There is no *or*, fool. You do *what* I tell you, *when* I tell you.'

I kept my chin up and looked past those razor-sharp, carefully manicured nails to her beast-yellow eyes. She was doing something with her lips, but it had only a superficial resemblance to a smile.

'Death lies ahead,' she said. 'Certain and unforgiving. Behind you lies opportunity.'

'Opportunity for what?'

'To choose as you wish.'

I didn't get it. 'Did Paul tell you to be deliberately obscure, or is this just a personal preference with you?'

No answer. Just that steady, predatory stare.

It clicked together in my head. *Duh*. 'You're not Paul's Djinn at all, are you? I just assumed you were, and you never told me different. Right?'

'Yes.' Teeth flashed. 'Now you can decide which question I've answered.'

'Doesn't matter, I didn't ask any of them in ritual. Let me try again. You're not Paul's Djinn at all, are you?'

'You can't outrun what's coming. Go back. You *must* make a choice.'

'Third time's the charm, sunshine. You're not Paul's Djinn at all, are—?' Before I could finish asking the ritual third, her hand was around my throat, choking the question off. I gagged, tried to pull free, and couldn't. Her eyes were full of fury.

'Ask me no questions,' she purred, 'and I'll tell you no lies, Child of Demons. *Go back the way you came.*'

She let the pressure ease enough for me to gulp in a breath and ask, 'Why should I?'

Rahel let go of my throat and snapped her fingers. 'You have two paths ahead of you. One lies down. One goes up. Choose.'

'Which one gets rid of *you?*' I croaked, and rubbed my throat. 'Look, enough with the Sphinx act. Just tell me what I'm supposed to do. Are you Marion's Djinn? Did she send you to get me to surrender? Well, I'm not giving up. Not yet.'

Rahel stopped and became utterly still. If I'd thought her eyes were unnerving before, they were downright creepy now.

'You are a fool,' she said very softly. 'I have done

all I can. You have been set on the path, you have been given signs.'

'Yeah? Like what? The radio in Westchester, telling me to come here?' Oh, boy. Her silence had the weight of a confession. I swallowed hard and kept going. 'The salt shaker back at the diner? Why send me into a trap?'

This time, she shook her head. 'If you can't see the yellow brick road, little Dorothy, then you are a fool, and there is no saving a fool. I only wish you weren't taking him with you.'

Him? Too many persons of the male gender involved in this. I didn't know which one she was talking about.

Before I could ask, brush crackled behind me. Rahel's eyes jumped from me to the person coming through the trees. It was David, and he didn't look surprised to see her. Or happy. He said something to her in a language I didn't understand, liquid and warm and beautiful as stars; her reply was long and sparked with harsh accents.

They glared at each other, stiff with tension, and then Rahel just – vanished. No showy exit, this time. She just *went*.

David stared for so long at the place where she'd been, I wondered if she'd really gone. 'Rahel,' he said finally. 'Here.'

'I'm guessing that's bad? Look, whose Djinn is she?'

He didn't answer me. Didn't look at me. 'Hurry.' He turned and walked away, back toward the truck.

I hurried.

After Star was burnt, she lingered on in the hospital for weeks, fighting for her life. Every day her breath came a little bit shallower; her heart raced a little bit faster. Pseudomonas cruised her blood. Pumping her full of antibiotics didn't seem to be working, and the Earth Wardens who'd tried to repair the damage had been completely defeated.

Sitting there at her bedside, holding her undamaged right hand, a thought came to me. I knew someone who *could* save her.

If I could find him.

Like Star, I'm not big on debate and thinking things over; the minute Lewis's name popped into my head, I went up into Oversight, far up, far enough that the planet curved away beneath me and night settled its cloak of stars around my shoulders. From up there, I could see little jets of flame that represented Wardens using their powers...little flicks like sparks from a flywheel. I waited up there, watching. It was impossible to distinguish the signatures of most Wardens – they were too similar, too homogenous. A few had characteristics, though. Marion, for one; her powers glowed stronger and in a deep blue green.

Martin Oliver, when he exercised his power – which was rarely – vibrated in a hot orange part of the spectrum.

I waited, and waited, and waited. The world turned, and I turned with it, watching.

Finally, I saw a soundless bloom of pearl-white. Not a jet, not a spark, but a *bloom*, like a fireworks blast expanding in all directions.

I fell toward it at top speed and stopped myself when I was close enough to determine where Lewis was at the moment.

I don't know why I didn't expect it, but I didn't, really.

He was in Yellowstone.

Six hours later, after enduring commercial air travel and two hours of jouncing around in a well-broken-in rental SUV, I came up on the area of Yellowstone that was blocked off to the public. The Warden on duty knew me. We exchanged the secret glowing-rune handshakes, and I went on in.

I smelt it before I came over the rise and saw it – a thick, ashen smell of death and bitter smoke. But nothing really prepared me for the devastation. Nothing could.

The valley stretched out as far as I could see, a black valley streaked with grey. No forest, nothing but ash and the skeletal black stubs of trees. There was a sense of...stillness. Of death so vast that no life could ever come there again, or would want to.

A sense of utter sadness.

Lewis was a dot of human colour in the middle of it, sitting on the hood of an SUV that looked like the mate to the one I was driving, only grey. Mine was red, but as I crawled it slowly over the ruined landscape it turned ash-grey, flecked with black. By the time I parked next to him, they were both camouflaged.

He looked...good. Filled out, no longer starving and sick. There was a sense of peace around him, and power. He was still tall and gawky, but somehow that fit now. He'd grown into it, and the gawkiness had become grace.

He didn't look surprised to see me as I climbed down out of the SUV and came around to face him. In fact, he smiled like he'd been expecting me for a while.

'Jo.' He nodded. I nodded back. 'Been a while.'

'You shouldn't be using all that power,' I said. 'You burn like a nuclear explosion in Oversight, you know.'

He shrugged. 'I knew you were watching. If I hadn't wanted you to find me, you wouldn't have found me.' He patted the hood of the SUV next to him. It was filthy, but I climbed up anyway. We didn't touch. 'Not too many people can see it, you know.'

'Really?' That boggled me; he'd lit up like Vegas in my eyes. 'Weird.'

'A bit,' he agreed. 'I'm guessing you didn't come out here just to catch up on old times.'

He was looking at me, but I felt the soft caress of power everywhere around me. Nothing I could understand, just a hint; I looked away from him at the burnt, blackened crematory of the forest and didn't see anything.

'You're doing something,' I said.

'Yes.'

'What?'

He gave me a slow, very slightly wicked smile. 'Seducing someone.'

If I kept very still, I could actually *see* it now. It was a mist, very faint, glittering gold in the sun. It was moving over the ground as softly and slowly as a lover's hand, spreading out from the epicentre of Lewis. I slid off the hood of the Jeep and reached down to touch my fingers to it, and felt a slow stirring of...life.

Lewis was pouring out life, like seed, across the mourning graveyard of Yellowstone.

'She needs help,' he said. 'She wants to live, but it's too much for her. I'm just helping her along.'

I felt the slow, warm tingle of it clinging to my fingers even after I climbed back up on the hood of the Jeep next to him. We sat in silence, watching the golden mist thicken and swirl and creep out across the land.

It was so beautiful, I wanted to weep.

'This is what you do,' I whispered. 'Oh, God, Lewis.'

'Some of it. You guys do a good job with the weather, but I pitch in now and again with Earth and Fire. I should've been here earlier. It wouldn't have been so—' He shook his head.

'You wouldn't have stopped it?'

'The fire? No. Things need to burn sometimes, and you have to know when to let them. But this got out of hand.' In the sunlight, his eyes were the colour of fine dark ale. 'There's a Demon trying to come through.'

'I have no idea what you're talking about.' Although I did, a little; there were whispers about Demon Marks, but nobody was very clear about them or what it meant. Lewis, however, sounded authoritative.

'Things like this happen because there's a kind of force acting on our world. Hurricane Andrew, that was another one. The floods in India. Those are signs that something's trying to break through into the aetheric.' He was holding a stick in his hands, turning it over and over, learning it with his fingers. 'Sometimes it succeeds in finding one of us to build the bridge. I think that's what this was. One of them trying to touch one of us.'

'Anyone in particular?'

'Don't know,' he confessed. 'Probably not. The problem is that the energy from the Demon's efforts doesn't go away, it accumulates up there, in the aetheric.' He shook his head. 'Never mind. Not important — you didn't come out here to get a lecture. What's up?'

'Star,' I said. All around me, the ground glittered with gold, with power, with potential. 'I need you to help her. She's dying.'

Lewis stopped turning the stick in his hands. He looked down at it as if surprised to find it there. 'Friend of yours?'

'Friend of yours, too. I remember her saying she knew you.'

He nodded. 'I met her here. I was young and stupid then; I didn't realise how much energy there was here. I nearly got myself toasted.'

It was so similar to the way I'd met Star that I had to smile at the memory.

'I can't help her,' he said. 'I've thought about it. I know she was — burnt.'

'Worse,' I said. 'Her power core was broken. That's what they tell me, anyway. That's what's keeping her from healing.'

He shivered a little. The colour of the mist around us changed subtly, from gold to silver, then back to gold. It clung to the skeletal limbs of trees like a coating of early frost.

'*Can* you help her?' I asked.

'It's not a question of *can*, Jo. Sometimes—'

'Sometimes you just have to let things burn,' I

finished for him. The air was warm and thick with the taste of smoke and death, and the hard metal hood of the Jeep felt too warm under me. 'But this is *Star*.'

He reached out and put his hand on my hair, stroking gently. Not letting himself touch my skin. I relaxed into the touch for the sheer pleasure of it. 'I know,' he said. 'Don't you think I *want* to?'

'I'm asking you,' I said. 'I'm asking you for a favour. You owe me one.'

His hand went still, but he didn't take it away.

'Lewis?' I asked. 'Please?'

The mist changed colours again, from gold to a pale green the colour of spring leaves. The colour change rolled across the valley slowly, in wavelike ripples.

The stick in Lewis's hand changed colour, too, from dead brown to a fine, delicate tan, the wood inside showing pale as flesh. As I watched, it sprouted a single, delicate leaf. Lewis slid off the hood of the Jeep and planted the stick carefully upright in the charcoal field. I could almost feel it rooting, growing, pulsing with life.

'It might not work,' he said. He might have been talking about the plant, but I knew he wasn't. 'Sometimes it doesn't work at all.'

'Try.'

He straightened up and turned to look at me. Around him, the mist rose into the air in whispering waves, like angels flying. It dissolved on the light of the sun, and then there was just a black valley, dead trees, a tall and graceful man standing there with his arms folded across his chest.

But the smell... The smell was different. Warm. Golden.

The wind smelt like life.

He nodded and said, 'Let's go.'

Six hours later, he was holding Star's hand, and that golden mist was moving through her, soaking into her skin, invading through her mouth and nose.

It saved her life. Lewis preserved what he could of her affinity with fire, but like me, he understood balance; to heal Star completely meant disturbing that balance beyond repair.

I don't think she ever knew he was there. When she woke up, two days later, Lewis was long gone, just a memory and a taste of gold in the air.

I never told her anything about it.

I watched the road behind us, once we were safely back in motion again, but I didn't see any lemon-yellow Djinn flying carpets in our trail. Not that she'd do anything that ridiculously *Arabian Nights*, of course, but when you're paranoid, staring out the back window seems like a vitally important occupation.

You're a fool. There is no saving a fool.

Whose side was Rahel on, anyway? Maybe nobody's. Certainly not mine. *Choose*. Choose what? Choose who? Why did the Djinn have to be so damn inscrutable, anyway? Was it just a personality flaw? I couldn't even assume she was really out to save David. In fact, as little as I actually understood about the Djinn, there was nothing I *could* safely assume about Rahel – I didn't even know where she stood in this strange little game.

Choose. So few choices I could make. I had the Mark. I could choose to give it to David... No. I wouldn't. I couldn't.

Choose. Dammit. The only thing I had left was...who to trust. Well, I knew something about that, at least. I couldn't trust Marion and her people; they'd do exactly what they were told to do by the Council, up to and including killing me. David – I already trusted him, in ways I couldn't begin to regret.

But I could commit to the one person I'd been avoiding dragging into this.

'Star—' I leant forward and touched her shoulder. Her dark hair dragged like silk on my fingers. 'Star, do you know anything about the Demon Mark?'

David couldn't quite control his flinch. He stared straight ahead, but I could feel the burn of his disapproval. As for Star, she turned her head, lips parted in astonishment, and then whipped back toward the road when a truck blared a warning. On the horizon, a flock of birds broke cover and wheeled like a tornado in the greying sky.

Star nodded toward David, plainly asking. I nodded. 'He knows.'

'Yeah? He knows about *what*, exactly?'

'The Wardens. All of it.'

'Really?' She cut an interested look his way, but he didn't respond. 'Well. OK, I know a little about it. Why? You got one?' She was kidding, of course. But in answer, I eased back the collar of my shirt and dragged it down to show her the scorch mark over my left breast. She whistled. 'Holy crap, Jo.'

'I need to know how to get rid of it,' I said.

'Obviously! OK.' She blew out an agitated breath. 'Damn, girl, that's a hell of a secret to keep.'

'If it's any consolation, you're the first one I've told.' True, actually. I hadn't told David, he'd known all along, or guessed pretty damn well.

'How'd you get it?' She seemed pretty shaken. I guess she had a right.

'Bad Bob. He kidnapped me and—' I didn't want to describe what he'd done to me; it was too chokingly vivid. 'Anyway. He died, I got the Mark.'

'Holy shit. Well...you could give it to somebody else. That's obvious.' She turned her attention back to the road, but her golden-bronze skin had taken on a paler tinge. '*Mira*, is that what you're looking to do? Pass it on? You know it won't go unless the person you try to give it to has more power than you do.' She flicked a glance at me in the rearview mirror, and her eyes widened. 'You *do* know that, right?'

I looked to David for confirmation; he didn't meet my gaze, which was confirmation enough. *Damn*. But that meant – no, that was impossible. 'Star, that can't be true,' I said. '*Bad Bob* gave this to me – you know he was one of the most powerful Wardens in the world. I can't be...'

If Estrella was surprised by that, she gave no sign of it. She just nodded. 'Well, *chica*, I guess you know something about yourself you didn't know before, then.'

'Bullshit!' I was, at best, a mediocre Warden. I wasn't – couldn't be—

'Straight up word of honour, JoJo. A Demon Mark can't go from stronger to weaker, only from weaker to stronger. It's a known fact. So if Bad Bob's Demon Mark traded up to you...' Her eyebrows rose. 'Welcome to the top of the food chain. Damn, girl, I knew you were strong. I guess I never knew how strong.'

'That's—'

'Impossible, yeah, you've said. But Bad Bob picked you to pass it to, so that settles that. Who else could have taken it for him? Lewis?' She made a rude noise to the road. 'Right. Like anybody can find *that* guy. Jeez, what are you going to do? Is that why the Rangers are after you? 'Cause of the Mark?'

I rubbed my aching forehead with the heels of my hands. 'Something like that. I find somebody to pass it on to. Whatever. What's the other option?'

'Well, you could, like, keep it.'

'Keep it! Jesus, Star, for crying out loud—'

'Hear me out. Look, everything I know about the Demon Mark, the farther it goes into you, the stronger you get. Maybe that's a good thing. Maybe – maybe that's what you ought to do. I mean, we *call* it a Demon Mark, but what do we really know about it? Is it any worse than the Djinn?'

'Oh, trust me on this, it's way worse,' I said, and had a grotesque sense-memory of the thing burrowing inside me, leaving that horrible violated slimy feeling in its wake.

'So you don't want to keep it.'

'God, no.'

Star's knuckles were white on the steering wheel. I watched her flex her fingers and shake them, one at a time. 'Well, that narrows it down. I guess you need to get yourself a Djinn.'

And I was back where I'd started. Helpless. Caught in the headlights of oncoming friggin' fate.

I wanted to scream at Rahel, wherever she was. *What fucking choice do I have?*

And then Star said, shocking me down to my shoes, 'Luckily, babe, I think I can help you out on that score.'

My asking what Star meant got me nowhere. She just kept giving me that secret little grin and telling me to wait and see; I could see David getting wound tighter and tighter, ready to lash out. He was scared. I was scared for him. God, she couldn't *know*...could she?

We pulled off at a gas station about five miles down the road. Star went inside to pay for the gas and to grab beverages and whatever passed for food; I got out to walk around in the cooling wind, shivering. The storm that had been following me was still on my trail. I could feel it like a tingle at the edges of my mind.

I don't know if you've ever been in that part of the world, but it's flat, and it seems to go on forever. The land can't quite decide whether it's desert or scrub forest, so it sticks clumps of stubby, twisted bushes together and surrounds them with reddish dust. There's no elegance to it, but there is a certain toughness. It's land that will fight you for every drop of water, every green growing thing you want to take from it. Even though I wasn't an Earth Warden, I could feel that, feel the awesome sleeping power of it surrounding me.

I didn't expect David to touch me, so the heavy warmth of his hands on my shoulders made me tense up before I turned to face him. I was hoping that meant I was forgiven, but I could see in his eyes that I wasn't. He was fully in human mode, walled off from me, but I could sense the power in him, too.

'Why'd you tell her?' he asked me. His hands stayed on my shoulders for a few seconds, then travelled up to cup my face with heat.

I thought of Rahel. 'Because it's the only choice I've had this whole trip that's really my own. I need to trust somebody.'

'Then trust me.'

'I do.' I looked up into his eyes and wished *he* trusted *me* – I could feel that reserve in him again, that doubt. 'I need help, David. You know that. If I can't get to Lewis – if he can't or won't let me get to him – I need help to fight off whatever's after me. Whether that's Marion, or some other bastard I don't even know...I can't do it alone.' And after it was out, I knew how that sounded.

'Is that what you are?' he asked. 'Alone?'

I can be a real bitch sometimes, without even meaning to. He let me go, stepped back to minimum safe distance, and shoved his hands in the pockets of his long olive coat.

'So it's you and Star against the world,' he said.

'That how it's going to be? Maybe she can even provide a Djinn for you. One that you don't know, so it won't be like eating your own pet dog.'

'Don't say that, dammit. I'm trying to change the rules of the game. I *have* to. The deck's stacked against us.'

'I already changed the rules. Look how much good it's done.'

Apparently, Djinn were capable of morning-after regrets, too. 'Fine. New rules. Rule number one: Let me do this my way. You've been herding me from one place to another ever since I left Westchester. You've been trying to tell me what to do, when to do it. And I can't live that way, David. I need to—'

'To what?' He glared at me, and I saw orange sparks flicker in his eyes. 'To make yourself a target? Tell the world you have the Demon Mark? Trust your *friend* to protect you?'

I watched his eyes. 'You don't like her.'

He stepped toward me, intimate and aggressive. 'I don't *trust* her. I don't trust *anybody* with your life.'

'Not even me?'

He growled in the back of his throat and stalked off toward the convenience store, where Star was paying for a stack of bottled water and portable calories. She was laughing with the cashier about something, but when she turned to wave at me, I saw the cashier watching her, studying her scars.

Everybody did. She had to know that, had to feel it all the time. She had to resent it, even if she never showed it on the surface. *God*. Could I have managed that? No. Never.

She hip-bopped the door open and came out with her armload of goodies. I grabbed some that were toppling and looked over her shoulder. The cashier was staring.

'Is he checking me out?' she asked.

'Uh-huh.' I didn't tell her the look wasn't so much admiration as there-but-for-the-grace-of-God fascination.

Star gave me her two-sided comedy-tragedy smile. 'I'm telling you, *chica*, guys dig scars. Makes 'em think I'm tough.'

I opened the passenger door and dumped the load in David's seat. Let him sort it out. 'News flash, babe, you are tough. Toughest girl I ever met.'

'Damn straight.' She offered me a fist. I tapped it. She raised her voice for David. 'Yo, boy, let's motor!'

He was watching the horizon. Clouds were creeping out there, doing something stealthy that sounded like barely more than a low mutter in Oversight. Too far off to concern us yet, but it was definitely my old friend the storm, coming back for more. The wind belled out his coat and snapped it behind him. I walked over.

'When she says *boy*, I think she means you,' I said. He squinted into the distance behind his glasses.

'I got the point.'

'And?'

He gave me a long, wordless look, then went back to the Land Rover, picked up the water and fast food, and sat himself in the passenger side. I climbed into the back. As Star shut the door, she looked quickly at David, then at me.

'Don't mean to get in the middle, but is there something I should know?' she asked.

'No.' We both said it instantly, simultaneously. It couldn't have been more obvious we were lying.

'O...k.' She put the Land Rover in gear and rolled the big boat out to the freeway. 'You down with my plan?'

'Star, I have no idea what plan you're talking about.'

She accelerated the truck and slid smoothly in between a red rollover-prone SUV and a station wagon held together with duct tape and baling wire. 'The one where I save your ass, babe.'

'I'm still waiting for a plan. That's an outcome.'

'Picky, picky... OK, here's the deal. I have a source in Norman who can put us in touch with an honest-to-God masterless Djinn. You know, the kind running around, ready to be claimed. Sound good to you?'

I didn't dare look at David. He handed me a water bottle, and I cracked the plastic ring and sucked down lukewarm liquid. It tasted like sweat, but my body was shiveringly grateful.

'Sure,' I said. 'Sounds fabulous.'

Norman, Oklahoma, was just twenty miles from Oklahoma City proper, but Star was making caution her new religion; we drove just about every cowpath and haypicker road in the county, watching for any sign Marion or her folks were on to us. Nothing. By the time we exited I-35 and crossed into Norman's city limits, it was getting close to sundown, and the burritos and bottled water were just a fond, gut-rumbling memory.

Norman's an old town, a strange mixture of pre-war buildings and hyper new neon. The local college ensured a steady parade of coffee shops, clothing boutiques, used CD emporiums, and bookstores.

'Who's your source?' David asked. He upended his water and drained the last few drops from blue plastic; I wondered if he was really thirsty, if he even really felt such mundane things as hunger and thirst. He'd eaten with me that first afternoon, I remembered. And in the diner. Maybe he was more flesh than spirit, after all. And hey, sex? Pretty much of the flesh.

'Excuse me?' Star asked.

'Your source. The one who told you about the Djinn.'

'Friend,' she said, which was no more illuminating than anything else she'd said for the past two hours. 'Which is all you need to know, seeing as how you're not in the Wardens.' She reached out and passed her hand over his. No glyphs lit up on his palms. 'Speaking of which, Jo, you owe me an explanation about how you and this cutie got together.'

She gave him a look that reminded me Star wasn't all fun and games; she'd once been a Warden, tough and very strong. Even if she didn't have full command of her power anymore, she could be dangerous. And focused.

'Joanne told me.' David pointed a thumb back over the seat at me. 'Not that I believe any of this, anyway. But it makes a good story.'

'Yeah?' Star's trademark smile flashed. 'You planning to write it up, print it in the newspaper?'

'More like the tabloids.'

'Makes sense. So why do you care who told me about the Djinn?'

'I don't,' he said, and shrugged, and pulled a book from the pocket of his coat. Nothing I recognised. The cover had a black-and-yellow road sign blazed on the cover; when I squinted, I saw it read BE CAREFUL.

Jesus, he was tempting fate, doing that in front of her.

The cover shifted again, into a Patricia Cornwell mystery, and he opened it to a dog-eared page and appeared to forget all about me.

Star was watching me in the rearview mirror. 'You heard about Lewis taking the Djinn, right? Three of 'em? When he bugged out?'

'I heard.'

'Well, rumour has it he let at least one of them go. It's just a matter of tracking him down, that's all. And I've got just the girl to do it.' She hadn't looked away. It was a little eerie, actually. Dark, dark eyes, pupils fading into irises. 'Once you have Lewis, what then?'

'Then he helps me figure out how to get this thing out of me.'

Her eyebrows slowly rose. 'Yeah? You really think he knows how?'

'Sure.' I was lying my ass off, mostly to myself, but it felt better than the uncertainty of the truth. 'If anybody does, he does.'

'OK, stupid question. What I meant to ask is, why would he? You got something special going with him?'

Oh, that was a subject I really didn't want to dig into, not with David sitting in the passenger seat, thumbing blandly through a book. Star didn't seem to care. She started to smile, but her eyes were going cold.

'Or you got something *else* going with him? You on some undercover mission, *chica*?'

'Yeah, sure,' I shrugged. 'Don't ask, don't tell.'

I meant it as a joke, and I wasn't prepared for the flash of sheer fury in her eyes. 'Fine,' she said. 'Keep your little secrets.'

'I don't have any secrets.' As soon as the words came out of my mouth, I realised I'd lied to her. Effortlessly. Without a second thought. And I didn't even know why, except that a yellow danger sign kept flashing into my head. I'd chosen to trust Star. I just...

...couldn't trust her.

She drove down Main Street, past shops just lightning up against the darkness...grocery stores...gas stations...incongruously, a condom shop. The Burger King on the corner was doing a brisk business in robbing college students of their lunch money. On the other side of the narrow street, gracious Plantation-style homes with Doric columns put on a brave front that the South would rise again.

She slowed and turned into a strip-mall parking lot pretty much identical to the six others we'd passed, and pulled the Land Rover into a parking space barely able to stretch to fit it. I squinted up at the sign, which hadn't yet been turned on against the falling darkness: BALL'S BOOKS.

It looked like exactly what it was: a used

bookstore, and not the corporate, regimented kind – the kind that conformed to the whim of an owner. I liked it immediately, but there was still a cold cramp in my stomach, and I couldn't think exactly how I was going to get out of this. More important, how I'd get David out of this.

I grabbed his coat sleeve as Estrella limped away, pulled him down for a whisper. 'Take a walk.'

'Where?' he asked mildly.

'Why should I care? I don't want you anywhere near her if she's going to—'

His hand covered mine, and some of his human disguise fell away; his eyes turned burning, swirling bronze, and I felt his heat pour into me and drive out the chill. His smile, though, was all guy. All David.

'It won't matter,' he said. 'If she can find me at all, it doesn't matter where I go. If you're so worried about me, there's something you can do to stop it.'

I knew what he meant. 'I'm not claiming you.'

He shrugged and took his hand away. 'Then I'll take my chances.'

Stubborn, infuriating...

Star tapped on the store window and gestured. David moved to the door and held it open for me, head down. I fought an impulse to kick him in the shins. As I walked past, he murmured, 'No matter what happens, you always have a choice.'

We stepped into cool silence and the smell of old

paper. To the right was a wall of corkboard packed with cards and papers of every description, no rhyme or reason to it that I could see; some advertised massages, some were photocopies of newspaper cartoons, some were just plain mystifying. David stepped around her and began to look through books – I thought at first he was stalling for time, but his interest in the contents of the racks seemed genuine. He really did love reading, after all. And I guess even Djinn need a hobby.

'Hey, Star,' said a voice from behind me. I turned to see a youngish woman sitting behind a table – well away from the cash register and counter – surrounded by books, a coffeemaker, and a butterscotch calico cat. She had brown hair cut in a shag and watchful cool eyes that struck me as capable and observant. 'New romances in – you want to look through the boxes?'

'Not today, thanks, Cathy.' Star exchanged what appeared to be a significant look with the woman. 'I need the book.'

If that seemed odd, asking for 'the' book in a store littered with them, the woman clearly didn't think so; she looked spooked, not confused. 'I thought we were done with that.'

'Almost,' Star said. She held out her hand, half-plea, half-demand. 'Come on, Cathy, just this once.'

Cathy shook her head, got up, and walked to the

back of the store. She opened a door marked NO ADMITTANCE.

'The book?' I asked Star. She shrugged, still watching the open door at the back.

'Took me years to track it down,' she said. 'Cathy finally bought it off the Internet for me. I told her she could have it when I was done with it.'

'What is it?'

Star smiled that lopsided smile. It wasn't comforting this time. 'It's a surprise. You'll see.'

Things thumped, back there. Cathy returned carrying a limp cardboard box, top closed, that looked like it weighed a considerable amount. She dropped it down on the desk and folded back the stained box wings.

'You're sure?' she asked. That silent communication again between them was nothing I could interpret. I didn't know Cathy Ball, but I felt like I should; on an impulse, I reached out and passed my hand over hers.

Glyphs shimmered, blue and silver. A Weather Warden. She looked up sharply and met my eyes; I smiled and showed her my matching set. Nothing eased in her body language. 'Star?' she said. 'You know I don't like other Wardens around here.'

I hadn't been expecting a hug, but this was a bit much; we're generally a pretty chummy group.

'Sorry,' Star said, not sounding too sorry at all. 'She's a friend. She needs our help.'

Cathy shot a look toward David, clearly asking the question. 'No,' I said. 'He's not. What've you got against other Wardens, anyway?'

'Nothing,' Cathy said, which vibrated like a lie all along my nerves. 'It's just that they're trouble. Bunch of power-hungry, crazy, egotistical jerks, generally. I like peace and quiet.' Her eyes narrowed at me. 'Take that business in Oklahoma City today. You wouldn't believe what a mess that was. The aetheric was screwed up from here to Kansas, all the way over to Phoenix. Took hours just to get the temperature variances back to normal.'

I threw a *save me!* look at Star, who was busy taking a huge leather-bound book out of the cardboard box and shaking off white packing peanuts. She ignored me, shoved the box off to thump on the floor, and eased the book down to the desk on top of a mound of category romances.

The cat that had been slinking inquisitively around Cathy's plate of doughnuts hissed around and skittered away, shooting past David into the farthest corner of the store. David had paused with the new Stephen King novel in his hands, staring at the book that Star had laid out, and I saw cinders of gold and bronze catch fire in his eyes. It was the real deal; I could see that from the intensely blank expression on his face.

'Star,' I said, 'Look, maybe this isn't the right time. I'm really tired, I'm starved – let's take this thing with us, get something to eat, maybe have a good night's sleep and talk it over. I'm trashed. Really.'

She flipped open pages that crackled like vellum. 'This won't take long.'

That was what I was afraid of. Cathy Ball sat back down in her chair, picked up a pen, and wrote something down in a ledger, but she couldn't take her eyes off Star for very long. I wondered what kind of history there was between them, because I could have sworn that the woman looked...scared. Of Star. Who didn't have a mean bone in her body.

'I'll need your Djinn,' Star said without looking up.

Cathy put the pen down. 'No,' she said. 'Not after last time.'

'I won't hurt her.'

'I said no, Star.'

Star looked up, finally, and I wasn't in the right angle to see her face, but I did see Cathy's. It went pale.

'*Chica*,' Star murmured, 'don't make me get all cranky with you.'

Cathy's lips pressed into a thin line, and a frown grooved between her brows, but she reached into the desk drawer and came out with a tiny little glass perfume bottle, one of those little sample sizes. She tossed it across the desk to Star, who caught it right-handed.

'I'll be in the back,' Cathy said.

Star didn't watch her go; she unscrewed the lid of the perfume bottle. No visible result, but I felt a surge of *something* behind me.

'Can I help you?' the Djinn asked. I turned to see her standing at an angle between me and Star, watching us both with bright, neon-blue eyes.

She was a child. Or at least she looked like she was no older than fourteen – dressed in a pale blue dress with a white apron. Long, long blond hair, straight, held back with an *Alice in Wonderland* blue band. Her heart-shaped face was sweet and innocent and straight out of Lewis Carroll.

When she looked at me, she frowned and wrinkled her nose. I knew she could smell the Mark. She looked from me to David, still standing like a statue in the general fiction section, but there was nothing to show she recognised who or what he was. She focused back on Star.

'Hey, Alice,' Star said, and held out the book. 'Hold this.'

Alice didn't move. She didn't resist, but she didn't comply. Star muttered Spanish curses under her breath and yelled Cathy's name. Twice. Cathy finally came to the NO ADMITTANCE door and looked out.

'Tell her to obey me,' Star said. Cathy rubbed her forehead.

'Do what she wants,' she said wearily. 'Three times only.'

Alice nodded. I was glad, for Alice's sake, that Cathy had put a limit on compliance.

'Hold this,' Star said again. Alice extended her arms and took the book from Star's hands. There was something about it that the Djinn didn't like; I could see it in the widening of her eyes, but Alice didn't – couldn't – protest. Star flipped pages and found what she was looking for, then gestured to me. I took a step closer and stopped when the girl looked at me with those bright, empty, desolate eyes.

'Here,' Star said as she grabbed my wrist and pulled me closer, next to her. 'Read this out loud.'

'What is it?' My legs were trembling, my heart pounding. The adrenaline was making my Demon Mark hiss and stretch inside me, and that only made my heart race faster, as if it wanted to escape.

'Hey, you want to fix this thing or not? 'Cause *chica*, the Demon Mark is nothing to screw around with. You let it get control of you, and you won't be the same.'

I looked down at the words, not words at all, some kind of symbols, and I started to tell her I didn't know what they meant, but something clicked in my head and I did know, I understood, I could hear the way the words were supposed to sound, taste the heavy flavour of them on my tongue. There was power in this thing. Earth power. Maybe fire. Certainly nothing I could control, though.

The words waited, *wanted* to be spoken. I opened my mouth, closed it, opened it again and heard the first syllable whispering and gathering strength and echoing in the sounding bell of my mind.

'Say it,' Star whispered. I felt her warm breath on my ear. 'It has to be you, *chica*, I can't do it for you.'

The Djinn, Alice. That was where this power was flowing from. She was holding the book, and the book drew power from her...I wondered if it hurt her. Her eyes were huge, doll-like, empty of emotion. Empty of fear. Her arms were shaking, as if the book were heavier than the world.

I hadn't heard him walk up to me, but now David was there, at the edge of my vision, almost glittering with intensity. He was still in human disguise, human form, but how much longer? How long until the words echoing in my head forced him to reveal himself?

I reached out, took the book from the Djinn's arms, and slammed it closed with a sound like thunder. The Djinn stumbled backwards, or floated; she looked drained and skeletal for a few seconds, then rebuilt herself into the sweet-faced little refugee from beyond the looking glass.

'No,' I said. I looked at Star and saw she was

staring at me as if she'd never seen me before, as if I'd grown two heads and goat feet. 'This is wrong, Star. I can feel it.'

'Wrong,' she repeated slowly. She reached out and put her hand over the place the Demon Mark had left its black scorching tattoo on my breast. 'And this isn't?'

'That wasn't my choice.' I hefted the heavy book. It smelt faintly rotten, felt damp and unclean. '*This* is. And I'm not doing it.'

Her eyes went flat and opaque, like Mayan flint. 'You can't keep it,' she said, and there was something terrible in her voice, like blood and lightning. 'I can't let you keep it, Jo.'

Her face was changing. Melting. *Becoming beautiful* the way she'd been back before Yellowstone. Taking on a kind of lush, lustrous glow that was too perfect, even for an airbrushed magazine model. An *inhuman* beauty.

'You don't deserve it,' she said. I could hear an echo in her voice now of something stirring inside me. '*I* deserve it. It chose *me*. I can't let you have it, Jo, not again. You've always been prettier and smarter and more powerful, and *you can't have this*!'

Ah, God, no, no, no. Not *Star*.

I remembered something Lewis had told me. There's a Demon trying to come through. Trying to touch one of us.

It had tried to touch Star. It must have succeeded,

in the end. That was how she repaired her fractured core, how she looked so lustrous and beautiful.

The Demon had given her what she wanted, just as mine had given Bad Bob everything he desired.

Except I couldn't sense a Mark on Star. I looked wildly at David, who was standing just a few feet away.

'She doesn't have one,' he told me. 'No Mark.'

'No,' she said. 'Not anymore. *He* took it away from me.' Star bared her teeth and didn't look so beautiful anymore. There was so much rage in her, so much despair. And yet, she was still Star. The same lovely, smart, smart-mouthed girl I loved.

She tore her gaze away from David and made an effort to pretend it was all normal again. 'I tried to make you listen, but you just kept coming. You knew, didn't you? You knew all about what was happening here. Had to be the *hero*. Had to *save* me.' Her pretty mouth twisted into something bitter and ugly. 'Barely saved yourself, back there in that stupid mall. Some great hero.'

Star. All this time I'd been thinking it was someone else, some invisible enemy. But my enemy had been right in plain sight. Jesus, I told her I was coming. No wonder she'd known where I was, how to track me. I'd made it simple.

'Feeling betrayed?' she asked. She stepped closer. 'Join the club, girlfriend. Not like you didn't betray me first.'

'Life sucks,' I said. Star took the book from my hands.

'Then you die,' she finished gravely. She flicked her eyes at the blond-haired Djinn, standing quietly with her hands clasped like a good little schoolgirl. 'When I give you the signal, I want you to transport me back to my house, understand? Me and whatever I'm holding in my hands.'

The book was in Star's hands. I wondered how I was going to get it away from her. Star didn't give me time to figure it out. She gave me a funny little half-smile.

'Third request,' she said. 'Alice, take the Demon Mark from my friend.'

I shouted a no, but Alice was already moving, reaching out for me and I couldn't move backwards fast enough. I tripped over a threadbare Persian carpet and fell against a table as her small pale hand reached out toward me...

...and David intercepted her, stiff-armed her back. Alice flinched from him and tried to come around the other side. David put himself in the middle and held her off. Star, standing off to the side, quietly watching, said nothing at all.

'Call her off!' I ordered. Star raised her hands and let them fall. 'Star, dammit, call her off. This is crazy!'

'Can't,' she said. 'Three wishes. I'm out of here, babe. Better let it happen.'

She waved to Alice, and instantly disappeared. With the book.

I yelled at David to hold Alice and I darted for the NO ADMITTANCE door at the back, where Cathy had gone. A blur streaked toward me, blue and white, and I slammed the door against it and stumbled back into boxes that tumbled over and spilt gaudy romance novels to the floor in a spray of heaving breasts and manly thews. I slipped on one and bruised my knee so hard, I saw red pulsing dots.

Alice blew through the door like it wasn't even there and reached out for me, and even while she did, I saw the terror in her eyes, the horror, the desperation. She knew what this meant. Eternal torment for her. And yet…she had no choice.

A blur of hot bronze collided with her and sent her off course, and I managed to clamber back to my feet and run down the narrow, dusty hallway. Pretty much useless, running, but I was out of options.

No. Wait. I wasn't. I sucked down gulps of air and tried to focus around the panic that was jackhammering my heart.

Alice got free of David again and flashed toward me. I stopped, turned, and put out my hands as if I might grab her in turn…

…and called the wind.

It blew down the narrow corridor, swirling,

ripping, tearing covers and ripping books into blizzards, hit Alice and tumbled her helplessly backwards. David, too. They both dropped from vapour into heavier flesh, but I just called more power, whipped the wind faster. The walls creaked around me, and the far door blew open with a splintering crash, spilling hurricane forces out into the bookstore where racks blew over and paperbacks were sent flying.

In my chest, something ignited. Sent feeders of blackness threading through my aching body.

I couldn't control it anymore. The wind ripped free of me, became wild and alive and dark, became a lover whispering over me, stroking my hair and pressing against me like a living thing.

David was screaming something into the wind at me. Telling me something I didn't want to hear. Something about the Demon Mark. It didn't matter. Not anymore. I could keep him away, could blow sweet little Alice back to Wonderland, could reduce this miserable little store to sticks and splinters. And I wanted to. God, I wanted all this filth to go away, quit clinging to me, quit holding me back from what I was becoming. Sticks and splinters, that was so easy. Bodies in the way? Hamburger. Gobbets of flesh, ground up between steel and stone.

Somebody was trying to stop me. They weren't doing very well, but they were trying. I opened my eyes and squinted through flying debris and saw someone standing against the wall, holding on to an iron bar for dear life. Her short brown hair blew out like a thistle, crackling with static and potential energy.

Cathy Ball. I blinked and went up into Oversight. She was scared, streaked in blacks and greys and hot liquid yellows, but she was fighting me.

I didn't have to stop. It would have been easy not to. But looking at her, so small against all the power burning in me, against the black writhing nest of the Demon Mark that was feeding and consuming and growing... I knew I *had* to try.

I let the wind fall. Alice, single-minded as ritual demanded, lunged for me.

'Stop!' Cathy commanded her, and she did, as suddenly as if physics had no meaning for her. Frozen in time.

'Tell her not to take the Mark,' I said. Cathy's face went pallid. 'Tell her.'

'Don't take the Mark,' she whispered. Alice relaxed, and the blue eyes filled up with emotion again – resentment, fear, relief, anguish. All hidden the instant she turned back to her master.

It didn't take Cathy long to get a handle on what was going on, or what we were all risking. She glanced at David just once, then focused on me and said, 'Get your Demon Marked ass out of my store.'

I swallowed a spark of anger. 'I'll pay for—'

'You won't do a goddamned thing except get the hell *gone!*' she shouted, and her face flushed red with the release of tension and fear. I didn't try to apologise. There was no apologising for what I'd done, or what I'd almost done, or what had almost been done to her Djinn.

Cathy watched me walk to the splintered, gaping door, out into the ruined bookstore. As I stumbled over broken racks and scattered books, I heard her say to her Djinn in a disgusted, shaking voice, 'Help me clean this mess up, will you?'

I made it outside before the panic attack hit me.

Well, this was about as low as I could go. On my hands and knees, shivering, gasping, crying like a baby. My whole body ached from the force of it, the need to get rid of the *thing* inside me and – worse – the horrible feeling of betrayal and grief.

Star wasn't who I thought. Maybe she hadn't ever been the person I'd thought she was. All this time I'd been believing in her, in our strong and unshakeable friendship, and for all I knew, that had all been a lie, too.

Star had made a deal, quite literally, with the Devil. Like Bad Bob, she'd opened herself, and something had crawled inside...and nobody, not even me, had known the difference.

I felt David's hands on my shoulders and leant back against him. So much comfort in his touch, and I didn't even know *why*. Why I trusted him, when I knew better… They'd all betrayed me, even Lewis. He'd told me to come here, but where the hell was he when I needed him? I'd trusted Star. I'd trusted Bad Bob.

How could I ever trust David? I barely *knew* him.

'Get up,' he said, and helped me to my feet. 'You have to go. Quickly.'

I couldn't. It was done, it was over, there wasn't anything left in me.

He half pushed, half carried me to the Land Rover. As he did, the timer on the outside sign for Ball's Books clicked on and lit us up in a cool yellow glow.

Amazingly, from the street, you couldn't tell a thing had happened inside the store. The plate glass windows were intact, and the front part of the store still looked normal.

'I'm not going anywhere,' I said numbly. David opened the door of the Land Rover.

'Yes, you are,' he said. 'I want you to drive. Go as far and as fast as you can. Don't let anything stop you. If Lewis is still out here, he'll find you.' He captured my face between those large, warm hands. '*Jo. Please. Last chance. Let me take the Mark.*'

'No,' I whispered. 'I can't. Please don't ask me again.'

'I won't.' He looked up at a flash of lightning. 'You have to go. *Now*.'

I tasted the tang of ozone, smelt the hot burn on the air. Power calls to power. I'd stirred up the aetheric, and that would help the storm that was hunting me. He was right. I had to go. If I stayed here, innocent people would suffer.

'What about you?' I asked. 'David?' I took his hands and held them tight. 'You're coming with me?'

The look on his face. If I'd ever had any doubt about how deeply Djinn could feel... 'I can't. She knows what I am, and she has the book. If you won't claim me—'

'She will,' I finished, and felt my skin pebble into gooseflesh at the idea. 'No. You can't let that happen.'

He smiled at me, very slightly, and ran his thumb across my lips. 'I can't prevent it.'

I could feel the nightmare closing in on me, clocks ticking, hearts racing, sands running out. I was dying and living and running all at once, and there was a storm inside me, black with thunder, white with lightning, and rain crawled in my veins.

He put his hand over the Mark. It didn't help. The storm didn't stop. Even when he kissed me – a long, gentle, lingering kiss that had the taste of good-bye.

'Remember me,' he whispered, with his lips still touching mine. 'No matter what happens.'

I felt him melt away like mist, and when I

reached out to touch his face, it was gone; there was nothing but the memory of him in my fingers and the taste of him burning my lips.

I screamed and screamed and screamed into the wind, but he didn't come back.

I drove the Land Rover out of town at high speed, not caring if anyone saw me; not caring about much of anything, really. Star would find me. Marion would find me. Hell, it really didn't matter *who* found me anymore, because it was all coming apart, I was coming apart, and David was *gone*.

Something flickered at the corner of my eye as I made the turn onto I-35, heading south for the Texas border. I had a stowaway in the passenger seat. *Unseeable is easier than invisible*, David had told me.

I reached over and grabbed Rahel by the wrist without looking at her, and when I turned my head, she faded into view, sunshine yellow still neon-bright and unnaturally stylish in the dashboard lights.

'I told you, you're a fool,' she said. 'Let go of my arm, Snow White.'

'I can hurt you,' I said. It was true. The Demon Mark had braided into me so deeply now that I had the power, power to smash and flatten and hurt even a Djinn. When David had vanished, the last reason I had to resist that power was gone.

What was the point of being human, anyway? To be hurt? To be abused? Screw it. I was done with that.

Rahel took me seriously, which was gratifying. 'Why would you? I'm not your enemy.'

'Baby, I'm no longer sure *who* my enemies are. My friends, either.'

She laughed. It was a rich Swiss chocolate kind of sound, full of delight. 'Well, you're learning.'

'Whose Djinn are you?'

She shook her finger at me, still smiling. 'No, no, not important, sweet one. We're past all that now. You know your enemy. It's time to fight.'

'Fight *what*?' I snarled. 'The Demon Mark? Star? Jesus, what exactly do you expect me to do? I never wanted any of this, you know. I just want—'

I just wanted David. I wanted that perfect night of peace. I wanted love with so much intensity, it brought tears to my eyes. *Oh, Star*. My whole soul mourned for the girl I'd known, the one I'd saved, the one I'd lost. It had happened by inches and years, and I'd never even noticed. But more than that, I mourned for *me*...for the me who had been destroyed when Bad Bob ripped away my sense of who I was in this world.

I let go of Rahel and put both hands back on the wheel. 'Leave me alone.'

She wasn't laughing now, or smiling, either. Whatever I'd expected to see in those hot yellow eyes, it wasn't compassion. 'The thing about being alone?' she said softly. 'So many choices. So many possibilities.'

'Yeah, I'm fucking blessed. Want to drop me a clue about what to do next?'

She shrugged. 'Whatever I tell you, you will not do it. Why should I burden you with advice for you to doubt and pick at like an unhealed sore?'

'Well, *that's* pretty.'

She leant back, put one foot up on the dashboard, and examined her neon-yellow toenails, which were displayed to advantage by a lovely pair of designer sandals in – of course – neon yellow. 'I'm no one's Djinn, Child of Demons. As you should know by now.'

'You're like David.' Saying his name hurt, and hurt, and hurt, turning a razor blade in the marrow of my bones.

She shot me a narrow, amused look, and her black cornrows rustled over her shoulders as she shook her head. 'Nothing like David, in fact. Nor do we share lineage.'

'You both belonged to Lewis, and you're still trying to protect him, wherever he is.'

She shook her head and sighed. She stroked her fingernails over her long, shapely toes, and where they touched, silver rings took form and glittered.

She examined the effect critically, cocking her head to one side. 'You understand nothing. It amazes me, still. Lewis did not free David. *You* did.'

I did? No way. No...

My heart thumped hard and stuttered.

Oh, God.

I had been on my knees in Bad Bob's house, fighting for my life... I had taken hold of an ancient wine bottle...and I'd smashed it into pieces.

Bad Bob's wine bottle.

Bad Bob's *Djinn*.

When we were fighting at the hotel, David had said, *I've tried to help you, I've tried to make up for*...for holding me down at Bob's order. For ripping away my defences and putting the Demon Mark inside me, a kind of rape that could never heal, could never stop.

That was why he'd shadowed me. Why he'd stayed with me. Why he'd dared me, begged me, and nearly forced me to allow him to take the Mark.

Because he'd done this thing to me in the first place.

I'd been waiting for him to betray me all this time, and the truth was, he'd done it from the very first second. He'd lied to me, kept lying, was *still* lying about it.

I swallowed a mouthful of acid and bitter truth. 'So he sent you in his place.'

She sniffed. 'Hardly. I have other...responsibilities.'

'Tell me, was I ever even close? Lewis's Djinn told

me to come here in the first place, or was that a lie, too?'

'The Djinn in Westchester once belonged to Lewis, it is true,' Rahel said. 'Freed, he serves him still. As do I. But we are limited in what we know, and what we can do.'

She stared hard at her toenails, then out at the road unrolling in the headlights.

Sunset was leaving the west, leaving a gorgeous trailing band of royal blue edged with early night, sprinkled with new stars. Somewhere the storm was looking for me, and I knew it would find me, if the others didn't find me first.

'So if he didn't lie to me, Lewis *did* come to Oklahoma.'

'Yes. As I told you.'

'So where is he now? And why isn't he helping me?'

She sighed, put-upon, just like the human being she almost resembled. 'Fool. You have everything at hand, and still you don't read the signs. Star has used the book before, yes? To claim a Djinn, or try to do so. Lewis came to stop her.'

I realised, with a hot jolt, that Star had been baiting me, trying to see if I knew where Lewis was, and if I'd come to help him stop her.

'Then where is he?' I asked. Rahel shook her head.

'You already know.'

And I did. Nothing else made sense. 'Star. Star has Lewis.'

Rahel beamed at me as if I'd finally taken my first toddling steps. 'See? You're not such a fool after all.'

Chapter Five

Extremely violent weather is expected in and around the Oklahoma City area for the next few hours, with hail and tornadoes possible. In the event of a tornado emergency, take cover immediately.

Star had Lewis. As in, had Lewis *prisoner*.

The words 'well and truly screwed' skipped through my mind, strewing flowers in their path.

'Can you grant wishes?' I asked Rahel bluntly. She looked faintly insulted. 'Well? Can you?'

'Please. Don't be ridiculous.'

'Ritual third. Can you?'

She smiled thinly. 'Can I what?'

'Grant wishes.'

'Thank you for playing, but you must put it in the form of a—'

'Question, I know. Skip the rules and just tell me, OK? I'm not getting any less demonic here.'

That zapped the fun out of her. 'If I wished.'

'Well, I wish you would all just stop *screwing with me!*' I put all my frustration and anger and terror into the scream, and even Rahel looked disturbed. She took her foot off the dashboard and sat up straight, staring at me. 'Look, I've done *nothing*, OK? I got screwed by Bad Bob—' *And David, oh, God,* '—and by you and by Star and now you're telling me the one man I was counting on to save my ass is in bigger trouble than I am. Please. Kill me now.'

'Stop the car,' she said.

'It's not a car. It's an SUV.' I had a bad thought. 'That "Kill me now", that was metaphorical...'

Her turn to bellow, and believe me, the bellow of a Djinn makes my pissant outburst look like an undernourished peep.

I swerved off the freeway. Luckily, there was an off-ramp about twenty feet ahead to the two-way service road; I bumped over hillocks and got tires back on tarmac, and exited with something like control.

'What the hell?' I asked. Rahel was looking behind us. There was a reddish glow gathering back there.

'Out,' Rahel ordered.

'Out's not such a good idea. *Driving* is a good idea—'

'Get out!' This was a yell, not an order, and

before I could even think about responding, she was out of the car, yanking the driver's-side door open. She dragged me over the centre console and leather seat and out onto gravel, and she kept dragging me, faster than I could get my feet moving. When she paused for a fraction of a second, I tried to get my balance, but then I was weightless, flying, and I had no idea how I could do that in the real world, but there were things moving so fast and a huge pressure at my back...

...and then I was down, flat on the ground, tasting blood and feeling numb. I rolled over and saw the fireball belching orange and black into the sky, and for a blank second, I didn't even connect it to the Land Rover. Not that there was much left of the Land Rover, and it for damn sure wasn't white anymore. Four melting tires, crisping paint, an interior that looked like a glimpse into a nuclear furnace.

Rahel was standing, untouched, a few feet away, staring at the inferno. Djinn were creatures of fire, they said. She glowed like a torch, beautiful, scary, sexy, and I could feel the heat from where I was standing.

Something was forming out of the wreckage of the fire and smoke. Something—

Something bad.

She turned her head, and her eyes were enormous, full of power and fury, the colour of boiling gold. In an eerily practical voice, she said, 'You need to run now.'

'What is it?' I scrambled up without much regard for bruises and cuts. Her face was calm and set.

'Just *run!*'

She didn't waste any more breath arguing with me. She shoved, I stumbled, almost fell, and then momentum and the desire to put distance between my fragile human self and what was coming out of that fireball took over, and I started to run.

I vaulted over the sagging barbed wire fence and fell into thick underbrush, most of it thorny. I thrashed through it with the strength of panic. Like Lot's wife, I looked back, and I saw that the fire from the truck was inexplicably looping out in a jet, streaking straight for Rahel. It hit her with so much force, I saw her yellow coat blow back like bird's wings, and then she was engulfed.

I couldn't stop. The underbrush was dry, all it would take would be a casual brush from that elemental *thing* that had erupted out of the Rover and I'd be nothing but charcoal and dental records. It was hard to work the weather in a panic, and I could feel things blocking me, forces in the aetheric that had control of the air, the water, the ground under my feet, the fire behind me—

I broke through the underbrush and found myself in a ploughed field. Neat dark-brown rows of earth, jewel-green seedlings just pushing out of the soil. A farmhouse sat at the far end, lit up like a kitschy craft fair painting. On the other side of the held, a grassy fenced area with brown, placid cows.

And a round metal stock tank for water.

I made for the fence, jumped it, felt air burning in my lungs and didn't know if it was the fire coming for me or an overload of panic. I fell into the cow pasture. As I rolled back to my feet, I got a look back.

The underbrush was burning. No sign of Rahel. There was nothing left of the Land Rover but a sizzling metal skeleton.

I ran for the stock tank. Cows trotted out of my way, amiably uncertain, and I hoped they wouldn't end the day as barbecue, but I couldn't do anything about that just now. I spared a look over my shoulder.

Fire boiled out of the underbrush in a straight line, burning a path straight for me. It hit the fence and blew a blackened hole in it.

Somehow, I knew – felt – it was Star.

I forced myself faster, faster, got both feet on the ground and jumped.

I dived into the ice-cold water of the stock tank and found the slimy metal bottom. My skin took the shock hard, and it was all I could do not to gasp in a big drowning breath, but I held on, and the icy slap of it wore off in seconds, leaving me numbed.

Something hit the stock tank hard enough to

rattle through the metal, and I saw a brilliant flare of orange and white sheet across the water, felt the temperature go up several degrees, and the thought came to me that if it went on for long, I'd boil like a lobster in a pot. Quite a lot of deaths to choose from, all of a sudden – burning, drowning, boiling – none of them really attractive.

I sucked oxygen molecules out of the water and made a breathable bubble, got my lips into it and refilled. I crab-walked backwards to the farthest part of the tank from where the fire was cantered, and peered through algae-murked water to see the metal glowing on the other side. Pretty soon my stock tank was going to become a stockpot. Did I have a chance of getting to the surface and hauling myself out of the tank and making it all the way to – where? – before getting fried? No. No, I did not.

Mastery over air and water didn't mean a damn thing right now, except that I could probably keep breathing right up until my skin boiled off and my eyes popped. Maybe I would lose consciousness before that. I hoped so.

It got dark all of a sudden. I wondered if my eyes had failed, but then my brain slowly crawled to the conclusion that the fire had stopped.

Somebody had hold of my hair and yanked. It hurt. I opened my mouth and yelled, or tried to, but all I got was a lungful of murky water, and then I was coming out of the water and into chilled air and I was on the ground, my face in the dirt, vomiting out green ooze.

I sucked in air, coughed, and felt the linings of my lungs burn like they'd never be clean again. Could you die of disgust? I coughed until I was shaking and weak, smeared wet dirt all over my face, and rolled over to look around. Hard to tell if anything else had been baked or fried – it was too dark – but I didn't smell barbecue, and I could hear the cows mooing in panic at the far side of the pasture.

Rahel stood over me, fresh and neon as ever. She stared down at me and said, 'I'm out of patience, Child of Demons. Do you love him?'

I coughed again, wiped my mouth, and gasped, 'What?'

'*Him.*' She waved her hand, and David was standing in front of me. David in Djinn form, hot bronzes and golds flickering along his skin, pooling in his eyes. '*Do you love him?*'

'Yes!'

Rahel snapped her fingers again, and we were standing somewhere else. Or no…I could still feel the wind on my face, feel the uneven stumpy grass under me.

But what I saw was a cellar. Dark, stacked here and there with boxes. There was a wooden worktable against the far wall, and on it…

On it lay the book from Cathy Ball's store.

Estrella stepped from the shadows behind me. I

jumped out of the way, ending up next to the sheer primal heat of Rahel, and I was grateful for the warmth because this place was cold and my heart was getting colder.

I sat up. Rahel helped me to my feet.

Estrella went to the book and opened it.

'No,' I whispered, and looked at Rahel; her face was impassive, but her golden eyes glowed like jack-o'-lanterns. 'Stop her!'

'I can't,' she said. 'I can't interfere in the claiming process.'

'The fuck you can't! Hell, set her house on fire…blow it down…*anything!*'

She rounded on me, gripped both my arms with talons hard as steel. 'If I could stop her, don't you think I would? Do you think I'd waste my time chasing after a filthy corrupted little witch like *you?*' She shook me hard. '*You* stop her.'

I fell out of my body, zoomed up into Oversight, and hurtled myself toward Oklahoma City. Star's house was somewhere around here…Where was she? She wasn't in the aetheric, wasn't using her powers…needle in a haystack…other Wardens appearing and disappearing like sparks in a fire, but without getting close to them, I couldn't see which was which, couldn't *find* her. I rocketed down the lifeline back into my body and screamed at the Djinn. 'Show me where she is!'

'I don't know. I can see, but I no more know

where this is happening than you do. It's within your powers. Find her.'

I felt a blind, anguished surge of panic. Sure, I could find her, if I had time...if I didn't have the Demon Mark eating me from inside out...if Star herself *wanted* to be found. No, there was nothing I could do, nothing my powers could pull up that would help me now. I needed something else.

My hand brushed something hard and angular that had made a whopping bruise on my left hip. I dug in my pocket and came up with...

...a cell phone. *Star's* cell phone. I punched buttons, and it lit up like a Christmas tree. Memory...memory... I paged through numbers I didn't recognise, names I didn't know.

Stopped on one I did. Star had called home to check her messages.

'Here goes nothing,' I said, and hit the CONNECT button.

In Rahel's illusion, Star was standing there with the book in her hands, mouthing words. I might be too late...

...and then she looked up, irritated, with exactly the same expression I knew I got when the phone rang at dinner. She shook her head, shrugged it off, and went back to the book.

'Pick it up,' I whispered. 'Come on, Star, please. Answer the phone.'

On my end, the call went to voice mail. I hung up and redialled.

Star was reading the book. Lips moving.

There was a flash of intense blue-white light, and when it faded...

When it faded, David was standing with Star, facing her across the book. Frozen. Rahel spat out words I didn't know, but the vicious anger in them was universal.

Star handed him the book. He took it without any change of expression.

'Too late,' I whispered. The phone was still ringing, a dull buzz in my ear. 'Oh, God, no.'

'Not yet. She has not claimed him yet, only trapped him.' Still, Rahel didn't sound overly optimistic. She reached out with yellow-tipped claws toward David, then let her hand fall back to her side. 'He fights.'

He would, I knew. He'd fight to the limits of his ability, and beyond, to stay free. The same as I would.

Star smiled at him and reached over to pick up something lying on the corner of the worktable. She put it to her ear.

'*Digame*,' she said. I watched her lips move in the illusion and heard her voice over the phone.

'Don't do it, Star,' I blurted. 'Please. Let him go. We've been friends a long time – it has to count for something. Don't do this to him.'

She jolted in surprise and looked around the room where she was, taking in every corner, every shadow. As she turned, I saw that indescribably alien beauty in her again. The beauty a Demon had given her.

'Jo? Jesus, you're slippery. I figured you'd be dead by now. No can do, babe. I need him.'

'You don't!'

'I need him.'

'You don't even *have* the Mark anymore! You're free!'

That pretty, false face distorted in anger. 'Yeah, exactly. I'm *healed*. Well, that's just great, isn't it? Except I can't go back to what I was. Scarred. Crippled. *Useless*. I need this one, Jo. I need him to *live*.'

I remembered the incredible strength of the fire jetting across the field toward me. A thing like that didn't come cheaply. She was weakened, and she needed a fresh source of power.

She needed David.

'I love him, Star,' I said. 'Please. Please, don't.'

She laughed. The same laugh, the same sweet, happy laugh that had kept me sane all these years, reminded me there was a normal world and normal friends and the hope of something beyond the Wardens.

The same lying laugh.

She walked up to David and trailed her fingers

over his face, down his neck. I felt an overwhelming urge to bitch-slap her into next week. She tucked the phone between her ear and shoulder and flipped pages in the book he held. 'Let's say I know what – and who – you're talking about.'

'I'm not fucking around, Star. You either let him go, or I come and take him from you. Understand?'

She found what she was looking for. She looked down at the words for a few seconds, then stepped back.

'You have no idea,' she said. 'No idea what I've done, or how hard I worked. I was a fucking *cripple*, Jo. Ugly, maimed, burnt out. Even *Marion* thought I wasn't worth bothering about. I barely had enough power left to light a match.'

I swallowed my anger and tried to sound reasonable. 'But you got better.'

'Oh, yeah, I got better. No thanks to any of *them*.' She was smiling now, but it was a hot, tight smile that looked like it hurt. 'No thanks to *Lewis*. He left me looking like a Halloween fright mask, you know. I felt him healing me, but he didn't have the guts to take it all the way. Just like you.'

She put the phone against her chest and said something to David, but there was no sound in the illusion. David didn't – couldn't – answer. Star finally put the phone back to her ear.

'Got to go, Jo,' she said. 'Things to do, Djinn to claim.'

She hung up and tossed the phone down on the table. I screamed into the cell phone, but it was too late, too late, too late.

Estrella took a Mason jar down from a shelf and set it on the floor next to David's feet. I don't know why I kept looking, except that not looking would have been a betrayal of everything he'd shown me about honour and loyalty, about forgiveness and responsibility.

I read her lips as they moved.

Be thou bound to my service.

Oh, Star, no. Please.

Be thou bound to my service.

Please stop.

Be thou bound to my service.

I felt the David I'd known snuff out like a candle, his personality and presence obliterated by the bonding.

He was Star's.

His eyes shifted spectrums, became a dark, lightless brown.

She took the book away from him and put it down, and his gaze followed her with the unsettling attention and devotion he'd once given me.

'He's lost,' Rahel said. Her voice had turned ice cold, hard enough to cut. 'Trust him no more. He cannot go against her.'

She let the illusion snap to darkness. I felt my knees give way and sank down in the grass again. I rested my forehead against my braced knees.

Rahel's hand rested briefly on my shoulder. Comfort? I don't know. But it did give me strength. I fought off the weight of panic in my chest and blinked against tears. My face felt hot, my skin too tight.

'I don't understand,' I said. 'Why is she doing this?'

'She doesn't have the Mark anymore,' Rahel said. She crouched down, fluid as a shadow, to look me in the face. 'She must have something to fill her emptiness.'

'Then where did the Mark—?'

The answer was in her sad, furious, outraged eyes.

'Oh, God,' I breathed. 'Lewis tried to save her. He took it from her. And now she wants it back.'

'Now you see,' Rahel said soberly.

I did. Vividly. Horribly. Lewis had so much power...more power than me, than anyone. Lewis had done exactly what his nature demanded he do – he'd stepped in to heal her. In doing so, he'd been vulnerable to the Mark, and that was...horrible. Lewis corrupted, without a conscience, with unlimited power...

Apocalypse never seemed like such a personal word before.

'Is he still with her?' I asked. She tilted her head to one side, then back. 'C'mon, Rahel, spill. I don't have time for Djinn games.'

'I think so. We have found no trace of him.'

'Why doesn't he leave?'

She blinked slowly. 'I think he can't.'

'Shit!' I slapped the ground hard enough to make my hand hurt. 'Why didn't you *tell me*?'

'What would you have done differently?'

'Well, *crap*, maybe I wouldn't have blundered right into the trap, you idiot!'

Rahel gave me a long, offended look that reminded me I was dealing with Power. Capital *P*. 'I am not responsible for the short-sighted nature of mortals, Snow White. I deal with you as we have always done with humans. It is not our nature to explain ourselves. We expect you to understand this.'

'Whatever. Man, if I make it out of this, we're going to have some classes in interspecies communication, 'cause you guys *suck* at it!' Shit. I didn't have time for this, the situation was out of control, and as somebody already falling, I had a bird's-eye view of the nasty landing. 'I need to get to Oklahoma City.'

'I can't take you there,' she said. 'I'm—'

'Yeah, free, I know. You can only travel the speed we do.' She looked pleased and surprised that I already knew. 'Get me to the closest car lot.'

She nodded. 'Hold on,' she said. She threw her arms around me in a full-body hug.

And my feet left the ground.

Now, I've flown in Oversight hundreds of times, maybe thousands – and I'm used to the sensation of the world falling away. But this was different. My body wasn't safely down on the ground waiting for me; my body was dangling in midair, at the mercy of a Djinn with an ugly sense of humour.

I let out a scream that came out more like a helpless *meep* and threw my arms around her, too, hanging on for dear life as we soared up into the cool air. Heat battered my skin, and when I dared to look down, we were passing over the blazing orange pyre of the Land Rover.

A bird dipped wings and darted closer to check us out; I read confusion in his dark little bird eyes and absolutely felt for him. I didn't know what I was doing in his airspace, either.

'You know so much of the Djinn,' Rahel said, grinning. 'Did you know we could do this?'

I shut my mouth before I could catch a bug in it.

Rahel touched us down on the corner of an intersection in Norman, about ten miles from where we'd started, and let me sit down and put my head between my knees to fight off the urge to puke. She found it amusing.

'You walk the worlds,' she said. 'Yet a little levitation bothers you?'

'A *little?* Hello, a *lot*,' I shot back, and swallowed. 'What are we doing here?'

Here being a closed, deserted car lot called Performance Automotive. Rahel gave me a look so exasperated, I was surprised she didn't just snap her fingers and make me into a white rat.

'Clearly, we are getting you transportation.'

Right, the Land Rover was a pile of smoking crap. 'We're stealing a car.'

'Unless they offer late-night test drives, I believe so.'

So, it was going to be straight-up grand theft auto. No problem. The idea of a car perked me right up, and besides, next to the death sentence ticking away inside me, prison sounded like a day spa. I had to get to OKC and find Star, and wheels sounded like a damn practical idea.

I scouted around for witnesses. Not much traffic in this part of town after sunset, especially with a storm coming; the predominant sound came from wind-snapped flags and the rattling hum of light poles shivering in the increasingly harsh wind. The few cars that did drive by didn't seem to be bothered by our presence.

Rahel waited for me to say something. I took a deep breath and obliged. 'I need something fast but invisible,' I said. 'High-end Honda, maybe an Acura, neutral colours. I want to blend into traffic. But first, take care of these security cameras.'

Rahel looked up at the shiny blind lenses stationed on the roof of the dealership and attached to two or three of the light poles. She stared for three or four seconds. 'It's done.'

'Really?'

'I fried the circuit boards,' she said. 'And also demagnetised the security tape.'

'Damn, you sure you've never done this kind of thing before?'

Rahel showed me fierce white teeth. 'I have done *every* kind of thing before, sistah.'

We stepped over the white-painted iron fence that wasn't designed to keep shoppers out, just cars in; there were some sweet machines parked on the lot, in a rainbow of yummy colours. I reluctantly ruled out the neon yellows, greens, and reds.

'That one,' I said, and pointed to the one that looked black in the peach gleam of the sodium lights. It was a BMW, a good solid production car. Not the highest priced set of wheels, not the lowest, but one that would do zero to sixty in under eight seconds without any mods at all. Best of all, it looked kind of like a family car, which meant it wouldn't be so easy to spot at a glance from a passing cop.

And, unless I missed my guess, it was dark blue, which was my colour.

Rahel nodded and walked over to do a slow circle of the car, never taking her eyes off it, and finally said, 'There is an alarm inside.'

'Can you disarm it?'

'Of course.'

'Go for it.'

'Done.' She shrugged. She put her hand on the door locks, manipulated electrical currents, and popped open the driver's side door. 'Now you should go, quickly.'

I started to. Really. And as I turned to get in, I saw *her*.

She was sitting all alone in the parking lot, gleaming dark blue with white racing stripes up her hood.

It was love at first sight.

I walked away from the Beamer without any conscious decision to do so. I heard Rahel asking what I thought I was doing, but I was locked on this unexpected beauty sitting there, waiting for me like God himself had put her there.

Rahel caught up with me as I came to a halt next to the car. *Car?* No, that was too small a word; it could have described anything from a Honda Civic to a Lamborghini. This needed a new word.

'What is it?' she asked impatiently. I put two fingers on the gorgeous metallic blue paint, stroking it.

'A 1997 Dodge Viper GTS,' I said reverently. 'V10, 7,990 cubic capacity engine, six thousand RPM. The fastest production car in America, top speed of nearly three hundred kilometres per hour. Faster than any Corvette, faster than the 1971 Boss

Mustang, faster than the goddamn *wind*, Rahel.'

Rahel looked unimpressed. 'It looks expensive.'

'About sixty grand, if you're lucky enough to find one.' The door was locked, of course, but I could feel the Viper issuing the invitation. 'Open it.'

'You told me you wanted to blend in and be difficult to spot. This…is not hard to spot.'

'Just hard to catch.' I flattened my hand against the paint and stroked her flared panels like she was a barely tamed tiger. 'She's the one. No question about it.'

Rahel shrugged, touched the door handle, and the lock popped up. I slipped inside with a sigh of pleasure; it felt like dropping into my favourite chair, with a purring cat curled up against me. Soul-deep comfort. I adjusted the seat, inspected the cockpit display, and felt a surge of love as strong as anything I'd felt for a car in my life. Even poor Delilah.

'I'll take it,' I said. Rahel looked perplexed. 'Please.'

She touched the ignition. The Viper shivered into purring life. The gearshift knob fit perfectly in the palm of my hand. Rahel closed the driver's-side door. I hit the button to glide down the window and said, 'Can you open the gate?'

'I live to serve.' She sounded bemused. Well, I guess she'd never witnessed the sacred bonding of woman and car before. 'Do you know where to go?'

'Away from you,' I said, and eased the Viper into gear. The power shifted to a low, trembling growl. *Sweet.* 'Actually, I have a pretty damn good idea what I have to do now. It's what you always wanted me to do, right? Go back to Oklahoma City. Get to Star.'

She smiled. 'Perhaps you're not as stupid as I feared.' Her hot gold eyes never blinked. 'Don't assume David will take your side. He can't, however much he wishes.'

Behind her, metal locks snapped and wrought-iron gates swung open with a soft moan, laying down the last token of the Viper's protection. 'God be with you,' she said. I idled, looking at her.

'How about you?'

She shook her head. 'At the last, I must be faithless,' she said. 'I have done what I could. Ask me for nothing more.'

I didn't intend to. As I slipped the Viper in gear, I slid up into Oversight to survey the stormline, and I saw the Demon Mark in me, an ugly black nightmare of tentacles and edges. I closed my eyes against the destruction of my soul and promised, 'I'm going to find a way to stop her.'

I let the Viper slip the leash and run.

The Viper – whose name, I decided, was Mona – hit ninety miles an hour on the way out of Norman, which barely required an effort on her part. She was a throwback to earlier cars, sensitive to touch, steering, braking, no computer-controlled minibrain to interpret between us.

The storm that had been chasing me for the last thousand miles was coming fast, gathering speed and rotation. I'd need to do something about that before I could make any move against Star; too much energy out there, too much risk that it could kick me when I was down. First, though, I was going to have to stop for gas. It was risky, not to mention pricey, but the dealership had left only an eighth of a tank in the Viper, and I couldn't afford to run out of gas.

I pulled into a roadside Texaco as a huge gust of wind blew through carrying grit and shredded papers and plastic bags; it had an earth-heavy, faintly corrupt smell that worried me. I pumped as much gas as my last few dollars would allow, paid the gap-toothed cashier, and headed back out into the wind. The temperature was dropping, and the white lace top, though fatally fashionable, did nothing to cut the chill.

Another gust blew my hair over my face. I clawed it back and realised that I had company.

A big yellow Nissan SUV had pulled up at the pumps between me and the Viper.

I slowed from a trot to a walk to a full stop. My heart hammered and went up to a level only cardio aerobics should have triggered. Fight or flight. God, I wanted to fight. I *needed* to fight, but whatever organs in my body controlled the flow of power were badly worked over these last few days, and even trying to gauge the wind speed made me ache.

Out on the freeway, a semi truck blew by, dragging an air-horn blast. The wind shoved me like a bully.

Marion Bearheart stepped out from behind the back of the SUV and stood watching me, hands in the pockets of her fringed leather coat. Her black-and-silver hair was contained in a thick braid that fell over one shoulder, and she looked strong and tough and resolute.

'Don't run,' she said. Somehow, I heard her even over the wind.

'Dammit, I don't have time for this!' I shouted. The words whipped away, but their essence remained. Her hands stayed in her pockets, but she took a step closer.

'Make time,' she said. And took another step. I wanted to back away, but there was something powerful and immortal in her eyes, something larger than my fear. 'I know you have the Mark.'

I wondered how long she'd known, or suspected. She'd been pretty careful with me, back on Iron Road – afraid of rousing the Mark? Or just putting it together afterwards?

'It's all right,' she said. The wind whipped unexpectedly sideways, then back; strands of hair tore loose from her braid and floated black and silver around her face. 'Joanne, trust me. This will all work out. Please, let's figure this out together.'

She held out her hand to me, silver-and-turquoise rings gleaming in the harsh lights of the gas station.

I took a step back. She tried again.

'Once your powers are gone, the Mark won't be able to feed,' she said. 'It will starve and wither. You'll live. I can make that happen.'

I couldn't live like that, not blind and deaf, cut off from the breathing of the world. Cut off from the aetheric. Like Star, I was just too deep in the world.

'I'm not the only one with the Mark,' I said. 'You know that, right?'

'One problem at a time.' Marion had a kind of fevered intensity about her, and I could feel her willing me to give in. But she hadn't used her power. Why not? She'd used it on Iron Road...Ah, of course, the storm. The more power we used, the worse the storm would get, the faster it would reach us. She was being responsible.

As I took another step back, arms closed around me from behind and lifted me straight off the ground. Erik. He was bigger than me, stronger, taller, and he'd taken me by surprise. I felt ribs creak when he squeezed. I kicked frantically at his shins, but if it hurt him, he didn't do more than grunt in my ear.

Marion walked up to me and gently smoothed

hair back from my face. She smiled. 'Don't struggle. I know, you made a terrible mistake, but it can be fixed, I swear. You're too valuable to the Wardens; I won't let anything happen to you.'

I stopped struggling. Erik let me down enough that my toes touched the ground. 'It's Star,' I said. 'She's turned on us. We have to stop her.'

Her eyes widened. 'Joanne, I expected something a little better from you than turning on the only friend you have left. Star's the one who told us you were coming. She wants you to get help. Accusing her won't make things any better.'

She slid her eyes past me to Erik. 'Put her in the truck.'

Struggling didn't do anything but make him squeeze harder and cut off half my air; I was reduced to kicking and screaming like a scared kid. Marion opened the back door of the Nissan, and I got my feet set on either side of the opening and pushed, hard.

Shirl, who'd come up on the other side of the truck, leant over and touched my foot. It burnt. I yelled, kicked out, and caught her right in the face with a snap that sent her rolling. Marion went after her. Erik staggered as a fresh gust of wind hit him squarely in the back.

I reached for that wind, whipped it around me like a cloak, and lifted me and Erik off the ground. He squawked like a chicken, and his grip loosened; I twisted the wind faster, spinning us in midair, and he let go to flail for balance he'd never get. Higher. Higher. Marion was reaching up toward us, but whatever magic she was summoning was no use; with the storm coming, there was so much potential in the air, so much power, it was as natural to me as breathing to counter her.

I split the mini-funnel into halves, stabilised myself in midair, and let Erik continue to turn and flail. *Faster*. The bastard had almost crushed my ribs. *Faster*. He was just a blur of flesh and cloth, screaming.

With just a little more, I could rip that cloth away, strip him naked, then begin to peel that pale flesh down to red meat and bone...

Jesus. I flinched because somewhere in me, something was licking its lips at the taste of that fear, that blood.

I let Erik drop into a heap on the concrete and held myself suspended ten feet above Marion's head, looking down. Shirl called fire, but Marion stopped her before the wind could whip it out of control.

'Your move,' I called down. The wind blew cold and harsh around me, black as night, streaming with power. It was sickeningly easy. I'd never felt so powerful, not even with a borrowed Djinn at my command. No wonder Bad Bob had let himself be consumed by this thing; it felt so...damn...*good*.

Marion knew better than to start a war here,

next to a town full of innocent lives. So did I.

That didn't mean we wouldn't do it.

She slowly lowered her hands to her sides and gave me one short, sharp nod.

'You know I could blow you away, don't you?' I asked. She looked ready to bite the head off a nail, but she nodded to that, too. 'You know I have the power to bury the three of you right here.'

'Do or don't, it's your choice.'

I was sick of everybody preaching to me about choices. 'No more fucking around, Marion. Don't try to smile to my face and stab me in the back, because I promise you, I'll hurt you. Now, I'm going after Star. You can either come along and help me get her, or you can get in that canary-yellow piece of crap and go home. But you are *not* taking me with you.'

Her eyes were ice, ice cold. 'It seems I was wrong about you. I thought you would do the right thing.'

'Well, it's all in the perspective.' I waited, hovering, while she thought about it. 'What if I can provide proof that Star's corrupted?'

'Then I'll take steps.'

We kept up the standoff for another few minutes, and then Marion nodded. Just once.

'Follow me,' I said. 'Don't get in my way.'

She bundled Shirl and Erik into the Nissan, then climbed up into the driver's seat. I lowered myself to a level where I could see her through the window.

Somewhere about half a mile away, a fork of lightning blazed through the sky. Sensitised as I was right now to the power, I felt it go through me like a rolling wave of orgasm. She must have read that in me, because for the first time – ever – I saw a flicker of fear in Marion's eyes.

'Try to keep up,' I said. I touched down on the concrete and let the wind slip from my control; it raged in a mini-tornado through the parking lot, slamming parked cars, scudding trash, kicking loose stones like a spoilt brat.

I stayed cool until I got in the Viper and then sat there, shaking, and felt the Demon Mark uncoiling and stretching inside me.

'I won't be like that,' I promised myself. But I already was. I'd hurt Erik, I'd thought seriously about killing him. It was only a matter of degrees now, of those slow descending steps to becoming what Bad Bob had been.

A monster.

I let the Viper fold me in its muscular strength; Mona was willing to run, and I was willing to let her. The first heavy drops of rain were falling around us as I sped out of the gas station, followed by the Day-Glo Nissan Xterra. We roared up the access ramp and hit I-35, heading for the heart of Oklahoma City.

❧ ❧ ❧

The storm was fast becoming a problem.

I watched it flowing toward me. The clouds had turned darker, edged with grey green; the light looked different seen through them. Lightning was a constant, hidden flicker somewhere up in the anvil cloud forming at the leading edge. It looked deceptively compact, but I knew it went up into the sky for thirty, forty, fifty thousand feet, a massive, boiling pressure cooker of force and power. Two miles after I left Norman, rain began lashing the road in sheets. Mona's windshield wipers worked on full speed just to keep the lane markers visible; lucky for me, there was no traffic except for the dimly seen SUV behind me. We were the only fools stupid enough to be driving.

Now that it was here, the green-and-grey pinwheel hanging so close over my head, I thought in a strange sort of way that I recognised it. It had a personality, this storm. A kind of surly intelligence. I had the sick feeling – and it was probably true – that this was the storm born of seeds I'd scattered on the coast of Florida in my fight with Bad Bob. Whether it came from me or had been birthed from the bloody womb of Mother Earth, this storm was now waking up to its own power and presence. Sentient. Able to control itself, alter its course, make decisions about how much damage to inflict, and where. There was no longer anybody manipulating the aetheric to control it; in fact, I could see lines of force constantly jabbing at it from a hundred different Weather Wardens, all trying to disrupt its patterns and all failing.

The more I looked at it, the more familiarity I felt. This was my storm. Created from my meddling. Fed by my reckless use of power. Dragged here by my subconscious, or my bad luck.

Overhead, the storm shifted and rumbled, and I felt it focus on me. Fine. At least this was an enemy I understood. One I could fight. I looked into its black, furious heart. I opened my mouth and screamed at it. No words, nothing but a tortured howl of agony. *Come on, you bastard. Come and take your best shot.*

When I stopped, there was silence. The storm muttered to itself and kept its own wary counsel; I'd surprised it, at least, even if I hadn't scared it.

I couldn't stop the storm without pulling power through my Demon Mark, and that would increase its rate of growth and burn away at what was left of my soul. Then again, I couldn't go back through the storm without it striking me with all its power and fury.

It was standing between me and Oklahoma City now. Between me and Star, me and David.

The storm stared at me. I stared back.

I pulled Mona off the road and got out of the car.

The Nissan ghosted to a caution-yellow stop behind me.

'Fuck you,' I said, staring up at this child of my power. 'Let's go to war.'

It started small. They always do. Just a breeze against my overheated face, tugging at the hem of my shirt and ruffling my sleeves. Combing through my hair like cold, unfeeling fingers.

Marion got out of the SUV behind me. I didn't turn around. 'Better take cover,' I said. Maybe she did; maybe she didn't. It wasn't something I could spare attention to check.

Overhead, the storm's rotation sped up. Clouds swirled and blended together. They spawned cone-shaped formations that twisted and turned on their own. Counterclockwise, all storms turn counterclockwise on this side of the world. The colours were incredible, grey and green and heart's-night black. Flashes of livid purple and pink from lightning discharging point to point across the sky.

I waited.

The wind snapped my hair back like a battle flag, even with a drenching rain; I used enough power to clear a bell of stillness around myself and immediately drew a lightning strike. I diffused it down into the ground and felt no more than a tingle, and the subtle, stealthy movements of the Demon Mark under my skin.

I told it to shut up. It was going to get a lot worse before it got better.

When the hail started – golf balls smashing out of the sky to shatter on the road around me at first – I extended my protection over the Viper, too; no point in winning the war and being stuck thumbing for a ride. The hail pounded harder, like white rain, growing into fist-size misshapen chunks that exploded like bombs when they hit. Ice shrapnel sliced through my clothes, cold and then hot as blood began to run. Hundreds of tiny cuts. I strengthened the shield around me, but it wasn't going to be easy to keep all of it out.

Out in the field to my right, dust and grass began to swirl and twist. A delicate streamer of grey shredded off from the clouds above it. Not much force to it yet, barely an F0, hardly more than a dust devil. The storm was testing me.

I chopped through the top of the baby tornado by freezing the air molecules. The sucking updraft lost force, and the dust funnel blew apart.

Round one to me.

I sensed something happening behind me, happening fast. Before I could even turn, I felt the tingle of another lightning bolt coming; I split my focus three ways into protection, diffusion, and moving my body to face whatever this storm was throwing at my back.

Another tornado, this one forming fast and ugly.

The full cone was already visible, shivering and dancing through the hard curtain of rain; it was lit from within by an eerie blue-white light. Ball lightning. I felt the hard plasmatic blobs of energy bouncing around inside the wind walls.

Tornadoes are simple, gruesomely effective engines of destruction. They're caused, by the humble updraft – the updraft from hell, driven by wind shear and Earth's own rotation. Imagine a column of air speeding three hundred miles per hour, straight up, blasting up into the mesosphere and erupting like an invisible geyser. As the air turns cold again, it sinks and gets drawn back into the spiral.

Sounds easy. When you're looking at that shifting, screaming wall of destruction heading straight for you, all the knowledge in the world doesn't help you maintain objectivity. This one was already formidably armed with found objects – pieces of wood, twists of wire torn from fence posts, nails, rocks, whipping grasses and abrasive sand. A human body trapped in the wind wall could be sawed apart by all that debris in a matter of seconds.

I went up into Oversight. The storm was grey with pale green, unhealthy light...photonegative, full of destructive energy and the instincts to deliver it with maximum damage. It circled up in the mesosphere like a vast clockworks. There were other Wardens there, working, but nobody came near me or offered to link; they were focused on working the weak points of the storm, trying to warm the air at the top and disrupt the engine cycle that was spawning tornadoes.

They wouldn't be successful. This storm had its parameters well under control, and it wasn't going to let us cut off its food supply. We had to be creative about this if we – if *I* – expected to survive. Truthfully, the rest of the Wardens probably weren't worried about my survival. They wanted to contain the storm where it was, over open country, until it burnt itself out. Any risk to me was a bonus.

Another lightning stroke was forming. Instead of diffusing the power, I channelled it, focused, and slammed that white-hot energy directly down into the vulnerable throat of the tornado roaring toward me.

It choked, stuttered, coughed on its own superheated breath. The residual heat on the ground radiated up, disrupting the cooling end of the cycle.

In seconds, the wind wall fell apart and fled back up into the water-heavy clouds, dropping its weapons of opportunity as it went. A thick whip of barbed wire snaked down from the sky and fell almost at my feet.

I grinned up at it and screamed defiance. 'That all

you got? You think you're going to stop me with *that?* Please!'

It hit me with more lightning, five times to be exact, one on top of the other. I fumbled the last, and it bled off into me, not enough to fry me but enough to scramble my already-abused nerves. I fell, rolled over on my stomach, and looked up into the heart of my enemy. There were no eyes to this storm, no face, but there was a kind of *centre*...the cold still place around which the rest of it rotated and screamed and rattled.

I stayed down, relaxed my body, and again flew up into Oversight. More chains were forming; it sensed weakness and was preparing a massive lightning attack. I snapped the links and drove the polarity back, all the way back, into the centre of the storm.

And then I did something that I'd been told never, ever to do.

I reached for the rotation of the storm itself.

It's a funny thing about momentum. It's a force multiplier for objects in motion, like kids on bicycles. But momentum only aids force when force operates according to logical, controlled rules.

When kids on bikes go too fast, they begin to lose control. Handlebars shake. Wheels wobble. Lines of force operate at angles instead of straight on.

Speed can be the enemy of momentum.

I didn't try to act in opposition to the storm – it

would be worse than useless; it would actually add to the fury of the energy circling me. No. I reached for the disturbed, chaotic winds operating at the fringes of the storm and *added* them to the storm, like a drain sucking in more water. I *fed* the storm. Pumped energy into it with abandon.

Other Wardens noticed what I was doing, and some of them tried to stop me. I shoved them back, hard. One or two had Djinn support, but I had the Mark; the power in me was black and hot and blending with mine to such an extent now that I didn't need a Djinn anymore.

One or two of the other Wardens fell out of Oversight and didn't come back. I didn't let myself wonder what I'd done. The storm was what was important. Spinning it faster, faster, pouring more energy into the sink until it was overflowing.

The storm was rotating, in the physical world, with a speed that was eerie to look at. Tornadoes popped and bubbled all over the underside of it as power struggled to regulate itself; but there was too much, no control, angles of force intersecting and cancelling each other out.

Faster. Faster. *Faster*.

I laughed out loud, looking up at the spinning pin-wheel, and the centre of the storm stared furiously back. Lightning was firing so continuously that the whole black-green-purple mass was lit within, pulsing with energy.

Not a single tornado touched the ground. A massive one formed in the air, almost a mile wide, struggling to reach damp earth and rip apart everything in its path. I warmed the air under it so quickly that rain turned to steam.

The storm readied another lightning bolt. The chain of polarity led straight to me, and it was as strong and inflexible as braided cable. No way I could break it.

Let it come, something in me said, something black and hard and riding the edge of my adrenaline. *Bathe in the power. It is your right.*

The idea was so diverting that I lost my grip on the air below the F5 tornado chewing its way out of the sky. Temperatures dropped.

The tornado hit ground, bounced, ripped up earth and plants and fence and began to roar toward me.

I felt the energy come up through my body. It arched my back, pulled a breathless scream out of my mouth, bathed every cell in my body with pure, primal force.

The thing in me ate it, and I felt it happening to me, felt the Demon change from the tentacled horror into a thing of ice and angles, grating on my bones, barely fitting beneath my skin.

I hardly felt the massive nuclear energy of the burn-off, the energy manifesting in visible light and heat.

I was transformed in the fiery inferno.

Made whole.

When I stood up, my shredded, melted clothes fell away, and I stood pure against the storm.

I stretched out my hand and touched the life inside it, caressed it, tasted the dark furious essence of it. Attuned myself to its vibrations and rhythms, learning it, *being* the storm.

And then I surrounded it with the enormous strength inside me, and I crushed it.

Twenty feet away, the enormous gnashing strength of the tornado fell in on itself, dead. The storm's energy patterns flared and tore.

In the breathless stillness, I heard myself laughing. Naked, soaking wet, infused with the furious power of the deepest darkness, I still found it funny.

I heard the unnaturally loud grate of footsteps on gravel, and came back to myself. Or what was left of my self now.

'My God,' Marion whispered. I turned my head to look at her and saw her flinch. 'What you did—'

'Saved our lives,' I said. I stood up, looked down at myself, and started feeling the shock take hold. So cold. So many cuts and bruises. I looked like a road map of been there, done that. 'Got any clothes I can borrow?'

They didn't want to come near me. Shirl stripped

off her flannel shirt, leaving herself the T-shirt; Marion dug a pair of loose blue jeans from a bag in the back of the Xterra. They tossed them to me, along with a pair of mud-caked hot pink Converse high-top sneakers. I pulled everything on without worrying about who was watching me; even Erik wasn't interesting in checking me out, right at the moment.

They hadn't even wanted to touch me. I couldn't say I blamed them.

I looked down at myself when I was finished and decided that I wouldn't win any fashion awards, even at the homeless shelter, but it would do. Good enough to die in, or kill a friend in.

You don't need to look good for that. You just have to look scary.

I'd made it seven miles down the road, almost into the Oklahoma City limits, when I ran into the first obstacle.

Wind wall. It was a ferocious east-to-west current whipping across the road at right angles, like a tornado lying down: It wasn't a natural phenomenon – at least, not anywhere other than high elevations with hair-trigger climates – but it was undeniably powerful; lose control, and the Viper would get slammed into a spin that might well turn into an end-over-end movie stunt, only without the padding and professional stuntmen. I could control a lot of things. Gravity and basic kinetic energy weren't among them.

I had one second to recognise the distortion across the road, one second more to make a decision about what to do. No time to focus or do any delicate manipulation.

I flattened the pedal and felt Mona jump forward like a champion racing for the finish.

The wind slammed the front left quarter panel like a speeding freight train, and the front wheels lost traction; I was going into a spin. If it had just been a single fast wind shear, that would have been one thing, but this was a fierce continuing blast, and as the car spun, it slammed directly into the back end, shoving the Viper toward the shoulder; I did exactly the opposite of what you should do; I turned the wheel against the skid, gave it more momentum, kept the car turning so that the momentum spun it like a top down the centre line. The wind kept buffeting me, but it was only adding to the car's rotational force, not slowing me down.

I gulped and hung on for dear life as the world beyond the windshield turned into a long brown-black-green blur...road, shoulder, field, road, shoulder, field...and then I felt the pressure of air against the car suddenly drop off.

I turned into the skid, smelt burning rubber and my own nerves frying, and the Viper fought me and fought the road like a bucking bronco.

I hit the brakes gently, gently, struggling with the wheel as we did one last, slow spin and jerked to a stop, still on the road.

I was about two inches over the dotted white line.

It would have been a real good moment to open the door and throw up, but I had no time for any of that. The yellow Xterra had been just a few hundred yards behind me, and a higher-profile vehicle stood no chance at all against that wind wall. The force would flip the truck over like a toy.

No time or energy to do it the careful way, the right way; I just brute-forced an equal and opposite force by slamming cold air down into the stream, and held it there while the Xterra blasted through. There was still enough wind to shake it, but not enough to flip it over.

I slipped Mona back in gear and popped the clutch, and we flew toward the city limits with Marion's SUV right on our tail. I expected trouble. In fact, I counted on it.

You can imagine how spooky it was not to have any at all, not even a hint, all the way into the suburbs, all the way to the merge with I-40. There was more and slower traffic now, and I had to slow Mona down from our breakneck gallop. Every passing car made me flinch, because this was a recipe for disaster; if Star wasn't choosy about the body count, this could end up in one of those spectacular forty-or fifty-car pileups, the kind that make the evening news and have the words 'death toll' in the tag line.

But nothing happened.

I got Star's cell phone and dialled it one-handed from memory.

'Crisis Centre,' said a voice that sounded too young and too friendly for comfort. What kind of grade school had they raided now? Had I been that young when I'd been on the Help Desk? Probably. It just raised chills and goose bumps to think my life and everybody's around me now might rest in the hands of somebody barely old enough to buy a legal drink.

'Hi, this is Joanne Baldwin, Weather. I'm in Oklahoma City, and I need to call a Code One general alert.'

Dead silence on the other end of the phone for at least ten seconds, and then a very quiet, 'Excuse me?'

'Code One,' I repeated. 'General alert. Look it up.'

'Please hold.' She was gone for thirty full seconds this time, and when she came back on, her voice was trembling. 'Um, Warden Baldwin? I've been told that you need to surrender yourself to the Wardens who are following you. Please.'

'Well, here's what *I'm* telling you: Oklahoma City is about to be a wide smoking hole in the road if you don't do exactly as I tell you. Call a Code One. Right now.'

She sounded stronger. There was probably a supervisor standing over her. 'Can't do that, ma'am.'

'Do *not* ma'am me, kid. Let me talk to whoever you've got quoting rules and regulations at you.'

I'd been right about the supervisor. There was a click, and a basso profundo male voice said, 'Jo, you got any idea how pissed off I am right now at you?'

'Paul?' I couldn't help it; beaten, scared, half-evil, I still grinned at the sound of his voice. 'Save it for later. I'm on my way to Estrella Almondovar's house, or I will be as soon as you give me the address. Marion and her crew are on my tail.'

'*Pull the car over,* and let them do their jobs! Jesus, Jo, Bad Bob was right all along about you. You got any idea what kind of hell you stirred up out there? Killer storm, followed by so much hellfire in the aetheric that we might as well call it a day and evacuate the whole friggin' state. And don't tell me it wasn't you. I *saw* you up there.'

'Shut up and listen. I've got a Demon Mark, so does Lewis, and we're about to go at it down here. If you don't want to be cleaning up a whole hell of a lot worse than just some blown-down shacks and road signs, I suggest you get off your ass and call a Code One, right now.'

He put me on hold. *Bastard.* I switched off and tossed the phone into the passenger seat.

Twenty seconds later, as I was squinting at exit signs, the mobile phone warbled for my attention. I flipped it open and said, 'Shoot.'

'1617 Fifty-Sixth Street,' Paul said. 'Code One's going in place. You're not serious, right? About going at it with Lewis?'

'I sure as hell hope not.'

I dropped the phone and downshifted, whipped the Viper around a family station wagon and two identical red Hondas, and saw the exit sign flash by over head. Fifty-Sixth Street, two miles.

The weather looked clear. Too clear.

It was just too damn easy.

I exited the freeway and took the turn at a screech that should have raised police attention in six states, but my luck was holding; no civilian cops taking a coffee break at the wrong intersection. I scratched the gear change and blasted through two yellow lights, had to stop for a red, and felt every nerve in my body snapping and shaking with the urge to move.

The neighbourhood was industrial, mostly blue-collar stuff like stamping factories and printing presses; the buildings were square, grey, and grimy. Saffron-coloured streetlamps gave everything a jaundiced look, and there wasn't a soul in sight on the sidewalks, only a few cars still hidden in parking lots behind chain-link and razor wire.

I'd gone four blocks when somebody stepped out into the street in front of me. I jammed on brake and clutch and rode the Viper to a shaking, screaming, smoking halt.

David was standing in front of me. He no longer had the road dude persona; this David was brown-haired, brown-eyed, dressed in a loose white shirt and dark pants that ended in a mist around his knees. This was the look Star had imposed on him, along with her will. I remembered the hot bronze of his eyes and felt a sharp stab of mourning.

Don't mistake foe for friend. Rahel's excellent advice, and yet, looking at him, I could only remember his hands touching me, stroking peace into my fevered skin. He wasn't just Djinn, not just a tool or a tap of power to turn on and off. He wasn't a slave.

And if he wasn't...maybe none of them were. Maybe none of them should be.

'Don't do this,' I said. I knew he could hear me, even through the closed windows of the car. 'Don't make us enemies. Please.'

'You made us enemies,' he said, and extended his hand, palm first.

I felt gravity increase around me, jamming me into the seat, holding me down.

The air around me turned thick and sweet and

poisonous. I gagged and stopped breathing, tried to reach for the automatic window controls, but he was too strong, too prepared. I felt my skin burning. The air had taken on a slight green tinge. Chlorine? Something worse?

He'd turned the car into a gas chamber.

I reached for the wind and slammed him hard enough to disincorporate him into mist, and in the instant before he could re-form, I jammed the window button and rolled all four down. Fresh air whipped in and blew out the poisoned fog, and I hit the gas and burnt rubber right at him.

He wasn't there when the front end arrived. I looked behind me, but saw nothing except Marion's Xterra crawling up the road in pursuit. I knew better than to think I'd lost him, but at least I had – no pun intended – breathing space.

I picked up the cell phone again. The line was still open, and I could hear Paul giving muffled orders in the distance. 'Hey!' I yelled. 'I need you! Pick up!'

'What do you need?' In a crisis, Paul was all about the facts, not the feelings. He'd hate me later, maybe kill me, but right now he'd made a choice and he'd stick to it.

'Djinn,' I said. 'Yours. Get it out here and tell it to block Star's Djinn, or I'll never make it there. He'll—'

A building tilted over the street in front of me. I screamed, dropped the phone, and twisted the wheel. It was an old, dilapidated thing of fire-ravaged bricks and blank glassless windows, probably due for demolition, but there was no way it should have chosen this moment to lie down right in front of me. I shifted gears and let the Viper scream at full power; a brick hit the roof with a bang, then another, and then we shot out from under the falling shadow and it collapsed behind us with a dull roar and a cloud of white smoke.

A light pole slammed forward into my path. I twisted around it.

A mailbox threw itself, trailing sparks and federally protected letters in its wake. I hit the brakes and slithered past it with inches to spare.

'Paul!' I screamed. 'Now would be good!'

Too late. David had mastered the timing now, and the next light pole was falling just exactly right – too far away for me to beat it, too close for me to stop. I hit the curb with enough force that I was afraid the Viper's tires would blow, but we bounced up, flashed by more wooden poles, kissed the finish on a dilapidated bus-stop shelter, and bounced out again into the street.

Into the path of an eighteen-wheel tractor-trailer, which was barrelling down the cross street. Nobody was driving it, and the load on the back looked suspiciously like a propane tank.

I went weirdly calm. The Viper was fast, but she wasn't supernatural, and I didn't have enough speed to make it, enough road to stop, or enough luck to avoid it this time.

Sorry, Mona. It was fun while it lasted.

Something flashed into the way. Some*one* – small, golden haired, dressed in blue and white like a fairytale heroine.

A Djinn had come to my rescue, but it wasn't Paul's; it was, instead, Alice in Wonderland.

She held up one small, delicate hand and brought the truck to a stop. Perfect control. She looked over her shoulder at me as I arrowed through the intersection, and I saw a smile on her lips, a neon-blue spark of life in her eyes that I hadn't seen before.

A whisper came through my car radio. *Go. I'll keep him back.*

Apparently, she was itching for a rematch from the game of keep-away at Cathy's bookstore. I made a mental note to thank Cathy later – preferably with chocolates and really fine booze – and felt the tension in my shoulders loosen just a little. At least I didn't have to fight David. Not directly.

No, I only had to fight Star. And myself.

I checked addresses when grimy industrial sections gave way to grimy lower-middle-class houses. Universally small, mostly of clapboard and in need of paint and new fences, they were crammed together like sardines with postage-stamp front yards mostly filled with weeds and rusting junk.

Estrella's house shone like a diamond in a sack of coal. Larger, well proportioned, gleaming with fresh paint and a neat white-painted fence. No weeds in the new spring grass, the only concession to lawn ornaments a heavy concrete birdbath with a cherub on top. It didn't look like the place to find somebody willing to kill in order to keep secrets.

I pulled the Viper to a halt at the curb and got out. Lights were on in the house, warm behind the window shades. The muted blue flicker of a TV screen made shadows in one of the bedroom windows.

All too normal. And I'd never expected to reach it this easily. That made it harder, somehow, bringing all my anger and fury had seemed easier when I didn't have to knock politely to do it.

I went up the steps and rang the doorbell.

'It's open,' Star's voice rang out. I swallowed hard, looked up and down the street, hoping to see Marion's yellow Xterra, but I was all alone. 'Come on in, Jo.'

I turned the knob and stepped inside.

The hallway was burnished wood, lovingly polished; a side table had faded photographs lined up, starting with two stiff-looking people in the formal dress of the mid-1800s, progressing by decades through Star's family. Hers was the last photo on the table. High school graduation, a beautiful girl, a winning smile, the devil's own laughter in her dark eyes.

I closed the door behind me and waited.

'In the kitchen!' she called. I smelt the mouth-watering aroma of fresh-baking peanut butter cookies.

Something very wrong about contemplating murder with the smell of baking in the air. As maybe she intended.

I walked down the hallway past a darkened formal living room, a brightly lit family room filled with warm colours and gleaming wood. The kitchen was at the back of the house, an old design, and I stopped in the doorway. Star was standing next to the oven, mitt on her hand, taking cookie sheets off the racks.

'Just a sec,' she said, and deposited the last grey pan on top of the bulky avocado-green stove. 'Ah. There. Now.'

She stripped off the oven mitt, turned off the oven. No more fake scars, not this time. She was showing me her true face. Untouched. Beautiful. False.

'You're wondering how this happened.' She touched the smooth bronze skin of her cheek. 'I was rotting to death in that hospital, and they couldn't – no, they *wouldn't* – help me.'

'Star—'

'Let me finish. All they had to do was give me a fucking Djinn, but no, they wouldn't do that. I hadn't earned it. They said I didn't have the temperament to handle the responsibility.' She glared at me. How had I missed all that hatred in her eyes before? All that bitterness? Had she covered that up, too? 'They left me with a face like a melted hockey mask. You remember?'

Of course I remembered. I couldn't move, couldn't speak. She reached for the oven mitt again, grabbed a tray of cookies, and began to savagely shovel the peanut butter rounds off into a white china bowl.

'Well, I didn't have to take that.' She finished scraping cookies off and dumped the pan in the sink. 'I could feel it out there. Waiting for me. All I had to do was accept it.'

She reached into the refrigerator and took out a jug of milk. She lifted it in my direction. When I didn't reach for it, she shrugged and put it on the counter, got out a glass, and poured.

'It felt like I was dying,' she said, and took a sip. 'Like my soul was burning out. But then it stopped hurting, and it became something else. Something real. Something with a purpose.'

'It's not purpose, Star. It's just suicide with a longer fuse.'

She picked up a cookie and bit into it.

'Also a really big bang,' she agreed. 'You think

that bothers me? I've been dying a long damn time.'

'Looks like you're feeling pretty good to me.'

'This?' She stroked her unmarked face. 'Yeah. It healed me. But it doesn't stay, not unless I find a way to get the Mark back inside me. I can already feel myself getting slower. Older. Twisting inside.'

'So why get rid of it?'

She slammed down the china bowl. 'I *didn't!* All I tried to do was feed the Mark. I needed a Djinn.'

Rahel had told me the truth, for once. 'The book. Free-range Djinn, yours for the taking. You claim them, feed them to the Demon.'

'Yeah.' She gave me a bleak smile. 'Should have been easy, you know? Only it wasn't. Because the minute I grabbed one, there was Lewis, showing up to smack my ass, and girl, he is one strong Warden. I thought he was gonna kill me.'

I'd moved a step closer to her without even realising it. I came to a stop, haunted by the fact that I'd always let my fondness for her blind me to just how selfish she really was.

'How'd he get the Mark?'

She glared. 'He *took* it. I didn't give it to him. The stupid bastard said he was trying to help me. I didn't want his help!'

Her belligerent tone didn't go with the too-bright shine in her eyes. Pain in there. Deep, anguished self-loathing. She went back to scraping cookies off sheet pans, dumping them into a bowl with quick, nervous motions.

'Then let him go,' I said. 'You can't get the Mark back from him, you said so yourself. It goes from weaker to stronger. Nobody's stronger than Lewis. It's finished.'

'No!' She almost screamed it at me, a raw physical outburst that sounded as if it scraped her throat bloody. 'I'll get it back. I have to!'

'How?' I sounded so logical all of a sudden. So calm. Maybe it was just shock, but all I really felt for her in that moment was sheer, sad pity. She'd been so glorious, once. So selfless. Seeing the ruin of that…ached in ways that I'd never expected.

Her dark eyes looked blind behind the glitter of fury, but this time her voice came out soft, nearly controlled. 'You gave me a way,' she said. 'I can't take the Mark from him, but your hot boyfriend Djinn can. And then I can order him to give it back to *me*. I can't make Lewis do shit, all he does is sits there and meditates, like he's thinking the damn thing to death. But I can make *David* do it.'

Fear went solid and slick as glass in my throat. I tried to swallow the lump. 'No, it doesn't work that way. If David takes the Mark he can't get rid of it. He'll be infested. Or worse.' If her Mark was as mature as it sounded, it might just devour him instead. I'd seen a Demon hatch, before. I didn't want to ever see it again. 'Give it up, Star. Please.

Let me try to help, try to think of something...'

She dumped the bowl on the counter between us. 'You already did think of something. You brought the damn Wardens here. If they find us, they'll take him away, take you away...and you know what they'll do to me, Jo. Gut me and leave me like I was before. A freak. Worse. A powerless freak. I can't live like that, and you know it.'

'Nothing you can do to stop it now,' I said. 'It's too late. I'm sorry. I really am.'

'Oh, there is something I can do. Nobody knows where the hell Lewis is, anyway, so it's no big thing. He disappears, you disappear...all I have to do is get rid of Maid Marion and her merry band of butchers out there. Maybe I'll get David to blow up their truck. I hate those damn SUVs, anyway, and they'll just blame it all on you.' Star finished scraping cookies from the second sheet pan, dumped it, and held out the bowl to me. 'Here. Have one.'

'Thanks, I'd rather choke on a razor blade. Which I'm not so sure you didn't bake inside those.'

She smiled, or tried to, and put the bowl down. 'So. We gonna fight now, or what?'

I looked at her over the bowl of cookies. My friend. My sister. My ghostly reflection of what might have happened if I'd been the one in the fire that day, because I'd always known I wasn't cut out for normal human life any more than Star was.

'Guess so,' I said. 'Because I'm taking Lewis and David out of here.'

'Thought you'd say that.'

She took another bite of cookie.

Behind her, the oven exploded into a brilliant blue-white ball of flame, which raced my way.

I dropped to the floor in a crouch and tossed every oxygen molecule out of the air around me for three feet in any direction. Fire needs O_2. It was an elementary tactic, but it worked; the fire blasted toward me, hit the shield of nonoxygenated air, and deflected around. The heat wasn't hard to control, either; after all, it was just molecules moving. I made them move slower.

When it was over, I wasn't even singed. I let go of the air bubble, stepped toward Star, and took a deep breath. 'You know, I was feeling sorry for you,' I said. 'Poor little Star, all alone in that hospital, burnt beyond recognition, boo-fucking-hoo. Did you ever stop to think about all those Wardens who *died?* Who never even made it out? Of course you didn't. Because it's just all about you.'

She laughed. It was a crazy sound. She held out both hands in front of her, palms up, and intense blue-white flames danced on the skin and reflected in her dark eyes. 'Yeah, like it ain't all about you, Jo. Bad Bob dumps a problem on you, and what do you do? Take off running like a scared rabbit to save your skin. You don't want to give up your powers any more than I do. You've put people in danger. Hell, for all I know, you killed some, too. So don't pretend we're not alike.'

'Oh, we're alike,' I agreed. 'See, that's why I *didn't* use David like some piece of Kleenex to save my skin. Because we're so fucking alike.'

'You gonna whine or fight?'

'I'm gonna win,' I said. 'Bank it.'

She bared her teeth. 'Yeah? Look behind you.'

I did.

There was a man standing there in the open doorway that must have led to the cellar of the house – tall, lanky, his face almost hidden by a growth of shaggy dark hair. He was wearing an ancient stained tie-dyed shirt and sweatpants stiff with grime. His feet were filthy. If I'd passed him on the street, I'd have dropped a dollar in his WILL WORK FOR FOOD CUP.

It was Lewis.

I turned around, put my hands out to my sides in the universal no-danger-here pose, and said, 'Lewis? Remember me? It's Jo.'

He was staring at me with eyes so wide and dark that they looked to be all pupil. Drugged, or worse. Completely mad.

He was staring at my breasts. Which was, to put it mildly, more weird than flattering in the current circumstances.

He looked up into my face, and I felt my knees turn to water at the sight of all the torment and confusion in his eyes. If Star didn't get punished for anything else she did, ever, she should be punished for this.

'Jo?' he asked, and it was an entirely normal voice, which was entirely *not* normal, given the way he looked. 'I'm really sorry about all this. I can't stop it.'

And then he walked up and slugged me, right in the face.

Fire and Weather don't go to war. We don't go to war because it's too dangerous, and we have no decisive advantages. Our powers counter each other very nicely, all the way down the line.

But when Weather fights Weather...that's when it gets nasty.

And that was exactly why I'd declared a Code One general alert, because I wanted the mystical world of the aetheric locked down tighter than a drum. A Code One calls every Warden able to respond, *everywhere*, to action. Locking down their patterns, whether of weather or fire or earth, in the same way you'd anchor boats in a storm or plywood your windows in a hurricane. Basically, it meant everything came to a stop.

Over Oklahoma City, the air was clear, still, and dead. Nothing was moving. Nothing *could* without a massive push, one large enough to toss off the controls of at least a hundred Wardens and their Djinn.

That wasn't likely to happen. Not even for Lewis.

Which at the moment of my opening my eyes didn't help much, because I felt like I'd been hit by a Mack Truck. I'm mostly insulated against lightning, I can sling wind and rain and hail with the best of 'em, but boxing...not my specialty.

I groaned and rolled over on my side and touched my throbbing chin. My lip was split. I explored it with the tip of my tongue, tasted fresh blood, and tried to figure out exactly what was going on.

Ah. It all came back. Star, the cookies, Lewis smacking the crap out of me.

The Code One lockdown.

I might have robbed Star and Lewis of options, but I also hadn't left myself a whole lot of room to manoeuvre.

Something brushed my face, light as cobwebs, and where it touched pain faded. I knew that touch, that warming sensation.

'She's awake.' David's voice, stripped of emotion. I opened my eyes and saw him sitting next to me. He didn't ask how I was, or say anything directly to me, but that touch – I had to believe that it had been David who'd done that, the *real* David. Was it possible for him to fight for control? To go against her? If Star knew...

'About time.' Star, of course; she sounded freaked, which made her sound callous. 'Jesus, girl, you're not exactly one of those TV kick-ass hero chicks, are you. One punch, you're down for ten minutes. My mama could have done better.'

'Get her down here, we'll go,' I mumbled. I wiped a trickle of blood away from my lips and sat up. 'It's over, Star. I've already spilt the beans. They're coming for all of us. Lewis'll probably get a Demon-ectomy, but you, you're toast, babe. They'll hoover you so dry, you won't be able to light a match with a nuclear weapon.'

She kicked me. Right in the stomach. I'd never been kicked in the stomach before, and it was not a special treat. I rolled over, pulled my knees up, and gagged through the pain. I wondered if she'd ruptured anything I couldn't live without. It would be a real bitch to end up dead, ripped up by this damn Demon I hadn't chosen, setting destruction loose on the aetheric, just because I'd taken a pointy-toed boot in the spleen.

'Don't,' Lewis said. He was sitting in the corner, resting his chin on his crossed forearms.

'Don't what?' Star shot back, and paced in front of me like a crack addict on a caffeine high. 'She *ruined* it! She brought them here...and now they *know*. I can't let them take me. I *can't*.'

Watching her, I realised David had been right when he'd warned me of the corrupting effects of living with the Demon Mark. Star had taken it; she'd lived with it in secret for a long time, and it had gnawed out her soul.

It made me wonder about Lewis. He had a towering amount of ability, but I wasn't sure anymore about his soul.

I was no longer sure about mine, either.

Star whirled on David and snapped her fingers at him. 'You. Get us out of here.'

'Where?' he asked without moving his eyes away from me. Dark eyes, a stranger's eyes. But he was still watching me with that eerie focus, the way he had before. *You don't own him completely, Star.*

She growled in frustration, walked over to him, and grabbed him by the hair. She forced his head up and made him meet her eyes. 'Hey. Look at me when I'm talking to you!'

He had no change of expression. If it hurt him at all, I couldn't tell. He didn't try to pull away. David, the poseable doll.

'I want to go to New York.'

'Specify,' he said.

She looked baffled. 'Grand Central Station!'

'Specify.'

He could, I sensed, play this game forever, down to making her identify the square inches of tile she wanted to plant her feet upon. Not only could she not do it, but she didn't even have the patience to try. She slammed his head backwards into the wall and let him go.

'Useless. Both of you. Unlimited power, my ass. I can't get either one of you to lift a finger.' She nudged Lewis with her toe, but he didn't respond, except to close his eyes; I felt a cold shiver and wondered what she'd done to him down here, what kind of hell a man who wielded near-unlimited power could experience to break him like this.

'Hey, Star?' I asked. I sat up, pulling my back closer to the wall, and reached out to lay my hand on top of David's, squeezed it in warning. 'Let's figure out how to get out of this alive. Both of us.'

She turned away and stalked back to me, dropped into a crouch by my side. Her dark eyes glittered like razor-sharp obsidian. 'What's your proposal?'

'Who says I have one?'

'Jo, I know you. You've always got an idea. It's usually crappy, but you always have one.' For just a second, there was a flicker, a memory of what she'd been. Who we'd both once been. *Oh, Star.* 'Remember when we built the anatomically correct snowman outside the dean's office? Not such a great plan, *chica*. But it had style.'

I remembered. I didn't want to, because it made things harder, remembering the outrageous fun of that winter night, our breathless giggles fogging the air. She'd been so stupidly innocent back then, and I'd been such a bad influence...

I had to be a worse one now. To save whatever was left of the girl I still loved.

I sucked in a breath that tasted of tears and said, 'Easy. Give Lewis up. Look, he's of no use to you, anyway. He's got the Mark, and he can't give it back to you. Even if he could, he wouldn't because he knows you're raving ape-shit crazy, and he'd rather die than see what you'd do with it. You're screwed, Star. Let him go, and you win points with the Wardens.'

She blew a raspberry that lifted the fine dark bangs on her forehead. 'Yeah, right. That's likely to happen.'

'It is if I tell them it was all my fault. I killed Bad Bob. I have the Mark. *And* I've been running away from Marion's crew for more than a thousand miles. I tell them everything was my fault, not yours. They'll believe it.'

She stared at me without blinking. 'Yeah? And why do I believe you'll *say* it in the first place?'

I gave her a slow, painful smile. 'Because you have something I want, Star.' I looked over at David, then back to her. 'Break his bottle and set him free. I'll go away like a good girl, Lewis is saved, everybody's happy.'

'Not me,' Star said. 'Not unless I get back what I had.'

I swallowed bile and said, 'Then you live to scheme another day.'

She frowned, grooving little lines between those fine black eyebrows, and studied me for so long, I thought she'd gone blind. 'That's stupid,' she finally said. 'Even if I do free David, I still have the book. I can take him back any time I want. What's the point?'

'Well, that's the second part. You let him destroy the book.'

She laughed. 'Never happen. Let me tell you *my* scenario, Jo. The house burns. They find bodies. Nobody's ever sure who belongs to who, except that me and my new *que lindo* Djinn end up living the sweet life on a tropical island, with nobody to know it. I don't need both you and Lewis, you know. I need only one of you, for David to take the Mark and give it to me. After that, you're all better off dead.' She smiled slightly, and it was bitter and ugly and hard. 'Well, *I'm* better off.'

She played with fire on her fingertips. She stared at it, then moved it closer to my face. Closer, as if she were trying to see by the light of it.

She set my hair on fire. I resisted the urge to scream and roll around, and beat it out with the palm of my hand. The smell of it lingered between us.

'Just a sample,' she said. 'How'd it feel?'

I froze the air around her, so cold, I saw frost form instantly on her skin. She cried out and jerked away in panic.

'About like that does,' I said. 'Don't push me. I'll give you freezer burn so deep, they'll have to microwave you to hear you scream. You start this, you know we'll both die. How does that help either one of us?'

Something wavered in her eyes. She reached out and pushed my burnt hair back from my face, and for a second there wasn't a gulf of years and secrets. 'You'd really do it? Tell them it was you?'

'Yeah,' I said. 'I will. Doesn't matter anymore – they won't let me keep my powers. I'm too far gone with this damn Mark. My life is over, Star. I know that. At least let me do something useful.'

Star nodded, looked at David, and got up to go to the worktable. She took a small bottle out of a drawer and set it down next to the book. She paused for a few seconds, looking up as if she could hear through the floor above us. Maybe she could. 'Company's here,' she said. 'Marion and her merry men, seven or eight at least. Enough to keep us busy, if we wanted to make a fight.'

'But we're not going to,' I said. 'Right?'

'Right.' Star lifted the bottle in her hand, looked at it from different angles. 'Weird, how a Djinn always has to be sourced in glass. You'd think with all the advances, we'd be able to use plastic. Stupid fucking rules.'

I didn't like her sudden change of focus. 'Star, it *won't work!* If you order David to do this, he'll be destroyed. Even if he's not, you can't order him to give you the Mark. He can't do it. Once he takes it, it won't leave him until it wins and eats him.' I was getting desperate – sweating, exhausted, scared. My head hurt. I could still smell the weirdly disorienting aroma of fresh-baked cookies wafting down from the kitchen. 'Come on. Let's all walk out of here alive, at least.'

She looked at me for a long, wordless few seconds, then cocked her head to the side. 'Why?'

'What do you mean, why?'

'Why do you want to save me? First Lewis, now you. Why?'

I couldn't even believe she was asking. 'Because I love you, Star. Don't you know?'

Her eyes filled up with tears, but none broke free. She blinked them away. They left a hard, unsettling shine behind. 'Love you, too,' she said. She turned the bottle, staring at the facets of glass. Held it up between us and let the light gleam through. 'You know, there's one thing I could do.'

I felt a cold surge of dread. 'Yeah?'

'Last resort, I could have David take the Mark, seal him in the bottle, and then it's your word against mine. Or maybe you go crazy, try to kill Lewis, he has to kill you, everybody dies in a tragic accidental fire but me, very sad. And you know, I think I like that plan better.'

She put the bottle back down and, without

turning around, said, 'David, go over to Lewis and take the Demon Mark out of him.'

'No!' I screamed, and lunged for her back. She fell against the table, and the bottle trembled on wood but didn't fall. Her hand closed around it. 'Dammit, Star, *no*, don't do this!'

'Take the Mark!' she yelled. When I tried to pull away from her, she twisted around and held me back, and the burning sensation in my skin wasn't a Djinn illusion; it was the real deal. 'Do it!'

David levitated up and slowly across the floor toward Lewis.

'David, don't! I'll say the words, please *don't do this*—' It was too late for that. He couldn't listen to me, couldn't obey me.

I ripped free of Star's grasp and threw myself at them just as David's hand reached down, *into* Lewis, and Lewis screamed.

Star threw fire at me. I dodged, but the fireball rolled under the stairs and flared up against dry wood. I didn't have time to spare to put it out; that was Star's specialty, let her deal with it. I reached out to grab hold of David and pull him away from Lewis.

My hand passed right through him – through both of them. Whatever was happening wasn't happening on this plane at all.

I threw myself up into Oversight and saw David the way he really was – a flaming angel, gilded and beautiful, with his hands deep inside the crystal perfection that made up the core of Lewis. Something black and horrible lashed out of Lewis, whipped tentacles around David's arms, crawled through the bridge and attacked. It was like seeing a butterfly being eaten by acid, and even though I couldn't hear David screaming, I could *feel* it. He'd suffer forever from this. It would never stop for him, until the end of time.

Lewis fell back against the wall and slid down. Now it was just David and the *thing*, wrapped together like predator and prey, pulsing and writhing and seeking supremacy. I felt the Demon Mark inside me break loose, feeding and screaming as if it could feel the presence of its kindred.

I didn't think. Didn't hesitate. Didn't allow myself even the smallest pause to feel fear.

I plunged myself into David on the aetheric, the way he'd plunged himself into Lewis, joining us together.

And my Demon Mark came into contact with the one wrapped around David.

Power calls to power – always has, always will.

The two Demon Marks went to war.

When you think of yourself as screaming, you usually think of it in your throat, or echoing in your ears, but this was something else. Something worse. It was as if my cells were screaming, each one equipped with a voice and agony to fuel it, and none of it would come out of my mouth. I was on fire. I was freezing. I was dying.

The Demon Marks inside me ate, and ate, and ate. My weather powers, first. When those were gone, the fighting Marks drained energy from my nerves and sent me crashing to the floor. Then they devoured microcellular energy that made up my life.

The last thing to go...the very last...was my sense of hearing, as the synapses of my brain were drained of energy and the Demon Marks howled.

Two snakes, eating each other.

Gone.

It was vastly empty, in the dark where I was. I had flashes of things – Star's melted-wax face, David's blazing copper eyes, the hot glow of his skin on mine. Bad Bob's scowl. The storm whirling to a stop overhead.

Smoke. The taste of smoke. This was what it must have felt like to Star, lying in the ashes while Yellowstone burnt around her.

I didn't want to die, but there was nothing left. Nothing.

And then it was all...gone.

The first thing I felt was heat. Not burning, just heat, blood-warm, comfortable, as if I'd fallen asleep in a perfect bath.

I was floating. Unformed. At peace.

'Open your eyes,' someone said. I didn't know I had eyes. Didn't know how to open them.

But they opened without my help, and I *saw*.

The world blazed in colours and auras, crystal and shadows. God, it was beautiful. This shattered ruin of a place, smoke and ashes...it was beautiful in ways I'd never imagined it could be. There were bones in the ashes, and they were beautiful, too. Graceful yellow-white bones with their curves and elegant strength.

So many people around me. Some here in flesh, some here in the Second World that I'd once called the aetheric. I knew all about that now. All about everything. The connection to sky, to sea, to earth, to stars. It was all inside me, and I was made up of fire.

'Come down,' the voice told me. I didn't know what it meant but then again, I did, and slowly drifted through the Worlds until I was in the First World, the world I'd known before.

David was holding me, and we were floating over a hot black bed of embers. Coils of smoke drifted in the sky, and they were so beautiful, I wanted to follow them. I felt a tug as thought instantly translated toward action.

'Stay with me,' he whispered, and the sound of it moved along my skin, inside my skin, through me in waves. I paused, caught.

This was real. The fire trucks flashing their lights

at the curb – they were real. The firefighters aiming hoses at the destruction that had once been Star's house – that was real, too.

There were bones in the basement. I could see them, shining in the charred wood.

'Can she hear me?' someone asked, and I looked in the basement but there was no one there. 'Jo, can you hear me?'

I focused and found there was someone right in front of me. He was heavy with flesh and wildly bright inside, and I wanted to reach out and sink into the fevered warmth of him but I knew, somehow, that it would be bad. And not just for him.

I blocked out the incredible glow of his spirit and focused on the real, the skin, the face. 'Lewis?'

He nodded. He was still ragged and badly dressed, but his eyes were clear. His soul was clear. If the Demon Mark had left him tainted, I couldn't see where, or how. *How strong was he, to survive that?*

'You know what you did?' he asked. I didn't, but I had no idea how to express it; evidently, he read it in my eyes. 'You took the Mark from David. Two can't exist in the same body. They destroyed each other.'

Ah. That would explain why I felt so empty, so full, so weightless, so powerful. I'd inherited something. But I didn't feel…well, evil. Just vast.

'Can she hear me?' Lewis asked, looking past me.

David was so warm against me, anchoring me against all the random currents that tried to pull me away. The smoke on the air, the heat rising off the fire – all so beautiful. Couldn't begin to believe how beautiful it all was.

'I think so,' David said. 'Jo. Concentrate. Make yourself flesh.'

I didn't know what that meant, either, until I did it, and then suddenly there was flesh around me, and it was hurting, and I went to my knees and took David down with me.

Make myself flesh. Wait, what had I just been before?

'What happened?' I whispered. My lips felt dry, as if I'd never tasted water. 'Star…'

'Star's dead,' Lewis said. 'She started the fire. I couldn't get her out – she wouldn't leave without the book.'

The book was gone. That was…good? Wasn't it?

Lewis reached out and touched my face, then jerked back and shook his hand as if it was burnt. Sucked his fingers. 'She's hot.'

'She can't control it yet,' David said. 'She'll learn.'

This didn't make any sense. Nothing made any sense. 'What happened?'

David's hand stroked the side of my face, down my neck, my shoulder. He folded me closer. My skin yearned toward his touch.

'You died,' he said. 'I felt you go. You'd taken

part of me inside you with the Demon Mark. When your body – was destroyed—'

I remembered the bones in the ashes and shivered. No wonder the graceful ivory curves had fascinated me.

'I died,' I said. 'It killed me.'

'I can't bring back the dead,' David was saying. 'No one can.'

I felt a flash of my old humour. 'Still here, though.'

'Yes.' He turned me in his arms to face him, and his eyes were bright, joyous copper, hotter than the sun, and I saw myself in them. A creature of fire. A black-haired, pale-skinned creature with eyes like the palest silver.

A Djinn.

'I can't bring back the dead,' he repeated. 'But I can create a new life in my image.'

He'd made me a Djinn.

'Oh, shit,' I said.

David's smile was hot enough to burn the world. 'That's not exactly how we put things, on this side.'

'Why not?'

His eyebrows quirked up. 'You know, I guess nobody ever asked that before.'

His arms folded around me, and I felt myself burning, and burning, and now it didn't hurt at all.

❧ ❧ ❧

There was nothing left of Star's house but cinders, by the time it was all done. There was a reason for that: Star had started the fire, but Shirl, Erik, and Marion had kept it blazing hotter than any normal fire could have sustained on its own. The firefighters had wasted tons of good Oklahoma water on the conflagration, but the Wardens had agreed that there shouldn't be any trace left – not of the book, of Star, or of any mortal remains.

It was quite a scene, on that Oklahoma City street in the fierce light of dawn. In and around the frantic fire department efforts, there was another agency at work, this one lots more powerful and lots more chaotic. By 8 a.m., there were nineteen Wardens on the scene – Marion and her team of eight, including Shirl and Erik; Sector and Regional Wardens for the area; State Wardens from anyplace close enough to matter...and Martin Oliver, National Warden.

They'd all come looking for Lewis, and this time, he let them find him. On his terms, for a change.

Oliver's first action was to authorise removal of the Code One I'd put in place; all around the world, air began to move, weather to breathe, the planet to flex its cramped muscles.

His second was to declare me a hero. OK, a dead hero, but still. I might actually get my memorial plaque up on the Association walls after all.

I stood on the sidelines with David, learning

how to be invisible – or unseeable. It took some doing, staying out of the way of people who had no idea you existed, but I was getting the hang of it. Staying in flesh was harder; there was so much to do, so much to feel, and the currents of the world kept pulling at me like they were playful children.

'We should go,' David finally said. Lewis was OK. He was huddled with Martin Oliver, a blanket over his shoulders, looking weary but far from the mess he'd been earlier. 'You can see him later.'

I slid my hand into David's. 'Go where?'

'Anywhere,' he said. 'We're free.'

I found myself staring at the Viper. Mona was still parked at the curb, crowded by emergency vehicles. I wished I'd parked her farther down the street, so that I could sneak her out of here...

Something electric and wild snapped inside me, like an internal shock.

The Viper vanished.

'Hey!' David yelped. I looked down the block. There Mona sat, gleaming metallic blue, ready to run. David stared at the mass of people, looking for any sign somebody had noticed. Lucky for me, there were only a couple, and one of them was drunk off his ass swilling Schlitz Malt Liquor from a quart bottle. The other one must have convinced himself he'd swallowed too much smoke; he just shook his head and moved on.

How many miracles happened every day, right in front of people? Unbelievable.

I felt a grin spreading over my face, filling me with delight. 'Man, that is so damn cool.'

'Yeah. And...try not to do it without asking first, would you?'

We walked down the block, and as we dodged around two cops taking statements from some neighbours still in pyjamas, we saw we had a visitor leaning against the Viper.

Rahel. She'd changed colours to an electric shade of green – pantsuit, hair beads, and nail polish all matched. Her eyes were still fierce hunting-hawk gold, and as she looked at me, I read something like pride in her expression.

'Well,' she said. 'I see you made your choice, Snow White.'

I'd always wondered why she called me that, and now I looked at the reflection of my flesh-form in the window of the Viper, and saw the midnight-black hair, the flawless white skin, the pale silver eyes. *Snow White.* As I watched, my lips grew fuller and redder.

Rahel laughed. 'See? I knew you had it in you.'

'You could've told me everything from the beginning. Made it a lot easier.'

She shrugged. 'I'm a Djinn. In time, you'll understand.'

She clicked her lime-green talons in complicated,

castanet rhythms and opened the driver's-side door of the Viper for me. As she bowed me in, she said, 'Welcome to your life, Ianna. Burn bright, live free, and remember that no human is your ally unless you hold his beating heart in your hand.' She winked. 'And have fun.'

As she shut the door, I looked at David. 'Ianna?'

'It suits you,' he said. 'Ianna's a name of power.'

'So's Joanne,' I smiled, and touched the ignition with my pale, fiery fingers. 'Better believe *that*.'

Mona roared to life, and the road stretched forever.

THE WEATHER WARDEN SERIES SO FAR...

The Morganville Vampires series so far...

Check out our website for free tasters and exclusive discounts, competitions and giveaways, and sign up to our monthly newsletter to keep up-to-date on our latest releases, news and upcoming events.

www.allisonandbusby.com